D0721888

Just One Kiss

Just One Kiss

Donna M. Schaff

Five Star
Unity, Maine

This novel is a work of fiction. Names, characters, places and incidents are either the product of the author's imagination, or, if real, used fictitiously.

Five Star First Edition Romance Series.
Published in 2001 in conjunction with The Knight Agency.

Set in 11 pt. Plantin by Christina S. Huff.

Printed in the United States on permanent paper.

Library of Congress Cataloging-in-Publication Data

Schaff, Donna M.
Just one kiss / Donna M. Schaff.
p. cm. — (Five Star first edition romance series)
ISBN 0-7862-3021-5 (hc : alk. paper)
1. Louisiana — Fiction. 2. Boston (Mass.) — Fiction.
3. French teachers — Fiction. I. Title. II. Series.
PS3569.C525 J87 2001
813′.6—dc21 00-067279

Dedication

For Dorothy Zilkowski—
aunt, sister, friend—
and woman extraordinaire

You said I could and would.
Thanks for all the love and support
In times of laughter and tears.

Chapter 1

Boston, 1874

"Alex! You're here!"

Alex Benedict grinned as the young woman flew down the front steps of the Boston brownstone and raced toward him. He barely had time to step down from the hansom cab before she threw herself at him, almost slamming him back against it.

"Watch it, Les, or you'll have me flat on my you-know-what in the street," he warned, but his grin broadened as his sister wrapped her arms around his neck and stood on tiptoe to kiss his cheek.

"Oh, Alex, I've been holding my breath, afraid that one of your business deals would interfere and you wouldn't be able to come." She laughed joyously. "Poor Aunt Lorna was beginning to lose patience with me, for each time the doorbell rang during the past week, I was sure it was someone delivering your telegram informing me that you weren't leaving Colorado after all. Oh, I'm so relieved—and so happy you've come!"

Alex winced as she lowered her arms and squeezed his waist fiercely. Leslie never did anything in half measures, and her breathlessly enthusiastic welcome was no exception.

He hugged her in return. "Now, darlin', you know that nothing would have kept me from coming to see my only sister being graduated from the Chatham Academy for Young Ladies."

"*And* to celebrate her eighteenth birthday," Leslie reminded him. "You haven't forgotten the party and the dance, have you?"

"Ah, yes, your debut. I could hardly forget, now could I, since you've been sending me wires almost every day reminding me that you're about to enter the realm of adulthood." His eyes twinkled. "Nice to see that you're managing to contain your excitement so—Ouch!"

Leslie had punched his arm playfully. "Stop your teasing. Oh, Alex, I *am* excited! I have so much to tell you."

Alex gently disengaged himself from his sister's embrace. "And I'm prepared to listen," he said with an indulgent smile, "but hold off until we're inside. I need to pay the cabby."

The driver had already set Alex's luggage on the curb and was waiting patiently. Alex handed him the fare plus a generous gratuity, whereupon the driver tipped his hat. "Many thanks, sir." Alex nodded and reached for a bag.

"Oh, leave those," Leslie said dismissively as she slipped an arm under his elbow and pulled him toward the house. "You know that Branson will be insulted if you carry your own bags." She shuddered in mock horror. "I've already put his nose out of joint, for I practically trod on his toes in an effort to reach the door before he did. Oh, dear, speak of the devil . . ."

Alex glanced up to find that his aunt's majordomo was indeed looking down his long, narrow nose at them. The stiffly postured man was thin to the point of emaciation and so tall that Alex, who was exactly six feet in height, had to crane his neck once he and Leslie had ascended the stairs and stood before the butler.

Branson snapped his fingers, and a footman immediately materialized to slip past them and retrieve Alex's luggage. "Welcome, Mr. Benedict," Branson intoned in his deep voice. "It's a pleasure to have you back with us, and, may I say, you're looking well."

"Thank you, Branson," Alex returned. "I'm glad to be back, and, yes, I'm feeling fit, despite having been so enthusiastically greeted by my sister. My toes are still quite sound, I'm happy to report. How are yours?" he asked with a straight face.

Branson's expression didn't change by so much as a flicker of an eyelid. His light blue eyes met Alex's squarely. "As yours, they remain securely attached to my feet," he replied with perfect solemnity.

Leslie pressed her face into Alex's sleeve to muffle her laughter as they walked past the man and into a large foyer.

At the opposite end, where a wide staircase led to the upper stories, a woman stood with her hands resting on the railing of the second-floor landing and shook her head fondly.

A smile played softly about Lorna Hall's mouth as she looked down at the two siblings so close together. Leslie was tall for a woman, so she was able to tilt her head almost onto Alex's broad shoulder, while he, in turn, rested his cheek against her temple. With their identical midnight-black hair and green eyes, they could almost be mistaken for twins. The only difference, excepting age and gender, was that Leslie's eyes reminded one of a verdant meadow, whereas Alex's were the smoky green of pine needles.

Lorna loved them both fiercely and thought of them as her own children, since she and her late husband, Burton, had never been blessed with any offspring of their own.

Lorna's smile wavered as she thought of her sister, Suzanne, who hadn't been much older than Leslie was now when she'd fallen madly in love with James Benedict, a planter from Georgia. How sad that she hadn't lived to see her children fully grown!

Lorna mentally corrected herself, for Suzanne *had* lived long enough to see Alex become an officer in the Confederate cavalry. But Leslie had been only nine years old when her mother died in the winter of '64. That was when James had sent Leslie here, to Lorna. Poor James. He'd joined his beloved wife in heaven just over a year later, shortly after Appomattox. That damned war, Lorna thought, had taken too many lives—and not all in battle. Oh, heavens, this was no moment to be maudlin! This was an exciting time for Leslie. Alex had arrived, and they should all be happy!

Shaking her head as if to clear it of her sentimental mood, Lorna smiled as she swept around the circular banister toward the staircase. "You naughty children!" she scolded fondly as she descended. "Will you never learn to leave poor Branson alone?"

Hearing the familiar voice, Alex immediately forgot his disappointment at failing to rile Branson. Giving Leslie, who was still clinging to his arm, a little tug, he took her with him as he went to the bottom of the stairs. His mouth curved into a wide smile. "Hello, Aunt Lorna," he greeted.

"Hello yourself, darling boy," she returned, causing him to grin. He was hardly a boy, but he had no doubt she'd continue to call him one until he was eighty.

He watched in wonder at her graceful descent. As always, she was elegantly dressed in the latest fashion, and her pale blue gown matched the twinkling gaze she directed at him. Her silver hair was artfully coiffed about her face and pinned into an impeccably arranged chignon in back. It gave Alex a pang to see his aunt, for she and his mother had been twins.

He wondered if his mother would have appeared as ageless as Lorna, had she lived.

"Aunt, I swear you haven't changed in twenty years." Wrapping his arms about her waist, he swept her off the stairs to give her a ribcracking hug before kissing her cheek.

"And you, my dear boy," she laughed breathlessly as she returned his kiss, "remain the charming liar. Still, I'm afraid the years keep creeping by. I warn you, Alex, you'll have to take more care with my person when I'm an old, frail woman!"

Alex chuckled as he set her back on her feet. "You'll never be old or frail."

She patted his cheek. "Ha! Stop trying to flatter me. Save your efforts for some sweet young thing."

Alex threw back his head and laughed. "Sweet young thing?" Leslie chuckled at his amusement. "Now, Aunt Lorna, you know perfectly well that sweet young things bore Alex to death. He much prefers naughty, dangerous women, don't you, brother dear?" she teased.

Alex abruptly sobered and peered down at her. "Is this my little sister speaking? My *innocent* little sister who shouldn't even know that naughty, dangerous women exist?"

"Phooey!" Leslie punched his arm hard enough to make him wince. "In case you haven't noticed, my head reaches your shoulder, so *little* hardly applies anymore. And I'm no longer a naive child, Alex!"

Lorna gently cleared her throat. "I think we'd best adjourn to the drawing room, dears. Branson . . ." She turned to find that, as usual, her majordomo was standing at attention only a short distance behind her and was already anticipating her request.

"Tea in ten minutes, madam," he informed her calmly.

Alex raised a finger to catch his attention, but Branson had divined his wishes, also. "You'll find the brandy decanter has been replenished, and there will be a cup for you on the tray, Mr. Benedict," he informed Alex before inclining his white-haired head and disappearing toward the kitchen.

Alex's grin flashed at Branson's unruffled demeanor. "That man always beats me to the punch. Even though Brannon and Benedict have offices in Boston, I don't get here often, yet Branson never forgets that I like a bit of brandy in my tea," he mused.

Lorna inserted herself between brother and sister, and taking each one's arm, she led the way to the drawing room. "Branson takes pride in remembering every detail about all my guests. Nothing you do or say will surprise him, I daresay. Give in and admit that you can't disconcert him. You've been trying since you were in knee pants, as I recall."

"And failed miserably all these years," Alex chuckled. "But I'll get him yet," he promised. "You'll have to tell me about your plans for Leslie's debut. If I'm to be thrust into staid Boston society for the next few weeks, I'd better be prepared," he teased as he walked to the fireplace. "God forbid I make a gaffe while in Branson's presence." He laughed and rolled his eyes. "I can't believe I said that. Lord, thirty-three years old and I'm still intimidated by that old devil!" Pulling a cheroot from an inside pocket, he raised a quizzical eyebrow at his aunt, who gave him a nod of permission. Lighting the slim cigar, he rested one elbow on the mantel and turned to watch Lorna gracefully spread her skirts before taking a seat on a sofa. His lips twitched as Leslie followed her aunt's example.

Comfortably ensconced beside Lorna, she glanced up and caught his expression. "What?" she asked.

"I'm merely finding it hard to believe that you've grown up on me, Les."

She laughed gaily at his consternation. "Well, I should hope so! Goodness, Alex, you didn't expect me to remain a child forever, did you?"

"No. But you've become a breathtakingly beautiful young woman. I suppose I simply wasn't prepared." A rueful smile tugged at his mouth. "How many of your suitors will I have to beat off while I'm in Boston?"

Leslie blushed prettily while Lorna patted her hand and replied for her. "You'll meet several of them at Leslie's birthday party. Your sister is a very popular young woman in our circle, and though her social life has been properly restricted up to now, I've made certain she's been introduced to a number of nice young men. Naturally, they are all of good families and have promising futures."

"And they're all boring, boring, *boring,*" Leslie interjected.

Alex's eyebrows rose at this statement.

"Well, they are," Leslie insisted. "They all do the same things, say the same things, think the same way. Lordy, they even all dress alike. It's as if someone had cast a mold and pressed them through, one by one."

Alex's amused glance met his aunt's. She smiled tolerantly and only shrugged, leading him to believe she'd probably heard this same refrain before. "No one among them piques your interest, Les?"

"No one among them makes my heart flutter, if that's what you mean," she stated flatly. "Not that it matters, for I'm not at all interested in matrimony." She narrowed her gaze at her brother. "So if you have any medieval notions along that line, forget them," she warned.

Somewhat surprised at Leslie's vehemence, Alex turned back to his aunt "Well. It appears you'll have to wait a bit longer before Les provides you with great-nieces or -nephews to spoil," he told Lorna.

"Oh? You don't intend to provide me with some anytime soon?" she teased.

Alex frowned. "No," he said abruptly. "I'll never marry again."

"Oh, Alex . . ." Lorna could have strangled herself. Marriage—*his* marriage—was a subject Alex never discussed. How could she have made such a terrible gaffe?

Exchanging a glance with her aunt, Leslie rushed in to cover the awkward moment. "I, for one, have too many places to see, too many things to do. Besides, Anne says that love is overrated and only leads to dependence."

Alex merely raised an eyebrow as he puffed on his cheroot.

Was "Anne" a schoolmate who espoused on a subject she knew nothing about in hopes of impressing Leslie? Encouraged, Leslie gushed on enthusiastically. "Anne also insists that women are entitled to the same freedom men allow themselves before they settle down. She believes women should have time to develop their characters without male influence. If a woman is allowed that, Anne says, then choosing her first lover will be an affair of the mind as well as—"

Alex choked on the smoke he'd inhaled and bent double, coughing and sputtering.

"Alex, are you all right?" Leslie asked, concerned.

Since he was unable to reply, it was just as well that Branson chose that moment to enter the room with a loaded tray. Glancing Alex's way, he set down the tray and inquired of Lorna, "The brandy, madam?"

"Exactly," Lorna replied as she quickly poured a small measure of tea into a cup. When she glanced up again, Branson was already standing before her, the decanter unstoppered. She held the cup until he'd filled it with brandy before indicating that he should take it to Alex.

His eyes watering, Alex tossed his cheroot into the fireplace and straightened to gratefully accept the cup. He quickly drained the contents.

"Another, sir?" Branson inquired with aplomb.

Alex cleared his throat. "No more tea for me. You may, however, leave the—Ah! I see you've already anticipated my needs," he added as Branson brought his other hand forward and produced the decanter. "Thank you, Branson. I'll just continue using this cup."

"Very good, sir." The majordomo inclined his head and sedately left the room.

"Darling, are you all right?" Lorna asked in concern as she filled two cups with steaming tea.

"I'll let you know in a minute," Alex replied as he poured a generous measure of brandy into his own cup before turning his narrowed gaze upon Leslie. "Who in hell—oh, sorry, Aunt—just what kind of girl is this Anne and why the devil is she speaking to you of *lovers?*"

Leslie returned his glare with one of mingled innocence and amusement. "Anne isn't a *girl,* Alex. She's my French instructor at Chatham's. Well, she's actually more than that. She's been my mentor and my friend, much like an older sister. I hated Chatham's at first, but Anne—it's really Madame DuBois, but I have her permission to use her given name in private—Anne made my life at the school bearable."

"By teaching you about lovers?"

"Oh, Alex, don't be so stuffy. It was an innocent conversation during which Anne told me I should never let myself be pressed into doing something I wasn't prepared for. She—"

"Prepared? In what way?" he asked sharply.

"She simply informed me that she had no doubt that many men would try to seduce me in the future and that I should therefore be very cautious and very particular, for men often wear masks to hide their true natures."

Alex could only gape, dumbfounded at Leslie's casual acceptance of this information. Who the hell was this woman offering intimate advice to his sister? What *kind* of woman was she? His questioning gaze met Lorna's. "Do you know this person?" he asked her.

His aunt smiled. "Of course. I've had several invigorating conversations with Madame DuBois and find her views refreshing. Frankly, I agree with her that it causes more harm than good to keep women too sheltered under the guise of protecting them. It leaves them unprepared for real life. Times are changing. Men need to stop thinking females are all fragile blossoms in danger of wilting on the vine if we don't have a male to depend on."

Alex could hardly believe what he was hearing. His aunt, a scion of Boston society, a woman who had lived her life according to a strict set of rules and restrictions, was actually a freethinking female rebel?

Lorna laughed softly at his expression. "I see I've shocked you, poor boy."

"That's putting it mildly," he muttered wryly.

Lorna chuckled silently. She reminded herself that Alex had been raised in the antebellum years when men played the dominant role and females were expected to be soft and sweet and quiescent. He was going to need some time to become accustomed to the fact that women's roles had changed and would soon change even more.

"Oh, Alex!" Leslie wailed. "You're not going to become stodgy on me, are you? Not after I've bragged to my friends and Anne about you, telling them that you're an open thinker who believes that all people have an equal right to freedom and happiness."

She had him there, Alex thought. "No, brat. You weren't wrong."

"Well, that's a relief! For a moment there I was afraid I'd have to use Aunt's teapot to knock some sense into you!"

"Good Lord! I only wanted assurance," he explained apologetically, "that this DuBois woman wasn't leading my sister astray."

"I hardly think so," Lorna cut in. "What I do think is that Leslie is fortunate to have had Madame as an instructor."

Alex silently scoffed. Anne DuBois sounded like nothing more than a man-hater, for her advice hadn't been very flattering to the male species. Yet he could hardly argue with it, since he himself would have to plead guilty to at least one of her claims—that of wearing the mask he wanted the world to see. "This DuBois woman," he ventured. "What's she like, other than boldly outspoken?"

"Oh, she's not bold at all. Exactly the opposite, in fact. She's rather quiet," Leslie replied. "She doesn't talk much about her past, but I do know that she's widowed, and she must have loved her husband very much, for she has such sad eyes. And sometimes she strikes me as being lonely, for she doesn't socialize with the rest of the staff." Leslie frowned. "Anne is the only part of Chatham's that I'll miss. Poor thing. I don't know how she can stand it there herself. Mrs. Busley is horrible to her. Actually, Mrs. B. is horrible to everyone, but she's particularly nasty to Anne. Mrs. B. is a witch."

"Leslie!" Lorna admonished.

"Well, she is! She constantly criticizes and browbeats Anne. Personally, I think she's jealous of Madame DuBois."

Alex's eyebrows rose. "Oh? Attractive, is she?"

Lorna opened her mouth to reply, but Leslie uttered an unladylike sound of exasperation and beat her to it. "Oh, Alex, you're just as bad as the young men I know. I swear you all think only about how a woman looks," she scolded.

"Don't you ever give any consideration to a woman's other attributes?"

Alex pretended to consider, but his eyes twinkled. "No. Not really," he drawled. "I admit I'm not particularly fond of crossed eyes or long noses or missing teeth," he continued. "On the other hand, I don't mind a freckle or two."

Leslie struggled to maintain a stern expression. "Anne is hardly cross-eyed or gap-toothed. And, before you ask, she doesn't have warts on her face, either."

"That's a relief. What about the rest of her?"

Leslie's mouth twitched. "Oh, you're impossible!"

"I know," he responded. "It's part of my charm."

At that, Leslie gave up and sputtered in helpless laughter, while Lorna smiled indulgently.

"Are you two prepared for our journey to Bellesfield?" Alex asked, changing the subject as he settled into a chair.

Leslie sobered. "Yes! I can hardly wait to see it again!"

"You realize, brat, that it won't be as you remember it?"

"I do realize that. I know the house was destroyed and that Bellesfield will never be our home again. But, Alex, you've built that wonderful school there, in Mama and Papa's memories. I'm dying to see it."

"As am I," Lorna added. "I think it's a marvelous tribute. You could have rebuilt the plantation after the War Between the States. Instead, you chose to give young men and women of all classes a chance for a future they might otherwise never have had. I'm so proud of you, Alex."

"Thank you, darlin'. Your approval means much to me. I should tell you both, however, that I need to attend to some business on this trip; therefore, I've changed our itinerary somewhat. Instead of going directly to Colorado from Georgia, I thought we'd take a little detour through New Orleans."

"New Orleans!" Leslie shivered in anticipation. "Oh, I've heard it's such a wicked city!"

He smiled at her in amusement. "And you can hardly wait to observe as much of that wickedness as possible, right?"

"Of course. I'm dying to see the Vieux Carré and the Garden District, and—Oh, and I can't wait to tell Anne about this! She'll be so excited for me!" Leslie exclaimed.

Alex's eyebrows rose a half inch. "Anne again?"

"Yes. Did I mention she's from New Orleans herself, and that her mother was French?"

"No, you didn't." Just how familiar with the sordid side of New Orleans, he wondered, was this DuBois woman?

Leslie abruptly slapped her palms to her cheeks. "Oh, heavens! That reminds me. I still have to address her invitation to my birthday party, for I want to hand it to her personally. I'd better do it now." She rose in a flurry of skirts.

"Don't forget Mrs. Busley's invitation," Lorna reminded her. "You can hardly invite one of the instructors without inviting the headmistress."

Leslie turned back, her nose wrinkled in distaste. "I know. I wish I didn't have to, though." Her face brightened. "But it will be worth it to have Anne attend my party. She's really a darling, Alex. I can't wait for you to meet her."

Neither could he, Alex mused, but he'd form his own opinion about the woman.

Lorna turned to him as the door closed behind Leslie. "New Orleans is a wonderful idea," she told Alex. "Burton's cousin, Louisa, still lives there, and she loves company. I shall write and tell her we're coming for a visit."

"Do," Alex murmured in a distracted tone.

Setting her teacup aside, Lorna tilted her head and studied her nephew. "Darling, what's bothering you?" she asked as she watched him drum his fingers on the arm of his chair.

"Hmm?" He lifted his head, frowning.

"You're suddenly deep in thought. What is it?"

"It appears to me that this Anne DuBois has had quite an influence on Leslie. You really approve?"

"Yes. I like Anne very much. You have doubts about her, I take it?"

"That remains to be seen," he replied noncommittally.

Doubts? Damn right he had doubts. He could hardly wait to tell Madame DuBois exactly what he thought of her espousing her worldly views to gullible young girls like Leslie. Why, the woman wasn't fit to teach. By God, maybe he'd have a talk with the headmistress, too, and let her know what kind of unsuitable educators she had on her staff!

Chapter 2

In the small auditorium, Alex shifted uncomfortably in his chair. Beside him, Lorna frowned. “It’s almost over,” she whispered. “Afterward there will be refreshments.” She leaned closer to him. “No brandy, I’m afraid.”

Alex groaned. Mrs. Eudora Busley, headmistress of the Chatham Academy for Young Ladies, had been speaking for what seemed like hours. A thin, pinched-looking woman of indeterminable age, she appeared as stern as Leslie had described, and her high-pitched voice was grating.

Bored and restless, Alex glanced around. The graduates were sitting in the front rows, their families and friends behind them. It amused him to see the rapt looks on the faces of the proud mamas. The papas, bless them, seemed just as eager to escape as he was.

His gaze returned to the small dais at the front of the hall. The three ladies seated there in stiff-backed chairs looked about as animated as statues while they listened to Mrs. Busley. He’d bet his last dollar that not one of them had so much as blinked during the headmistress’s boring monologue.

Well, what could one expect? They were practically replicas of Mrs. B. Take the one on the left there, the one who kept her eyes downcast. Wearing a hideous brown dress with a prim white collar, she looked like a dull little wren as she sat stoically with her hands clasped. Gads! No wonder Leslie was so glad to be free of this place.

Ah, finally! Busley was calling the names of the graduates . . .

Alex skeptically eyed the untasted cake on his plate. "I don't suppose there's such a thing as a smoking room in this place?" he whispered as he set the plate back on the refreshment table.

Leslie tossed him a disgusted glance. "Honestly, Alex, it's a girls' school, not a saloon or gentlemen's club."

Alex grinned down at his sister. "Now, what would you know about saloons?"

Leslie almost stamped her foot. "Why do I have to keep reminding you that I'm no longer an ignorant child? Really, Alex, you'll just have to wait for your cigar until we get home. Besides, I want you to meet Anne DuBois."

"Ah, yes. The paragon of rectitude who doesn't find it contradictory to preach against uncalculated involvement with the other half of the human race—us poor, lowly males."

"Stop it, Alex! You make her sound stiff and awful, and she's not like that at all. But she *is* shy around strangers, so be nice to her," she warned as she slipped her arm beneath his.

He came to a sudden halt. "Good God, Les, I'm not in the habit of frightening ladies. In fact, I'd venture to say that most find me a bit attractive."

"Most find you *extremely* attractive. I'm sure it hasn't passed your notice that my classmates have all been drooling since you walked in." She laughed. "As have their mothers!"

"Oh, Lord, save me from marriage-minded mamas and their eminently marriageable daughters," Alex muttered.

"Well, you won't have to worry about Anne, since she's neither. Come along, now. She's over in that corner speaking to Mrs. Winters, a patron of the academy."

Alex went good-naturedly. Besides, he was prepared to

give the woman a piece of his mind. The sooner this was over, the sooner he'd be able to return to Aunt Lorna's to enjoy that cigar. And a snifter of brandy.

He was heartily sick of hearing about the DuBois woman. Leslie hadn't stopped singing her praises for the last two days, nor had she ceased bemoaning the fact that she'd soon have to say good-bye to the French instructor.

Alex was half convinced that wasn't a bad thing.

But when Leslie led him toward two ladies who were conversing in a corner of the room, Alex barely noticed the straight back that was all to be seen of one, for his gaze immediately latched on to the female facing in their direction. Her wheat-colored hair provided a perfect frame for her sky-blue eyes. He quickly scanned the rest of her. Nice. He preferred full-figured women, and this one bordered on voluptuous.

Just then she laughed and said to the other woman, "Ah, *oui!*" before catching sight of him and Leslie. She fell silent as her blue eyes returned his bold appraisal.

Aha! Madame DuBois was, Alex thought, exactly what he'd expected—a woman of experience. Possibly, just possibly, he'd have to rethink his plans for her. Suddenly he was envisioning the prospect of an interesting diversion to pass his time in Boston.

Alex eagerly stepped in the blonde's direction, but at the same moment an older couple came up behind her and spoke to her, forcing her to turn her attention to them. "Guess we'll have to wait," he murmured to Leslie.

But Leslie tugged on his arm and led him forward. "Madame DuBois," she called.

The other woman turned to face them.

Oh, hell! It was the wren.

She didn't seem all that old, but how could one tell?

She was wearing odd, pink-tinted spectacles that made her

eyes look muddy brown. Which figured, Alex thought, for she had heavy dark eyebrows and dull brown hair, which was pulled back and pinned into a tight knot. So tight, in fact, that Alex wondered if she had a perpetual headache, which would account for the fact that her skin was so pale that she looked almost unhealthy.

Then she smiled, and Alex was taken aback at her wide, generous mouth and perfect white teeth.

"Leslie!" she exclaimed in an almost breathless manner.

"Hello, Madame DuBois. I've brought my brother to meet you. Madame, may I present Alex Benedict?"

The woman's smile faltered, and since she hadn't so much as looked his way yet, Alex could swear that she'd been prepared to pretend he was invisible. Now she took a deep breath and stiffened her shoulders before turning to him.

Alex felt pity for the drab creature. He smiled, hoping to put her at ease. "*Enchanté,* madame," he said as he made a proper bow. She blinked in surprise. After one startled upward glance, she lowered her gaze to somewhere in the vicinity of his tie before gingerly extending her slim white hand. Alex grasped it, suddenly bedeviled into pressing his lips to her knuckles in the French manner, but he'd barely touched her cool fingers before she snatched her hand away.

"Pleased to make your acquaintance, Mr. Benedict," she murmured. Good God! Leslie hadn't been exaggerating when she said the woman was shy. Good thing at least two feet of space remained between them. Anne DuBois would probably turn cross-eyed with fear if a man got any closer.

How could this be? He'd expected a polished Frenchwoman of distinction, of sophistication. Of *experience!* Certainly not this prim, aloof female who spoke so softly he had to bend his head to hear her velvety voice, which was at such distinct odds with her stern appearance. That dulcet tone better suited a siren, a woman of passion, than this shriveled-up excuse for a female.

Ah, hell, she was such a sorry-looking thing, he no longer had the heart to tell her what he thought of her views. What did it matter, anyway? Leslie would no longer be under her influence.

"Likewise," he replied, his thoughts already wandering, wondering if it would be rude to step away—toward the blonde.

"Madame—" Leslie began.

"Leslie, since you're no longer a student," Madame cut in gently, "I think we may safely drop the formalities for good. From now on, I'm Anne, even in public."

Leslie flushed with pleasure. "Thank you . . . Anne. Oh, I almost forgot! I have something for you." She reached inside her reticule, pulled out an embossed envelope and handed it to the other woman. "It's your invitation to my birthday party."

"Oh, Leslie, it's very thoughtful and sweet of you to invite me, but I'm afraid I won't be able to come. You know Mrs. Busley frowns on the staff's socializing with the students."

Leslie wrinkled her pert nose. "Exactly. That's why I'm inviting her, also. Besides, as you just pointed out, I'm no longer a student, so how can she object?"

A soft laugh escaped Madame, bringing Alex's attention back to her. At least the woman was capable of humor.

"Why, you're absolutely right!" she exclaimed.

"So you'll come?" Leslie asked eagerly.

"Well . . ."

Alex tuned out the murmur of their voices as he glanced surreptitiously toward the blonde. His mouth curled in satisfaction when he noted that her own glance kept darting his way even as she conversed with the older couple.

Hands linked behind his back, he shifted restlessly from foot to foot, barely paying attention to the conversation taking place beside him as he waited for the couple to leave.

"Oh, you must come!" Leslie implored. "Aunt Lorna is planning a fantastic dinner and she's engaged an orchestra for dancing afterward, and—"

"It sounds wonderful, Leslie," Anne interrupted mildly. "I'd be delighted to come to dinner, but I hardly think I'll be dancing."

"Of course you will! Why, Alex will—" Leslie turned to her brother and jerked his sleeve to attract his attention. "Alex!"

He started, guiltily aware that he'd breached good manners by ignoring his sister and Madame DuBois. Regretfully, he turned away from the intriguing blonde. "What is it, Les?"

"You'll dance with Anne, won't you? At my party?"

His eyebrows went up at the sudden trap he saw springing before him. "I beg your pardon?"

"At my birthday party. Oh, do pay attention, Alex. Anne is reluctant to come, for she's afraid she'll feel uncomfortable and out of place," she stated bluntly. "But you'll dance with her, won't you?"

"Really, Leslie, it's not necessary to . . ." Madame DuBois stammered, and Alex saw that her pale cheeks now flamed with color. Once again he felt a twinge of pity.

"Oh, most certainly. I'd be honored," he lied. Damn Les and her impulsiveness!

Leslie ignored the glare he threw her way. "You see?" she pointed out to the other woman. "Now you must come."

The smile she gave his sister was more a grimace, yet her tone remained placid. "Thank you, Leslie. I'll be most happy to accept your invitation."

"Good! Then that's settled. Now, Alex, keep Anne company while I find Mrs. Busley and hand her invitation to her." And with that, Leslie was suddenly gone.

An awkward silence fell, until their simultaneous utterances.

"Mr. Benedict, I—"

"I apologize for Les—"

Alex chuckled good-humoredly, but she failed to respond in kind. In fact, her gaze through those awful spectacles was flitting nervously about the room, as if seeking escape. It was all too easy to read her uneasiness, Alex decided, and the one laugh he'd heard from her had likely been an aberration. She obviously didn't have any sense of humor. She was a bloodless, solemn prude. "I'm sorry," he said soberly. "You were saying?"

She straightened her spine. "Feel free to withdraw your dance invitation, Mr. Benedict," she said stiffly, focusing on something over his shoulder. "In fact, I'd prefer it. Frankly, I'm a bit out of practice, anyway."

I'd wager you are, Alex thought indelicately. She'd probably faint if a man put his arms around her, even to dance. But then it suddenly occurred to him that *she* was making excuses to get out of dancing with *him,* and he found himself inexplicably irritated by the polite rebuff. "How can that be?" he drawled, his eyes glittering with challenge. "I thought all Frenchwomen learned to dance before they could walk."

Her gaze jerked back to his. For just an instant he thought a flash of temper brightened the murky eyes behind the spectacles. He decided he'd been mistaken when she looked away again and replied in an even tone, "If you're insinuating that all Frenchwomen are frivolous, Mr. Benedict, I can only conclude that you've met very few. I assure you, Frenchwomen are no different than women everywhere. The majority are too busy struggling to survive to give much thought to dancing."

He could almost feel her hostility in waves, and since she didn't know him at all, he suspected that she reacted that way to all men. Damned if she *wasn't* a man-hater, then. Perversely, that fact made him want to retaliate. Childish of him, perhaps, but . . .

"You may be right," he said smoothly. "In which case, you can hardly turn down the opportunity to correct my misconception, can you? Besides, you never said you didn't know how to dance, only that you're out of practice. Leslie will verify that I have very staunch toes, Madame. So, shall we say the fifth waltz?"

Madame remained as still and silent as a fawn in hiding. Wondering what it would take to get some sort of reaction from her, Alex pushed on. "It will also give us a chance to discuss some of the subjects I understand you and Leslie have often conferred about," he added.

At least that got her to look at him again. "I'm afraid I don't know what subjects you're speaking of, Mr. Benedict," she said in her soft voice, a small frown creasing her forehead.

"Why, marriage, lovers. Yes, I do believe we must make time to have a chat," he said smoothly. "I'm curious to know how one goes about choosing a lover. I'm even more curious about how you—" he deliberately, slowly perused her from her face down to her feet— "came by this wealth of knowledge." Before she could do more than gasp at his sly implication that she hardly had the physical attributes to attract any lover, he took her hand, and this time he did kiss it. "I'll be looking forward to our dance. *Au revoir,* Madame."

It was with relief that Anne DuBois closed the door to her spartan room in the staff quarters at the school. She was never comfortable in social gatherings, particularly those of mixed company.

So small it was almost cell-like, the room contained only a minuscule dressing table with a stool, one armoire, a well-worn armchair, and a narrow cot, with her battered trunk at its foot. The sole signs of color were the cot's bright quilt and a small vase of red miniature carnations.

Anne pulled the stool out from beneath the dressing table and sat down before removing her spectacles. She didn't need them for seeing; they were but tinted glass, made to special order.

Unmoving, she stared at her reflection.

The sherry-colored eyes looking back at her revealed nothing. She saw simply Anne DuBois, a middle-aged, prim schoolteacher with a carefully blank expression, and it occurred to her that the bland countenance she was now studying had become so much a part of her, she even wore it in privacy.

Uncapping a jar of cleansing cream, she smoothed it over her face. Then, using a soft towel, she wiped off both the cream and the layer of pale powder beneath to reveal a glowing pink complexion. Lastly, she rubbed away all traces of the dark grease pencil she'd used to fill in and thicken her eyebrows. When her face was clean, she slowly unpinned the tight bun at her nape and shook her head to loosen her hair, then brushed it until most of the pomade she'd applied was gone and her tresses began to spring back into their natural curl as they fell against her shoulders. Later she'd wash out the remaining pomade and the dulling coffee rinse she'd begun substituting for the more expensive dye that dried and frizzed her naturally auburn hair.

The person now reflected in the mirror was much younger, with a face that only she saw, and then, so seldom it was almost that of a stranger.

Perhaps it was. What had happened to that person? That young woman named Rianne Forrester, whose true age was but twenty-three? Where had the once-vibrant girl of twelve, full of life and eager to taste it, gone? Had either of them really existed?

Of course they had.

But no trace of them remained now—perhaps because she'd taken on the persona of a mature widow and lived with it for five years. Good God, was it really that long since she'd arrived in Boston?

That had been an accident of fate. When she'd fled New Orleans and her former life, she hadn't had the luxury of time to choose her destination. She'd bought passage on the first ship to sail, frantic to get away from Lance Paxton, from the fury she'd seen on his bloody face.

When she'd learned that Boston was the ship's port of call, she'd been relieved, actually. She didn't believe Lance would think to look for her in a Northern city.

But the money she'd snatched from the dresser where Lance had laid it after emptying his pockets had almost run out. She'd been down to her last dollar by the time she'd been in Boston a week, and she'd desperately needed to find some means of support. She'd known it would be difficult, for all she'd ever been trained to do was to be a charming hostess and to properly please a man.

Hardly the kind of talents an eighteen-year-old girl on her own could safely fall back on in an unfamiliar city filled with strangers.

She'd purchased a copy of the *Globe*, hoping to find work in its classified advertisements. Her age precluded her obtaining a position as a housekeeper, and she shrank from the idea of becoming someone's paid companion. She didn't know how to, actually. She'd just spent five years in near seclusion. Except for her beloved nanny, Mimsie, her only companions had been the stiff, cold servants hired by Lance to watch her every move.

She'd carefully studied the advertisements in the *Globe* until she found one for a French instructor at a select school—The Chatham Academy for Young Ladies.

She'd never taught anyone anything, but she knew French. She'd grown up multilingual, for French was her mother's language. Too, as part of her "training," for an entire year Lance hadn't allowed her to speak anything *but* French. She had no references, of course; she would have to say that they hadn't yet arrived from New Orleans and hope that if she obtained the position and worked hard, perhaps the school would be so happy with her efforts that they'd forget about the references.

Her immediate concern was that the requirements specified that "only spinsters or widows of unquestionable character need apply."

She made inquiries and learned that the headmistress of the school was very particular. So she'd purchased the glasses and dulled her riotous hair with pomade and dye, applied a grease pencil to her eyebrows and heavily powdered her normally creamy complexion—and she had become Anne DuBois, a widow from New Orleans.

Even so, Mrs. Busley had been reluctant to hire her. But Chatham's last French instructor had eloped suddenly—a development over which the headmistress was still furious—and she was in a quandary, for the new school term was about to begin. So Mrs. Busley had agreed to give "Madame DuBois" a trial.

Rianne *had* worked very hard. She'd ingratiated herself with the other staff members, managed to charm the students, and run herself ragged trying to gratify Mrs. Busley's constant demands, strict rules, and miserly ways. Still, the position barely provided a living.

Initially Rianne had hoped to make enough money to set aside a little nest egg. She didn't much care for Boston. She hated its cold winters and even colder society. She didn't dare go back to New Orleans, but the West beckoned—an enormous expanse of land with few inhabitants and vast opportunities. Yet at the slow pace she was putting money aside, she'd never get there.

Rianne sighed.

She supposed she hadn't any choice but to stay on at the school for a time. But she would definitely have to ask Mrs. Busley for an increase in salary. After all, she'd had none since she'd first started teaching, and French instructors weren't exactly numerous in Boston. Mrs. Busley would have to search hard to find someone with "Madame's" ability. Though she wasn't Eudora Busley's favorite instructor, the headmistress couldn't deny that her rapport with the students was excellent, her French impeccable.

But, Lord, she was tired of Eudora Busley and her unending, unbending rules. And, oh, how she envied Leslie Benedict, who was free to travel with her brother all the way to Colorado Territory!

But the thought of Alex Benedict sent a spurt of anger through Rianne's veins. Certainly she conversed with other men—fathers and brothers of her students, primarily—but they were always polite and respectful. None of them had ever looked at her in Alex Benedict's condescending manner. Nor had any of them been so disgustingly rude.

Well, truth to tell, Alex Benedict wasn't at all what she'd expected. Leslie had often spoken of her brother, always in glowing terms, and Rianne had received the impression that the man was practically a saint and she'd pictured him as a mild-tempered man. Never would she have believed he would be so tall, so debonair. So damned arrogant! Oh, he was attractive enough.

Rianne stirred restlessly. All right, he was *extremely* attractive. She'd been so struck by his appearance, in fact, that her tongue had almost frozen to her teeth when she looked up at him and found those unfathomable, heavily-lashed green eyes assessing her.

Then there was that smiling mouth, which had almost coaxed her to respond in kind. That soft drawl, which reminded her of the things she'd loved and left behind: smooth, slow Southern speech, balmy breezes and steamy nights, the scent of magnolias . . .

Enough! Handsomeness meant nothing. Beautiful faces could very well hide ugliness. Hadn't she learned that at Lance Paxton's hands too well? Alex Benedict could be such a man, as well. The safest course of action would be to keep her distance, which was what she should have done from the beginning with Leslie.

If she hadn't broken one of her own rules—to refrain from forming a friendship with anyone—she wouldn't be feeling so agitated now. But she had let herself be drawn to Leslie, had even become the girl's friend. Perhaps it was because Leslie was open, so frightfully eager to experience life.

Hard to believe she'd been like that herself once. Only she hadn't had a brother to protect her.

Leslie was lucky to have one. Alex Benedict was surely a womanizer—Rianne hadn't missed those warm glances he'd exchanged with Mrs. Winters—but she had no doubt that he would be a lion when protecting his sister.

Oh, yes, Alex Benedict could be a dangerous adversary. Why, mere minutes after they met, he'd managed to crack her carefully constructed defenses and almost forced her to abandon the meek and subservient demeanor she'd learned, with much pain and difficulty, to wear. She'd had to bite her tongue to keep from responding to his rudeness in kind.

If Alex Benedict thought she would dance with him at Leslie's party just to be the object of his rude scrutiny and biting sarcasm again, he was mistaken. She didn't have to take that from anyone, especially a man who was a scoundrel, a rake, a . . .

Rianne scowled and grabbed her hairbrush, forgetting she'd already used it earlier. Alex Benedict wasn't worth her thoughts. She didn't like him at all, despite the fact that he was Leslie's brother.

He'd managed to breach that invisible wall with which Rianne had surrounded herself and ripple the waters of the deep well of anger within her.

It wouldn't do. It simply wouldn't do. She couldn't permit herself to feel so . . . so *alive!*

Chapter 3

"I still don't know how you managed to cajole me into this," Alex complained good-naturedly.

Sitting beside him in Aunt Lorna's runabout, Leslie grinned. "Well, I thought that, since you're paying for my new wardrobe, you might want to give it your approval."

"All right, I approve."

"Not good enough." Leslie laughed. "Give in, Alex. Besides, it's my last fitting; it shouldn't take too long. You might even enjoy it."

"Sitting at a dressmaker's for even an hour is hardly my idea of enjoyment," he grumbled.

"I suppose you'd do it willingly enough if the woman was your lover instead of your sister," Leslie said slyly.

Alex's brow rose a half inch. Bantering with his little sister was enjoyable, but this fixation she had with the subject of lovers was disconcerting. He didn't give a damn what Aunt Lorna *or* Anne DuBois said. His not-yet-eighteen-year-old sister shouldn't even be thinking about the subject, and he told her so.

"May I remind you that in a couple of days I *will* be eighteen?" Leslie was clearly exasperated. "And give me some credit. I'm intelligent enough to know that my brother, being a male, is hardly celibate."

"Dammit, brat! My love life is not a subject I care to discuss with you, nor is it something you should even be aware of!" Alex was clearly perturbed.

"Why not?" Leslie returned calmly. "Just because men wish women to be subservient doesn't mean we have to conform. Nor does it mean we can't think for ourselves. Anne says a woman is no less entitled to have opinions than a man is."

Alex frowned. "Anne again. The sound of that name is beginning to irritate me. You shouldn't take to heart everything she's told you, Les. I seriously doubt she's an expert on the male of the species."

"How would you know? You've only just met her."

"Yes, well, I'm beginning to think I should have vetted the Chatham Academy and its staff before Aunt Lorna and I sent you there. I'm not convinced that your beloved Anne has been the right sort of influence."

"Honestly, Alex. I've attended Chatham's since I was twelve. Anne wasn't even there my first year. And now that I've graduated, it's too late to worry about it, isn't it?"

"That depends on what other knowledge Anne has passed on to you about men and lov—about men."

Leslie's tone was one of smug satisfaction. "You'll just have to wonder, won't you?" Her green eyes were sparkling with suppressed laughter.

"Or I could make it a point to have a long discussion with her, couldn't I?"

Leslie lowered her gaze and idly played with a button on her glove. "Well," she said mischievously, "I do believe you'll get your chance, since she's meeting us at the dressmaker's."

Alex's head snapped about, and he glowered down at his sister. "*What?*"

"Anne is meeting us at the dressmaker's," Leslie repeated. "I offered to stop by the school for her but she refused, because she had other errands to run first."

Alex groaned. "If I'd known *she* was coming, I wouldn't have agreed to accompany you."

Leslie's head jerked up. "You don't like her?" She was astonished and disappointed.

"Let's just say she's not the type of woman who holds my interest," he responded cautiously. He didn't want to upset Leslie or risk her volatile anger, for it was plain she thought highly of the Frenchwoman. "If you asked her, why am I here? Perhaps I could drop you off and—"

"Oh, no, you don't! You promised, Alex!" Leslie wailed. "I asked Anne because Aunt Lorna is too busy with the arrangements for my party, and I'd like to have a woman's opinion, but I value yours, too. You have impeccable taste and an eye for women's fashion."

"Something your Anne obviously doesn't," he muttered, "considering her own atrocious attire."

"It's not her fault if she doesn't have the money to spend on clothing," Leslie defended hotly. "Besides, Mrs. Busley has restrictions on staff wardrobe. But I happen to know Anne has as good an eye as you do. We've spent hours studying *Harper's Bazar* and discussing style."

Alex muttered something that sounded suspiciously like "what style?" before tugging on the reins to halt Aunt Lorna's matched bays.

Anne DuBois was indeed waiting at the dressmaker's establishment. She rose from her chair and returned Leslie's exuberant greeting with that warm, unexpected smile that was, in Alex's estimation, her sole redeeming feature, before turning to him.

"How nice to see you again, Mr. Benedict," she murmured with no inflection whatsoever in her tone, implying that she didn't think it nice at all.

So she didn't like him. Well, he didn't much care for her, either. "The feeling's mutual," he returned with the same equanimity.

She didn't so much as blink as she turned away to attend to the conversation between Leslie and the owner of the establishment, Mrs. Porter. In short order the three of them were following the dressmaker to the back of her shop.

Alex found his gaze focusing on Madame DuBois's apparel as he trailed behind her. Lord, he could not imagine how Leslie thought that this creature had taste and style. The hat she wore was unadorned. Not a feather. His gaze moved lower. The dull olive suit didn't have so much as a touch of braid.

Still, the cut was quite good. The masculine style of the jacket hugged her waist—which he noticed was almost small enough for his hands to encircle—and draped her hips quite nicely.

In fact, he noted with some surprise, Anne DuBois had a very acceptable figure. Trim, not voluptuous, but with curves in all the right places and a smoothly rounded bottom . . .

"Oh!"

Alex jerked back at her exclamation, chagrined to realize that he'd been so engrossed he'd failed to realize she'd come to a halt. He had walked right into her. "I *beg* your pardon!" he blurted, feeling abruptly like an awkward adolescent.

She didn't acknowledge either him or his apology, merely stepped carefully away, and Alex felt even more foolish.

"Make yourselves comfortable," Mrs. Porter invited. "I'll escort Miss Benedict to the dressing room. We'll be back shortly."

As if by unspoken agreement, Alex and Rianne separated, he going to the settee on one side of the room, she to the other. It wasn't until they were both seated that either of them realized they had put themselves in the position of having to face one another across a space of less than ten feet.

Two pairs of eyes flitted about the room in pretended casualness. There was not much to see, for it was fitted out like a small parlor, with only the two sofas and several tables.

The table in front of Rianne held a bound volume of fabric swatches. She pounced upon it eagerly, flipping the pages while pretending to finger the samples, but her mind was elsewhere.

On Alex Benedict, to be specific.

The unexpected feel of his hard thighs against hers when he'd bumped into her had unnerved her. He'd been so close, she'd even caught a whiff of his scent. Not bay rum as Lance had used, but something more subtle, more tantalizing.

Oh, would Leslie and Mrs. Porter never return?

This is ridiculous! Alex thought. He'd been a boy of fourteen the last time a woman had come this close to unnerving him. Of course, it had been her beauty that had done it, and God knew the woman sitting across from him had little of that. No, it was Madame's aloofness, her unattractive, placidly blank face that made him feel like some lowly creature. Irked, he decided to challenge her, simply to see if he could ruffle *her* feathers.

He opened his mouth, preparatory to doing precisely that, but the dressing room door opened, and Leslie sailed in, followed by Mrs. Porter. Leslie swirled to a stop in the middle of the floor. "This is the gown I'm wearing for my birthday party. What do you think?" she asked.

The dress was white, as befitted a debutante. Gauzy puffed sleeves supported a low neckline, while a faille overskirt was hitched to a demi-train underskirt in horizontal puffs by garlands of white roses.

Alex stared at the bodice. "Don't you think it reveals a bit too much, er, skin?" he asked cautiously.

"Certainly not. This is an evening dress, not a walking suit," Leslie informed him with a sigh of exasperation.

"The neckline is actually quite modest," Mrs. Porter added. "But we could add an insert if—"

"Absolutely not!" Leslie cut in. "Alex, I'm a woman. I have a bosom. You might as well get used to it."

A choking sound jerked Alex's gaze to the woman sitting across from him just in time to see her cover her mouth with one gloved hand and lower her head. She coughed softly.

Alex's eyes narrowed in suspicion. Could Madame have been laughing at him? Not possible. She had no sense of humor. "Anne, inform my overprotective brother that this gown is perfectly decent," Leslie pleaded.

At that, Madame's head rose, and she shot a quick glance in Alex's direction. Though her expression revealed nothing, he thought that her eyes were gleaming behind those awful spectacles. Before he could form his expression into a retaliatory glower, she rose and approached Leslie.

"Perhaps your brother simply needs to become accustomed to seeing you in something other than school clothes and day wear," she replied calmly before walking around Leslie to study the back of the gown. "The dress is beautiful, and the style suits you."

"Ha! You see?" Leslie chortled with a triumphant glance at her brother.

Alex shrugged. "I seem to be outnumbered."

"You are," she retorted. "The dress is perfect. Almost. If only . . ."

"What?" Alex asked. "You've decided you don't like it after all, brat?"

"Oh, I love the style. It's just that I wish I could wear

something other than white. I'm really, really sick of wearing white and pastels."

"It looks fine with your complexion and black hair."

"Your hair stands out wonderfully against—"

Alex and Rianne exchanged startled glances as they both spoke at the same time.

Rianne looked away first. "It's a requirement, Leslie," she reminded gently. "Once you've passed your eighteenth birthday, you'll be able to wear brighter colors. Haven't you already ordered other gowns?"

Leslie brightened. "I have, and I'm never going to wear white again if I can help it."

Alex appeared shocked. "You damn well better on your wedding day!"

"I've told you, Alex, I may never *have* a wedding day," Leslie retorted. She turned to Mrs. Porter. "Well, it seems my brother and Anne approve of this gown. Shall we show them some of the others?" She disappeared through the doorway, the dressmaker following.

Alex and Rianne's glances met. "Never let it be said that my sister doesn't have a mind of her own," he noted.

"Leslie's a very intelligent young woman," Rianne offered.

"I was thinking more along the lines of *stubborn.*"

"Oh."

Alex frowned when she bit her lip. "You find my concern for my sister amusing?"

"Not at all. I find it rather endearing . . ."

Endearing? Hell, she made him sound like an absent-minded, elderly uncle.

". . . even if a bit excessive," she finished.

Alex felt a spurt of anger. All right, so maybe he was inclined to be overprotective, but this woman had no business telling him to what extent he should care for his own sister. Crossing his arms over his chest, he narrowed his gaze on her. "You don't much like men, do you, Madame?"

"I wouldn't know," she replied placidly. "I haven't had much to do with them."

"Yet you were married once."

Her only response was to lower her lashes.

Alex's anger and frustration grew. More often than not he affected a devil-may-care attitude, and he was a natural tease. Most women found both traits charming and responded to his teasing in kind. This one didn't appear amused.

In fact, Leslie seemed to be the only person granted Madame's rare smiles, which were really wonderful. She looked much younger, more approachable, when she smiled.

Right now, however, he didn't care whether she smiled or threw something at him. He just wanted to provoke a response.

"I'll wager you didn't much like marriage, either," he drawled.

Her shoulders stiffened, but she said nothing.

"What was it? Did your husband offend your feminine sensibilities on your wedding night? Were you shocked to discover that the gentle man who'd courted and charmed you was nothing more than a male animal? Or do I have it all wrong? Did he seduce you beforehand? Tell me, Madame DuBois," he drawled, "was *your* wedding gown virginal white?" The insinuation was clear.

Alex felt a moment's satisfaction when her pale skin turned even whiter. He knew he was being deliberately crude, but the woman's demeanor grated on him and he wanted to crack that stillness, that composure.

Even now, her face showed no expression as she spoke. "That, Mr. Benedict, is none of your business," she replied calmly, and she turned her head to stare unseeingly at the opposite wall. Rianne clasped her trembling hands tightly in her lap. Alex Benedict had surpassed ill manners; he was downright contemptuous. Why was he baiting her so? He had no right to be so rude. No right at all. Her trembling came from the sight of Leslie, so young and so innocent, in the white gown which had reminded her of a similar gown . . .

The dress had hung in her closet in the little Creole cottage on rue Dauphine for almost a month. It was the most beautiful dress she'd ever seen. It *was* virginal white, of course. She'd never worn anything else.

But this dress was special . . .

It was all gleaming satin, cut in simple lines, but its sleeves and bodice and hem were trimmed with lace stitched by nuns—the only ones who produced that particular kind of lace, usually worn by Creole brides. Rianne knew that because the dressmaker had mentioned it several times during the fittings.

"You can't wear it until the eve of your eighteenth birthday, pet," Lance had warned. "I'm taking you to your first opera, then dinner. Afterward, sometime past midnight, we'll return home." His smile was genuine, the one that made her stomach flutter. "It's going to be a special night—a very special occasion—for both of us," he added.

He could only mean that the minister would be waiting when they came home. Her heart thudded with excitement but, as usual, she lowered her lashes and said demurely, "Yes, Lance."

She wanted to ask him about the veil. Surely for her wedding she should wear a veil, too, made of the same lace.

But she didn't ask. Lance didn't like being questioned. He frowned and became abrupt, she'd discovered, and since she couldn't stand his being cross with her, she'd learned to accept everything he told her, do everything as he expected, and never presume to ask questions.

Besides, why should she? He was all she had. Her father had been killed in the War Between the States, when she was almost twelve, her mother in the same carriage accident that had killed Lance's father, when Rianne was thirteen.

She would have been left orphaned and penniless, with no one but Mimsie, if it hadn't been for Lance. He was the one who had broken the terrible news, who had made the arrangements for her mother's burial, who had told her that not only would she continue to live at the house but that she was now his ward. He'd promised he would see to it that she lacked for nothing.

She'd been relieved. She'd been grateful. And he'd kept his word.

He provided only the best clothing and food, hired the best teachers. She learned dancing and appreciation of music and art, how to entertain and be a perfect hostess, and she improved her French. If her innate intelligence made her impatient that her lessons only touched on the basics of science, mathematics, and geography—geared as they were toward nothing more than shaping conversational abilities—she never disputed her tutors. And if sometimes she felt she was treated more like a delicate flower than a person, she never rebelled.

She'd learned to adore Lance.

She'd believed that he was grooming her to be his bride.

Strangely enough, though, Mimsie looked at her sadly whenever Rianne mentioned it. Odder still, Mimsie had never liked Lance. Once, shortly after Rianne turned sixteen, she'd overheard the two of them arguing furiously. It had been during one of Lance's weekly visits; he always came on Sunday afternoons and stayed to have a late dinner with her.

This particular evening, she'd thought him already gone.

Mimsie had helped her prepare for bed and left the room, but Rianne had been too restless to sleep and so had slipped downstairs to find Mimsie and ask her to prepare a tisane.

She'd heard voices in the small salon and, curious, had tiptoed closer to discover who was visiting.

"Dat girl is meant for better things!" she'd heard Mimsie say.

To Rianne's surprise, it had been Lance who replied. "That's not for you to say." His voice had been cold.

"She be my baby. *Ma petite papillonne d'or.* My little golden butterfly. I was her mama's mammy, and when li'l Rianne was born, I come hers. Dat give me every right."

"Oh, yes, her mama—my father's whore!"

"Miss Claudine was a good woman—a good wife when she was married to Masta Forrester. After he was kilt, the bank took the land. She had nuthin' to live on and a chile to care for. Yer pa gave her a choice when he made her his mistress. But you ain't givin' my girl a choice. Mebbe she don't want—"

"Listen, old woman, I'm the one who's supporting Rianne. Where do you think she'd be without me? She'd be selling her wares in some bordello—would've been from the time her mama died." Lance had laughed derisively. "She'd be worn out by now, used by every man who had the price. She's a damned sight better off with me. So don't try to tell me what I can or can't do with Rianne. She's mine, and if you don't like it, you can leave."

"No! I cain't leave my baby!"

"Then keep your mouth shut and your thoughts to yourself, old woman!"

Rianne heard a chair being shoved back and guessed that Lance was leaving. She fled to her room, instinctively knowing he wouldn't like finding her eavesdropping.

Afterward, she lay in bed, uneasy for the first time. She'd never heard Lance actually shout before. It must have been Mimsie's fault. Mimsie should have known better. It wasn't her place to tell her employer what to do.

Rianne had not understood what the argument had been about, except that it had involved her.

Lance had called her mother a whore. She had no idea what a whore was, nor had she understood any of the other implications. Her greatest fear was his threat to make Mimsie leave.

Oh, God, not that! Mimsie was the only person left from the life she'd once known. Lance had gotten rid of the other family retainers, replacing them with stiff, stoic minions who answered only to him. Mimsie couldn't leave!

The next morning, when she confessed her eavesdropping to Mimsie, the old servant hugged her fiercely and assured her she'd been mistaken. "I ain't never gonna leave, missy. I's gonna stay wit' you 'til the day I meet my maker." Rianne was so relieved that she forgot to ask her other questions.

Or maybe she was afraid to ask. She only wanted everything to continue as before, for Lance to remain attentive and pleased with her and for Mimsie to stay with her.

It had just been a misunderstanding. Lance hadn't meant anything by it.

So she convinced herself, and then she forgot about the disturbing conversation she'd overheard, for Mimsie stayed on, and she was there on the eve of Rianne's eighteenth birthday, to help dress her in that gorgeous satin gown.

The last white dress she'd ever worn . . .

Alex gritted his teeth. Did nothing ruffle the woman's composure? Hell, she must have water running in her veins. Just now, she looked about as warm as Arctic ice as she stared at a painting on the wall to his left, as if he wasn't even present.

"Oh, but it is," he said grimly.

Rianne started. She'd been lost in her memories. "I beg your pardon?"

"I was asking you about your marriage, remember? You told me it was none of my business. I beg to differ. You've had a lot of influence on Leslie. She's been quoting you without cease. Since you agree that I have a right to be concerned, you must surely agree that I have a right to know upon what you base those opinions she's been spouting."

She met his hard gaze unemotionally. "Yes. All right. What do you want to know?"

"How long have you been widowed?"

"Ah . . . five years."

"Did you love him? Was it a happy marriage?"

Rianne's nails bit into her palms. "I . . . yes. For a time." She saw a gleam of triumph light his eyes and felt her face warm. Why had she tacked that on? Why couldn't she simply have said yes and left it at that? Oh, she was no good at dissembling. She hadn't really had to before. No one had asked her specific details about her supposed marriage. Everyone had merely accepted that she was a widow.

"Which one? You loved him, or it was a happy marriage for a time?"

"I *thought* I loved him," she mumbled, so rattled that she wasn't even aware that she'd emphasized *thought.*

"Aha! So the romance didn't last. What happened? Was he cruel to you? Did he beat you? Starve you? What?" he goaded.

"Mr. Benedict, I can't answer those questions. I don't *have* to answer," she said desperately, praying that her voice hadn't quaked. Oh, God, she couldn't lose control!

"Did he take a mistress? Is that why you told Leslie that men aren't what they seem? Or did your husband discover that *you'd* taken a lover and cuckolded *him?*"

Rianne gasped at his blatant crudeness. *"Really!"* She was sure that her voice was squeaking, like a rarely-used wheel. Her hand went to her throat. "Your questions are much too personal, sir, and exceed the bounds of propriety!"

Alex sat back, smiling. Her slim fingers had begun stroking her throat, slowly at first, then faster. He didn't think she was even aware of the revealing gesture, but she was clearly agitated. He'd managed to finally break through that aloofness, and damned if he wasn't enjoying her discomfiture.

"Well, at least I've learned one thing about you, Anne," he drawled, deliberately using her given name. "You quite clearly detest all men, not just me."

"I—"

"Here I am again!" Leslie's voice suddenly interrupted. "This is my favorite gown. What do you think of it?"

Alex and Rianne both glanced up to find her wearing an evening gown of pale jade shot through with gold that shimmered with each step she took.

"It's lovely!" Rianne exclaimed, effectively distracted from the man sitting across from her. Rising to her feet, she approached Leslie and fingered the fabric. "Oh, it's silk! Gorgeous!"

"The fabric is very special," Mrs. Porter informed her, "and quite rare."

Leslie turned to her brother. "It came in on one of your ships, didn't it, Alex? All the way from India."

"Yes, it did. We saved it specially for you and Audra."

At Rianne's questioning gaze, Leslie explained. "Audra is Nick Brannon's wife, and Nick is Alex's partner. Hence, the name of their company, Brannon and Benedict. They own vast shipping and railroad lines, not to mention gold mines in Colorado Territory. That's where their headquarters are now, and that's where we'll be going after New Orleans."

"I see," Anne murmured. Lord, she hadn't known he was so wealthy, too.

"Still, there's something wrong with this dress," Leslie said. "I feel it, but I don't know what it is."

Rianne stepped back to study it. "I wonder . . . perhaps if the bows were removed from the sleeves? The gown doesn't really need them. They're superfluous."

"You may be right. What do you think, Alex?"

"I think Anne's correct. The bows only detract from the classic simplicity of the lines. Don't you think so, Mrs. Porter?"

The woman came to stand beside Rianne. "Bows are all the style, but . . . hmm. They're only held by a few stitches. Let me snip one off, and then we'll see." She proceeded to do so.

"Oh, yes!" Rianne exclaimed. "Much better."

Leslie glanced toward her brother, who nodded approvingly.

"Please remove the other bow, Mrs. Porter."

The dressmaker did so, while Leslie addressed both Alex and Rianne. "There's only one more gown I want you both to see. You don't mind, do you?"

"Not at all," Alex responded coolly, though his mouth wore a tight smile. "Anne and I are enjoying becoming acquainted, aren't we, Anne?"

"I . . . yes," Rianne replied, striving to match his tone. Unaware of the tension, Leslie beamed at them. "Good. I'm so glad you two are getting to know each other. You're two of my favorite people, you know. Anne, you will return to the house with us for tea after we've finished here, won't you? Aunt Lorna is expecting you."

"I don't think—"

"Yes, why don't you?" Alex cut in. "It will give us a chance to get to know one another *even better.*"

He was laughing at her. Daring her to refuse. Oh, how she'd love to accept, just to show him she wasn't afraid of him or his laughing insults. But as much as she hated to admit it, she was.

Thank goodness, she had to be back at the school within the hour. "I'd love to have tea with you and Mrs. Hall, Leslie, but I can't today. I'm running errands for Mrs. Busley, and the school's driver will be here shortly," she replied.

Leslie accepted the refusal good-naturedly, but she and Mrs. Porter were no sooner gone, and Rianne had no sooner reclaimed her seat—being careful not to look at Mr. Benedict as she did so—than he clicked his tongue at her.

"Tsk, tsk."

Her head shot up before she could prevent it. *"What?"* She bit down on her lip. She'd practically shouted it.

"Be careful, Anne. Your animosity is showing."

She refused to speak to him at all after that, and they sat in silence—except for the sound of his unconcealed chuckles.

Chapter 4

In the receiving line, Leslie—flanked by her aunt and Alex—was accepting felicitations from the guests.

"How are you, Mr. and Mrs. Thornby? So nice to see you both again. Thank you for attending my birthday celebration." Then, in an aside to Alex, she murmured, "What time is it?"

"Almost seven."

"Oh, dear. I wonder what's happened to Anne . . . Oh, hello, Mrs. Saldorn. Yes, it's exciting to finally reach eighteen. Thank you so much for coming." Leslie waited until the woman moved on before whispering again into Alex's ear. "You don't think Anne's decided not to come, do you?"

"I'm sure Madame DuBois would have sent her regrets if that were the case, Les," he replied absently.

If the damned woman had decided just that, it was fine with him, for he wasn't looking forward to dancing with her. He regretted his rash baiting of her at the dressmaker's. It had barely caused even a ripple in her placid demeanor. The woman was a real bore.

"That's true," Leslie agreed. "And Mrs. Busley is a stickler for protocol. I'm sure they've only been delayed."

"Mmm." Alex didn't hear Leslie, for the delectable Sylvia Winters, who was standing across the room, had just turned to smile at him, her blue eyes beckoning.

Now *there* was an interesting piece of femininity! He'd finally gotten Leslie to introduce him to her at the commencement, and he and Mrs. Winters had spent an enjoyable fifteen minutes in conversation, during which time he'd learned that she was a descendent of one of Boston's founding fathers and therefore highly ranked in society. She was also a widow who was wealthy enough to live as she pleased, within her own code of discretion. She hadn't flaunted her interest in him, but she hadn't been coy about it, either. She'd made it clear she was available, and Alex intended to avail himself.

"Alex, you will remember to dance with her, won't you?"

"Hmm?"

"Anne! You'll dance with her, won't you?" Leslie repeated.

"What, Les?" Alex sent the lovely widow a smile that promised "later" as he returned his attention to his sister. "Oh, dance. With Anne DuBois. Perhaps."

"Oh, Alex, you promised!" Leslie wailed.

He rolled his eyes. "Oh, all right, Les. But you owe me."

"Thank you, Alex," she murmured in appropriate gratitude. "I want Anne to feel welcome. Oh, I wish she'd leave that school and come with us."

Alex glanced down at his sister, surprised at this new notion of hers. "You mean to Georgia and New Orleans?"

"Yes. I think she'd love it, and she'd make an interesting travel companion."

Alex almost rolled his eyes. He and Leslie often thought alike, but in this they were definitely at odds. He couldn't understand Leslie's infatuation with a woman who seemed to have as much life in her as . . . as a doorstop. "Now, Les . . ." Alex reached out to shake the hand of the man standing before him. "Quite right, Mr. Mathers. I'm always happy to visit Boston again. Now, Les," he continued as Mathers stepped past, "don't you think you're carrying this sudden friendship too far?"

"Sudden? Alex, I've known Anne for years."

"All right, all right," he conceded. "But what makes you think she isn't content at the school? I doubt she'd care to give up a secure position to accompany you to Bellesfield and New Orleans."

"Why wouldn't she? New Orleans was once her home, after all. And she was fascinated by the stories I've told her about Bellesfield."

Alex glanced down at his sister. "How could you have many? After all, you were sent away when you were nine, after Mother died. And you were only six when the Conflict began. Surely your memories can't be pleasant."

"Six is hardly a toddler. And I do remember happy times. I remember the houseparties and the dances, and—Oh! She's here!"

"Who's here?"

"Why, Anne, of course."

Rianne trailed miserably behind a huffing Eudora Busley.

She hadn't expected so many people to attend Leslie's party. She hated noisy crowds. Her life was secluded and sometimes lonely, and large groups made her nervous. Already her skin felt clammy, and it was becoming difficult to breathe. One of the pins holding her hair in its usual tight bun was digging into her scalp, giving her a slight headache.

Of course, it didn't help that the bodice of her one dressy gown was made of black velvet, with long sleeves and a slightly scooped neckline. She felt itchy and hot. One glance at the colorful gowns of the other women, and she felt horribly out of place, too.

She really did not want to be here. And yet . . .

And yet it was strangely exciting, too, though she couldn't

understand why she should have this odd thrill of anticipation.

As if she couldn't control her gaze, it went straight to the receiving line and immediately found Alex Benedict, who was standing at his sister's side.

It would have been difficult not to be drawn to that imposing figure. His black hair was slicked back, revealing a proud forehead. His chiseled features were softened by a small smile that played about his mouth as he gazed across the room.

He was insolent and arrogant, she reminded herself.

Rianne squared her shoulders. Whatever else happened, she wasn't going to let him intimidate her. And if he *dared* give her that condescending look again, she'd . . . she'd . . .

"Come along, Madame DuBois. We're late enough as it is," Mrs. Busley scolded as she handed her wrap to a footman. "We wouldn't be in this humiliating position if you'd remembered to inform Harold that he couldn't have this evening off, thus forcing us to hire a cab. A hired cab, indeed! I've never had to depend on one before."

Rianne sighed and bit her lip to keep from retorting that her employer had never told her to speak to Harold, the school's carriage driver. Mrs. Busley was becoming forgetful. Everyone at the school knew it. She knew it herself but was too stubborn to admit it. Not that it mattered. She blamed everyone but herself for her own shortcomings.

"Mrs. Busley! And Madame DuBois! How lovely that you could come." Lorna Hall greeted them with a warm smile. A little pang of nostalgia swept through Rianne as she watched her converse with an overly effusive Mrs. Busley. Leslie's aunt was charming and gracious, and very loving with Leslie. Mrs. Hall brought back memories of her own mother.

Mrs. Busley finally moved on to Leslie, giving Rianne a chance to return Mrs. Hall's greeting. "Thank you for inviting us. You have a charming home. So many lovely, old French pieces."

Though she and Leslie were friends and she had been introduced to Leslie's aunt years ago, their encounters had all taken place at the school. Determined to keep their personal friendship private, Anne had gently refused all Leslie's invitations to Lorna's home.

"Thank you. You're familiar with Louis the Sixteenth style, then?" Lorna laughed at herself. "But of course you are. I keep forgetting that you're French yourself."

"Only half, on my mother's side," Rianne corrected absently, for once again her gaze had been drawn to Alex Benedict. She was disconcerted to find that, though he stood tall and silent with his hands clasped behind his back, his cool green gaze was pinned directly on her. She quickly turned back to Lorna. "I've never owned any pieces, myself." That was true enough. The little house in New Orleans had been filled with French treasures, but she'd never claimed them for her own. "You're very fortunate."

Lorna laughed. "Exactly what I tried to tell my husband. Poor Burton. He was always terrified that he'd crash to the floor if he sat in one of the chairs. Of course, his study was furnished much differently, with very serviceable, sturdy furniture. It still is. I shall give you a tour of the house one day."

"I'd like that very much."

"Good. Now I'd better cease chattering, for Leslie has been fretting all evening that you wouldn't come."

Rianne turned to take Leslie's hand and squeeze it. "Hello, Leslie. I'm sorry we're late."

"It doesn't matter, now that you're here. I only hope that you'll enjoy yourself, Anne."

"I'm sure I will." But she knew she wouldn't. The scent of roses filled the warm room. A scent that plunged her stomach into quivering unease. Oh, God, how humiliating it would be should she faint! Particularly right in front of . . .

"*Bonsoir,* Madame DuBois."

Rianne lifted her chin and gave him her hand, determined to impress upon him that his opinion was worthless. "Mr. Benedict," she returned coolly, meeting his gaze. "How very . . . *nice* to see you again," she added, her slightly caustic tone giving the lie to what seemed a simple social comment.

As she'd intended, he caught the inflection immediately, for his eyebrows rose in surprise. Just a fraction, but enough to give her a small feeling of triumph. She sent him a fleeting smile and turned, prepared to step away immediately toward Mrs. Busley, who was waiting for her.

She was brought up short when he wouldn't release her hand.

"You haven't forgotten, have you?"

"I beg your pardon?" she said, turning her head slightly to look at him over her shoulder.

"Dear me!" he replied mockingly. "Are all women so fickle? You promised me a dance, did you not?"

Rianne's gaze fell to his mouth, which quirked in the most fascinating manner. "Oh! I . . . Well, yes. Of course." As she recalled, she hadn't *promised* him any such thing, but she realized he had no intention of forgetting. What she could do, however, was make sure she was unavailable by the time the fifth waltz came around. How convenient for her that he'd specified the dance!

"*Bon!* I'm looking forward to it," he murmured as he released her hand.

I'll bet you are, Rianne thought scornfully. *I'll bet you're just itching for another chance to be rude and insulting to me!*

Mrs. Busley appeared at her elbow. "Come along now,

Madame DuBois! It's most impolite, monopolizing Mr. Benedict's time this way!"

Rianne's cheeks warmed. Her conversation with him had lasted barely a minute, and though it had been a slight battle of wills, an eavesdropper—which Mrs. Busley had certainly been—could have found nothing improper in it. The headmistress had no call to chastise her. Rianne's eyes sparked angrily, clearly visible even through the pink lenses of her spectacles, yet she said nothing as she let herself be led away.

"Old bat!" Leslie murmured loud enough for only Alex to hear. "I think she's just jealous because you didn't ask *her* to dance! Poor Anne. How she puts up with that woman, I don't know."

Alex hadn't missed Anne's spark of rebellion, either.

So the little widow wasn't quite as mousy and subservient as she appeared! Perhaps it would be worth the dance after all, to see if he could bring light to those muddy eyes again.

But all he said to Leslie was, "I agree. However, keep in mind that no one is forcing her to teach at Chatham's. It's her choice. I think your guests have all arrived. Shall we join the party?"

The hundred guests were seated at ten large round tables. The delicious dinner was perfectly prepared and served, yet Rianne ate almost nothing. She played with her food and desperately tried to avoid the sight and scent of the arrangements of white roses on the table. For once she would have been glad to have the distraction of conversation, but the young man seated to her left had eyes only for the lovely brunette across the table from him.

The elderly gentleman on her right, who had introduced himself as Major Collins, did make an attempt, but then he became curious and began to ask questions about her background. Rianne mumbled evasive answers, and he finally gave up trying to converse with her at all.

Thereafter Rianne tried to ignore the roses by focusing on the other guests at her table. She felt awkward and out of place, despite that she was well versed in all the social niceties and capable of hosting a dinner party such as this herself. She'd spent years learning the rules and obligations. She merely hadn't had much opportunity to put them to practical use.

When dinner was over, Rianne gratefully left the table and the roses, only to be filled with dismay when she discovered that the ballroom was also decorated with roses. Hanging baskets of roses, vases and urns filled with roses. Their perfume was overwhelming. Her chest felt constricted.

By the time the dancing commenced, Rianne was desperate to escape. She searched the room for Mrs. Busley with the intention of informing her that she wasn't feeling well and wanted to leave. But she was unable to find her employer, so she began to make her way to the door, intending to leave a message with the majordomo.

Unfortunately, she was waylaid by the mother of one of her students who insisted on thanking her for taking extra time to tutor her daughter. Rianne was so distracted, attempting to count the waltzes, that she hardly heard the conversation.

By the time the woman finally stopped chattering, the orchestra was halfway through the fourth waltz. Since she was still on the opposite side of the room from the exit, Rianne slipped behind a pillar to hide in the hopes that Alex Benedict wouldn't find her.

She tensed when footsteps approached but relaxed when she recognized Major Collins's voice.

"Alex, m'boy!"

Rianne held her breath. Oh, no! She was sure she'd seen

Mr. Benedict at a distance conversing with a group of men, but here he was, no more than six feet away!

"Major," his deep voice replied. "Nice to see you again."

"Same here, m'boy. Same here. I've been meaning to have a word with you about the railroad company you and your partner, Brannon, have started. Might be interested in investing. Thought perhaps you and I could have a little chat about it."

"I'd be happy to, Major. But I'm afraid I can't tonight."

"Of course! Of course! Didn't mean right now, you know, it being your sister's birthday. Besides, a young man like you should be enjoying yourself. How is it you're not dancing?"

"As a matter of fact, I'm promised for the next dance and was just seeking my partner."

"The intriguing Mrs. Winters?" The major chuckled. "Saw the looks you exchanged with her at dinner. Can't say I blame you, son. Was young myself once, and the widow is a delicious morsel."

"Actually, I was looking for the lady who was sitting next to you at dinner. Madame DuBois. You haven't seen her, have you?"

"You mean that quiet little thing? Hmm, can't say I have. Must say I'm surprised, though. Why dance with her when you could partner Sylvie Winters?"

"I promised my sister I'd dance with Madame."

"Oh, I see. A pity dance, hmm?"

Rianne cringed. She strained to catch Alex Benedict's reply, but heard only an indecipherable murmur.

"Trying to save a poor wallflower, I gather. Good of you, son. We men have to do our duty, no matter how onerous, don't we?"

Another murmur, then the sound of footsteps again as both men moved away.

Rianne shrank back even farther behind the pillar, mortified.

Of course she'd known that Alex Benedict hadn't wanted to dance with her, but did he have to announce it to everyone?

She'd leave. Right now. No doubt Mr. Benedict would be relieved to escape his "onerous duty."

Turning, she fled, using the pillars to shield herself, but when she reached the last one, she was dismayed to see a crowd of people blocking her path to the door.

And then the orchestra began the strains of another number.

Oh, God, the fifth waltz! And she was trapped!

Leaning back against the pillar, she bowed her head and closed her eyes. *Just a few minutes,* she told herself, and took a deep breath. *Only a few minutes, and then I can make my way around the edge of the crowd and . . .*

Rianne opened her eyes—and found herself looking down at a pair of glossy black shoes.

Her head shot up. Alex Benedict stood before her, one eyebrow raised in query, one corner of his mouth crooked. "I believe this dance is ours, Madame DuBois?"

Oh, Lord! Where had he come from? "I . . . ah . . . I . . ." She couldn't stop stammering. How was it that he had the ability to make her feel gauche and tongue-tied?

Alex frowned. "Are you feeling well, Madame DuBois?"

Her chin rose. "Of course. Perfectly fine."

"Ah, then perhaps it's only that you'd prefer another dance partner?"

"I'm sure you're well aware that you're the only man who has asked me to dance!" she replied more sharply than she'd intended. "But I'd rather not, if you don't mind."

He frowned at that. "Ah, but I do. I'm a man who keeps my word. Therefore . . ." He grasped her hand and led her out to the dance floor so quickly that she had no time to think about it, much less protest. In another moment, he'd about-faced and pulled her into his arms.

She fumed silently. Apparently, he was also a man who didn't understand the word "no."

She considered dragging her feet or stepping on his toes, but pride forbade it. She'd be the one to look like a fool, not he.

He didn't speak, either, for the first few steps. Then he swung her into a wide arc. "You led me astray," he murmured near her ear. "You dance beautifully."

"I never implied I couldn't dance. I merely said that I hadn't danced in a long time."

"How long?"

She glanced up to find that his eyes were sparkling with laughter. Was he mocking her? "Several years," she mumbled.

"I see. Since you were widowed, then?"

"Widowed," she repeated lamely, glancing about desperately, praying for escape. She caught a glimpse of Mrs. Busley on the sidelines, staring at her and Alex with a frown of disapproval. Oh, wonderful. Where had the headmistress been earlier, when Rianne had been looking for her?

And then Rianne noticed that several other people were staring at the two of them. Staring and whispering and . . . and probably laughing at her, poking fun at her.

Her partner suddenly whirled her about, sending her head spinning. She faltered and missed a step. "Oh! Mr. Benedict, would you please not move about in circles so much?" she gritted.

"You *are* ill!" Alex's voice was concerned.

"No. Yes. I . . . I need some air." The heat of the crowded room, the overwhelming scent of roses, the whirling—suddenly it was all too much. "I . . . I'm sorry. Please excuse me." Jerking free, she pushed past him. He called her name, but she ignored him as she quickly maneuvered her way through the crowd.

Where *was* that blasted door?

Chapter 5

The crowd suddenly shifted, and Rianne caught a glimpse of a doorway and the empty hallway beyond. Thank God!

In the hall, she realized she'd forgotten the location of the powder room. Desperately, she ran through an open doorway and found herself in a small anteroom, which was being used to hold the male guests' coats and hats.

Only one small lamp lit the warm, stuffy room. Even more heated from her frantic dash, Rianne rushed to open the window, then leaned out to breathe deeply of the night air. It felt wonderfully reviving on her face, so she gripped the sill with both hands and leaned out even more. Her spectacles slipped down her nose. Using one hand to push them back, she lost her balance and nearly fell out the window. As she jerked back, her clammy fingers slipped off the sill. She wobbled precariously.

"Oh!" Spectacles forgotten, she flailed her arms wildly.

Suddenly, unexpectedly, hands clamped about her waist.

She gave a small scream and lunged forward to grasp the edges of the window, whereupon she clung on fiercely as the hands tried to pull her backward. "What are you doing?" she screeched.

The hands became arms that slid around her waist. "It's all right. I've got you."

Rianne was so surprised to recognize Alex Benedict's deep voice directly behind her ear that she let go.

Unprepared for the abrupt release, Alex stumbled backward. She slammed into his chest, forcing him back even more. His calf banged into a long narrow table covered with silk top hats. He fell onto it, realized that he'd landed only on the edge and that they were about to go over, and tightened his hold to break her fall. The two of them crashed onto the floor together.

They ended up in a tangled heap of legs and arms, except that Alex's hands had slipped—and were now clasped tightly about Rianne's bosom as she landed, back to his chest, atop him.

Stunned, they both lay unmoving.

"What the devil are you doing?" Rianne finally managed to gasp. She tried to lunge forward, only to yelp in pain and fall back upon him.

"Hold still!" Alex growled.

"Stop pulling my hair!"

"I'm not, dammit! It's caught on my shirt button. Wait . . . I can't see from this angle. I have to flip you over."

"Flip me over?" Rianne promptly found herself lying on her stomach, his heavy body on top of hers.

"Why aren't you releasing me?" she hissed. "Do so at once!"

"I'm trying to see where your hair—Ouch!" The last came as the top of her head clipped his chin. "Hold still, dammit!"

"Alex!"

"Madame DuBois!"

At the sound of outraged voices, Alex and Rianne froze and slowly turned their heads toward the doorway.

Lorna Hall stood aghast, her hand clutched to her throat, while Eudora Busley peered over her shoulder. Standing behind them with Mrs. Busley's wrap and Rianne's cloak over his arm was Branson. His eyes looked like two big saucers and his mouth was a wide O.

"Well, I never! What, may I ask, is the meaning of this shocking display, Madame DuBois?" the headmistress demanded in an outraged squeal.

"Now, Mrs. Busley, I'm sure there's a perfectly reasonable explanation. Isn't there, Alex?" Lorna asked hopefully.

Rianne felt Alex's chest heave above her. "Give me a minute, and I'll think of one," he muttered.

Embarrassed beyond words, Rianne shifted in an attempt to slide out from under him. It was only then that she realized that one of his hands still clasped her bosom. Horrified, she rose to pull his hand away and thrust it aside. She closed her eyes in mortification. She didn't even want to think about what this looked like to the others.

Cautiously, she opened one eye to squint down the length of her body—only to discover that her skirt was raised above her calves. She jerked on it, but it was caught between herself and Alex. She wasn't going to get it loose until he freed her hair. "Will you please hurry!" she hissed at him.

"I'm trying! If you'd just stop squirming . . ."

Rianne flailed her arms in frustration, banging him with her elbow.

"Oomph! Watch it!" Alex growled. "Those are my ribs."

"Oh! Sorry!"

"Branson," Alex called. "Do you suppose you could close your mouth long enough to give us a hand here? I can't see where her hair is caught."

Branson snapped his mouth shut. "Er . . . Ah . . . certainly," he stammered as he placed the cloaks on a table and hurried forward to do Alex's bidding.

"Great! Twenty years I've been trying to fluster you, and all it took was an unplanned tumble in the cloakroom," Alex groused as Branson bent on one knee and gently worked free the strand of Rianne's hair that was twisted around a button on Alex's waistcoat.

"I've got it, sir. Need a hand up?"

"No, but you could help the lady," Alex said. He waited until Branson had stood Madame DuBois back on her feet before scrambling up to assess the damage. Impatiently, he pushed back his hair which had fallen over one eye, and turned to her. Her spectacles lay crookedly across her nose, and several loose strands of hair were hanging around her face.

After each quickly glanced at the other, Alex tightened his tie and tugged on his cuffs while Rianne straightened her spectacles and smoothed down her skirt.

"Alex?" Lorna prompted tentatively.

"Madame DuBois! I insist that *you* explain this immediately if you please!" The headmistress moved forward, her mouth pinched more than usual, as if she'd just been forced to swallow a lemon.

"It . . . I . . . We . . ."

Alex took pity on her and jumped in with an explanation. "I feared she was about to fall from the window."

She snorted in disgust. "I was *not* about to fall!"

Well, perfect! He was trying his damnedest to extricate her—them—from this predicament, and she had the gall to dispute him! "Oh. Then perhaps you were merely checking the height from the ground to see if it was feasible for you to climb down the side of the house?"

"I wasn't going to climb down, either! Why would I do something so ridiculous?"

"Exactly! Why would you? I must admit, I've never had a woman prefer climbing out a window to dancing with me," he said dryly.

"Oh, don't be silly," Rianne scoffed. "Although dancing with you wasn't exactly pleasant, it wasn't the most horrible experience of my life, either."

Alex scowled at her. "You could have fooled me. Perhaps I misunderstood," he snapped. "It was my discernment that you were somewhat distraught when you left the dance floor so abruptly."

Her face flushed. "I was not *distraught!* I only needed a breath of fresh air. It was stuffy in the ballroom, and . . . and I was afraid I was about to faint."

"Really? I wouldn't have thought you the fainting type," he sneered.

Stamping her foot in frustration, she shouted at him. "I'm not!" she fumed, contradicting her previous statement.

"Forgive me," Alex drawled. "The next time I'll let you lie where you fall, be it the dance floor *or* twenty feet to the ground." He shrugged. "Makes no difference to me."

Rianne drew herself up. "Do that. And keep in mind that I don't need your help. I don't want it."

"Children! Please, enough arguing," Lorna chided.

Alex sighed. "You're right, Aunt. As I tried to explain, I thought Anne was about to—" he raised an eyebrow in Rianne's direction "—*fly* out the window since she was leaning out so far. I was attempting to prevent her from falling. The table tripped me and we fell. That's all."

Mrs. Busley huffed. "Ha! An unlikely story! You cannot expect me to believe it. The position we found you in was most shockingly indiscreet." She turned to Rianne. "Well, I don't know why I should be surprised. I've felt there was something impure about you. For that reason I was most reluctant to employ you. I see now that I was correct in my assumption."

"Really, Mrs. Busley . . ." Lorna started.

"Impure!" Rianne's chest heaved with indignation. Oh! This was too much! To think that she'd meekly subjected herself to Mrs. Busley for five years, to her constant fault finding, her stringent rules, her prudish, hypocritical standards. And now this! Control suddenly shattered within Rianne, and years of submission and rigid control turned into hot, liquid anger. She let it flow through her veins, and she fed on it. "Let me inform you, Mrs. Busley, that the only impurity in this room is in your mind!" she spat furiously.

Alex leaned to whisper in her ear. "Good one, Anne."

"Thank you," she retorted without so much as a glance in his direction. "Now please keep quiet! I'll attend to you in a moment." If she'd been looking at him, she would have seen that, instead of humbling him, her words had brought a look of surprised admiration to his face. But she wasn't, and Alex said nothing more.

Mrs. Busley, however, gasped in outrage. "I never! How dare you? You have no right to speak to me that way!"

"And *I* never!" Rianne mimicked. "*You* have no right to judge me, nor have you any reason to disbelieve Alex!"

"Aha!" Mrs. Busley pointed an accusatory finger at Rianne.

"You see, Mrs. Hall? This was no 'accident'! They use each other's given names! Madame and your nephew know one another intimately, I have no doubt!"

Lorna objected gently. "Really, Mrs. Busley, I hardly think—"

"Why, you old hypocrite!" Rianne cut in, drawing everyone's attention back to her. "Do you think I don't know about your midnight trysts with the dancing instructor? Ha! The entire staff knows."

Mrs. Busley's mouth worked like a fish's as she clutched her throat in shock. "Mr. Godfrey is strictly a staff member," she squeaked. "He has been for twenty years."

"Oh? Is that why he creeps to your quarters every Saturday past midnight and doesn't sneak back until after two? I suppose you'll be telling me next that you and he practice the dance steps he's to teach the students!"

"Oh, bravo, Anne," Alex murmured.

"Stop it, Alex! You're not helping matters," Lorna scolded.

"I didn't intend to. I rather thought Anne was doing a good job, herself. My, my. The virtuous Mrs. Busley and—" he turned to Rianne "—who did you say?"

"Mr. Godfrey, the dance instructor. He's in his fifties and quite dapper. Wouldn't you agree, Mrs. Busley?" Rianne asked sweetly.

Crimson-faced, Mrs. Busley wobbled on her feet. "How dare you spread such lies, you wicked creature! Oh, I'm going to faint!" she threatened as she clutched her throat.

"The window is still open," Rianne suggested tightly. "In fact, I'd be happy to help you—"

Mrs. Busley shrieked and stumbled back as Rianne took a step toward her. "Help! Keep her away from me! She's dangerous!" Her eyes rolled back. "I *am* going to faint!"

"Alex . . . Branson . . ." Lorna pleaded.

Alex was tempted to let Mrs. Busley swoon. In fact, he hoped she'd fall flat on her face. Still, he couldn't ignore his aunt's plea, so he moved forward to take the woman's right arm while Branson took her left. Together they guided her to a seat, but once there, the two men exchanged looks. By silent agreement, they released her at the same time, whereupon Mrs. Busley collapsed into the chair and closed her eyes as her head fell against the high back.

"Branson, water," Lorna ordered as she stood over Mrs. Busley to fan her mottled face.

Branson nodded and left, his reluctance to do so apparent. Alex could hardly blame him. It *was* a good show. He was rather enjoying it himself, and damned if he was going to miss the ending. He went to lean against a wall, hands shoved into his pockets, one ankle crossed over the other.

When his gaze met Anne's, he gave her a smile of encouragement but received only a fierce glare in return. Her cheeks were flagged with color, and she was still breathing heavily, her chest heaving in fury. Good for her! The timid mouse had roared.

He only wished those ridiculous spectacles of hers had fallen out the window. He wanted to see her eyes. He'd bet anything that they were shooting sparks. Golden sparks, perhaps. The brief glimpse he'd had when her spectacles had slipped had proved that her eyes weren't muddy brown but lighter and brighter.

Branson was back so swiftly, Alex wondered if he'd run. He was carrying a tray with one glass. Lorna stopped her fanning to take it from him. "Here, Mrs. Busley. Drink this."

The headmistress's eyelids fluttered. "What? Oh, yes . . . Thank you, Mrs. Hall. I can't tell you what a shock this has all been." She sipped from the glass.

"Are you feeling better now?" Lorna asked.

"I . . . yes, a bit."

"Good. I really think we should adjourn downstairs to a more private room. Another guest could wander in here at any time."

At that Mrs. Busley seemed to recover fully as she jerked to her feet. "There's nothing more to discuss," she stated. She aimed her finger at Rianne. "You may no longer consider yourself a member of my staff."

Lorna tried to smooth ruffled feathers. "Oh, Mrs. Busley, that's a bit harsh, isn't it?"

Mrs. Busley drew herself up even more stiffly and looked down her nose at Anne. "I have a reputation to uphold and standards to meet. It's obvious Madame DuBois is a detriment to both."

"What reputation? What standards?" Rianne scoffed. "Your liaison with Mr. Godfrey is no secret."

"You are a liar!" Mrs. Busley shrieked. "You must go! Now! Tonight! I simply cannot tolerate your kind at my school."

Alex straightened. "Now look here, Mrs. Busley . . ." he began.

"I really don't think . . ." Lorna said at the same time.

"No."

They both turned to look at Rianne. She was standing rigidly, her chin jutting proudly. "There's no need for either of you to speak in my defense," she said, her tone once again contained. She stepped forward until she was directly in front of Mrs. Busley. "I wouldn't continue to teach for a dirty-minded, sour-mouthed individual like you if you offered me the contents of the Bank of Boston, you old hypocrite. You can't dismiss me, Mrs. Busley, for I've just resigned."

With those words, she tugged at the waist of her dress, snatched her cloak from the table where Branson had dropped it, thrust back her shoulders, and walked toward the door. It was a moment before anyone realized she was leaving.

Lorna was the first to react. "Madame DuBois—Anne—wait!"

When Rianne didn't pause, Lorna appealed to her nephew. "Alex, stop her! She can't leave like this."

Alex moved swiftly to step in front of Rianne and block her exit. She stared at him coldly.

"I won't ask you to kindly step aside, Mr. Benedict, since

we both know that kindness isn't in your nature." She took a deep breath. "The first moment we met I concluded that you were an arrogant lout with the manners of a bully. Your actions since then have only reinforced that impression. I don't intend to be the target of your snide comments or your mockery any longer. And I'm sure you'll be happy to know that you are relieved of any 'onerous duty' you feel you may have toward me, for I, Mr. Benedict, have had enough of *you*. So please get out of my way!" she hissed.

Alex's eyes narrowed and his mouth curled downward. "Since you've seen fit to spout your opinions of me so freely, let me share mine of you," he replied, his voice as angry as hers. "I knew even before we met that you were an opinionated, man-hating shrew." Ignoring her outraged gasp, he stepped aside and bowed mockingly. "You are free to leave, madam. *Merci* for the dance," he said stiffly. "I'm sure we're *both* relieved that it will never occur again."

Rianne stormed outside, but slowed her steps when she saw the coaches and carriages lining the street. The drivers were standing in small groups, talking and laughing, some enjoying smokes, while they waited for their passengers. A few glanced at her curiously before dismissing her and turning back to their companions.

It was only then that she realized that her cheeks were wet with tears of anger and frustration. Brushing them away with her ungloved hands, she came to an abrupt halt.

She didn't have any money with her. She couldn't hire a cab, and the school was ten blocks away.

Resigned, she flung her cloak over her shoulders and set out to walk. At first her steps were brisk, fueled by rebellious fury. Gradually they slowed, both because her evening slippers were too thin for outdoor wear and because she began to realize what she'd just said. And done.

She pressed her hands to her burning cheeks, her thoughts replaying the horrifying incident.

Oh, heavens! She'd never spoken to anyone as rudely as she had tonight. Never!

She'd been reared to be a genteel, soft-spoken lady. One who never raised her voice in argument or anger. Yet tonight she'd shouted at Mrs. Busley and screamed at Alex Benedict like a fishwife! And the things she'd said!

Well, it wasn't as if Mrs. Busley hadn't deserved them. The nerve of that evil woman accusing her of improper behavior with Alex Benedict—a man she didn't even like! Who could? He was arrogant. Insulting. Mocking.

Oh, Lord! Had she really called him a bully and a lout? Well, he'd called her a man-hating shrew, hadn't he? That was even worse.

Rianne's lips thinned as she pushed open the gate to the school grounds and limped toward the building that housed the staff quarters.

There was no reason for her to feel guilty. No reason at all. It was *his* fault that she now had blisters on her feet. And it was *his* fault that she'd been forced to resign.

As she reached the statue of entwined cherubs that served as a centerpiece for a small fountain, Rianne stopped again.

She'd resigned! She'd really done it! No more Mrs. Busley breathing over her shoulder. No more worrying about doing or saying the wrong thing. No more having someone else tell her how to act. Who to *be*. Ha! No more Anne DuBois, middle-aged, prim and proper widow! For the first time in her life, she had no one to answer to. She could be who she wanted to be!

Oh, what a heady feeling!

Rianne's laughter pealed out over the darkened grounds as an unfamiliar feeling of freedom crept over her. Pulling the pins out of her hair, she tossed them carelessly into the air. *"Yes!"* she cried into the night as she danced joyously around the fountain. Her skirts swirled and her hair flew around her face.

"Yes, yes, *yes!*"

Chapter 6

"May I have the salt, please?"

About to take a bite of delicious, honey-basted ham, Alex stopped his fork midway to his mouth and glanced across the table at Leslie. They were the first words she'd spoken to him since she'd joined him at the breakfast table.

That she'd come down for breakfast was in itself unusual, since it was only seven in the morning, and neither Aunt Lorna nor Leslie were early risers. Alex had expected to breakfast alone, as he had the last few mornings, before going to the offices of Brannon and Benedict.

Even more unusual was that Leslie had spoken to him.

When she'd learned of the incident involving Anne DuBois and Mrs. Busley three evenings ago, she'd been furious—with *him*. She had dismissed his arguments and taken Anne's side, accusing him of bullying poor Anne and being the direct cause of her lack of employment.

Poor Anne, indeed! In Alex's estimation, she'd given as good as she'd gotten. And it was *she,* after all, who had resigned. He did feel sympathy for her. In honesty, he admitted that pride would have forced him to do the same had he been in her situation.

It was just that he couldn't understand why the women of this household seemed to think *he* was responsible. Aunt Lorna hadn't been very pleased with him, either. And no doubt if Anne were here, she'd still be blistering his ears, too.

Women! How was it that they banded together to blame men for all their troubles? How was it that *he'd* become the ogre in this situation? He didn't have a blasted thing to feel remorseful for.

Well, perhaps he could have tempered his tongue a bit.

"The salt, Alex?" Leslie reminded him sharply.

Though she'd just spoken to him, she wasn't looking at him, Alex noted, but somewhere past his shoulder. Her nose was tilted in the air, her mouth set in a mulish line.

"If you don't pull that stubborn chin back a ways, it's going to end up in the sauce bowl," he teased as he held the salt pot out to her.

Refusing to acknowledge his comment, she only tilted her chin higher and reached for the salt without meeting his eyes. Alex sighed in exasperation. "Dammit, Les. You've barely spoken to me in three days. How long is this silent treatment to continue?"

Leslie stared at him. "As long as it takes for you to find Anne and apologize to her," she retorted coldly as she sprinkled salt liberally over her scrambled eggs.

Alex set his fork on his plate and pushed it away, scarcely nodding at the maid, Betsy, who promptly came forward at Branson's silent signal to remove it. "I am not going to chase after that woman! Why should I?"

Leslie shoved her own plate away, also ignoring Betsy as the maid came around the table to remove her salt-covered eggs.

"Because, brother dear," Leslie replied, her eyes glittering with anger, "it's your fault that Anne lost her position. And it's your fault that she's disappeared. Furthermore—"

Alex raised a hand. "Wait! Wait just a moment. We've had this argument before. How many times and ways must I say that it was *not* my fault? And what do you mean she's disappeared?"

"It is *too* your fault, Alex! And I mean, Anne's *disappeared!* Aunt Lorna and I were worried about her, so Aunt sent a carriage to the school the morning after my party, but Anne had already left. She'd told another instructor she was going to a hotel, but she didn't say which one. Why did you ever let her leave the house? And how *could* you have been so callous to her?"

"Your Anne insulted me first. What did you expect me to do? Run after her? I just told you—I'm not in the habit of running after any woman, particularly this one."

Leslie glared at him from across the table. "Oh? Then what, pray tell, do you call your pursuit of the Wild Widow?"

"The wild who?" he asked, pretending ignorance.

Leslie was clearly not falling for it. "You know perfectly well I'm speaking of Sylvia Winters. She's earned the sobriquet, you know. She has a reputation."

"Interesting," Alex murmured noncommittally. "If I'd known that, I'd have made certain to further our acquaintance." In truth, Leslie had it right. He had been spending evenings—and a good part of his nights—with the delectable widow, and she was, indeed, wild.

"*Zut!* Don't play the innocent with me, Alex."

"Your education hasn't been as thorough as I thought. Someone neglected to wash your mouth out with soap," he muttered as he took a sip of coffee.

"It's only a mild swear word. And it doesn't sound as bad in French. I'm also familiar with a few Italian and Spanish swear words."

"That's hardly something for a young lady to brag about!"

"Ha! You're no angel, so stop frowning at me that way. And stop trying to change the subject. You left my party with the Wild Widow. I know perfectly well that you spent that night—and each consecutive night since—with her. After all, you come home in the early hours of the morning, your clothing saturated with her perfume. Heavens, I could smell it even before I ran into Branson carrying your jacket and trousers downstairs to be brushed and aired. How could you? How could you spend your time with a woman who isn't worth—"

"Leslie!" Alex's tone held warning. "My private affairs are none of your concern! Nor do I care to discuss them at the breakfast table," he added sharply, with a slight nod in the direction of Branson and Betsy, who were fussing with the food on the sideboard.

Leslie slapped the table in frustration. "Fine! Then let's discuss what you're going to do about Anne!"

"I'm not going to do a damn thing about her."

"Oh! You are so cold and heartless, Alex Benedict!" Leslie shouted, having lost all patience.

"I am not responsible for her!" Alex shouted back. "Besides, how was I to know she'd leave the school that night?"

"Well, do you blame her for not wanting to subject herself to more of Mrs. Busley's condemnation? Oh, I could just smack you, Alex. You don't even care, do you?"

Branson suddenly appeared at the table with the coffee server. "More coffee, Miss Leslie? Mr. Benedict?" he interjected.

Alex and Leslie turned their frustration on him. "No!" they retorted in unison.

"Very good," Branson concurred without even blinking. "Betsy and I shall return to the kitchen. If you need anything else, you have only to . . . shout," he said pointedly.

Alex and Leslie exchanged sheepish looks, but Branson had already turned away. Neither of the two combatants saw the slight smile that played about the majordomo's mouth as he shooed Betsy out of the room before him.

"See what you've done? Branson will give me that disapproving look for days now, all because you made me so angry, I forgot to act like a lady."

"Dammit, Les. This has nothing to do with Branson. Neither does it have anything to do with the Wild—with Mrs. Winters. You just want me to feel guilty about your friend, Anne!"

"Well, I'm worried about her. Aunt Lorna and I are both convinced she doesn't have the resources to stay in a hotel for very long, and she can hardly find another position without a reference—which we all know Mrs. Busley will withhold, the witch!"

"You've got a point there," he muttered.

Leslie's eyes suddenly filled with tears. "That's why we have to find Anne. Why *you* have to."

"Why do *I* have to?"

"Really, Alex. You can hardly expect Aunt and myself to drive all over Boston and inquire at every hotel. Please, Alex. Maybe you weren't directly responsible, but if it hadn't been for you, Anne wouldn't be in this predicament."

Alex propped his elbows on the table and dropped his head into his hands. He felt himself weakening, helpless against his sister's tears. "God!" he groaned. "You're going to harp until I'm wallowing in guilt, aren't you?"

Leslie sniffed. "Yes," she replied in a small voice.

"I swear," Alex said as he lifted his head, "if you cry, I'm going to move into my office downtown until the day we leave for Georgia!"

Leslie only sniffed again.

"Oh, hell," Alex sighed, knowing he was defeated. It wasn't just Leslie; ingrained within him was a core of decency that wouldn't allow him to ignore a woman in distress.

Besides, in a way, he did feel responsible for Anne's losing her position. *Partially* responsible, he amended.

"I'll see what I can do," he agreed without enthusiasm. "But convincing her to return with me—if I even find her—may be another matter entirely. She doesn't exactly like me, you know," he added wryly.

"Well, you can hardly blame her, can you? Not after you called her a—" At Alex's warning look, Leslie swallowed the word. "It might help if you apologized."

His eyes narrowed even more. "Will you at least try to be nicer to her?" Leslie pleaded.

"Depends on whether or not she's nice to me," he groused.

Leslie ignored that comment and beamed at him. "Thank you, Alex. You're the most wonderful brother in the world."

His stern look told Leslie that she was pushing her luck. Getting to her feet, she came around the table to hug him ferociously before running out of the dining room, leaving Alex scratching his head.

Damned Frenchwoman! He couldn't believe he was going to do this—run after a woman who had a tongue like a virago's. What was it she'd called him? An arrogant lout. A bully.

She'd given *better* than she'd received—though calling her an opinionated, man-hating shrew might have been a touch too much. But apologize? Never. Damned if he'd feel guilty merely because he'd returned her insults.

She'd surely surprised him, though. She'd aimed some pointed arrows at Mrs. Busley, too. The little mouse had turned out to have sharp teeth! The memory twisted Alex's mouth into a reluctant smile. Damned if he didn't feel a touch of admiration for Madame Anne DuBois.

The lovely euphoria Rianne had so joyously celebrated on the school grounds was short-lived.

The newspaper in her lap rustled as she shoved her fingers into the unruly curls at her temples and threw back her head to relieve the strain in her neck. Her feet hurt. She was tired and depressed, and once again she felt trapped.

Freedom was fine—if one could afford it. Unfortunately, she couldn't.

As she'd done for the last two days, she was once again studying the employment section of the *Globe*. It was so frustrating to admit that she wasn't qualified for a blasted one of the help-wanted advertisements.

Thus far she'd applied for a clerical position, only to be told she was too young. She'd almost been hired as an assistant in a butcher shop. The owner had seemed interested—until his very pregnant wife had stepped out from the back room, taken one look at Rianne, and brusquely informed her that they weren't hiring, after all.

Perhaps she should have applied as Anne and not as herself.

Lord, she was back where she'd started five years ago! The only difference was that she had a bit more money now. Still, a hundred dollars wasn't going to last long, especially since she was now forced to pay for her room and board.

She wondered if it would be enough to buy passage out West. Surely it was enough for a train ticket, at least, but she didn't know how long the journey would take or how much money she'd need for food and other necessities along the way.

She wasn't even sure where she'd go, exactly. San Francisco sounded exciting, but it was so far away. There weren't many big cities between here and there, except for Chicago, of course, but that hardly qualified as the *real* West. She wanted to go somewhere new and . . . and perhaps even a bit untamed, where no one would know her and she could be whoever she wanted to be.

Rianne sighed. Not that she'd figured out who she really was as yet. It was frightfully confusing, this breaking the bonds of restraint and discovering the hint of a new individual—someone she felt she *should* know but didn't.

Well, it wasn't surprising. She'd only ever been whatever others had wanted her to be.

She did know, however, that she wanted to claim her real name again. It had been years since she'd last done so. Surely it was safe now. Maybe Lance had stopped searching for her. Maybe he thought she was dead.

Oh, God, she fervently hoped so.

The unexpected banging on her door had her bolting upright. She stared at the wooden panel, wondering who could possibly be calling. She'd paid a week's rent in advance, and she certainly hadn't ordered room service—not that a hotel as inferior as this one offered such an amenity.

The knock came again, even more demanding this time. She let the newspaper slide to the floor as she slowly rose. "Yes? Who is it?" she called out apprehensively.

"It's Alex. Alex Benedict. Open the door, Anne."

Rianne froze. How in heaven's name had he found her? And why? She neared the door and asked, "What do you want?"

"I want you to open the door."

"I don't think I wish to." She was almost sure she heard a muttered curse from the other side of the panel.

She jumped at the sound of a palm slapping against the wood.

"Open the damned door!"

"No. I have nothing to say to you. Go away."

"You had plenty to say to me the other night. Look, we can do this the easy way, or we can do it the hard way. If you don't unlock the door, I'll have to break it down. Don't doubt me, Anne. This door is so flimsy it wouldn't keep out a two-year-old."

"You wouldn't dare!" Rianne stepped back cautiously, just in case.

"Oh? I gave you fair warning, lady. Stand back."

"No, wait! Wait, I . . . give me a minute." Silence. "Did you hear me? What are you doing?"

"I'm observing the hand on my watch. You have fifty-four seconds left."

Rianne gasped. She didn't doubt he'd do what he'd threatened. "Just hold on!" she gasped as she whirled and ran to the dresser. A quick glance in the murky mirror was enough to show that her hair, which she'd let down earlier, was flying in disarray. Oh, heavens, she couldn't let him see her this way!

Blast! Was it only minutes ago that she'd thought she was finished with "Anne"? That it would be possible to become Rianne again and be done with the charade?

All of Rianne's bravado fled, and she had no time to question why she wasn't ready to face Alex Benedict without the guise she'd invented. She only knew that he would ask questions, dig and dig, probably even ridicule her until she became furious again and spit out all her secrets. Yes, she had to become Anne again. It was her sole protection.

"Forty seconds," said the voice from the other side of the door.

Shoving a handful of hairpins between her teeth, Rianne fumbled with the cover of the pomade jar. She scooped up far too much, then splayed droplets all over the dresser in an attempt to scrape some back. She quickly rubbed the goo into her hair, then twisted it into a knot. "Ouch!" She'd poked herself with a hairpin.

"Thirty seconds."

"Oh! Ah . . . choo!" The sneeze was caused by the cloud of white powder she'd just slapped onto her face. She frantically waved the flying talc away as she searched for the grease pencil. It took a few precious seconds before she found it under the powder puff she'd dropped. Her hand shook as she darkened her eyebrows.

"Fifteen seconds."

Her apprehensive gaze flew to the door, and her hand jerked, leaving a dark streak from the end of her eyebrow almost to her hairline. Dropping the pencil, she ran to the door. "I'm *coming*. I'm—oh, wait a second!"

Running back to the dresser, she snatched up her spectacles and jammed them onto her face before running back to unlock the door. She was breathing hard as she stood aside to let Alex in.

Only he wasn't there. What? Rianne poked her head out to cautiously peer around the doorway. He was leaning against the wall next to it, ankles crossed, arms over his chest, eyes closed.

Eyes closed?

Rianne's glance fell to his empty hands. "Why, you don't even have your watch out. You lied!"

He opened one eye to peer at her before dismissing her accusation with a shrug. "I lied," he admitted unapologetically. "What can you expect of a bully and a lout?"

Rianne bit her lip. Despite his casual stance, he looked angry. Suddenly she felt as if she were sixteen again and had done something disappointing. Years of having proper behavior drummed into her, of having to apologize for every mistake, came to the forefront. "I'm sorry, Mr. Benedict," she said in a small voice. "I've never spoken so rudely to anyone before. Truly, I'm not normally shrewish. I don't know what got into me."

His other eye popped open, and he straightened. "Stop that!"

She stared at him, wondering if he'd lost his mind. "What? Stop what?"

"Don't apologize, for one thing. If you do, then I'll be forced to do so, too, and I make it a habit never to apologize if I can help it. And stop wringing your hands that way, as if you've caused the greatest catastrophe in the world."

Rianne glanced down. She hadn't even been aware that she was nervously twisting her fingers.

"Don't disappoint me now, Anne. I rather enjoyed your surprising outburst the other night. It proves that you aren't a complete doormat." Alex noticed that she seemed taken aback at his blunt assessment. Then he took a closer look at her. "What in blazes have you done to your face?" he asked, stepping nearer.

Rianne backed away and touched her cheek self-consciously. "Why, er, nothing."

Alex stared at her chin, at the big blotch of what appeared to be pale powder. His gaze rose to her eyebrows, which just reached the tops of her spectacles. Funny, he'd never noticed before that they were lopsided, with the right one a quarter inch higher than the other. And her hair looked . . . *oily!*

A door down the hall opened, and a middle-aged man in shirt-sleeves stepped out and stared at them. The look Alex gave him had him retreating immediately. The door closed behind him.

Alex turned to grasp Rianne's arm and smoothly maneuver her into her room before closing her door.

She turned to confront him. "What are you doing here?" she asked breathlessly.

Instead of replying immediately, Alex perused the shabby lodgings. A battered trunk, unopened, sat next to the door, a large satchel on the bed. The dresser held only bare essentials—a couple of jars, a puff, a comb and brush—all sprinkled with white powder. A modest nightgown and robe lay on the foot of the bed.

"I see you haven't quite made yourself at home yet. Good. It'll save you the trouble of packing again," he drawled.

"Packing? Why would I do that, Mr. Benedict?"

He stared down at her, frowning. "Don't call me that. It makes me feel like a doddering old man. Why, I can't be more than a year or two younger than you are."

Rianne's chin dropped. He really did believe she was middle-aged. What would he say if she announced that she was ten years younger than he?

She surprised herself by wanting to laugh. Perhaps it was because he'd dismissed her apology so easily instead of berating her as she'd expected. Still, she didn't dare laugh at him. It wouldn't do. It just wouldn't do. She fought the urge, swallowing convulsively.

"And since we'll be living in the same house for a time," he was saying, "you might as well get accustomed to calling me Alex."

Her amusement fled. "Living in . . . What are you saying?"

"I'm telling you that you're coming back to Aunt Lorna's with me."

She gaped at him. "I most certainly am not!"

"You most certainly are," he contradicted firmly. "Aunt has invited you to be her guest. I'm under strict orders to bring you back with me." His mouth curled down, as if he found the thought distasteful.

"I see." She certainly did. He didn't want to be here, and he didn't want to take her back with him, but he was under *orders.* "I take it this is another of those 'onerous duties' you've been assigned?" she asked coolly.

He stared at her until she blinked. "That was unfair. If you overheard my conversation with Major Collins, then you know damned well that I wasn't the one who referred to our dance in that manner."

"Oh? I didn't hear you disagreeing."

He shrugged. "The major's notorious for his lack of diplomacy. Those of us who know him simply ignore it. Are you going to let an inane comment keep you from accepting Aunt Lorna's invitation?"

"I don't care what Major Collins thinks of me. I don't even care what you think of me," Rianne retorted. "Neither do I intend to be anyone's newest charity." She walked to the door and opened it. "Please thank Mrs. Hall for me," she said stiffly as she stepped aside, waiting for him to leave, "and inform her I must refuse."

He walked to her and closed the door.

"Now listen here—" she began to protest.

"No, you listen to *me!*" His eyes sparked angrily. "What you and I think about each other has nothing to do with Aunt Lorna. It's also no reason to insult her for being concerned and caring. Secondly, I've just spent the last six hours searching the city for you. And third, I've already been raked over the coals by both my aunt and my sister, and damned if they're going to chastise me again because I failed to bring you back with me!

"You have two choices: One, you can concede gracefully, pack, and come with me on your own two feet. Or, two, I can carry you out over my shoulder." Then, to her astonishment, he walked to the bed, stretched out upon it, clasped his hands behind his head, crossed his ankles, and closed his eyes. "Take your time deciding. I'll just have a short nap while you think about it."

She stared at his recumbent figure in dismay. "What are you doing? Get off my bed immediately."

"Uh-uh. I had a late night, and I've spent half the day chasing all over Boston after you. You owe me a few winks."

Rianne crossed to the bed and stared down at him in dismay. His long lashes didn't so much as flutter. He was perfectly still except for the rise and fall of his chest as he breathed evenly.

"Mr. Benedict?"

No response. Rianne bit her lip. He couldn't have fallen asleep that fast! Reaching out, she tentatively poked his shoulder before jerking back her hand. "Mr. Benedict?" Still no response. She gave him a harder poke, in his ribs.

He didn't even blink.

"Alex!"

One eyelid rose, revealing a cool green stare that sent her stumbling back.

Alex pushed himself upright. "Ah, now we're making progress. Does the use of my name mean you've changed your mind?" he asked.

Rianne frowned as she considered. Leslie was a dear, and Mrs. Hall was a sincere person; she wouldn't have extended the invitation if she hadn't meant it.

Then, too, there was the problem of her own shortage of funds and lack of employment. Why not accept? It would give her time to find a new position—it would be two weeks before the two women would be leaving with Mr. Benedict . . . Alex. Still, the thought of spending even that short a time in the same house with him . . .

"If it's the thought of my presence that gives you pause,"

he said, startling her by reading her thoughts, "I won't be around very much. I dedicated my first several days in Boston entirely to Leslie, but I'll be spending the rest of this week and all of next in my offices. You probably won't even see me except at dinnertime." He startled her even more by grinning. "I'll try to refrain from loutish, bullying behavior. I'll even forget you called me names if you forget I called you one." His eyes gleamed with mischief. He looked like a boy who'd just promised to keep his hands out of the cookie jar but didn't mean it.

She responded with a small smile. "Does that mean *I* can't name-call again?" she asked. She'd surprised him, she saw when his eyes widened appreciably.

"Not unless I deserve it," he replied, "and I can't promise that I won't. Look, can we at least agree to try to be civil to each other?"

She tilted her head and studied him from behind her ugly spectacles. "Define the word *try,*" she responded dryly.

Alex's mouth curled at her unexpected cheekiness. Each time he thought he had the woman figured out, she surprised him.

"Let's say that we agree to disagree without characterizing the other unfavorably."

She pretended to consider. "I suppose I can learn to bite my tongue if I'm tempted, can't I? All right, then. I'll come. Give me a few minutes to pack."

A few minutes was all it took. When she was finished, she turned to find him standing by the door, her cloak draped over his arm. "That's it. I'm ready," she told him.

"Good. Now, then . . ." He opened her cloak and held it out. Rianne walked to him, then turned her back to him to allow him to drape the garment over her shoulders.

The top of her head came to his chin, Alex noticed. She

must have been in a hurry when she dressed her hair, for several strands were sticking out of one side of her knot. To his surprise, he saw that the ends were slightly curled and more auburn than mousy brown, though it was difficult to tell with all that greasy stuff smeared over her scalp.

He grimaced, thinking she would look much better if she would simply loosen her hair and rid herself of those dreadful spectacles. Perhaps he'd have a word with his aunt. Possibly with a little direction from Lorna, Anne might manage to look more acceptable. Poor woman. She obviously didn't know how to make the best of the few attributes she had—like her figure. Decent clothes would set it off—and thus deflect attention from her hair and face.

"What about my trunk?" she asked as she whirled around to face him.

"Let's get you into the carriage first, then I'll come back and have the clerk help me carry it down."

In less than ten minutes it was done, and they were on their way to Lorna Hall's tall brownstone on Beacon Hill.

Rianne sat across from him, relieved that he wasn't attempting to converse. In fact, he appeared to have fallen asleep—unless he was merely faking again!

Still, it gave her a chance to study him surreptitiously from under her lashes. He had strong features—sharply defined cheekbones and a straight, chiseled nose. His chin jutted just enough to prove his obstinacy but was softened by a slight cleft right in the middle. Her gaze fell to his full-lipped mouth, which at the moment drooped in relaxation. He really was a most attractive man but then, she didn't know many, so it was difficult to make a comparison. She knew that *she* found him so, and she suspected that other women did, also.

But appearances could be too deceiving, she reminded

herself. Hadn't she learned that with Lance? She'd once thought his blond good looks the epitome of male elegance, and, like the man across from her, he could be charming when he chose. Deceptively so.

God, what a foolish child she'd been!

But she was a child no longer. She was a woman who had been hurt and betrayed, not only emotionally but also to the point of having been forced to fight for her life.

Alex Benedict would never hurt a woman physically. She was certain of that, but she also knew that he was capable of scarring a woman forever without so much as touching her. No doubt he had a score of such women in his past.

She brushed that thought aside. It was no concern of hers, for there was absolutely no chance that she'd ever be one of them.

Chapter 7

"Well, well, what have we here? Sweeping my aunt off her feet, are you, Branson?" Alex was amused.

Rianne stood beside him in the entrance foyer of Mrs. Hall's home and gaped at the scene before her. At the bottom of the stairs stood Branson, holding Mrs. Hall in his arms!

The majordomo's face turned a dull red. "I'm afraid Mrs. Hall has been injured, sir. She took a fall down the stairs—"

Rianne's valise thunked as Alex dropped it and rushed forward. "Is she conscious?" he asked apprehensively.

Lorna peered up at Alex. Though her face was tear-streaked, she managed a wan smile. "Of course I am. It isn't as if I landed on my head. I merely twisted my ankle and knee."

"Thank God! Here, Branson, give her to me."

Branson transferred his burden to Alex, who asked him if he'd sent for a doctor.

"I haven't had a moment to yet, Mr. Benedict."

"Yes, of course. Where's my sister?"

"Miss Leslie has gone shopping, then to dinner, with Mrs. Thornby and her daughter."

"Send the footman—what's his name? Oh, Douglas. Send Douglas to fetch the doctor now," Alex ordered. "In the meantime—" He halted, glancing about as if he didn't know quite what to do.

Rianne slipped out of her cloak and let it fall atop her valise. Peeling off her gloves, she moved forward. "Perhaps you should carry Mrs. Hall into the drawing room," she suggested.

"The drawing room. Of course." Alex walked slowly in that direction.

Rianne turned to Branson. "We'll need ice for Mrs. Hall's injuries," she requested quietly. "Crush the ice first, and bring two large towels."

"Yes, ma'am," he responded, relieved at her calm tone. "I'll bring it myself." He disappeared toward the kitchen.

Rianne followed Alex into the drawing room and waited until he'd carefully placed his aunt on a sofa. "How are you feeling, Aunt?" he inquired solicitously as he knelt before her.

"It hurts," she admitted, "but not half as much as does my pride."

Moving quickly, Rianne gathered several pillows and brought them to the injured woman. "We need to keep your leg elevated, Mrs. Hall," she said. "But I may have to hurt you even more to get these cushions beneath it."

Lorna nodded and reached for Alex's hand. Cautiously Rianne raised the injured leg and slipped one pillow under her knee, the other under her ankle. "That should feel better. Even more so once Branson brings the ice. Ah, here he is now."

Branson had indeed entered, followed by a maid.

"Thank you, Branson." Rianne turned to the maid. "If you would just clear that table in front of the sofa . . ." It was done, and four pairs of eyes watched curiously as Rianne took the towels and knelt beside Alex to lay them out upon the table. In no time, she had spread the crushed ice down the middle of each towel and rolled two long, narrow pads of them. Twisting about to face the sofa again, Rianne was careful to preserve Mrs. Hall's modesty by reaching under the woman's skirts to wrap one ice package about her knee, the other her ankle.

"There," she said, kneeling back. "That should keep the swelling down and take away some of the pain."

"How did this happen, Aunt?" Alex inquired.

"Oh, Alex, it was such a silly thing. I was coming downstairs and glanced up—I don't even recall why—when my foot slipped off the edge of the step. I landed on the side of my ankle and when I tried to grab for the railing, I turned my knee."

"Is it very painful?"

"Only if I move my leg." Lorna patted Alex's cheek. "Don't look so worried, dear. It's bearable, especially now." She turned to Rianne. "Thank you, Anne. You have a gentle touch. I'm sorry for the dramatics. This wasn't exactly the way I'd intended to greet you."

"Please, Mrs. Hall, don't worry about that," Rianne said. "I'm only sorry that the timing of my arrival is so awkward."

Lorna reached out and clasped her hand. "Of course it's not! If anything, it was a blessing, for you knew just what to do. My maid, Yvette, would have known, but she's off today."

"Perhaps I should send Douglas for Leslie after he's returned with the doctor," Alex suggested.

"No!" Lorna replied. "Don't do that." She took in the worried faces surrounding her. "Will you all stop looking so glum? Really, it isn't as if I've broken my foolish neck. Branson, watch for the doctor. Betsy, you take Madame DuBois up to her room and see that she has everything she needs. And you, Alex, can bring me a glass of brandy."

"Are you sure?" he asked, frowning.

Lorna managed a laugh. "Quite sure. I have nothing to do but wait until the doctor arrives, and I think I'm entitled to a small brandy."

Alex kissed her hand and rose. "Yes, ma'am. You're entitled to anything you want."

Rianne stared at Alex as he went to fetch the brandy, for she was seeing him in a new light—that of a caring, considerate man. His sincere concern for his aunt was obvious.

For the first time, Rianne realized that there was much more to Alex Benedict than his brash, arrogant, bullying manner. Did he use it to hide his true character from everyone or just her? Her musings were interrupted when Betsy stepped forward. "Ma'am? I'll take you up to your room," she told Rianne.

"What? Oh, yes. Of course." Rianne turned to follow the maid but was brought up short when Alex called her name.

"Thank you, Anne," he said. "I'm glad you were here to give assistance."

She blushed in pleased embarrassment. "I am, too," she replied softly.

"How is it that you knew what to do?"

"One can hardly spend ten months of the year in the company of a hundred active girls without any of them suffering an occasional injury," Rianne explained. "I've nursed many a sprained ankle before."

"Lucky for us," he said, smiling.

Rianne followed Betsy, automatically responding to the maid's inquiries. She was hardly even aware of the beautifully appointed room she was shown to, which was ten times larger than the one she'd had at the school.

Once Betsy left, Rianne leaned against the closed door and covered her warm cheeks with her hands. Goodness! When Mr. Benedict—Alex—flashed a genuine smile rather than his usual mocking one, it was difficult not to give him one right back.

Well! What a surprise this day was turning out to be! She'd started out worrying about her future and never expecting to see either Leslie or Alex or Mrs. Hall again, and now, here she was, in this very feminine, very pretty room as their guest.

And she'd discovered that Alex was a much nicer man than she'd first thought. Fascinating!

Her hands dropped. Oh, no! What was she thinking? Hadn't she sworn, five years ago, that she would never, ever again fall prey to any man's charm? And hadn't she told herself—only an hour ago—that Alex Benedict was a particularly dangerous man? She would have to be careful to keep her distance. It shouldn't be too difficult. She had only to remain "Anne DuBois"—a woman he thought older than himself, and unbearably plain. Hardly the type to interest him, she was sure.

Besides, he would be here for but another few days. Afterward, he would leave, and she'd never see him again.

See? It's simple, Rianne, she scolded herself as she went to unpack, ignoring a little, niggling feeling of regret.

Rianne loved staying at Lorna Hall's elegant home. Everyone made her feel so welcome. She was given all the gracious consideration a close family friend would receive. She had beautiful accommodations—grander than any she'd ever had before. She should have been delighted.

Instead, she was filled with unexpected guilt.

She was here under false pretenses. In her mind, assuming the identity of Anne DuBois, French instructor, had been acceptable; it had been a matter of survival. But Anne DuBois, houseguest of Lorna Hall, felt dishonest.

She couldn't rid herself of the nagging conviction that she

should have admitted her duplicity—at least to Leslie and Mrs. Hall. They were women, too. Perhaps they'd understand. But Alex . . .

Well, she admitted that she was a coward when it came to him. Despite his charming smiles, he was intimidating. She didn't understand him. Her experience with men was so limited, she often couldn't tell whether he was joking or being sarcastic.

She hadn't seen much of him in the three days since her arrival. Once he was assured that his aunt would recover, he'd been leaving early each morning for his offices downtown. He returned only to have dinner with them, then usually left again.

His sister wasn't happy about that behavior, Rianne knew. Only last evening she'd overheard an argument between Leslie and Alex. Rianne gathered that Alex was seeing a woman Leslie didn't approve of, and she had told him so. Alex had laughed and instructed his sister to keep her pretty nose out of his business, a suggestion that had sent Leslie flying out of the room in a huff.

Rianne had wondered who the woman was. It wasn't any of *her* business, either, but she was curious. Despite her own wariness of the man, there was no denying that he was attractive. And eligible.

Why had he never married? Most men of his wealth and social stature would be concerned with heirs and would have produced at least one by now. Perhaps he was pursuing this woman Leslie didn't like with that objective in mind. It would be too bad if the courtship caused a rift between brother and sister, but . . .

Rianne's musings were interrupted by a knock on her door.

"Anne? May I come in?" Without waiting for a reply,

Leslie pushed open the door and entered. "Oh, good! I was afraid you'd be napping."

"No. I came up to read the paper." Rianne raised her eyebrows, for it appeared that Leslie had about her an air of barely suppressed excitement. Her eyes were shining, and she was smiling in a self-satisfied manner.

"You're still looking for another position." It was a statement, not a question. Leslie leaned forward and snatched the newspaper out of Rianne's hands. "Forget it," she said mysteriously. "You're coming to have tea with me in Aunt's room. We have a proposition for you." Without waiting for acquiescence, Leslie grabbed Rianne's arm and steered her out of the bedroom.

"Leslie! What in the world—?"

"Wait until we see Aunt," Leslie said enigmatically.

Laughing, Rianne allowed herself to be guided out the door. Leslie's enthusiasm was impossible to resist.

Lorna Hall was lying on a chaise longue, the tea service already arranged on a table nearby. She glanced up when Leslie and Rianne entered the room. "Ah, here you are. Come in, and we'll have tea, and then we'll talk. You'll pour, Leslie."

"But, Aunt—"

"After tea, dear. After."

Leslie attempted to tamp down her excitement, and Rianne kept her curiosity at bay while they had tea and spice cake, chatting idly. Finally, when Lorna set her own cup aside, Leslie, without asking, took Rianne's from her and placed both their cups beside Lorna's before leaning forward eagerly.

Lorna smiled at her fondly before turning to Rianne. "You know that Dr. Howell insists that I stay off my feet for several weeks?"

"Yes." Rianne had been present when Dr. John Howell arrived to tend to Lorna's injuries. He'd been a close friend of Lorna's husband and lived only a few houses away. He had just seen his last patient when Douglas came for him.

After examining Lorna, he pronounced that her ankle was only sprained, but that her knee was, indeed, badly twisted. She was to stay off her feet for several weeks, perhaps longer. "If you try to walk on it any earlier, you may do permanent damage, Lorna," he'd told her.

"Oh, dear. That won't do at all. You know that I was planning to travel with my niece and nephew, John."

He shook his head sadly. "I'm afraid that is out of the question."

"But—"

"No. Absolutely, unequivocally, no. Do you want to use a cane the rest of your life, or worse, be confined to a rolling chair?"

Lorna didn't, of course, and so she was ensconced in her rooms upstairs, with the servants willingly seeing to her comfort. Leslie and Rianne visited her several times daily, and had their tea with her.

Now Mrs. Hall was studying Rianne in a considering manner, and Rianne wondered if she'd unwittingly committed a terrible gaffe.

"You also know that Leslie and Alex and I were to leave week after next," she told Rianne. "Our plans were to take the Rolling Palace to Atlanta, then on to Bellesfield."

"Excuse me, but what's the Rolling Palace?" Rianne asked.

"It's Leslie's name for Alex's private railroad car. Well, it actually belongs to Brannon and Benedict. Alex and Nick had the car specially built since they do so much traveling. It's very comfortable and decorated in a lovely manner. Much quieter and cleaner than the public cars," Lorna explained.

"I see. And Bellesfield?"

"Bellesfield is—was—the family home I've told you about," Leslie replied. "It was destroyed during the war, but Alex has turned it into a trade school. I haven't been there since I came to live with Aunt Lorna. Anyway, from Bellesfield, Alex plans to again take the train to New Orleans. After that, we're going on to Colorado. The entire journey will last perhaps three months."

"Yes, you mentioned that."

"Alex has business matters to attend to, also, during this trip," Lorna said. "Leslie would have been on her own quite a bit, which was one of the reasons I was accompanying them. Unfortunately, I can no longer do so," she added, indicating her propped-up leg, "and Alex can't delay this trip. Which is where you come in, Anne."

"I? I'm afraid I don't understand how—" And then, she did. Rianne glanced from Lorna to Leslie—who was barely containing her excitement—then back. "Oh, my. You want me to chaperone Leslie," she stated flatly, even though a thrill of anticipation ran up her spine.

"Exactly," said Lorna.

"Oh, Anne!" Leslie jumped in. "It's the perfect solution. You have no position, you've always said you'd like to travel, and you'll be able to see New Orleans again. Please, please say you'll do this!"

The mention of New Orleans immediately dissipated Rianne's excitement and her breath hitched in her throat. She rose swiftly. "I'm sorry, Leslie, but I can't. I'm grateful to you—and to you, Mrs. Hall—for thinking of me, but I just can't." She began to pace the room, her hand massaging her throat in agitation.

Leslie's face fell. "But, Anne! Why not?"

"Is it money, dear?" Lorna asked gently. "You would be paid a salary, of course."

"Oh, no! No, it's not that. It's, it's—" Rianne whirled about. Leslie and Lorna were both staring at her with identical expressions of disappointment. "You don't understand." She took a deep breath. "Oh, dear you've both been so sweet to me, I can't deceive you anymore. I must tell you the truth. I'm not who you think I am."

Leslie's expression changed to bafflement. "Of course we know who you are, Anne!"

"No. No, you don't," Rianne insisted. "My real name isn't even Anne DuBois," she blurted. "It's *Ri*anne Forrester." Wringing her hands, she began to pace again. "You see, I've been dishonest with you—with everyone. I was forced to leave New Orleans rather abruptly and had to assume a disguise. I can't even tell you why, but I'm quite sure you will no longer think me a suitable companion for your niece, Mrs. Hall," she added, turning to look directly at the woman. Expecting to see disgust, Rianne was surprised to see sympathy.

"Anne—Rianne—please sit down," Lorna urged. "Here, beside me." She waited until Rianne reluctantly acceded to her request, then reached out to take Rianne's hand in hers. "What *can* you tell us?" she asked quietly.

Rianne shook her head in misery. "Only that I had a good reason to leave New Orleans. The circumstances . . ." she bit her lip. "My parents had both died by the time I was thirteen. I was made the ward of a man who was our neighbor, when we still had a plantation. This man—" Rianne swallowed. "This man took over my life, and then, when I was about to turn eighteen, he did something that made me believe my life was in danger. I had no family to turn to, few I could ask for help without endangering them, too. I had no choice but to flee New Orleans."

"So that's how you came to Boston," Leslie stated, wide-eyed. "My heavens, but you were brave! I never would have found the courage to do such a thing."

Rianne shook her head miserably. "I wasn't brave, Leslie, just desperate. You are much stronger than I could ever be."

"I wouldn't be one bit brave if I were on my own, as you were," Leslie insisted. "You see, I've always had family to rely on. Even after *I* was orphaned, I have always had Alex and Aunt Lorna. Unlike you, I would be lost on my own."

Rianne didn't think this was the time to tell Leslie that she *had* felt lost. Lost, alone, and frightened to death. "So you came directly from New Orleans to Boston?" Lorna prompted.

"Yes. I found passage on the only ship that was leaving immediately. Then, once I arrived in Boston, I needed a way to support myself." She explained how she'd become Madame Anne DuBois so that she could obtain the teaching position at the Chatham Academy.

Lorna nodded in understanding. "I see nothing wrong with that. Sometimes a woman has no resources but her own brain, and, as far as I can tell, that's exactly what you did." She bit her lip and hesitated. Finally, she asked, "Rianne, I don't mean to pry, but is there anything more I should know about your life in New Orleans?"

Rianne knew that Lorna hadn't asked out of curiosity but out of concern for her niece and the girl's reputation. "Mrs. Hall, I assure you that I didn't do anything that would cause the authorities to seek me." Lance Paxton wouldn't even consider bringing them into it. He would want to exact his own revenge. "I mean, I'm not a criminal, and I wasn't a . . . well, a loose woman. I had a very strict, very secluded upbringing." She laughed unsteadily. "Actually, I was hardly any kind of *woman*. I was barely eighteen at the time, and very naive."

Leslie, who had been listening in rapt attention, gasped. "Eighteen! But you just said you came to Boston directly from New Orleans. You've been here five years. Why, that makes you—" Her eyes widened.

Rianne nodded. "Twenty-three."

"But you look at least thirty," Leslie blurted, then blushed guiltily. "I mean, that is—oh, do forgive me. I didn't mean to insult you, Anne. I mean, *Rianne.*"

"You haven't." Rianne smiled to reassure Leslie. "In fact, you've given me a compliment, of sorts. As I said, I made myself look older primarily to obtain the position at Chatham's, but I admit it suited other purposes, for I was afraid that the person I'd fled would come looking for me. He had a likeness of me, taken shortly before my eighteenth birthday, and he would have used it to track me down."

"You aren't really a widow, then, either?" Lorna asked.

"No," Rianne replied simply.

"This person, he wants to do you harm?"

Lorna Hall was no fool, Rianne thought. And though she knew she could trust the woman, she simply couldn't tell her everything. It was all so humiliating. "Yes," she said simply. "He feels I've wronged him, and he isn't above exacting revenge."

"I see. Do you think he's still searching for you?"

"I don't know. Perhaps not. It's been a long time. He may even have given me up as dead. But I don't dare return to New Orleans, so you see why I can't become Leslie's companion."

"Then what *will* you do?" Leslie asked, concerned.

"I'm not sure. I've thought about going West, but I don't have enough—that is, I'm not in a position to do so yet."

"Hmm." Lorna pursed her lips in thought. "You know, Rianne, you wouldn't have to travel as far as New Orleans.

You could still accompany Alex and Leslie to Georgia. They can continue on from there as planned, while you could travel on to Memphis or St. Louis, and then go West from there. As for Leslie's being in New Orleans—well, she wouldn't be on her own while Alex conducts his business, for I've already written to a cousin of my late husband's who lives there. Louisa is also a widow, and her daughter and son-in-law live with her. Both women love to socialize, so I daresay they'll enjoy taking Leslie about."

"Oh, do say you'll come as far as Bellesfield," Leslie pleaded.

"Well . . ."

"It would be to everyone's mutual benefit," Lorna coaxed. "You would help us out, and we'd see to it that you had a new start."

Rianne was torn. On one hand, she was excited at the prospect, and what Mrs. Hall said made sense. On the other hand . . .

"What about Alex? Mr. Benedict? Wouldn't he have to approve, first?" she asked, cringing at the thought of facing him as a prospective employee. He didn't think much of her now. What would he say once he knew about her deception?

Instead of replying, Lorna studied Rianne's face carefully. "Do something for me, dear, will you?" she asked.

"Yes. Of course."

"Sit yourself at my dressing table and take down your hair. You may use my brush. Your complexion isn't normally that pale, is it?" When Rianne shook her head, Lorna smiled. "I thought not. Use my face cream, too. I'd like to see your real appearance."

"Oh, yes. I would, too," Leslie chimed in as she followed Rianne to the table. "Here, you do your face, and I'll take down your hair and brush it."

Leslie did so as Rianne removed her spectacles and used the cream and the towel Leslie handed her to scrub her face. "Rianne, are you dyeing your hair?"

"I have been, yes." Her voice was muffled beneath the towel.

"Why, your hair isn't really brown at all, is it?" Leslie murmured as she wielded the brush. "I suspect it's auburn, and it's so thick and wavy. Goodness, Rianne—"

She broke off as she lifted her head to glance into the mirror. Her hand froze in mid-stroke as she stared at the reflection of a young woman with a heart-shaped face, a flawless complexion, and sherry-brown eyes flecked with gold and fringed with long lashes. The heavy brows were gone; the ones she was seeing were delicately arched.

"Oh, my! Why, Rianne, you're *lovely!*" Leslie gushed.

Rianne frowned at her reflection. In her mind, she was passable. Oddly shaped face, common brown hair, ordinary brown eyes.

"You don't believe me?" Leslie asked, observing Rianne's doubtful expression. When Rianne shook her head, Leslie turned to send her aunt a silent plea.

"Turn around and let me see," Lorna ordered from the divan.

Leslie stepped back, and Rianne twisted about on the stool to face Lorna, whose eyes widened in shock.

"Oh, dear. It won't do."

Rianne leaped from the stool. "I knew it! Alex will be angry when he sees me like this, won't he?" she asked miserably. "He won't accept me as Leslie's companion."

Leslie's laughter pealed, startling and confusing Rianne. "I'm sorry," Leslie gasped. "It's really not funny, yet . . . Oh, Lord! Alex will take one look at you and decide you need a chaperone as much as I do."

Lorna chuckled. "Exactly what I was thinking, Leslie. Alex may be a man of the world, but he was reared to believe that women should be protected at all times—particularly young ladies. He can't help it. Look at how overprotective he is with you." Abruptly, she sobered. "There's another problem that concerns me, however. Alex also has an eye for pretty women. He might become attracted to Rianne, and that *definitely* won't do."

Rianne blushed at the idea that Alex would find her attractive. She didn't believe it; he was much too sophisticated, while her ingenuous single experience with a man had been disastrous. Perhaps her social standing had once been equal to Alex Benedict's, but she was now a woman with a questionable past and few resources. Mrs. Hall recognized that, and Rianne could hardly blame her for wanting to protect her nephew.

Still, traveling as Leslie's companion, even if only partway, would have been a lovely solution to her problems. She would have been much nearer to her goal of the West.

"Of course it won't do," she agreed, trying to hide her disappointment. "I understand perfectly, and I'm grateful to you for allowing me to stay in your home, Mrs. Hall. I'll do my best to find another position before Leslie and Alex leave."

"No! Oh, no, my dear! You misunderstand. I don't mean that it's impossible—" Lorna frowned in thought. "I still think you'll make an excellent companion for Leslie." She sighed. "You'll have to do it as Anne DuBois, though. Yes, I think we could manage it."

Rianne gaped at her, while Leslie clapped her hands in glee. "Aunt, do you mean to say you still approve of Rianne as my companion?"

"Well, certainly. Mind now, I'm not fond of deception. In this case, however, I quite understand why you did it, Rianne.

You began this before you ever knew Leslie or me or even Alex, so it wasn't as if you intended to deliberately deceive us. It was a matter of survival, and as far as I'm concerned, it's still that—at least until after Bellesfield. We just won't tell Alex yet that you aren't going on to New Orleans. Do you think you can stand to continue being Anne DuBois for a while longer?"

Rianne laughed. "I've put up with her for all these years, so, yes—another month or so will be nothing."

"Good girl!" Lorna smiled and patted Rianne's hand. "But I don't think we'll have to drag it out that long. The main thing is not to let Alex see you as Rianne before Bellesfield. Once there, he can hardly abandon you, can he? Hmm, let's see . . ." She then proceeded to issue instructions in a fast, no-nonsense manner.

Rianne was to begin wearing her hair in a slightly looser style. She was to stop using that "awful white powder" once she was on the train. As for her eyes—"I suspect you don't really need those spectacles," Lorna surmised.

"No, ma'am. I don't."

"I didn't think so, but you shouldn't forgo them just yet. And keep penciling your brows. Even with small changes, your appearance will be improved, but I doubt Alex will notice them. You'll be on your way, and once you've left Bellesfield, you can become your true self entirely."

"I'll do as you say, Mrs. Hall," Rianne assented.

"Leslie, I think this calls for more shopping expeditions," Lorna advised her niece. "Let's see if we can outfit Rianne with something more colorful."

"Oh, yes!" Leslie enthused. "We have time! There are several excellent ready-to-wear shops, and there's always Mrs. Porter. She's very skilled with last-minute creations."

Rianne's face warmed. "I really don't need much," she

murmured, almost wincing at the thought of parting with the money. Certainly she couldn't afford more than a gown or two, nor could she afford the dressmaker's prices.

"Oh, but I didn't make myself clear," Lorna cut into her thoughts. "The additions to your wardrobe will be my gift to you, Rianne, for being such a special teacher and friend to Leslie all these years."

"Oh, no! I couldn't possibly—"

"Yes, you can," Leslie cut in. "Aunt loves to buy clothes. As a result, I have more than I can ever wear. I think she secretly bemoans the fact that I'm not a triplet," she added, lessening Rianne's embarrassment. "In fact, I have some things you may be able to wear, too. We're almost the same shape from the waist up. I'll bet they'll only need shortening."

"I don't know what to say," Rianne murmured, overcome by the generosity of these two women. "Thank you both. Thank you for your offer of a position and for . . . for . . ." Rianne's eyes filled with tears. It had been so long since anyone had shown her such genuine kindness.

Lorna waved her off. "Please! I should be thanking you, for Leslie might not have been able to go on this journey if you hadn't agreed to accompany her, and she's been looking forward to it so much."

Rianne knew she was gaining much more than was Leslie, but she was too choked up to speak, so she simply nodded. Leslie leaned over to hug her. "Oh, I'm so glad you've agreed. We're going to have such a wonderful time. It will be a grand adventure, don't you think?" She clapped her hands in glee. "And that's what we shall call it—our 'Grand Adventure'."

Rianne nodded. A Grand Adventure! She'd never had a happy adventure before, nor someone to share it with. "Yes, I believe it will be. I'm looking forward to it, Leslie."

On the chaise, Lorna stretched leisurely. "Now, girls—all this planning has worn me out. I think I'd like to take a nap."

Rianne rose. "Of course. I'll return this to the kitchen," she offered as she gathered the cups and saucers onto the tray.

"Rianne . . ."

She turned back. "Yes?"

"You need to put up your hair again before you go down," Lorna reminded her.

"And don't forget your spectacles," Leslie added as she ran to fetch them.

"Oh, yes! Thank you." Rianne donned the spectacles, bringing a smile to the other women's faces. "What is it?"

"I can't believe what a difference those awful things make," Leslie replied. "You have beautiful eyes, but through those tinted lenses they look so murky, I can't tell what color they really are."

Rianne found herself grinning back. "That was the general idea, but I think they're horrible, too."

After Rianne left, Leslie went to her aunt and kissed her cheek. "Thank you, Aunt Lorna. I know you did this to keep Alex from foisting one of those awful creatures he's been interviewing the last two days upon me, but you also did it for Anne. Oh, dear, I'm going to have to remember that her name is Rianne—you really did this for her, didn't you?"

"Well, the poor girl needs a helping hand. And I feel for her. It's obvious that she's not had an easy time of it."

"She ran away from a cruel husband, didn't she?" Leslie asked with discernment.

"I'm afraid so."

"Is that why you were so sweet to her?"

"Partly. The other reason is that I admire her."

"Truly?"

"Truly. Unfortunately, in our society, husbands practically own their wives, and the law allows it. It takes courage for a woman to leave a man who's abused her."

"Yes, I suppose it does," Leslie mused. "Now I understand her views on men and marriage. Also why you said it wouldn't do after you saw what she really looks like. You were worried that Alex could become enamored of Rianne, and that would become terribly complicated, wouldn't it, since she's married?"

"Exactly. I would hate to see either of them hurt. Leslie, sometimes you surprise me with your insight and maturity."

"I don't know why I should, Auntie, dear. After all, I had you to teach me, didn't I?"

"I did the best I could," Lorna said, smiling, "and I have to admit I'm proud of how you turned out. And Alex, too, of course, though I didn't have much to do with his upbringing."

Leslie turned serious. "Speaking of Alex—how are we to convince him that Rianne is to be my companion? I don't think he much likes her, Aunt, though I can't understand why."

"It's not a matter of like or dislike. From what I've observed, I believe Alex is bewildered by Rianne. He doesn't understand a woman like her—one who is self-contained, even shy, yet unafraid to speak her mind." Lorna laughed. "It may do him some good to learn that there's a variety of women in this world. Alex has become much too cynical. He's also wary of . . . involvements, which is why he only sees a certain type."

"Hmm. The loose and easy type, you mean?"

"Exactly. They're safe, you see. There's no danger of his

becoming emotionally engaged."

"Do you think that's it?" Leslie asked thoughtfully. "He never speaks of Father's death, or . . ." Leslie bit her lip. "I know I'll never stop missing my parents, yet Alex has lost so much more. I suppose I've lost sight of that fact, for to me, he's always been my strong, confident brother. Is he still grieving, do you suppose? Is that why he doesn't seem to care about marrying again?"

"Yes, I'm sure that's it," Lorna replied quietly. Then, because she'd long ago promised Alex that she would never tell Leslie what had really happened at Bellesfield all those years ago, she gently changed the subject. "I'll speak to him about Rianne tonight."

"Oh, good. Are you sure he won't flatly refuse to allow her to accompany us?"

Lorna patted Leslie's hand. "I'm sure. If he balks, I'll tell him I gave my word. Alex was nurtured on honor from the day he was born. He'll have no choice but to agree."

Chapter 8

Alex stared at his aunt in disbelief. "Tell me you're not serious!"

"Of course I'm serious!" Lorna exclaimed. "This is an ideal solution to our dilemma."

Alex ran his fingers through his hair and blew a breath of exasperation. "Les put you up to this, didn't she?" he asked, pinning a narrowed gaze upon his aunt. "I should have known when she refused to interview the two women from the agency."

"True, Leslie doesn't care for the idea of traveling with a stranger, but she certainly didn't put me up to anything. She simply suggested the idea, and I happen to think it's an excellent one."

"Right. And who gave *her* the idea? I don't trust Anne DuBois. She gives the appearance of a meek, little mouse, but I have a mighty strong suspicion that demeanor is just a cover. What do we really know about her? It's possible she may even be dangerous."

"Dangerous? Oh, for heaven's sake, Alex! Don't you think you're overreacting?"

"No. Look at all those radical ideas she's put into Leslie's head. They don't sit well with me, I can tell you. In my opinion, they'll only confuse Les and could very well affect the rest of her life. I don't want my sister becoming a facsimile of Anne—a desiccated, unloved, unwanted prune."

"Oh, Alex! Anne's not like that!" Lorna protested.

Alex stretched his long legs out before him and leaned back to link his fingers behind his neck. "Isn't she? I'll wager that her marriage was never consummated. I can't imagine any man bedding her. She probably raised such a ruckus on her wedding night that the poor fellow had a heart attack. Wouldn't be surprised if she smiled all through the funeral, too."

Lorna gasped. "What a terrible thing to say!"

He grinned, unabashed. "It gets worse, Aunt Lorna. Frankly, I'm not thrilled about spending the next few weeks in Anne's company. The woman has almost no sense of humor, is painfully shy, and her feeble attempts to converse are excruciating to watch. She can barely meet one's eyes. On top of that, she's not exactly pleasant to look at. In fact, I'd meant to talk to you about that. Can't you do something to improve her looks? Surely no one should be that pale. And her hair is awful. I think she uses more pomade than some of those young fops who were hanging around Les the other night."

"Well, I suppose I could make some casual suggestions," Lorna replied, trying hard not to smile. In almost the same breath, Alex had insulted Anne, then pleaded for assistance for her.

"Good! And see what you can do about those hideous spectacles," Alex added, grimacing. "Perhaps we can convince her to at least change them to clear lenses."

"I'll try, but you must realize that I may not be able to accomplish much of anything in so short a time. Also, these matters call for subtlety, and I wouldn't want to hurt Anne's feelings."

"What feelings? She has ice water in her veins."

Lorna frowned at Alex, genuinely puzzled at his attitude.

True, he'd hardened over the years. Most of the time he deliberately donned a devil-may-care attitude, but Lorna knew that beneath that mask he still harbored caring, protective attributes for his family and for those less fortunate than he. So why was he so heartless regarding Anne—*Ri*anne? "That comment is beneath you, Alex," she said sternly. "For goodness sake, the poor girl has no family. She was orphaned as a child, then married to her guardian at a young age, and I don't believe he was very kind to her. She's a woman alone who has need of our compassion and generosity. I can't believe you have such unkind feelings toward her."

Two slashes of red appeared on Alex's cheeks. He rose and went to stand at the window, shoving his hands into his pockets as he looked out. "I agree that Anne needs a helping hand, and I have no quarrel with that. But the plain fact is, she's such a pitiable creature, it would be too easy for Les to think she has to be her savior and become overly attached to her."

Lorna stared at her nephew. He wasn't making any sense. Why would he be so averse to the idea of Leslie's becoming attached to that "pitiable creature" when he had himself expressed a genuine concern for Anne—Rianne? If he really believed his own callous notions about Rianne, why had he bothered to ask her to try to make Rianne more appealing? A thought began to glimmer in Lorna's mind—that perhaps Alex didn't really think that Anne was quite as pitiable as he let on. "Leslie is already attached to Anne," Lorna said quietly. "I don't think that's so terrible. Why do you?"

Alex turned back to her. "What if she's just using Les?"

"In what way?"

Alex waved a hand to indicate the room. "The woman is practically destitute. She's probably never lived in so grand a house. What if she's clinging to Les in hopes of gaining an advantage? I don't want my sister hurt. Nor you, for that matter."

"Anne isn't like that," Lorna said firmly. "You forget that she and Leslie have been friends for several years. As to Leslie, she's a grown woman now. You can't keep her from experiencing life to the fullest, which means she must learn to handle her own disappointments. You know better than some that the world's not perfect, that we must all bear our own burdens, take the bad with the good. Otherwise we're not really living, are we?"

Alex reclaimed his chair and took his aunt's hand in his. Studying it, he spoke quietly. "Bearing our own burdens is hardly the same as being the cause of pain to others." He lifted his head to meet Lorna's gaze. "How does one live with the guilt, Aunt?" he asked bleakly. "Tell me, for I've been trying for almost ten years, yet I can't rid myself of the thought that I should have been able to prevent the deaths of those I loved."

Lorna squeezed his hand. "You have nothing to feel guilty for, Alex," she said gently. "For God's sake, you were wounded and taken prisoner. You couldn't possibly have gotten back to Bellesfield in time to prevent what happened there. You must believe that it had nothing to do with you—that it was ordained by a Higher Power. I beg you, Alex, stop doing this to yourself," she pleaded.

"As you said, we all have our own burdens to bear. Mine is guilt. Don't try to take it away from me, Aunt. It fuels my determination not to make the same mistake."

"Oh, my dear Alex," Lorna replied, shaking her head. "It's not a mistake to care for someone. To have a lover and companion who will share your life, your laughter and joy and, yes, even your sorrows. Love makes all things bearable and fills your heart with peace and joy."

Alex looked weary as he rubbed the back of his neck. "And what about the pain you suffer when all that's taken from you, Aunt? Have you forgotten that?"

"Of course I haven't forgotten. I loved Burt dearly. He was my entire life. What we had together was wonderful. I think of it, and him, daily, and feel blessed. Don't you see that I would only have dishonored his memory by becoming bitter?"

Alex smiled at her ruefully. "Is that what I've become? Bitter?"

"To an extent, yes, but you've turned it inward. Outwardly you wear an uncaring air. Sometimes I think that, though you're alive and breathing, you're not really here."

"At times I feel as if I'm not." Alex sighed and sat straighter. "So, how did we get on this subject anyway? We were speaking of Anne, I believe."

Lorna knew not to push. Besides, Alex had become an expert at hiding his emotions. The last time he'd revealed his deepest feelings to her had been when he'd returned from Bellesfield in '65, devastated and close to spiritually destroyed.

But Lorna had to say one more thing. "Yes, we were speaking of Ri—of Anne. I've just realized that you and she both seem detached at times. She's suffered, also, Alex. You may have more in common with her than you think."

Alex grimaced. "Lord, I hope not," he replied, ignoring Lorna's comment. "The woman irritates me. If I affect her the same way, it's going to be a hell of a trip." Then he grinned. "On the other hand, a little stimulus will keep things from becoming too boring."

"Does that mean that you're agreeing to have Anne?"

His eyes sparkled and he devilishly quirked an eyebrow.

"*Having* her is the last thing on my mind, believe me!"

"Alex, you're outrageous!" Lorna tossed a small pillow at him.

Alex batted it away, laughing. "I know. It's one of the reasons women can't keep their hands off me," he replied audaciously before dropping her hand and rising to bend over and kiss her cheek. "Yes," he said as he turned and strode to the door. "Les can have her little friend for a companion. I don't suppose I ever really had a choice. It's either take Anne or be on the receiving end of Leslie's anger for the next few weeks. Frankly, I don't much care for that cold-shoulder act she does so effectively."

Lorna chuckled. "Leslie will be so pleased. It will work out, Alex. You'll see. You won't be sorry."

Alex had already stepped into the hall, but he turned to poke his head back through the doorway. "So you say, but I have the damnedest feeling I'm going to be very sorry, indeed."

"You're late, Alex," Leslie greeted him smugly as he walked into the dining room, where she and Rianne had just seated themselves.

"Sorry, I had some things to see to," he replied casually as he pulled out his chair.

Leslie exchanged a questioning look with Rianne, but when Alex offered nothing more, she said to him, "You'll like the soup tonight. It's asparagus."

"Good. I'm starving," he responded as he sat down and spread his napkin. Betsy came forward and ladled soup into his bowl. Silence reigned for a few minutes, until Alex glanced up and saw two pairs of eyes focused on him. "What is it? Have I dripped on my chin?"

"No! Nothing like that," Leslie hastened to assure him. With another quick glance at Rianne, she turned her attention back to her own soup. "Are you going out again this evening?"

Alex studied his bowl to hide his smile. Les was obviously bursting to ask him the results of his discussion with their aunt. He decided he wasn't in any hurry to reveal its outcome. His sneaky little sister deserved a bit of anxiety. "I thought I would," he replied casually. "How about you two? Any plans?"

"I purchased some books on New Orleans the other day. I think we'll stay in and browse through those."

"Oh?" Alex glanced from one woman to the other. Anne, he noticed, was engrossed in studying her spoon, as if debating whether or not to lick it. She hadn't said a word, as yet. Lord, she was the quietest woman he'd ever known. "Are you helping Leslie plan her itinerary, Anne?"

"Rianne," Leslie stated firmly.

Alex's own spoon halted halfway to his mouth. "Rianne? Who's that?"

The hand belonging to the person in question jerked, knocking over a glass of water.

"So clumsy. I'm terribly sorry," Rianne murmured as she tried to mop up the water. Betsy finished the task and replaced Rianne's soaked napkin.

Rianne glanced up to find Alex regarding her curiously. Well, there was no help for it now that Leslie had let the cat out of the bag. "That's me. That is, my name isn't Anne, it's really *Ri*anne. After meeting Mrs. Busley the first time and discovering how . . . conventional she was, I was convinced she would think my real name too exotic. Therefore, I shortened it to Anne."

"I see. Rianne, hmm?" He made no further comment about her name, only studied her more intently. Finally he said, "You've done something different to your hair."

"Not really." She touched it self-consciously. She hadn't completely discarded Madame DuBois's persona, but as Mrs. Hall had suggested, she'd begun to compromise.

She was wearing a new dress, moss green in color, but very simple and modest, yet Alex had seemed to notice only her hair. She'd loosened it slightly and netted it at her nape in a soft chignon. Without the heavy pomade, her curls showed more body. Also, since she'd stopped using the dye when she left Chatham's, they were beginning to regain their natural color.

"It seems brighter," Alex noted.

Rianne gave him a wan smile in reply before tossing a quick glance at Leslie, who winked at her.

Alex turned his attention to Leslie. "You said you were planning your itinerary," he reminded her.

"What? Oh, yes. Rianne's been helping me."

Alex waited until Betsy removed the soup bowls and set the next course before them. "Les," he said, after swallowing a mouthful of his cod, "I'm not promising you'll see all the places you'd like to see. I may not have the time to take you, and some of them may not be suitable for you to visit alone."

"For heaven's sake, Alex, you *are* becoming stuffy!" Leslie pushed her fish around her plate and sighed dramatically. "I suppose," she said innocently, "that I should have expected it, though, with your advancing age . . ."

Rianne lowered her head to hide her smile. It was fascinating watching the ease with which Leslie manipulated her brother. What would it be like, she wondered, to have such an easy, relaxed relationship with a man? Alex, aware that he was being manipulated, attempted to keep his own lips from twitching and failed. "You little devil! What a thing to say to your esteemed brother. All right," he capitulated in response to Leslie's eager look. "I'll think about it. But only if you promise not to traipse off anywhere on your own. We still have to agree on hiring someone to be your companion and chaperone." He eyed her narrowly. "Something that would already be accomplished if you wouldn't keep refusing to interview the candidates I've selected."

"Oh, Alex, I saw them from upstairs. One looked like a peacock with her garish clothes and the other—she actually had the nerve to look Branson up and down as if he were a creature from another planet before she stuck her nose in the air and sniffed—actually *sniffed*—at him! Now I ask you, would you want to be stuck with someone like that?"

Alex shook his head in pretended exasperation. "We've so little time left, Les. We're going to have to find someone soon."

"Well, actually, weren't you upstairs speaking to Aunt Lorna earlier?"

"As a matter of fact, I was." Alex took his time buttering a roll, knowing that Leslie's impatience was increasing. He chanced a glance at Rianne. Her head was bowed as she idly rearranged the food on her plate. Alex would have wagered anything that she wasn't even seeing the cod, that her attention was focused on his and Les's conversation.

"Well?" Leslie burst out. "What did you and Aunt Lorna speak about? The weather? The stock market? The journey we're soon to take? *What?*"

"Hmm. The weather, yes. Stock market? I believe we discussed the value of one of her investments, yes. I don't recall that she mentioned anything *specific* about the trip, however." Alex said innocently before biting into a roll, "Is there any reason she should have?"

"Well, I . . . uh . . . ah . . ." Leslie stuttered, perplexed.

"How about you, Rianne? Do you think Aunt Lorna might

have a reason to speak to me about the trip Les and I are taking?"

Not expecting Alex to address her, Rianne dropped her fork. It landed on her lap, splattering chunks of fish over the bodice of her dress. She was mortified when she glanced up and saw that Alex was staring at her chest sympathetically. She dabbed at herself frantically, ruining her second napkin of the evening.

"I . . . ah . . ." Lord, why did her tongue have to tie itself into knots every time he focused those startlingly beautiful eyes upon her?

"It isn't fair putting Rianne on the spot, Alex," Leslie complained.

"Why not? She's adept at tongue-lashings. She can always give me another one." His eyes twinkled as he turned to address Rianne. "Feel free, Rianne."

This time she recognized that he was teasing her. A smile spread across her face. Strange, but lately it seemed he was making her smile. "I'll pass, but that's not to say I won't ever be tempted. Especially since you're such an excellent subject for practice," she dared to respond.

At this, Alex threw back his head and laughed. Leslie joined in, while Rianne found herself chuckling.

Goodness! Had those cheeky words actually come from her own mouth? Dinner proceeded with much conversation and laughter after that. Rianne was almost sorry to see it end, but it did, and she and Leslie adjourned to the drawing room, while Alex stepped out onto the terrace to smoke a cigar.

"Why did you tell Alex my real name?" Rianne whispered as she and Leslie sat down.

"It's too confusing to try to remember which name to use," Leslie replied. "I didn't think Alex would question it, and he didn't. Many people use shortened versions of their names."

"I have to admit it makes me feel better—a little less deceitful, anyway," Rianne remarked.

"Of course it does. You're such an honest person, Rianne, these last few years must have been difficult for you."

Rianne was surprised at Leslie's insight. *It's getting more and more so all the time!* she silently agreed. She didn't think herself honest at all, for though it had been an enormous relief to reveal to Leslie and Mrs. Hall part of her story, there was so much she couldn't tell them. Couldn't tell anyone. She sighed. Guilt was weighing heavily on her. "Why do you think your aunt didn't bring up the subject of my accompanying you?" she asked anxiously as she sipped her coffee.

"Perhaps she hadn't time enough before dinner. She'll do it. If not tonight, then tomorrow."

"Do you think your brother will agree?"

"Don't worry. Aunt will convince him. Alex may sound and act gruff at times, but inside he's a softy. He does have a temper, as do I, but it takes a lot for either of us to get really angry. Except, of course, at each other. And that's because we're so much alike. You don't have any brothers, do you?"

"No, I was an only child. My father died when I was eleven, and after that . . . Well, I've never been around many men," she admitted. "I wouldn't even know how to begin to manage one the way you do Alex."

Leslie grinned. "Once you've spent some time with him, you'll learn how, too. You simply have to remember to pretend he's always right, then do as you wish and convince him that it was what he wanted in the first place."

They were still laughing over that when Alex entered the drawing room. He refused when Leslie asked if he wanted coffee. "No, what I'd like is for Rianne to accompany me to

Uncle Burt's study. I have some matters to discuss with her."

Leslie plopped her cup and saucer onto the tray, ignoring the coffee that splashed over the sides as she jumped to her feet. "Blast you, Alex!" she yelled, hands on her hips. "Aunt *did* speak to you about Rianne, didn't she? You were just tormenting me at dinner. Oh, I could smack you!"

"Let this be a lesson to you," he smirked. "Two can play at your secrecy games, but I'm better at them than you."

"Oh! You're a rascal, Alex Benedict!" Leslie sputtered.

"And you love me for it, don't you?" Alex chortled, causing Leslie to join in helplessly.

Rianne's wide eyes went from one to the other. She couldn't understand how two people could be angry at one another yet laugh at the same time!

"Rianne?"

Still wearing a puzzled expression, Rianne immediately rose to follow Alex, but when he stepped out of the room to let her precede him, she glanced back in worry.

Leslie smiled reassuringly and waved crossed fingers.

Chapter 9

In the study, Alex indicated that Rianne should take the chair in front of the desk, while he went to sit behind it—and stare at her thoughtfully. She sat and stared back through her spectacles, once again glad that he couldn't see her eyes clearly. Was he angry?

"I can't quite decide if you're genuine or if you're just a very clever woman, Rianne DuBois," he said without preamble.

Rianne blinked. Oh, dear! He was back to addressing her formally. This certainly didn't bode well. She was on guard, convinced that her earlier, improved opinion of Alex had been a mistake.

She sat stiffly silent as she tried to stare him down. Her attempt was hopeless, of course, for he merely leaned back and balanced his chair on its two rear legs, then proceeded to pick up a pencil and tap it on the desk as he waited, his narrowed gaze pinning her as effectively as if he were physically restraining her.

Rianne finally sighed in defeat. "I don't know what you mean," she said cautiously. "Clever in what way?"

"In being even more manipulative than Leslie—and most other women of my acquaintance."

"I've *never*—" She jumped when his chair crashed down.

"You know damned well you've managed to ingratiate yourself with Leslie and Aunt Lorna. No doubt you slyly hinted that you would make an excellent companion and—"

"I did no such thing!" she protested. "It was their idea, not mine. I didn't even know they were considering it until they spoke to me. Anyway, Mrs. Hall led me to understand that you have the final word."

He smiled in self-mockery. "When a man lives in a household of women, he seldom has the final word. He's only allowed to think he has."

"Still, they'll do as you wish," Rianne said stiffly, her voice calm though she felt terribly hurt at his accusations. "As I was about to say, if you don't like the idea, then say so, and I'll leave."

"Right, and I'll be left to deal with Les's fury and Aunt's scolding. Uh uh."

Now Rianne was confused. "What are you saying? That you *want* me to accompany you and Leslie?"

"No, I don't want it. You're stubborn, opinionated—"

Rianne almost snorted in derision.

"—and you hold a number of negative views of men. I'm not convinced you're a good role model for Les."

"Oh? You'd rather she be a simpering miss who's afraid to open her mouth other than to say 'yes' and 'whatever you wish'?" As she had once been herself, Rianne thought ruefully. "She's a young woman with a mind of her own. To break her spirit would be the utmost cruelty."

"I don't want her spirit broken. I just don't want her being led to believe that all men are ogres."

Rianne gasped. "I *never* told her that."

"Perhaps not. But it's obvious that your own experiences, whatever they may have been, have appreciably dimmed your vision of the male species."

Rianne bit her lip. Perhaps she *had* been too fervent. Still, that didn't give him the right to scold her as if she were a child, nor to sit tapping that blasted pencil while he stared at her as if considering what her punishment should be.

But he surprised her with his next words.

"You know, Rianne," he said mildly as he tossed down the pencil and leaned forward, "sometimes you irritate the hell out of me."

She stiffened. "Why do you say that?" she asked cautiously.

"Because I can't figure you out. You shift from being painfully shy to vociferously expressing your opinions. You're a widow, yet you're the worst example of a dried-up spinster I've ever met. You sometimes act as if you're afraid of me, yet you aren't afraid to defend my sister or yourself against me."

Rianne fumed silently as he continued.

"I never know what to expect from you next. One minute you're a timid little mouse, the most subservient creature I've ever met, and—"

"I am not!" she denied hotly, though she knew it was true. When had she ever had a chance to be otherwise? "Aha!" Alex said triumphantly. "You see? Now you're the mouse who roars. You only do it when you're impugned, though. On the other hand, if you feel *you've* insulted someone, you fall all over yourself apologizing."

Rianne's cheeks burned, for she couldn't deny either of Alex's assessments. She was still trying to unlearn the lessons of restraint and humble acceptance, still discovering that she was free to express her opinions and that no one was going to quash signs of rebellion, as Lance had done.

The second lesson—always apologizing—was more difficult to unlearn, since she'd spent years trying to please Lance, to become the woman he wanted and expected. Each time she'd failed to please him, he'd raised his eyebrows and waited silently until she'd apologized. Sometimes she hadn't even known what it was she was apologizing for.

She'd sworn that no one would ever again catalogue her deficiencies as if she were being graded. Yet she wasn't sure if that was what Alex was doing.

"You need to make yourself clearer," she told him. "I'm not sure if I'm being criticized or praised for my inadequacies."

"Ah, so you admit to them."

Rianne glanced about the study, then back at him. "Excuse me, I didn't realize I was in a courtroom."

He grinned at her, unabashed. "That's something else that intrigues me—your quick wit. Seems at odds with your character."

Rianne sighed. It seemed he was leading up to a refusal. He didn't want her to be Leslie's companion, else why would he be discussing her shortcomings? Well, then, she had nothing to lose by letting him know what she thought of *him*. "You've already dissected my character. When do we get to vivisect yours?"

To her surprise, he laughed. "I believe you've already done so—the night of Leslie's party. You may have missed a few points, though. Let's see. Did you include charming? No? How about lovable?"

Despite her irritation with Alex, Rianne suppressed a smile. "Sorry. For some odd reason I can't seem to get past your arrogance."

He laughed again. "I'll make a deal with you. I'll attempt to be less arrogant if you stop apologizing each time you think you've offended me. I have a thick skin, Rianne. I can take it. I'd rather you tell me what you really think instead of hiding under that cloak of demureness."

She flushed. "I didn't realize apologizing had become a

habit. I promise I'll try to do better. Or less, as the case may be."

"Good. In return, I'll promise to remind you each time you forget," Alex told her. "That being said," he continued, "I've told Aunt Lorna that you may come with us, but—"

"You're hiring me?" Rianne cut in, surprised.

"Didn't I just say I told my aunt so?"

"Why, if you dislike me so much?"

Alex's mouth curled downward. "I never said I disliked you."

"Oh. I see. You think I'm a scheming, man-hating woman who's led your sister astray. You don't trust me, yet you claim to *not* dislike me. Forgive me, but I find that contradictory."

"I repeat, I never said I didn't like *you*. What I don't like are mysteries. You're an enigma, Rianne DuBois, and I'm going to find out what makes you tick."

"Why?"

He shrugged. "Up until now, I've never met a woman I can't decipher. I refuse to accept that you should be the first."

Rianne bit her lip to keep from retorting that he'd no doubt had scores of women to practice on, but she didn't intend to be one of them. Her secrets were hers to keep, and Alex Benedict was the last person to whom she would reveal them.

She would have to keep her guard up. She'd already seen examples of his stubborn nature. He was too forceful and too demanding. Devious, too, as she'd just learned through witnessing his game with Leslie.

"Well, have you nothing to say to that?" he asked her.

Rianne shrugged, pretending indifference. "Do your best," she replied calmly. She knew immediately that she'd made a mistake when his eyes flashed. Instead of lessening his interest, she'd managed to expand it.

"Oh, I intend to," he said smugly, "for I can't resist a challenge. Worried?" he taunted when he saw her wince slightly.

Her chin shot into the air. "If I were, I'd certainly never admit it to you," she bit out.

"Aha! You see? Already I've learned something else about you. You have pride. Very good, Rianne."

She couldn't help asking. Her curiosity was too great. "You said 'something else.' "

"I know you're stubborn, and that you have a temper. But with each new facet I uncover about you, I'm more intrigued."

"Oh, for heaven's sake," she burst out, "there's nothing more to know. I'm just a person!"

Alex grinned. "Really worried now, aren't you?"

Rianne gritted her teeth. "May we please get off the subject of my personality and finish our business?"

"Hmm. I did get a bit side-tracked, didn't I? Let's see, we were discussing your employment. I think I was about to say that you may come with us, but only if you follow my dictates. No more downgrading men, no encouraging Les to visit inappropriate places. You will check with me first, is that clear?"

"Certainly," Rianne replied tersely.

"I'll be watching you, Rianne. I warn you."

Ha! Rianne thought rudely, but she kept her mouth closed and merely nodded.

"Good. Now the matter of salary," Alex said. "Some of the decisions, I'm relieved to find, have still been left to me. I suggest two-fifty."

"Two hundred and fifty?" When he nodded, Rianne tried to hide her disappointment. That was only half her yearly salary at the academy. Twenty dollars a month was hardly enough to finance her trip West. Still, it was better than nothing.

"That's strictly salary," Alex added. "Your board and keep are included, of course."

That certainly helped. "That's quite acceptable, Mr. Benedict. Thank you."

"I thought we'd agreed that you would call me Alex."

"Did we? As I recall, you practically *ordered* me to use your given name."

He eyed her sternly. "Then obey."

She hated that word. *Obey. Yes, Lance. No, Lance. Of course, Lance.* As his ward, she'd had no choice; it appeared she didn't now, either. She needed this position. It was her ticket to freedom. "As you wish," she replied formally.

Alex frowned as he studied Rianne's expression. She seemed suddenly detached, withdrawn into herself. What had he said to bring that on? All right, so he'd tested her. She'd passed the test; her reaction had proven to him that she hadn't planned this venture.

He hadn't been surprised at Aunt Lorna's suggestion that Anne—Rianne—be Leslie's companion. Considering that Les was so fond of Rianne, and his aunt's approval, he'd been expecting it. He hadn't been convinced it was the right course of action, however. Rianne as a teacher was one aspect. Rianne as a constant companion, another. He wanted Leslie to enjoy this trip, and he wasn't so sure that Rianne knew *how* to enjoy herself.

Still, she had shown hints of humor. A touch of sparkling wit. Perhaps she simply needed to relax and enjoy herself.

Maybe this trip would be beneficial to her as well. Maybe it would reveal the real woman beneath that wary, unattractive exterior. Looks weren't everything, after all. Though, come to think of it, he'd noticed a subtle change in her at dinner . . .

He studied her more carefully. Her hair was softer, wavier,

and it no longer seemed mousy brown but burnished with a touch of red. She wasn't nearly as pale as he remembered, either. Her cheeks flushed a becoming pink as she became aware of his perusal. No, she didn't look too unattractive, except . . . "Do you really need those blasted spectacles?"

Rianne blinked, surprised at his question. "Yes, of course," she said, touching the frame self-consciously. *They're my protection from you.*

"Will you take them off so I can see your eyes?"

"No," she replied curtly.

All right. He wouldn't force the issue, but sooner or later he was going to get those tinted lenses off her and see what she was hiding behind them. Just as he intended to peel away, one by one, all those layers of protective armor she wore.

He would have to do so gently and cautiously. Before his aunt mentioned Rianne's past, he'd already discerned pain.

Like recognizes like, eh? said a voice in Alex's head. *Your Auntie was right. You and Rianne aren't so different, after all.* Alex willed the voice to disappear, but it ignored him and continued to nag. *You can't help being intrigued, but you don't like it one bit. Afraid you'll become too involved . . .*

Alex quickly pulled a ledger out of a drawer and opened it. "Having traveled with Les and my aunt in the past," he began, "I'm aware that women need to shop before packing, so . . ." He began writing. In a moment he ripped out a draft and handed it to her. "This is an advance on your first month's salary, Rianne."

"Thank you." She glanced at the draft in her hand. Then she took a second look and blinked in shock. "Oh, goodness!"

"I thought we agreed on the figure. Is it not enough?"

"Not enough? Mr. B—er, Alex. This draft is for two hundred and fifty dollars!"

"Yes. I'm quite aware of that since I just wrote it."

"But—" A *month's* salary? When he'd said two hundred and fifty dollars, she'd calculated that amount on an *annual* basis. This was too much, and she told him so.

"It's not too much, Rianne. It's no more than Brannon and Benedict pay their clerks, and believe me, keeping my sister out of mischief entails much more responsibility."

"You pay office clerks this much each month?" she asked in disbelief.

"Nick Brannon and I believe that employees who are fairly reimbursed for their work are both satisfied and loyal. We pay them well if they're deserving."

"But you don't . . . you just made it clear that you're uncertain about me. That you don't even trust me. Excuse me, but this salary contradicts all you said."

"Perhaps I should also have mentioned that I know that you're mature and steady. You proved, when Aunt was injured, that you can remain calm in an emergency. Leslie seems determined to enjoy New Orleans completely, and since you're familiar with the city, I'll feel relieved knowing you're with her while I'm attending to business."

Rianne squirmed restlessly. She could hardly blurt out that nearly everything she'd told Leslie about New Orleans she'd learned either from books or from the servants in the little house on rue Daphine. After her mother, Claudine, had been killed and Lance came into her life, she'd not been allowed much freedom.

Nor could she admit that she wouldn't be going to New Orleans with them. Mrs. Hall had warned her not to tell Alex that. It would be another thing she'd keep from him.

"Rianne?"

Her head jerked. "I'm sorry. You were saying—?"

Alex rose to his feet and extended his right hand. "I know we've had some differences since we met, but there's no reason we can't set those aside in order to make this a memorable event for Leslie." When she only stared at him, he quirked an eyebrow. "Come, come, Rianne. Take this as *your* challenge."

"All right. I will." Rianne let him shake her hand.

"Incidentally, I like the name Rianne. A shame you haven't used it all along."

Rianne ignored his unspoken question and left the study, her mind a jumble of confusion. First he'd accused her of being manipulative. Then he'd insisted that he didn't dislike her—before threatening to learn all her secrets. He'd said he thought her mature and steady, then he'd turned around and tossed her a challenge. The man was so blasted contradictory! She didn't think she'd ever understand him.

Forget it, Rianne, she told herself. *He may be curious about you, but the last thing you need is to try to figure him out. You thought you knew Lance well, and you didn't know one true thing about him.*

No. Curiosity was too close to involvement. Even if she and Alex should actually became friends, which she sincerely doubted, it was safer to keep herself removed from him.

That would be easier, though, if she could rid herself of the excitement she felt at the thought of spending the next month or so in his company.

Not good. Not good at all.

Chapter 10

"Oh my." Rianne's tone was one of hushed awe. "Oh *my!*" she repeated.

"Grand, isn't it?" Leslie asked from beside her.

"It's more than that. It's so . . . so *elaborate!*"

"Is that a problem?" Alex stepped past a young, red-faced porter and onto the platform, where another porter was stacking trunks and luggage and baskets of food. Making his way through the maze, he slapped his hat against his thigh to rid it of raindrops and entered the railroad car. It had been raining most of the morning, and though the precipitation had now let up, the skies were still brooding and it was unseasonably cold.

"Rianne is having difficulty believing what she's seeing," Leslie told him as she snapped her umbrella shut.

Alex set his hat on a small table and shoved his hands into his pockets. His mouth was twitching. "Oh? You think the Rolling Palace may be too ostentatious?" he asked Rianne.

She blushed guiltily, worried he might have taken her words as criticism. "Oh, no! It's charming. I was simply taken by surprise."

"It may look elaborate, but Nick and I had her built by the Pullman Company specifically for comfort. Go on, look it over."

"Oh, thank you!"

Alex's watched as she stepped forward and eagerly opened

a folding door. "Oh, my heavens! It's a kitchen!" she exclaimed.

Alex's smile broadened at her amazement. "We bring our own cook and valet on extended trips or when we entertain clients and associates. I didn't this time, since we'll be on the train only two days."

Alex followed Rianne farther into the coach, leaving Leslie to deal with the porters. He found himself wearing a pleased grin as he watched Rianne walk about, her expression one of awed delight as she took in her new surroundings.

Rianne was impressed by the soft patina of the hand-carved oak walls and cupboards, the wicker chairs and sofas upholstered in hunter green to match the carpet, the blue and green striped curtains covering the wide windows.

Alex lifted the seat of one sofa to demonstrate how it lifted and folded out into a platform wide enough to sleep two people. The mattresses used to pad the platforms were tucked away in drawers under each sofa. When he swung open one of the hinged "cupboard" doors, Rianne saw that they, too, were sleeping berths.

"Goodness," she exclaimed, "this car can easily sleep six people!"

"And there's more," Alex said mysteriously as he led her to the far end.

"How long is this coach?" Rianne asked curiously.

"Nearly fifty feet." Alex slid open a door to reveal another area. "The observation room," he announced proudly.

It was small, but had large windows on either side. Two wicker chairs sat in front of one, a table and chairs before the other. The sofa and berth were against the back wall. Like the other room, it was beautifully appointed with a mirror and excellent prints on the walls, hanging brass kerosene lamps and . . . Rianne winced. A vase of fresh dewy roses sat on the table.

She back-tracked toward the doorway, but it was blocked by Alex's imposing figure.

"You don't like this room?" he asked perceptively.

"Oh, no. That is, I do. It's lovely. I thought perhaps we should get back and help Leslie, er, arrange the luggage." She hesitated, biting her lip.

Alex frowned down at her. Why was she suddenly so nervous? Then he realized that she was waiting for him to step aside.

What the devil *was* her problem? Just when she'd begun to behave normally, leading him to believe that traveling with her might not be so unpleasant, she resumed her "shrinking violet" act.

And she infuriated him when she did that! Dammit, he wasn't odoriferous or uncouth or so damned ugly that women couldn't stand to look at him. Most women found excuses to further their association with him, while Rianne—Hell, it was obvious she couldn't get away fast enough! "Don't look so damned worried," he snapped. "Your virtue, Madame, is safe. Not," he added, "that it was ever in jeopardy to begin with."

Shocked at his cruel tone and icy eyes, Rianne was abjectly humiliated—and unexpectedly hurt by his crushing words. She struck back without thought. "A blessing, and one for which I'm profoundly grateful!"

He bowed mockingly. "*Touché,* Madame DuBois! After you," he said coldly as he swept his arm forward to indicate that her way was clear.

Face flaming, Rianne started to step past him. Why, why, did those awful memories of the past inexplicably intrude upon her present? She really couldn't blame Alex for becoming angry. He deserved an explanation, but she didn't know if she had the courage to give him one. It had been too long since she'd revealed her innermost feelings to anyone.

Alex straightened in time to see distress crease Rianne's forehead. Her hand came up to stroke her throat. She lowered her head and took a cautious step forward, and when he didn't move, she began to edge carefully around him.

She stopped. "It isn't you," she said in her soft voice. "It's just . . ." She took a deep breath. "I can't abide the scent of roses and . . . and being in a small room with a m—with another person brings back unpleasant memories. I'm sorry if I offended you."

Alex looked down at her bowed head. She looked abjectly miserable. His anger immediately dissipated. She had just trusted him with a secret from her past. It wasn't much, but it was one layer peeled away. He felt like the worst kind of heel.

Stepping in front of her, he lifted her chin with the knuckle of his forefinger. "I'm the one who's sorry, darlin'. I shouldn't have jumped to conclusions like that. Thank you for explaining. I'll take the roses with me when I leave."

Rianne was too stunned to reply. His abrupt change from anger to gentleness unsettled her. She knew that his eyes were a glacial green when he was angry, but when he was amused or looking at his sister or his aunt with tenderness and warmth, they turned a darker green, just as—

Just as they were now, looking at her!

And he'd called her "darlin'."

Rianne told herself it meant nothing. He was merely contrite for what he'd said, trying to charm his way back into her good graces. That was all there was to it, so why was her heart beating such a rapid rhythm? "You look as if you can't decide whether to forgive me or slap me." He gave her a devilish grin. "Care to try for both?"

"I—" Rianne jumped when Leslie suddenly spoke from the doorway.

"What in the world are you two finding so interesting in here?" she asked, looking from one to the other curiously as she peeled off her gloves.

"Roses," Alex replied.

"Roses?"

"Uh—huh. Rianne was telling me she hates my roses," he explained to his sister, and to Rianne's surprise, he winked.

At her. "Oh! I didn't know they were from you," she said.

"Alex always has roses sent to our rooms when Aunt and I travel with him," Leslie said. "Despite his numerous bad traits, he's a very thoughtful person."

"What kind of an underhanded compliment is that?" Alex complained good-naturedly.

Leslie ignored her brother's query and patted his cheek affectionately before she stepped back into the other room. "Believe it or not, Rianne, he can even be sweet at times."

Sweet? Up until a few minutes ago, Rianne would probably have laughed. Until he'd chucked her under the chin and given her that look and called her darlin', she'd have said he was bad-tempered, infuriating, intimidating, underhanded—but not sweet.

Now . . . well . . . Perhaps he *did* have a few redeeming qualities, after all.

"I don't think she agrees, Les," Alex called after his sister. "She's awfully quiet on the subject." Laughter glittered in his eyes.

Rianne tilted her head and pursed her lips as she squinted at him. "Hmm. I was just trying to recall whether 'thoughtful' and 'sweet' were among that list of your traits we discussed. I don't believe they were."

"I deliberately left them out so you could discover them for yourself. A man can't reveal all his good qualities at once, you know. Women become overwhelmed by such abundance."

Rianne snickered. She tried to contain it by placing a hand over her mouth, but the giggle escaped and became laughter.

Alex shoved his hands into his pockets and rocked on his heels, grinning at Rianne's amusement. It occurred to him that this was the first time he'd heard her laugh. The sound was full-bodied and melodious, unlike the irritating high-pitched squeals or giggles of some women. Nice. Infectious, too. As to her mouth . . .

Rianne wiped a tear off her cheek with the tip of a finger. "Despite your *abundance* of wondrous traits, 'arrogant' is still at the top of the list."

"Hmm."

She saw that Alex wasn't smiling; he was staring at her in the oddest way. Oh, dear. She'd probably offended him again. She sighed. "I should be helping Leslie."

"Hmm?" Alex said absently, still staring at her mouth."Leslie. I should be helping her with the luggage."

"The luggage?" What was the matter with him? Alex wondered. He didn't usually get so distracted. All right, so he'd just realized what a beautiful mouth Rianne had. What of it? Every woman deserved one good feature.

Alex jerked his hands out of his pockets. "It's time for me to find my own compartment, so I leave the Rolling Palace to you ladies. But first—" He went to the table and removed the vase of roses. "I'll find another place for these."

"Thank you. They're beautiful, but . . ."

"No apologies, remember? Though I must say, you're perhaps the only woman I've met who doesn't like roses." He studied her for a moment, recalling the little she'd told him, then he smiled reassuringly. "No matter. They aren't the only flowers in the world."

Leslie didn't need any help with the luggage, Rianne discovered. Thanks to the porters, the trunks were already neatly stacked against the walls. Rianne's battered trunk looked sad next to the shiny new one that had been a gift from Leslie. It was filled with lovely new clothes—the result of a whirlwind of shopping with Leslie and the help of Mrs. Porter, who had responded to Lorna Hall's urgent request by appropriating and altering part of a wardrobe that had been meant for another customer.

"Let's unpack the things we'll need for the next couple of days," Leslie suggested. "Then we'll set out the food Aunt Lorna's cook sent along." When she received no reply, she turned to find Rianne standing in the middle of the room, staring at the floor. "Rianne? Rianne!"

Hearing her name called, Rianne looked up to see that Leslie was observing her, concern etched on her face.

"Are you all right?" Leslie asked.

"What? Oh, yes. I'm fine."

"Did Alex say something to upset you?"

"No, of course not." Rianne sighed as she sank into a chair. "It was I who upset him."

Leslie gathered her skirts and sat in the other wicker chair. "How?" she asked bluntly.

"Oh, Leslie—it's just that I've never been very comfortable around men, and sometimes your brother can be intimidating and so . . . so . . ."

"Brusque? Direct? Impatient?" Leslie asked, smiling tolerantly.

"Yes, yes, and yes."

"True. Alex is all those things, but I can hardly fault him for it, since I'm afraid I share the same traits. Still, I can see that it would be unsettling to someone who doesn't know him well."

"Yes, but somehow I always seem to do or say the wrong thing and make him angry." Rianne's mouth curved self-mockingly.

"That is a bit odd, since Alex generally does an excellent job of hiding his feelings. You should know, however, that his anger doesn't usually last very long. Hmm." Leslie pursed her lips in thought. "Hmm," she murmured again. Then her eyes flashed with amusement. "Actually, I wouldn't worry about it if I were you. It's probably good for him."

"That I make Alex angry?" Rianne asked, disbelieving.

"Uh-huh. It beats indifference," Leslie said.

Before Rianne could ask what she meant by that, Leslie rose and took Rianne's hands to pull her to her feet. "Come on. Let's get at those trunks."

Rianne glanced about questioningly. "Where are we to put our things?"

"There's a small closet just inside the doorway to the observation room, and we can set our toiletries in here—" Leslie went to the wall separating the little kitchen from the main room. Secured to it were two hanging cabinets, one on each side of the doorway. Going to one, Leslie reached up to pull on the knob. The front of the cabinet was hinged, as were the berths, and folded down to reveal several shelves. *"Voilà!"* Leslie proclaimed. "Our dressing tables."

Rianne applauded. "How wonderfully clever!"

"The Rolling Palace has all kinds of little storage nooks. I'll take this one, and the other's yours. That reminds me, which bed do you want?"

"It doesn't matter."

"Let's do it this way, then, so we don't have to step on each other's toes, I'll sleep in here and you can have the observation room."

Rianne agreed and prepared to unpack. She set her spectacles on the sofa-bed next to her trunks and bent with the intention of kneeling. At that moment, the coach lurched forward. She was thrown off-balance and toppled onto her side. She sat up quickly, slapping her palms against the floor to brace herself. "What was that?" she squealed in alarm. "Are we moving?" She tried to struggle to her feet, but another jerk of the train landed her flat on her back.

Leslie looked down at Rianne sprawled on the floor, her eyes wide with apprehension, and she began to laugh. "Yes, the train's starting to move. But you look as if you're glued to the floor," she choked.

"Right now, the floor seems the most secure place *to* be," Rianne moaned. "Pass me the glue pot."

Rianne's pained tone had the opposite effect on Leslie. She fell to her knees and sat on her heels, laughing helplessly. "I'm s-sorry," she sputtered, "b-but I can't help it. Your eyes are as wide as saucers, and your skirts are up to your knees. You look as if you've been tossed off a train instead of boarding one."

Rianne grinned ruefully. "And well I might! You could have warned me, you know."

"Haven't you ever ridden a train before?"

Rianne shook her head and pushed herself into a sitting position. "Never. Am I going to have to spend all my time on the floor?"

"No, of course not. We're starting to move faster now, and once we've reached full speed, you'll feel only a slight rocking motion. You'll get used to it quickly and won't even notice."

Rianne was relieved. "I was afraid you were going to tell

me I had trainsickness—you know, like seasickness."

"Oh? Were you seasick on the voyage from New Orleans to Boston?"

"Horribly, for the first two days. It was so humiliating, because I was the only one to suffer the malady. I was sharing a cabin with three other women. When my stomach first rebelled, I spent most of my time kneeling over a bucket, until the others began to complain. So I graduated to hanging over the rail outside. When I wasn't retching, I was praying to die."

"How awful!" Leslie sympathized. "But the train won't be like that. No one ever gets sick on a train."

"That's good to know." Rianne grinned. "I'd hate for anything to spoil our Grand Adventure."

Chapter 11

Rianne couldn't sleep.

Despite the soothing, rolling motion of the train, she remained awake. Everything was so new and exciting to her, and she wondered what lay in the future.

Finally she gave up on slumber. Groping for the matches, she knelt on the bed to light the small sconce lamp over the headboard. It gave off only a small pool of light, but that was enough for her to find her robe and draw it on over her nightgown as she slid her feet into her slippers.

She stepped into the main room and stopped when she came to Leslie's sleeping berth. She listened for any sounds or movements coming from the bed, for almost immediately after their "picnic" dinner, Leslie had complained of feeling tired and achy. She'd sneezed several times while preparing for bed, too.

Leslie stirred, moaning quietly as she turned over onto her side, but her breathing sounded normal, so Rianne tiptoed past her. She could vaguely see silhouettes of furniture at this end of the coach and she groped her way to the platform door. Opening it carefully, she slipped outside and went to the railing, which she clasped tightly as she leaned slightly forward over it.

The rush of air created by the train's speed whipped her robe about her legs and loosened the ribbon binding her hair.

It was gone before she could catch it, thus freeing her hair to stream behind her.

She didn't mind. The feeling of speed and freedom was exhilarating. Keeping her thighs pressed against the rail, she lifted her head, raised her arms and laughed at the crescent moon.

A sudden flash of light to her right spun her around in alarm. Her breath hitched when she saw a man standing on the platform of the connecting car, his head bowed, and the light coming from between his cupped hands.

Rianne's hand went to her throat. Hoping she could slip back inside unobserved, she side-stepped cautiously to her own door. The man lifted his head and let the wind blow out his match, but the flame stayed lit long enough for her to recognize Alex.

Apparently she wasn't the only one who was having trouble falling asleep. But what was he doing here, near the Rolling Palace? "My Lord! You almost frightened me to death!" she sputtered, for the wind was now at her back, and strands of her hair were whipping over her face, threatening to both blind and gag her.

"Can't hear you!" Alex yelled over the noise the train made clattering over the tracks.

"I said—" She'd thought she was shouting until Alex shook his head.

"Stand away, Rianne!" he bellowed.

She pressed her back against the wall of the coach and held her breath as he leapt over the four feet separating his platform from hers and came to stand beside her. He spoke loudly into her ear. "Scare you?" he asked, laughing.

"Yes! Both times!"

"Sorry," he said as he leaned back against the wall. "I didn't know how to announce myself *without* startling you."

The end of Alex's cigar glowed red as he took a puff. "I was afraid if I yelled, you'd scream and faint."

"Need I remind you that I've never fainted in my life?" she scoffed, pulling strands of hair from her mouth and eyes. "But I admit I was frightened when you jumped. I'd been out here earlier, and when I found I had only to look down between these two cars to see the railroad ties whizzing past, it made me dizzy. I've never been on anything this fast before." She glanced up to find Alex's bent head only inches from hers, his ear almost pressed to her mouth in an attempt to hear her. She slid backward a few inches.

He turned his head to look down at her. "This is your first time on a train?"

"What? I can't hear you." Hair filled her mouth once again. She struggled to gather it at her nape.

Alex tossed his cigar over the railing. "Here, use this," he yelled, offering her his handkerchief.

"Thank you," she said as she took the scrap of white cloth. She had to clench it in her teeth, for she needed both hands to gather her hair at her nape.

Before she'd managed to do so, Alex took her elbow and turned her about. She glanced up at him questioningly. Jabbing his finger toward the door of the Rolling Palace, he opened it so that they could both slip inside to the little kitchen.

"Impossible to converse out there," he explained.

"Leslie's sleeping in the next room," Rianne whispered in warning as she managed to tie the handkerchief around her hair.

"No need to whisper. Les has always slept like the dead."

"Oh." She stared up at him, but it was too dark to see more than the glint of his eyes, which was good. That meant that he couldn't see her clearly, either. She leaned back against the narrow kitchen table, at ease. "What were you saying outside?"

"I asked if this is your first train ride."

"Yes. I'm regarding it as the beginning of our Great Adventure, as Leslie calls it." She laughed softly. Here, in the near dark, she felt comfortable with Alex. She was sharing a normal, friendly conversation with a man, which in itself was unusual. That the man was Alex gave her an unfamiliar, warm, fuzzy feeling.

Alex smiled at Rianne's enthusiasm. So that was why she'd been laughing at the moon. It had been an expression of joy. How long had it been since she'd had that in her life?

Her Great Adventure, hmm? "Then we'll do our best to see that you aren't disappointed on this trip," he told her. "Have you traveled before?"

"Only when I took that horrible cargo vessel to Boston." She chuckled softly. "In my estimation, that shouldn't even count as travel. So, no, I've never been anywhere before. That's why I'm excited about this opportunity."

He could see that she was, for she was bubbling over with it. She sounded as young and vivacious as Leslie.

Good God. She'd never been on board a large passenger ship, never traveled by train. Never traveled at all. So chances were she'd never stayed in an exclusive hotel or eaten in a fancy restaurant. Just what kind of life had Rianne led? She'd probably once been a normal, happy child. Mischievous, certainly. Daring, perhaps. So what had happened to her after she was orphaned? Who could have had enough influence over her to impel her into her current manner of subservience?

The man who'd been her guardian, then her husband.

What kind of a bastard had he been? Alex was surprised to realize that instead of feeling pity for the woman he'd known as Madame DuBois, he was filled with fierce anger toward the man who had taken over a young girl's life—Rianne's—then continued to assert his control by marrying her. Had she had any choice in the matter? Alex doubted it.

From the little Aunt Lorna had told him, he suspected that the bastard had abused Rianne. He'd met men of that ilk before. They were bullies, intent on breaking the spirit of the women they'd pledged to honor, forcing subservience upon them, often abusing them, emotionally and physically.

Sadly, society usually looked the other way, and those poor women were condemned to a lifetime of ill-treatment and unending torment.

Was that what had happened to Rianne? It occurred to Alex that, tonight, she was as relaxed as she'd ever been with him. He considered it too good an opportunity to pass by. Now was his chance to probe.

So it wasn't an admirable action to take. He really *shouldn't.*

Damned if he wouldn't, though! "Had you always lived in New Orleans?" he asked casually.

She didn't answer for a long moment, leaving Alex to think that she'd suddenly reverted to wariness. But then she spoke.

"Well, not always in the city. My father had a sugar cane plantation to the north. Belle Bayou," she said wistfully.

"A happy coincidence!" Alex rejoined. "Our plantation was named Bellesfield by my French great-great-great-grandfather, who settled it."

"Really? My mother was French, also."

"What happened to Belle Bayou and your parents, Rianne?"

"Papa was killed in '63. I don't even recall where, but afterward, Maman couldn't hold on to the land, for Papa had mortgaged it heavily. We lost everything, and Maman and I moved into a small house in the city."

"Aunt Lorna mentioned that you were orphaned at a young age." She stirred restlessly at that. Alex could tell she was staring at him in the dark, and now she *was* wary. "That was all she told me, really," he said gently.

"Yes," Rianne replied quietly. "Maman was killed in a carriage accident."

Seeing her shiver, Alex immediately slipped off his jacket to drape it over her shoulders. She murmured her thanks. He waited, but she didn't offer any more information.

Alex crossed his arms over his chest and settled back against the stove again. "You probably know that Leslie was orphaned at nine."

"Yes, but she was lucky enough to have Mrs. Hall and . . . and you," Rianne said shyly.

"You have no brothers or sisters?"

"None."

"Aunts? Uncles? Cousins?"

"My father had a younger brother, but he, too, was killed in the Conflict. Maman met and married my father in France. She had two sisters, and I believe there were several cousins in France, but I never met any of them. My . . . er, my guardian wrote to them after Maman died. He—"

"Your guardian. Who was he?" Alex cut in.

"The son of one of my father's friends," she said tersely. "Anyway, he, Lance, claimed that he never received a reply from my French relations."

"*Claimed?* You didn't believe him?"

"I had no reason to disbelieve him then." Alex felt rather than saw her shrug. "Since . . . well, it doesn't matter now."

Alex shoved his hands into his pockets. Very telling, he thought. Rianne felt she'd been deceived, and her tone had hardened when she spoke of the man who had been first her guardian, then her husband.

Obviously his own assumptions had been on track. The man had been a bastard. He'd brow-beaten Rianne, probably convinced her she was worthless and dependent on him. Who knew what other cruelties Rianne had endured at his hands.

Alex remembered the young banker in New York with the cowed, frightened wife he treated like a worthless object. Alex had abhorred the banker's attitude and felt justified in pulling his company's substantial accounts out of that particular bank even though he knew that wouldn't prevent the bully from continuing his actions.

In Rianne's situation, however, he felt a surprising stab of violence toward her husband. But the man was dead, and Alex was enjoying her company tonight, appreciating her sharp wit and occasional flash of impish humor.

The clock on the wall of the main room began to chime. Separately and silently, Alex and Rianne each counted off until the last beat was done and the clock fell silent once again.

"It's midnight!" Rianne exclaimed. "I had no idea—" she broke off, caught by a wide yawn. "Oh, dear," she said, covering her mouth with a hand. "I do believe I'm ready for bed now, too, if you don't mind."

Alex's chuckle came out of the dark, followed by his voice.

"You are exceedingly polite, aren't you?"

She stiffened. Was he going to ridicule her again? "My mother taught me to be a lady at all times," she said defensively.

"I'm sorry. I meant no insult. I've been fortunate to make the acquaintance of many women, but they don't usually ask my permission to retire. Actually, the majority of the women I know usually *invite* me to bed."

Had he really said . . . ? Yes, he had. She found her lips curling irresistibly upward, and she realized that she wasn't as affronted by his arrogant, bold manner as she had been. It was a deliberate ploy on his part. He *enjoyed* provoking others into a response—not to be cruel, but to tease. Truthfully, she was finding his little repartees rather appealing.

Even more enjoyable was trying to best him.

"Really? How horribly confusing that must be for you," she said, tongue in cheek.

Alex's hesitation told her that he was attempting to decipher her tone. Was she serious, he was wondering, or was she simply baiting him—ushering him into a verbal trap? Rianne stifled a giggle.

"Why do you say that?" he finally asked cautiously.

"However do you keep all those women straight in your mind? It must cause you no end of headaches. Do you carry a little book with all their names and other pertinent information in it? Heavens, it would have to be a very *thick* book, wouldn't it, since you travel so much? Why, you must have made the 'acquaintance' of scores of women!"

Alex was almost choking in an effort to keep his laughter contained.

"Are you all right?" Rianne asked him silkily.

"I will be, just as soon as I strangle a certain woman whose tongue flouts convention almost as well as mine."

"Why, Mr. Benedict, I do believe there's a compliment in there somewhere."

"I do believe you're right, Madame DuBois."

They shared a moment of quiet laughter before falling silent. Rianne racked her brain for something more to say. For two people who had just admired one another's witticisms, this pause was rather awkward.

She finally thought of something. "Oh! I meant to ask

what you did with the roses. I do hope you didn't toss them over the side."

"No, I had the porter take them into the ladies' coach and distribute them."

"Really? That was sweet of you."

"Sweet, eh?" Alex chuckled. "Does this mean you've changed your opinion of me?" he asked.

"Not exactly."

"Uh-uh-uh," Alex chided. "Come, come, Rianne. You've shown little timidity in voicing your conclusions. Don't disappoint me with faint-heartedness now."

"All right. I don't think I can go so far as to reverse my opinion, but I will amend it. I've decided you're a loutish bully only some of the time," she retorted.

Alex chuckled again. "You're always truthful, aren't you?"

Rianne stirred restlessly, once again filled with guilt. If he really knew the truth, he'd probably throw her off the train! From the next room, Leslie suddenly stirred, then coughed. "I think she's coming down with a cold," Rianne whispered.

"I doubt it. Les is never ill."

Rianne frowned. "She was sneezing when she went to bed."

"She probably caught a chill from the last two days of rain. It's been unusually cold for this time of year."

"Hmm." Rianne stifled another yawn. She was very tired.

Alex must have recognized her fatigue, for he straightened. "I'm sorry. I'm keeping you from your sleep." How he found her hand in the dark, she didn't know, but he did so and squeezed it gently. "Good night, Rianne. Be sure to lock the outside door after I leave."

"I will. Good night, Alex."

He slipped out the door. Rianne locked it, as directed, then went to her berth, yawning.

It wasn't until she began to untie her robe that she realized she was still wearing Alex's jacket. It smelled of cigar smoke but also held other, more intriguing scents. Something slightly tangy, like citron. A minty odor. And something sharper that she couldn't define. It was a soothing, masculine scent, and one unlike anything she'd come across before. But for all she knew, thousands of men used the same scent.

She had no way of knowing, for she'd never worn a man's jacket before. Or been as close to a man as she'd been to Alex.

Her hand stopped stroking his jacket.

Her eyes widened in sudden awareness.

It was true. She'd spent nearly half an hour standing only a foot or so away from Alex, and she'd been at ease. More, she'd conversed with him without mumbling or stuttering—and she had managed to refrain from apologizing even once. Alex had even complimented her.

Well! Maybe she would be able to conquer this awful legacy Lance had left and become a woman who wasn't afraid of shadows and was no longer woefully short of self-confidence. Perhaps even a woman who could learn to trust a man again—at least enough to be friends with him.

She'd like to be friends with Alex, if he was willing.

Certainly he was bad-tempered at times, but it didn't happen often. He didn't hurt anyone, and it didn't seem to take him long to recover from his fouler moods. That wasn't so bad.

Rianne smiled as she carefully folded Alex's jacket and set it on a chair. Still smiling, she removed her robe and climbed into her snug berth.

This time, the rhythmic rocking of the train lulled her into relaxing sleep.

★ ★ ★ ★ ★

Rianne didn't have any idea how long she'd slept when she was awakened by a sound. She lay alert, waiting for it to be repeated.

It was, and she realized it was Leslie, coughing and moaning, calling Rianne's name.

She was on her feet instantly, fumbling with the matches until she managed to light one lamp. Hurrying into the main room, she lit another. Dropping the box of matches, she rushed to Leslie and fell to her knees before her bed.

"Rianne?" Leslie's voice was weak. Her hair was tangled about her face, and when Rianne reached out to smooth it back, she became alarmed at the heat of Leslie's skin. The girl's face was also sheened with perspiration.

"Yes, it's me. You have a fever, Leslie. How do you feel otherwise?"

"Awful. Stomach hurts, head hurts." She tossed restlessly. "I'm thirsty."

"Yes, of course. I'll bring water." Rianne ran to the kitchen area, realized she didn't know where the matches were kept, and had to run back to retrieve the box she'd used earlier.

Her hands were shaking as she lit the hanging lamp. Kneeling before the table, she opened the cupboard beneath it and pulled out the half-full cans of water—one earmarked for drinking, the other for washing.

Cups—where were the cups? And towels. She wanted to wet a towel.

She managed to gather what she needed and carry it back to the bed. Slipping her arm under Leslie's head, she lifted it enough to put the cup to her mouth. Leslie gulped the water greedily before Rianne let her sink back onto the pillows. Rianne folded the towel. "I've brought a damp cloth for your head. It may feel cold at first," she warned Leslie before placing the towel over her forehead. Leslie shivered violently and tossed her head. "Les, you have a fever. You should keep this in place in order to bring it down."

Leslie nodded almost imperceptibly but moaned softly when Rianne replaced the cloth.

"Do you need the chamber pot?" Rianne asked anxiously.

"No, but now I'm cold." Leslie was indeed shivering, even though her face was still damp with sweat.

Rianne scooted to the drawer beneath the other sofa and began pulling quilts and blankets from it. She piled two onto Leslie and tucked them around her. "Better?"

"Mmm." Leslie's eyelids drooped.

Placing the back of her hand against Leslie's cheek, she found it still warm but not as much as it had been before. Still, she was worried. Though Leslie's malady was similar to a form of ague that had once struck the Chatham Academy—debilitating, but not deadly—she had no way of being certain.

Perhaps there was a doctor on the train.

"Les, how do I summon the porter?" She received no reply. "Leslie?" Still none. The girl was once again asleep.

Rianne rose to her feet, biting her lip in indecision. She was going to have to search for the porter herself—if she could even find one awake at this hour. Alex had said something about the porters' lounge, but where was it? This was strictly a passenger train, she knew, and it wasn't very long, but she couldn't remember how many cars it had in all. She did recall that the Rolling Palace was at the rear of the train, with only the caboose behind it.

Might she have to traverse the entire train to find a porter? She shuddered at the thought. She'd seen some rough-looking men board the train. What if she had to enter their cars? Wait! Alex had told them he was in the F car. Compartment twelve. Perhaps she'd reach his car first, and then he could fetch a porter. Actually, she should have thought of seeking him out right away. It was his sister who was ill, and he'd be upset if Rianne *didn't* tell him.

Making up her mind, Rianne quickly pulled the skirt and shirtwaist she'd worn earlier on over her nightgown, then slipped her boots on without bothering with stockings. Her coat was in the armoire, so she grabbed Alex's jacket and donned it as she checked on Leslie—the girl was still asleep—and then quickly left the Rolling Palace.

Chapter 12

On the platform, Rianne was brought to a sudden halt.

She'd forgotten about the gap between the Rolling Palace and the car in front of it.

Clenching the rail tightly, she cautiously leaned over to look down. The glimmer of metal and the clickety-clack of the wheels reminded her that they were traveling fast. Faster, as she'd told Alex, than she'd ever gone before. Too, the platform on the other car was much narrower than the one on which she stood, leaving her precious little room for maneuvering.

Jumping the gap had seemed easy when Alex did it, but he was a man, with more strength. Besides, she'd never leapt from a moving conveyance of any kind before.

Despite the chill of the night, Rianne began perspiring as fear knotted her stomach. Oh, God, she didn't think she could do this! If she should fall . . .

Closing her eyes, she let go of the rail and staggered backwards until she slammed up against the Palace door, her palms spread at her sides.

Rianne took deep breaths, until her racing heart slowed.

She had two choices. She could either gather her courage and take that leap, or she could be a coward, retreat back into the Palace and wait for Alex or someone else to come to their aid in the morning. But if Leslie worsened in the interim . . .

Rianne was disgusted with herself. Leslie was counting on

her, and here she was, dithering like a helpless old lady.

Stiffening her spine, she gathered her skirts and focused on the door of the opposite car. Though she desperately wanted to close her eyes, she didn't, for fear she'd miss the other rail. She said a quick prayer, then counted off. One . . .

Two . . . *Three*—and then she was in the air.

Mercifully, both hands closed over the cold iron railing, and for an instant her toes touched the reassuring solidness of the floor. But her own momentum carried the rest of her body forward, and her feet went out from under her. She yelped in pain as one shoulder slammed into the side of the car, bouncing her off to spin toward the railing and crash into it face first before finally landing on her knees. She huddled there, holding her breath and praying that she was through flying about like an inept acrobat.

Rianne slowly opened her eyes and got her bearings. She'd made it! "Yes!" she shouted victoriously.

She had not done so without suffering a few bumps and bruises, she discovered as she pulled herself to her feet. She sucked on her numb fingers and lifted her skirt to find that her knees were badly scraped and oozing blood. Her already swelling cheek hurt like blazes, as did her shoulder.

Still, the pain didn't lessen her elation. What *did* was the thought that she was on a mission.

Everyone was asleep in the first car. A family of four huddled together at one end, two elderly ladies snored on benches, and a young mother slumbered with a baby bundled on her lap. Rianne smiled when she saw that two women were holding Alex's roses.

She tiptoed past them to the other end of the car and opened the door to slip outside. It was with relief that she saw she wouldn't have to leap between these cars, for they were connected by a short walkway.

Crossing, she cautiously entered the next car and was dismayed to discover that it contained only sleeping men of all sizes and ages, draped over seats and benches in varying positions, some with their snoring mouths open. Rianne wrinkled her nose. The car smelled foul, and it resounded with rumblings, and other indecipherable sounds. Did all men have such disgusting nighttime habits? she wondered.

Averting her eyes as she passed, she hoped desperately that none of the men would awaken. If they did, she would be mortified! *And Lord,* she prayed, *if I have to walk through more cars, please don't let them be filled with men.*

At first she only heard gruff voices and laughter as she entered the next car. It was impossible to see anyone clearly, for the coach was filled with thick, acrid smoke. It began to seep through the door she'd just opened, and Rianne had a sick feeling that her prayer hadn't been heard.

As the air cleared, she saw two upholstered chairs occupied by sleeping men. Another man was draped over a table, his head on his arms. And at the far end . . .

Rianne hesitated. Her feet seemed glued to the floor. Only men occupied the car, and several of them were awake. Seated in chairs about a round table, they seemed to be frozen in place. Two had cigars halfway to their mouths, one had his head tilted back and a glass at his lips, another held a deck of cards in one hand and, in the other, a single card in mid-air. The last two had their backs to her, but as they became aware that something unusual was happening, they twisted about to see what had caught their companions' attention.

Rianne stared at the men. They stared back at her.

Finally the one who had been about to take a drink set his glass down and appraised her boldly. "Well, well," he said, with an unpleasant smile. "What have we here, gentlemen? A little diversion, eh?"

Sitting to his right, a gargoyle-faced man with a thick neck tossed his cards onto the table. "Mebbe the pretty lady's lookin' for company, Black."

Though Alex's jacket was buttoned, Rianne hugged it to herself. She didn't like the avaricious manner in which the two of them looked at her.

More movement ensued as the other men stirred. One elderly gentleman pushed back his chair. The man who'd first spoken snickered and said, "Damn, Greenwood, you ain't gonna send the little lady away, are you? Hell, if she joins us, we could have us a party. Or if she don't want to look at all your ugly mugs, maybe she and I—Oomph!"

He was cut off as the man on his other side elbowed him in the ribs. "Shut your mouth, Black. Can't you see she's a *lady?*"

Some of the others growled words to Black, also, and he fell silent, though his avaricious gaze remained pinned on Rianne.

She looked up as the elderly gentleman approached her. "I do believe you've lost your way, miss," he said in a deep drawl. "This is the gentlemen's club car."

Rianne greeted him with relief. "Thank you, sir. I see that now, but I'm afraid I must still walk through it."

The man frowned. "Young lady, you should be in your own coach and not out at this time of night—especially alone."

"But, sir, you don't understand. I'm traveling with another lady, and she's taken ill. I must fetch her brother, but he's in the F car. How else am I to reach it?"

His frown deepened. "The F car is a men's sleeping coach. You cannot enter it alone. Perhaps you should return to your own car and allow me to fetch him for you."

Rianne hesitated. He looked like a trustworthy gentleman, but how could she know for certain? He had been playing cards with these other unsavory-looking men. What if she left and he became distracted and forgot to fetch Alex? The thought of jumping that platform and entering this coach full of men again filled her with dismay. She shook her head. "I have taken responsibility for the gentleman's sister. This is something I must do."

"I see. It's a matter of honor, then?"

"Yes, exactly!"

"Then there's nothing for it but for me to accompany you." He bowed gallantly. "Percival Greenwood, at your service."

"Oh, thank you, Mr. Greenwood!" Rianne said fervently. She stepped forward, but he took her arm to stay her.

"Forgive me. Manners dictate that you should precede me, but in this case, I think it better if you follow me. Stay close."

Rianne nodded. Mr. Greenwood smiled reassuringly, then turned to lead the way. She held her head high and once again averted her eyes as they neared the table. She was startled into looking that way, however, when one man murmured, "Good evening, miss," in a respectful tone. Most of the others followed his lead.

"Good evening, gentlemen," she replied, deliberately avoiding glancing in the direction of the two who'd addressed her so crudely.

Mr. Greenwood led her into the next car. Rianne saw that it was a sleeper, for a narrow aisle divided two rows of curtained berths, one row stacked above the other. They weren't very wide, and she wondered how anyone actually managed to sleep on them without rolling off onto the floor. The only light came from a small lamp burning over the opposite door.

Beneath it, she saw the letter *G*. Thank goodness! That meant Alex's car should be the next one.

It was, indeed. This car seemed more modern, for it had compartments instead of berths. Actual rooms, with doors.

"Which is his?" Mr. Greenwood asked in a low tone.

"I believe it's number twelve," Rianne whispered back.

The numbers were painted above the doors. Mr. Greenwood led her to the one marked 12 and stepped aside.

Rianne knocked cautiously. "Alex?" she called softly. She received no reply, so she tried again, louder this time. "Alex, it's Rianne. Please open the door."

She heard a stirring inside the compartment, then a crash, followed by a loud curse, followed by a scraping sound as someone fumbled with the lock.

"Whoever you are," Alex growled as the door swung open, "you'd better have a damn good reason for knocking at this time of—" He broke off as he saw Rianne standing at his door. Rianne fell speechless, too, for Alex was wearing nothing more than his pants. The light from the lamp above the door revealed broad shoulders and a beautifully sculpted chest. A matting of dark hair ran straight down its middle and disappeared into his trousers.

Alex rubbed his eyes. "Rianne? What the hell are you doing here?"

Her gaze flew to his face. His jaw was faintly shadowed, his eyes had a somnolent look to them, and his hair was rumpled. He looked boyishly vulnerable. Rianne's heart lurched. That warm, fuzzy feeling filled her stomach again.

"Rianne!"

She jerked at Alex's bark. He was staring down at her.

"What are you doing here? Do you know what time it is?" he growled at her. "Have you lost your mind? Do you have any idea what kind of men you could run into on this train?"

Alex was alarmed at the risks she'd taken.

"Yes. That is . . ." She tossed Mr. Greenwood a helpless glance.

He stepped forward into Alex's view. "The young lady isn't alone, sir. I took the liberty of escorting her here."

Alex rubbed his head, disarranging his hair even more. "Why? What's going on, Rianne?"

"This is Mr. Percival Greenwood, Alex. I'm here because of Leslie. She's ill."

Alex's eyes filled with alarm. "What is it? How bad is she?" he asked as he snatched his shirt and jammed his arms into it. He glanced up. "Did you come from the Rolling Palace to the club car on your own?" he asked as he quickly buttoned the shirt.

"Of course. I had no choice."

"You came across on your own? From car to car?" She nodded. "Bloody hell! You could have fallen. You could have—"

"I didn't, and that's all that matters," she told him quietly.

Alex's reply was to nod, but the look he gave Rianne caused her heart to lurch a little. It was almost worth the terror of leaping from car to car on a moving train to see that glitter of admiration in his eyes!

When Rianne realized that he was unbuttoning his trousers to secure his shirt, she whipped around and turned her back to him. Her cheeks pink, she hastened to reassure him. "I don't think Leslie's in any real danger, Alex. In fact, I believe she has only a form of ague, but I was worried that it might worsen, and I had no idea if there was a doctor on board, so I decided to fetch you."

"You were right to come," Alex said as he finished buttoning his shirt and sat down to pull on his socks and shoes. He glanced up at Rianne's companion. "I thank you, Mr.

Greenwood, for your aid in bringing Madame DuBois to me."

"It was my pleasure, sir."

Alex grabbed his coat and extinguished the lamp. "Let's go," he said as he closed his door.

The three of them moved quickly, until they stood outside the club car.

"This is where I leave you," Mr. Greenwood announced as he offered his hand to Alex. "Glad I could be of service," he said before turning to Rianne. "Madame, I bid you good night."

Rianne smiled at him. "Good night, and thank you, sir. You've been most kind."

Mr. Greenwood disappeared into the men's sleeping car while Alex turned to Rianne. "Stay close to me," he ordered. "The men using the club car often stay up the entire night, and not all of them are trustworthy."

Rianne didn't have a chance to inform him that she'd figured that out for herself, for he was already leading her inside.

Alex stopped inside the door, for instead of the raucous talk and laughter he'd expected, only two men occupied the car, both sitting silently at a table, looking oddly expectant. One was shifty-eyed, with the smooth-looking hands and clothing that identified him as a professional gambler. The other was dressed in rougher clothes, and he was ugly and big as a bull.

Rianne tugged on Alex's sleeve. "There were a dozen men in here earlier. What happened to them?" she whispered.

Alex didn't reply, but he was wondering the same thing. The two men said nothing, but Alex was alert, his muscles tense. He nodded at the pair. In return, they scanned his tailored suit in derision and dismissed him.

Alex's eyes narrowed. He wasn't fond of compromise, so he dressed what he was—a businessman and a gentleman. Under the dapper clothing, however, was a toughened body. On occasion he ran into an idiot who mistakenly thought his choice of wardrobe meant he was a weakling. Most of the time a deadly look was enough to warn off a troublemaker, but sometimes it wasn't.

He hoped this wasn't going to be one of those latter times, but he doubted it. The lascivious way these two fellows were eyeing Rianne promised trouble. It didn't bode well that the car had emptied of its other occupants, either, for from Rianne's question, it seemed several others, including Mr. Greenwood, had smoothed her passage past these two the first time.

He had only himself to see to her safety, and it seemed prudent to get her out now. He hoped he wasn't going to regret leaving his pistol packed in his trunk in the Rolling Palace.

He took Rianne's arm protectively. "Move ahead of me," he told her curtly, still watching the two out of the corner of his eye. He led her past their table. They'd reached the middle of the coach when, from behind them, a chair scraped and a voice called out.

"Hey, little lady! You ain't planning on lettin' Mr. Fancypants crawl into your bed now, are you? 'Cuz I gotta tell you, he don't got the right equipment, does he, Gumm?"

Rianne's face flamed, but she continued moving, reassured by Alex's hand on her arm and his growled order to "Keep walking."

The other man chortled. "You got it right, Black." Then he addressed Rianne. "If Fancypants falls short, pretty gel. You come on back, and we'll show you the kind of equipment a *real* man has."

Alex halted. When Rianne looked at him questioningly, he lowered his head to speak in a low, grim tone. "I want you at that door in two seconds, Rianne. Then I want you out of here. Can you get across to the Palace on your own?" At her nod, he ordered, "Then do so and lock yourself in." The coach was padlocked from the outside when in storage, and not much thought had been given to an inside lock. Alex knew it was flimsy and wouldn't keep a determined man out, much less two of this ilk. But then, he didn't intend for these two to be in any shape to try. They'd insulted a woman under his protection.

Besides, no man called him fancypants without paying a heavy price! Rianne didn't immediately obey. The tension in the car was palpable. She realized that Alex was in danger and wanted to plead with him to come with her, but one look at his face and she knew he wouldn't. She shivered. His eyes were green ice, his mouth a narrow slash. Though he was still facing her, he wasn't seeing her. His attention was focused on the two men behind them.

"Hey! Whatcha doin' over there?" one bellowed.

"Betcha the little lady is telling fancypants that she don't want his company no more, Gumm. Maybe she wants a real man." This brought loud guffaws from Gumm.

Alex cursed under his breath. "Get going *now!*" he urged Rianne, and he shoved her to send her toward the exit.

She scurried to reach the door and safety. But once there, she was compelled to turn back. Surely Alex didn't mean to confront these brutes? One man against two—one of whom was four inches taller and must be a hundred pounds heavier than Alex? Oh, God! It would be suicide.

She stood aghast, helpless, hands pressed over her mouth, as she watched Alex approach the two men. The skinnier one was standing near the front of the table, one foot casually propped on a chair and a forearm resting on his thigh. Gumm, the big one, still sat behind the table, heckling Alex.

"Come on, fancypants!" he taunted. He was flexing thick fingers, beckoning Alex forward. "I can take you from here. Don't even have to get up."

"Damn, Gumm, you ain't thinkin' of mussin' that pretty face now, are you?" Black smirked. "Hell, just knock him out for a while. 'Til mornin', maybe. That'll give us time to party with the pretty lady."

Rianne's stomach recoiled at the insinuation and with fear for Alex. She watched him walk toward the two cocky, grinning men as if he were on a Sunday stroll.

Alex was considering his options. Chances were good that the gambler, Black, had a derringer tucked into an inside pocket, so he had to go down first. That wouldn't be too difficult. The man was soft.

His companion, however, presented a different problem. Now if he were Gumm, he'd be on his feet, trying to intimidate with his size, but Gumm was still sitting, his lower torso concealed by the table. It was a pretty good bet that Gumm was concealing a gun there, too, which meant Alex had to incapacitate him *before* he got his hands on him.

His plan clear in his head, Alex stopped a foot short of the table. "I reckon you boys didn't have mamas to teach you manners and respect for a lady," he drawled softly. "Know how I can tell?"

The question clearly baffled the two men and took them off guard. "How?" Gumm replied before he could stop himself.

"Stands to reason. Even a fool can see that both of you are nothing more than low-down, dirty sons-of-bitches." Alex waited only an instant to let that soak in before he grasped the edge of the table and heaved. It crashed right onto Gumm's lap, knocking over both him and the chair.

Ignoring his high, piercing scream—so at odds with his size—Alex reached for Black, who hadn't yet had time to react. Grabbing the man by his collar and jerking him forward, Alex smashed his right fist into the man's jaw, then released him.

Black collapsed limply.

Alex turned toward Gumm, but the giant was faster than Alex had expected. He was already up on his knees. With a howl of fury, he heaved off the table and shoved it toward Alex, causing Alex to lose precious seconds as he was forced to sidestep.

A furious bellow warned him. He whipped around just in time to see Gumm lower his head and charge, but he had no chance to brace himself. Gumm's head and shoulders slammed into his stomach. Air escaped his lungs in a swoosh, and he staggered backward into another table, scattering bottles and glasses onto the floor.

Alex got his feet tangled in a chair. Cursing, he kicked at it until it went flying into a wall. He looked up to see Gumm charging him again, tossing chairs out of his way as if they were twigs.

Acting reflexively, Alex managed to shove his fist into Gumm's belly. Gumm didn't grunt nor falter, and Alex's feet left the floor. He found himself looking at the top of Gumm's head, at pink scalp showing through his greasy, thinning hair.

Gumm's massive arms were wrapped around Alex's upper torso, squeezing . . . squeezing . . .

Alex's lungs began to burn and black spots floated before his eyes. Gumm was going to either suffocate him or crush his ribs.

Or maybe both.

Alex had belonged to a boxing club at his university many

years previously, but he'd never had a three-hundred-pound giant for an opponent before. This was no time for niceties. Fisting his hands together, he pounded on Gumm's head. When Gumm made the mistake of glancing up, Alex swung his joined fists into his nose and felt the satisfying crunch of bones.

Gumm yelped and immediately dropped Alex to clasp his smashed nose. He stared at the blood on his hand, as if surprised to discover that he was bleeding.

Alex didn't wait for Gumm to recover. He took several breaths and swung again, aiming for Gumm's already injured face. He got in several good punches, but so did Gumm, and his were more powerful.

Alex didn't have Gumm's size or strength, but he had quickness and agility and brains—the latter something in which he was sure Gumm was deficient. Gumm's weight was also a liability. It took a massive amount of energy to move that huge body. It was a matter of outlasting Gumm and timing his punches. He was in control of himself, but Gumm was losing his.

"Getting tired, Gumm?" he taunted. "That big belly of yours is slowing you down, isn't it?" Alex circled Gumm, laughing as he dodged punches.

Paralyzed at the door, Rianne had watched in horror as Gumm staggered, dangling Alex in the air. Alex was a big man, but he'd looked like a child in Gumm's mammoth arms.

She gasped as Alex freed himself, then she held her breath again as, instead of retreating, he did a silly little dance around the giant and—Oh, no! Alex was actually laughing! The foolish man! Couldn't he see that it made Gumm more furious? Gumm's expression was murderous!

She had to do something. If she didn't, Gumm would surely kill Alex! She scanned the room desperately, searching for a weapon—something, anything she could use against Gumm. Her gaze settled on a leg that had snapped off one of the chairs.

She grabbed it, finding it satisfyingly heavy, and wound her way through more overturned chairs and littered shards of glass toward the battling men. Just as she came to where Black lay on the floor, he groaned and tried to sit up.

"Excuse me," Rianne said politely. Then she calmly brought the heavy chair leg down onto his head. He dropped without a whimper.

When she looked up again, Alex and Gumm were still circling one another, exchanging occasional punches. Both of them were breathing heavily and sweating. Gumm's nose was still bleeding, and Alex had a small cut on his brow dribbling blood into his eye. He dragged a sleeve over it, but it kept flowing, and Rianne knew that it could blind him at just the wrong moment. Alex might not survive if Gumm got his hands on him again. Edging toward them, Rianne managed to get behind Gumm.

Lord, he was too tall for her to reach his head. Glancing about desperately, she spied an overturned chair, dragged it closer to the men, and set it upright several feet behind Gumm. Scrambling onto it, she spread her feet for balance and prepared for battle. "Over here, Alex!" she screamed, jumping up and down, rocking the chair precariously. "Move him over this way!"

Both men froze and turned to her, astonishment written on their faces.

"Bloody hell, Rianne!" Alex bellowed. "I told you to get out of here!"

"I know, but—Alex, look out! Oh, no!" Rianne covered her eyes with her empty hand.

Gumm wasn't smart, but he was clever enough to take advantage of Alex's distraction and land a right to his jaw. Alex almost went down but recovered barely in time to avoid a left. Rianne peeped through her fingers. Neither man was paying any attention to her as they resumed their odd dance. She rested one hand on her hip. "Well, really!" she complained. "Anyone else would appreciate my help!"

Whether Alex was forcing it or not, the men *were* moving closer to her, she noted. She held the chair leg in readiness. When Gumm slipped and staggered backward, toward her, she closed her eyes and swung.

Triumphant, she heard Gumm bellow, but when she opened her eyes she saw that the brute hadn't gone down as she'd hoped.

"What'd you do that for, lady?" he yelled, and there was definitely murder in his eyes as he reached for her.

Alex gave her a hard shove to move her out of Gumm's reach and punched Gumm's broken nose once again.

Rianne fell backward, her legs flew into the air, and she landed on a table, skittering across it on her bottom before falling off the other end. Her back smacked into a wall, and she slid down it to the floor.

Dazed, she sat there, wondering why the back of her head hurt. Her gingerly probing fingers found a lump already forming on her skull. It was wet, and when she looked at her fingertips, she found a trace of blood. She must have struck the wall with her head when Alex had pushed her off the . . .

Alex had done it, not Gumm! Oh, this was too much! Here she was, trying to save his life, and he'd pushed her off a chair! It was not to be tolerated! She'd had enough. It was time for Alex and Gumm to call it quits. They'd both drawn blood, were both exhausted—and what was the purpose in continuing, anyway? Alex had certainly avenged her honor by now.

She was still hearing the sounds of panting and cursing

and shuffling feet. How could she make them stop?

Then Rianne spied the gun. It was lying just beyond her toes, beneath the table. Scrambling to her knees, she crawled to it and tried to lift it. She hadn't expected it to be so heavy; the long barrel clanked against the floor as she wrapped her fingers around the grip. She was going to need both hands.

She knew nothing *about* guns. She'd never even held one before. But how difficult could it be?

She was dismayed to discover that the gun's weight pulled her arms down as she rose to her feet. Just as she'd expected, Alex and Gumm were still trying to beat each other to death.

Rianne walked around to the other side of the table on unsteady legs. Positioning herself so that they could clearly see her, she raised her arms in front of her. "Stop!" she yelled. "Stop, or I'll shoot!"

Both men ignored her.

Rianne lifted the gun higher, closed her eyes, and squeezed the trigger.

The blast was deafening. Worse, it reverberated around the closed club car. When it finally stopped, silence reigned.

Opening her eyes, Rianne saw Alex and Gumm standing almost shoulder to shoulder, staring up at a large hole in the ceiling as dust and slivers of wood rained down upon them.

The revolver visibly trembling in her hands, Rianne nodded in satisfaction. "Th-there!" she stuttered. "That's mu-much better!"

Two pairs of eyes locked on her. Finally "Your woman's crazy. You oughta chain her up somewhere. She coulda killed us both!" Gumm informed Alex sourly.

Alex didn't reply. He cautiously approached Rianne, his hand extended. "Rianne, give me the revolver." She jerked it toward him. Both he and Gumm immediately ducked in reflex.

Still bent over, Alex carefully turned his head to look at her as if she were indeed insane. "God almighty, woman!" he snapped as he slowly straightened again. "Not that way! Take your finger off the trigger, *then* hand it to me."

"Oh." She did as he directed. Alex gingerly took the revolver from her by the barrel.

Gumm came to stand beside him. "Are you still here?" Alex asked, turning to him.

"Hell, yes. Look here, mister, what say to calling it a draw? It's getting too damned dangerous in here, what with a crazy woman smashing people's heads in and shooting off guns."

Rianne sniffed in affront. "I'll have you know I'm as sane as anyone—present company excluded!" she protested.

"Be quiet, Rianne," Alex ordered, not even glancing her way. "We don't call this quits unless you apologize to the lady, Gumm."

The man was disbelieving. "Apologize to *her?* Hell, she ought to be apologizing to *me!*"

"You damned well better do it!" Alex flipped the revolver around and pointed it at Gumm's groin.

Gumm blanched. "Ah, hell!" he said, lowering his head to stare at his boots. "I'm sorry, lady. We didn't mean no harm. Black and I ain't seen another lady as pretty as you on this train. Sorry, ma'am," he mumbled.

"Look at the lady when you say that," Alex snarled, jerking Gumm's head up.

"It's all right, Alex," Rianne cut in. Relieved that she wasn't going to have to drag his body out of here after all, she beamed at Gumm. "I'm quite willing to accept your apology, Mr. Gumm, but let this be a lesson—"

"Enough, Rianne!" Alex snapped.

She turned to him in surprise. "Really, Alex, you could at least let me finish. I was about to—" She broke off, blanching as she saw his face clearly for the first time.

It was grimy with dust, and blood was still running down it, dripping onto his white shirt. She glanced at Gumm and found that he looked even worse. His ugly face was covered with blood.

Her hand went to her temple. "Oh!" she mouthed.

And then she quietly collapsed onto the floor.

Both men stared at the little heap.

"Gumm . . ."

"Yeah?"

"*Now* we'll call it quits," Alex said, and he slammed the side of the revolver against Gumm's head. The giant fell onto his back with a huge thud. Sparing him not a glance, Alex shoved the revolver into his pants and, with a sigh of resignation, bent over Rianne.

Chapter 13

Alex carried Rianne draped over his shoulder, muttering all the way.

Gumm was right. She was a damned menace—and a nuisance. She didn't have the sense God gave sheep, and everyone knew they were the dumbest creatures on earth.

Bloody hell! Why hadn't she stayed put and summoned a porter to wake him instead of running through the train on her own, not to mention leaping from platform to platform as he was doing now? One slip, one false move—He shuddered at the thought of Rianne's falling beneath the train.

As if that weren't bad enough, she'd carelessly entered a club car full of men and whetted their carnal appetites with that wavy, burnished hair and eyes the color of warmed sherry.

Ah, hell! Why'd he have to remember that now? He'd meant to wait until he'd seen to her injuries before reflecting on Rianne's sudden transformation.

Yes, he'd noticed there was something different about her when she'd come to his compartment, but he'd been rushed, too worried about Leslie, to analyze the transformation. It wasn't until Rianne had climbed up on the chair in the club car and screamed at them that he'd realized she wasn't wearing spectacles. He hadn't had time to give *that* much thought, either, while Gumm was trying to beat his brains out.

It was only when she'd shot the revolver and he'd turned to look at her again that he'd finally comprehended.

She'd stood there, arms trembling with the weight of the smoking revolver, eyes filled with a combination of fear and fierce determination, her wild and tangled hair framing her face. A face that had glowed with excitement.

Prim, spinsterish "Anne" was gone. That shy, timid woman who'd been unable to meet his eyes when they were first introduced, the one who became silent and cold when he'd taunted her and wary when he'd teased her, had been transformed into a woman of fire and passion. A young goddess, by God.

He hadn't been able to stop looking at her—until Gumm had grunted lustily beside him.

The thought of how she'd put herself in danger almost made him want to strangle *her!*

When he'd told her to leave the club car, had she obeyed? No. She hadn't even had the sense to tuck herself safely away in a corner, for God's sake! Instead, she'd thrust herself into the fracas.

She'd tried to bash in Gumm's head, then damn near killed *him*—Gumm didn't count—by firing a powerful Remington .44 with her eyes *closed,* for God's sake! The culminating offense had been her gall to *smile* at Gumm when he apologized, as if he were a little boy offering her a handful of dandelions.

By God, Alex thought as he shifted Rianne in preparation for jumping to the Rolling Palace, she had some explaining to do!

Inside, he deposited her onto the sitting room sofa, then checked the pulse in her neck. Her color was good; she was breathing normally.

The woman who swore she never fainted, had.

Alex was relieved. She'd be all right for a time; he had a few other matters to attend to before he could see to her.

The only light came from one lamp and the one in the observation room, leaving most of the sitting room dark, but Alex didn't take the time to light another sconce. Instead, he fell to his knees in front of Leslie's bed and removed the cloth from her forehead to smooth back her hair. She felt warm but not feverish. Her eyelids fluttered at his touch.

"I'm awake, Rianne," she murmured.

"Hey, Les. How are you doing, darlin'?"

Her eyelids fluttered. "Alex?"

"Yes, it's me. How are you feeling, baby?"

A small smile played about her mouth. "You haven't called me that in years." She sighed. "I don't feel as awful as I did awhile ago, but I'm thirsty, and my feet are cold."

Alex frowned. A number of quilts and blankets already covered her. Slipping his hand beneath them, he found that both the sheets and Leslie's nightgown were damp from perspiration. "Darlin', it's necessary to get you out of this bed and into a dry one. Same with your nightgown." He thought for a moment. This berth was the only one made up in here, which meant that Rianne must have been sleeping in the observation room.

Alex pulled the covers off Leslie and slipped his arms under her. "I'm going to put you in Rianne's bed for now."

"Where is she?"

"She's asleep on the sofa," he said after a quick glance told him that Rianne *was* either asleep or still unconscious. "Can you sit up?" he asked Les as he carried her into the other room and placed her in a chair.

"Yes, but don't ask me to walk just yet."

"I won't. In fact, I want you to stay put," he ordered as he peeled the quilt off Rianne's bed. Going back to his sister, he set about wrapping it tightly about her.

"Good Lord!" she gasped. "Alex, what's happened to your face?"

"Had a little difference of opinion with someone I met," he replied, grinning.

"But who? Why?" she asked, scanning him carefully. "And what are you doing with that revolver tucked into your pants?"

"Darlin', I have no time to answer questions right now. Too many things to do. You said you were thirsty. How does hot tea sound?"

"Lovely. The kettle's beneath the table, and a tin of assorted teas is in the cupboard above it. Use the water in the yellow can," she reminded him.

Alex grabbed the tieback from the curtains separating this and the sitting room and took it with him into the kitchen. After he'd lit the lamp there, he tied one end of the cord around the handle of the door. He looked around for something to attach the other end to, then recalled that the door opened to the inside.

Finding the metal utensils hanging above the stove, he grabbed two spoons, pulled the cord through the holes in the handles, then tied the end of the cord to the hanging lamp above him. The spoons jangled noisily when he swatted them. Good enough. At least he'd have warning if someone tried to break in.

That done, he set the revolver aside and filled a teakettle and a pot with water and set those on the stove. Then he went into the sitting room, lit the lamp hanging from the ceiling, and headed for the women's trunks.

Opening the nearest one, he carelessly tossed clothing aside as he rummaged through it, looking for a fresh nightgown. It didn't matter to him if the trunk belonged to Leslie or Rianne; he just wanted his sister in something dry.

A quick glance at Rianne—she'd turned onto her side, a reassuring sign—and he returned to Leslie. She hadn't stirred, except that her eyes were closed and her head was drooping to one side.

Alex gently shook her shoulder. "Les? Les, wake up."

She opened her eyes and looked at him. "I'm cold all over again," she complained, shivering.

"We'll have you dry and warm in no time," Alex assured her as he went to the closet for towels and a bed sheet, then brought them to her. "You're going to have to help me, Les," he told her. "Do you think you can pull this sheet up under your nightgown, wrap it about you and dry yourself with a towel before you slip into the fresh gown?"

Leslie waved him away. "Some things one simply *has* to do for oneself," she said pertly, though her teeth were chattering. "I'll manage. Just bring that tea, will you?"

Back in the kitchen, Alex saw that the water was steaming.

Leslie was going to have to wait a bit, though. Now that he knew she wasn't mortally ill, he had to see to Rianne.

As if on cue, a groan came from the still figure on the sofa. Alex filled a small basin with warm water, grabbed a cloth, and pulled a chair to the sofa. He set the basin on the floor and dampened the cloth. It was only when he began to gently wash away the grime and a few drops of blood from her face that he saw the swelling on her cheek. Anger surged through him. If he found out that Gumm or Black had touched her in any way, he'd go back to that car and empty the Remington into them both!

Now that her face was cleansed and she wasn't wearing those awful spectacles, which he now suspected were unnecessary, he saw that the bushy eyebrows he'd become used to seeing had been replaced by delicately arched ones. Her face was heart-shaped with a flawless, creamy complexion—except for a smattering of intriguing freckles over a perky nose.

Damn, she didn't look a day older than his sister!

She reached out to clutch his wrist and hold it tightly against her breast. "Mimsie, thank God you're here. Is . . . is he gone?" Her voice was a hoarse whisper, full of fear, and tears ran from the corners of her closed eyes.

Alex didn't know who Mimsie was or whether Rianne was speaking of Gumm, but he could feel her heart beating frantically against his palm. "Yes, he's gone, darlin'," he reassured her quietly.

She opened her eyes. "He'll be back! He'll come after me!" she cried as she twisted her head from side to side, searching the room as if afraid the monster would suddenly appear and devour her.

Alex knew that she wasn't seeing *him,* even though he was so close her breath brushed his face. "It's all right, darlin'," he said soothingly. "I'll see that no one comes after you."

"Promise?"

"I promise. You'll always be safe with me. Now lie down and sleep. That's it," he murmured as she put her head down and closed her eyes. "That's it." Alex brushed back the hair from her forehead. When he saw that she was once again asleep, he rose and pulled more blankets from the berth above.

About to put them over her, Alex realized that she was wearing the coat he'd given her several hours earlier. He lifted her again and held her upright against his arm and eased off the jacket. Once that was done, he removed her boots, then placed a pillow under her head and tucked the blankets around her.

The clock began to chime as he took Leslie's tea in to her. She'd managed to climb into Rianne's bed and was propped against the pillows, waiting. “Heavens, is it really four in the morning?”

“It is,” he affirmed as he handed a steaming mug to her and perched on the side of the bed with the glass of brandy he’d brought for himself.

Leslie took a sip from her mug, then sniffed the contents.

“Did you put something in here?” she asked.

“A small dollop of brandy. I figured it would settle your stomach and help you sleep.”

“I see you’re indulging in more than a dollop.”

“It’s been a hell of a night,” he sighed as he took a generous sip of brandy.

“So it seems, by the way you look. Are you going to tell me about it?”

“Tomorrow,” Alex promised. “Or rather, later today.” He rubbed the back of his neck. “Thank God we’ll be in Atlanta by dinnertime. I made hotel reservations for only one night, but I think we’ll stay longer. You’re ill and Rianne’s exhausted. We could all use a few days to rest and recuperate.”

“I won’t object. Did I hear you speaking to Rianne earlier?”

Alex swallowed the last of his brandy. “No,” he lied. “She’s still asleep.”

“She’s not ill, too, is she?” Leslie asked, concerned.

“I don’t think so. She’s just exhausted.” And well she might be, Alex thought, and he smiled to himself. She’d had quite an evening.

“Has she been up all this time taking care of me?” Leslie asked. “She must have. I vaguely recall her speaking to me. Poor dear. I suppose that why she’s worn out.”

“I suppose,” Alex muttered, not bothering to correct Leslie’s assumptions.

She finished her tea and sighed with satisfaction. “I feel

better now, all warm and cozy. Thanks, Alex." She yawned widely as she handed the mug back to him. "I'm exhausted myself. I think I'm ready for sleep again," she said as she snuggled down into the pillows.

Alex made sure she was tucked in, then turned off the lamp.

"Night, Les." His sister made no reply. She was already asleep. Rianne was sound asleep, also, he saw as he stood staring down at her. She'd curled up into a small ball and had one palm tucked under her cheek. She looked like a fragile little girl. He reached over to tuck a wisp of hair behind her ear and then he grinned as he remembered how she'd looked holding the smoking Remington. She might be vulnerable, but she wasn't fragile.

She was, in fact, turning out to be a remarkable woman!

Alex jerked his hand away from her. *Don't even think about it,* said that little inner voice.

He turned off the ceiling lamp and the wall sconce, leaving only the small kitchen one lit, and went to tend his own injuries. He soaked his hands in warm water to wash off the encrusted blood from his raw knuckles, then flexed them as he dried them to verify that he had no broken bones. Rinsing out the cloth he'd used on Rianne, he glanced into the mirror.

He looked like hell. The cut above his eye had stopped bleeding, but it was also encrusted. He didn't scrub it, knowing that would open it again, and used the cloth to rub away only the dried droplets and smears on the rest of his face.

When he was finished, he discovered that his left eye was swelling shut, the skin around it already turning blue-black, as were two areas on his jaw.

Leaving the lamp lit, he took the revolver with him as he went back into the sitting room. Dumping Leslie's damp bedding in a corner, he got a pillow and quilt for himself, removed his boots, and lay down on the quilt, covering his torso with his jacket. His nose wrinkled, and he sniffed, realizing that the coat contained a strange mixture of familiar scents and something more feminine. Flowery. It wasn't unpleasant, so he pulled the jacket up to his chin and settled down.

It had, as he'd told Les, been one hell of a night.

Damned confusing. Surprising, too.

It was Rianne who kept surprising him.

Alex creased his brow in thought. What was he supposed to do with a woman who was part mouse, part wildcat?

He should be furious with her, for one thing. Probably with Leslie and Aunt Lorna, too. They had to have known about Rianne's disguise when they'd plotted to retain her as Leslie's companion.

What else did they know? Just what had happened in her past? Why had she felt it necessary to hide her attractiveness? What in her past would drive her to do such extremes?

Rianne hadn't been dreaming earlier when she'd clutched his hand and voiced her fear. She'd been in another time, another place, reliving memories that sent her into a chilling panic.

Why? And if that bastard of a husband of hers was dead, who was she was so terrified of? A ray of bright light fell across Rianne's face. She wanted to remain asleep, but it bored persistently into her eyelids.

She opened her eyes, then quickly shut them again. The sun was shining through the window next to her, directly onto her face. She turned her head aside and tried again, squinting this time. She found herself staring at an unfamiliar ceiling of narrow slats of polished wood, a beautiful brass lamp hanging from it. Why was the room so narrow?

Glancing straight up, she saw what appeared to be a strange, coffin-sized box above her bed. It startled her so that she jerked upright, then moaned and clasped her forehead as she was overcome by dizziness.

She jerked again as a hand closed over her nape. "Hold it! Not so fast. Here, lower your head for a moment." The hand pushed her head forward, until her chin was almost on her chest.

Rianne relaxed when she recognized Alex's voice. From the corner of her eye she could see his legs and part of a chair beside her bed.

He held her long enough for her confused brain to recall where she was and some of the events of the night before. Except that she couldn't remember anything after the fracas in the gentlemen's club car. "What happened last night? How did I get back here?"

"You fainted. I carried you."

"I couldn't have! You didn't!"

"You did. I did." Alex was firm.

Rianne frowned. The last thing she recollected was an awful pain in her head, and before that, seeing Alex and Mr. Gumm's bloodied faces. Oh, Lord, she didn't want to remember *that.* "I didn't *faint,*" she insisted. "I think it was this bump on my head that knocked me out." She touched the lump and winced. Twisting about, she tried to free herself from Alex's hold. "Let me up."

"How *did* you get that lump?" Alex asked grimly.

"From you, when you practically threw me across the room," she told him.

"When Alex *what?*" Leslie screeched from the doorway of the observation room where she'd just appeared.

"He—Will you *please* let me up," Rianne said, swatting at Alex's free hand. "I'm all right now."

He released her, only to bark, "I did *not* throw you across the room!"

"That's right. You merely *shoved* me so hard I slid across the table and into a wall. And you just found the lump to prove it!" Rianne was angry, yet she noticed that Alex still looked awful. His hair was in disorder, and dark circles cupped his bloodshot eyes, one of which was bruised a bluish black.

Alex raked his fingers through his hair, mussing it even more. "Dammit, I merely gave you a little *push* to move you out of Gumm's way. One swat from *him* and you'd probably still be unconscious. You ought to thank me."

Rianne glared at him. "*Thank* you? My initial opinion of you was right. You're an arrogant lout, Alex Benedict. It was *I* who was trying to save you from getting killed or, at the very least, having all your bones broken!"

"Oh, I see," he sneered. "You were saving me from Gumm so that you could kill me yourself—with a revolver you could barely lift."

Leslie's jaw dropped. She was swiveling her head back and forth as she absorbed this exchange.

"Mr. Gumm!" Rianne gasped. "What did you do to him?"

"I put him out of commission."

Rianne stared at Alex. "My God, you didn't kill him, did you?"

"No, I merely invited his head to meet Mr. Remington."

"Who? Oh, you mean the gun?"

"It's not just a gun, it's a revolver."

Rianne waved a hand impatiently. "Whatever. The man apologized as you told him to. Why did you knock him out?"

"Because you smiled at him."

"Oh." She had no idea what he meant by that. Did he mean she had a nice smile, or did he mean he didn't think she should smile at men like Gumm?

Sometimes, she decided, Alex enjoyed being deliberately obtuse, just to confuse her.

". . . sense," Alex said.

Rianne realized he'd been speaking to her and made an effort to pay attention. "What?" she asked.

"I was saying that none of this would have happened if you had used a bit of common sense. You have only yourself to blame," he stated.

"Will someone please explain what's going on? Or what *went* on last night?" Leslie pleaded. When the other two ignored her, she sighed and sank into a chair to wait out the argument.

"It was not my fault!" Rianne protested. "We were almost safely out of the club car. *You* were the one who decided to avenge my honor—or some silly thing—and almost got yourself killed."

Alex's eyes narrowed. "Silly! *Silly?* No man insults a woman in my care! And I had no intention of getting killed. I was doing fine, in fact, until *you* decided to join the fracas. You should beg my forgiveness for being such a blasted nuisance!"

Rianne crossed her arms over her chest. "Are you saying you expect *me* to apologize to *you?*" she asked, disbelieving.

"It wouldn't be amiss."

Her chin set mulishly, Rianne gave him a look of disdain. "Humph! All I did was try to save your life, and this is the thanks I get. I am *not* going to apologize! I'm not! Why should I? Besides, you were the one who told me to stop saying I'm sorry."

She had him there, Alex thought, and he burst into laughter.

"Oh! Oh, you are *such* an infuriating man!" Rianne pushed

the covers aside and tried to slide around him to climb out of bed. She almost fell back into it, for she was stiff and sore all over. Her head and cheek hurt, her shoulder ached, and her knees almost wouldn't bend.

"Does this mean you no longer think I'm sweet?" Alex asked, grinning devilishly.

Rianne bit down on a groan and forcibly pushed herself out of bed, whereupon she tried to stomp to the observation room. The best she could manage was an awkward limp. At the doorway, she turned back. "About as sweet as a poisonous snake," she hissed before jerking the curtains closed. Unfortunately, she couldn't shut out Alex's laughter.

Leslie's wide-eyed gaze moved from the swishing curtains to her brother. "*Now* will someone please tell me what this is all about?" she demanded.

In the observation room, Rianne tried to shut out Leslie and Alex's murmurs as she assessed the damage to her body. She rotated her arm, wincing at the ache but deciding that she could live with it. Falling into a chair, she lifted her skirt and nightgown to look at her knees. As she'd expected, they were scraped and needed washing with soap to prevent infection. She sighed. That meant she'd have to go out to heat water. Perhaps she'd wait a while, until Alex left. Surely he'd want to wash, also, and shave.

A look into the mirror showed that her right cheek was slightly swollen and discolored. She sighed. She'd have to find her face powder . . .

She stared at her reflection, aghast. Oh, no! Alex had seen her like this! She'd washed her face before going to bed, then hadn't even given a thought to donning her spectacles when she'd gone for Alex.

Maybe he hadn't noticed. The lighting in the coaches wasn't very bright. He'd been occupied with other matters in the club car. And once he'd brought her back here, Leslie had been his concern.

Surely he'd simply placed her on the sofa, covered her, and left her to sleep. And this morning, well, they hadn't spent much time together.

Rianne tried to convince herself that he hadn't had an opportunity to really look at her. Still, uneasiness sat heavily in her stomach.

Well, there was only one way to find out. She needed water to wash. She would wear her spectacles on her way to the kitchen and see what reaction they evoked from Alex.

She scanned the table where she'd left them last night, but they weren't there. Maybe they'd fallen.

She was on her hands and knees, peering beneath the table, running her hands under the chairs, when the curtain swished open behind her. Thinking it was Leslie, she called out. "You haven't seen my—?"

"Looking for these, by any chance?" a masculine voice asked.

Rianne gasped and peered over her shoulder to find Alex leaning nonchalantly against the doorframe. She scrambled to her feet, her face pink with chagrin. "You could have knocked," she said, guilt making her sound irritable.

"I did, but you didn't reply. I repeat, looking for these?" He was twirling her spectacles idly by one stem.

"I . . . er, yes." She took a hesitant step forward and reached for them.

Instead of handing them over, he brushed past her and went to the window behind her. Rianne's jaw dropped when he slid it open, then tossed out her spectacles.

Alex brushed his hands in satisfaction as he came back to her. "Been wanting to do that for a long time," he told her as he pushed her chin back into place with one finger. Then he shoved his hands into his pockets and left, whistling.

Rianne was confused. Where was the Alex Benedict she'd first met? The one who'd pushed and probed, asking personal questions? The one who'd ridiculed and taunted her about her past? This didn't seem like that man at all! That man would have demanded an explanation, been furious, even ordered her to leave him and Leslie at Atlanta.

Of course, that could still happen.

Rianne cautiously peered out from behind the curtain. Leslie was busy in the kitchen. "Is he gone?" Rianne asked her.

"Yes." Leslie dried her hands. "I've just made some coffee. I think we could both use it. My goodness, Rianne—Alex told me about last night. I could hardly believe it!"

Rianne sighed as she sank into a chair. "Neither can I. It seems like a bad dream." She looked up in surprise when Leslie came to sit in the opposite chair and chuckled.

"Bad dream? I'm jealous. I missed out on all the excitement."

Rianne laughed. "Leslie, only you would say such a thing. You must be feeling much better."

"I am. For a few hours I thought I was going to die, but . . ." She shrugged. "I guess I'm too stubborn. Alex insists I'm to see a doctor when we reach Atlanta, but I really don't feel it's necessary, do you?"

"Remember when there was an epidemic of influenza at the school?" Rianne asked her.

"Is that what I had?"

Rianne nodded. "It seems likely, but it wouldn't hurt to have a doctor take a look at you, just to be sure. The only thing that puzzles me is why I didn't catch it. We've been almost inseparable for days. How is it that you became ill and I haven't?"

"Hmm. That is odd. We went shopping together, to Mrs. Porter's together . . ." Leslie snapped her fingers. "I know! Remember that last fitting you had? It was about four days ago, I believe. Aunt Lorna had asked me to stop at—"

"—the orphanage!" Rianne finished for her.

"Exactly. We were running late, so I dropped you off and went on my own. I remember it was very quiet, and the directress said that some of the children were ill. She reassured me that the doctor had been by and it wasn't serious, but I was so rushed that I didn't ask questions."

"That's it, then." Rianne tilted her head as she heard the sound of sizzling behind her. "The coffee's done. No, you stay put, and I'll get it. Do you want some biscuits, too?"

"I think my stomach will welcome food now."

In short order Rianne had prepared a tray and set it on the table between them. Leslie happily devoured two biscuits, then reached for another. "I feel like a pig. Do you want one?" When Rianne didn't reply, Leslie glanced up to find her frowning, deep in thought. "Hello," she sang. "Are you still with me?"

Rianne jumped. "Oh, sorry." She set her mug back on the tray. "I was just wondering . . . Leslie, do you realize that Alex has now seen me as I really am?"

Leslie's eyes widened. "Uh-oh. No, I didn't think of that. Was he very angry?"

"That's just it. He hasn't said a thing about it. Don't you think that's strange? You know him much better than I do, of course, but he doesn't strike me as the type to take kindly to being deceived." Still frowning, Rianne absently drummed her fingers against the arms of her chair.

Leslie set her mug beside Rianne's. "He's not." Her own forehead creased in thought as she tapped *her* fingers against her lips.

They sat for a minute or two, silently brooding. Finally Leslie offered, "Something odd's going on here."

"Isn't that what I just said?"

"Mmm. He's playing some sort of game."

"Hmm. He likes playing games with people, doesn't he?"

" 'Fraid so."

"I don't like being the mouse to his cat."

Their fingers stilled, and they exchanged worried glances.

Rianne bit her lip. "The thing is, I never know—"

"—when he's going to pounce," Leslie finished.

Chapter 14

Rianne and Leslie were packed and ready when the train pulled into Atlanta in midafternoon. Alex hadn't reappeared since morning, but he came for them now, followed by two porters. He'd already made all the arrangements, he told them. A hired carriage, a wagon for the trunks, and reservations at the hotel awaited them.

They flanked Alex as they left the Rolling Palace and walked toward the row of waiting carriages and cabs. "You two are sharing a corner suite, while I'm next door." He glanced at his sister. "The doctor's coming in two hours, Les."

She looked at him in disgust. "Been busy, haven't you?"

"Sarcasm won't get you out of this one, Les. Neither will pouting," Alex told her firmly. "The doctor is going to take a look at you, and that's final."

Rianne bent her head to hide her smile as Leslie craned her neck behind Alex's back and rolled her eyes at her. But the girl didn't say another word until they were all inside the carriage, Alex sitting across from her and Rianne.

"I'll see the doctor," she declared imperiously, as if granting a royal favor, "as long as he doesn't interfere with my dinner. I'm starving."

Rianne turned away, pretending to look out the window but once again hid a smile. If she wasn't mistaken, brother and sister would soon be in the midst of one of their spats.

"We'll see what the doctor says," she heard Alex reply noncommittally.

"What?" Leslie cried. "Surely he won't tell me I'm not allowed to eat dinner!"

"He may keep you on a bland diet for a time."

"Oh, phooey."

"Likely he'll also insist you dine in your suite instead of the hotel dining room."

Leslie's jaw fell.

"You could relapse if you don't follow his orders," Alex said before she could voice her opinion at this turn of events. "You don't want a relapse, do you?" he added emphatically, looking at her intently while nodding surreptitiously in Rianne's direction.

Leslie's eyebrows rose as she finally comprehended. "No, I . . . of course I don't want a relapse," she replied. "I really should follow the doctor's orders, shouldn't I? I'll definitely have dinner in my room. Yes, that's what I'll do."

Surprised at Leslie's acquiescence, Rianne turned to her and offered, "I'll dine with you, then."

Two pairs of green eyes connected. "No!" Leslie and Alex exclaimed in unison.

Rianne cast a perplexed glance from one to the other. "No?" she repeated, oblivious to the silent exchanges occurring.

"No," Alex said definitively. "Leslie's still weak and tired. She should have her dinner quietly, then retire immediately after."

"Yes," Leslie agreed lamely. "Immediately after."

"Besides," Alex added, "you'll hardly want to share the same, most likely bland, dinner, nor would Les want you to. Isn't that so, Les?"

Leslie sent her brother a glare that promised retribution.

"Of course not," she gritted. "You two just have your six-course meal. Enjoy it. Feel free to have dessert, too. No need to worry about me."

Alex grinned at her unrepentantly.

Rianne frowned. "I still think—"

Leslie patted her hand. "Rianne, you've already spent most of the time on the train waiting on me. I'd feel terribly guilty if you were to miss out on a sumptuous meal in the dining room. I hear the decor is absolutely gorgeous, also."

Rianne slowly turned her gaze to Alex. He was watching her, satisfaction gleaming in his green eyes and a hint of triumph on his lips. Why was he looking so smug?

He crossed his arms over his chest. "You will, of course, join me for dinner in the hotel dining room, Madame," he said.

It was not an invitation but an order.

Uh-oh! She was back to being Madame again. Rianne closed her eyes briefly. Was the cat sharpening his claws and preparing to pounce?

"What could I do?" Leslie lamented as she shook out the dress she planned to wear the next day. "When Alex takes on that narrow-eyed, mulish expression, even I know enough to back down."

"I'm not blaming you, Leslie. Heavens, Alex intimidates *me* most of the time." Rianne sank onto the closest bed. "I wonder what he has in mind," she mused.

"So he knows what you look like," Leslie said as she hung the dress in the closet and began to set her toiletries on one side of the long dressing table. "What's the worst that can happen?"

"He can fire me. Tonight. He *will* fire me."

Leslie turned about, her hands on her hips. "He will *not* fire you. I admit Alex can be a cad at times, but I truly can't see him abandoning you here all alone. His sense of honor won't allow it." She came to sit beside Rianne and squeezed her hand. "Blast it! If only I had access to my trust account, I'd pay your wages myself."

"You have a trust account?"

"I do. Alex set it up for me when I was still a child," Leslie explained. "But I don't have access to it until I'm twenty-one, and even then only to the interest." She grimaced. "I'm not allowed to touch the capital until I'm either twenty-five or married. Alex was definite about that, but he keeps me apprised of the facts and figures, so I know that the fund is substantial. I'm a wealthy woman, Rianne. Or I will be. Despite Alex's many flaws, no one can fault his generosity."

Rianne smiled. "You're not fooling me, Leslie Benedict. I suspect you really think your brother is perfect. You only pretend to be angry with him on occasion, and he with you, but you both enjoy your little squabbles. The truth is, you adore him."

Leslie laughed and acknowledged this truth. "Guilty! Alex has always been my hero."

Strangely, Rianne understood why. Despite Alex's complexity, she knew that he would never let down or betray the people he loved. Rianne felt envy, but she brushed it off. The one thing she'd never allowed herself was self-pity. "I'll wager," she said, smiling, "that Alex returns those sentiments."

"Of course. We understand each other, you see." Leslie hopped off the bed. "Enough of this. It's time you got ready for your dinner with him."

Rianne winced. "For my inquisition and trial, you mean?" she asked dryly.

"Just tell him the truth—you donned the disguise in order to obtain the teaching position. You don't have to tell him anything else."

"Easier said than done. Your brother can be brutally persistent."

"True. So don't let him make you angry. Stay calm and unruffled—you do that very well—and if all else fails, use tears. Alex turns to mush when a woman cries."

"I can't do that, Leslie!" Rianne was appalled.

"Of course you can. Tears are one of the few natural weapons women have."

Rianne was awed. Where had Leslie learned this feminine ingenuity? "I'm not practiced enough to use such tactics. Alex will know immediately that I'm faking," she improvised. The truth was that she hadn't allowed herself to cry since her mother died. She didn't think she knew how anymore.

"Do as you think best, then," Leslie said. "Now, I think you should wear that azure gown. Which trunk is it in?"

That particular gown was very classic, with simple lines but a low, square neckline. "I was thinking I'd wear the hunter green," Rianne said doubtfully, for she'd never worn a stylish evening gown before.

"Uh-uh!" Leslie shook her head. "It's very nice, but it has a high, button-up collar. Not at all a gown to wear at dinner. You want something a bit more sophisticated. Now that Alex knows what you look like, why not flaunt it? Besides, knowing you're looking your best will give you confidence."

Rianne wasn't so sure of that. And she had her doubts about "flaunting" herself. She was habitually careful to *not* draw attention to herself.

Still . . .

If she was about to attend her own execution, she could at least die with dignity. "The blue it is," she sighed.

Alex arrived at seven. While she apprehensively gathered her gloves and fan, she kept glancing at him as he stood inside the door, speaking to Leslie.

Except for last night and this morning, Rianne had never seen him appear anything other than impeccable. Tonight he wore a beautifully tailored black dresscoat with gray vest and trousers, his broad tie perfectly arranged.

She smoothed her hair nervously, convinced she could never match his elegance. She lost even the small bit of confidence Leslie had given her as he glanced her way and said simply, "Good, you're ready. Les, I bid you good night."

"It will hardly be that," Leslie groused. "I'm sure my stomach will be growling and keeping me awake." Alex chucked her chin and laughed, but she frowned at him. "Alex, kindly remember that Rianne is my friend," she warned.

"Now, Les, I plan to have pheasant for dinner, not Rianne, despite the fact that she looks delicious." His laughing eyes turned to Rianne.

Rianne didn't know what to say to that. She felt gauche and very much out of her element.

Her face must have revealed her confusion, for Alex took her arm, bid his sister good night once more, and escorted Rianne to the elevator.

They reached it at the same time as two elderly couples did. They exchanged pleasantries as they waited. When it finally arrived and the attendant slid open the doors, Alex and Rianne waited to let the others enter first.

It was not a very wide elevator, and the ladies' voluminous skirts took up considerable room. The two older gentlemen held a murmured conversation at the back, leaving their spouses in the middle, while Rianne and Alex were forced to stand face to face between the group and the attendant. The two men continued to talk; the other four remained silent. Rather than staring at Alex's chest, Rianne pretended to observe what she could see of the walls, the floor, the other ladies' hems. She glanced up and found two pairs of curious eyes alternately studying her, then Alex.

Rianne hated being stared at. She quickly lowered her head and nervously fiddled with her fan as she focused on Alex's glossy black shoes. It was a relief when the elevator suddenly jerked to a stop and the attendant opened the doors.

Rianne walked out with pink cheeks to step into a huge hall. At least two dozen people were milling about, while others filled the sofas and chairs, socializing in a subdued manner, as if they were in a sanctuary. Many of them turned to glance toward the elevator. Since she was the first to exit, she once again felt the object of scrutiny.

Several young men stood in a circle, conversing. When they saw her emerge from the elevator, they turned toward her. To Rianne, it appeared that they were appraising her, laughing as they made comments among themselves. Another gentleman glanced past the woman standing before him. When the woman turned to follow his gaze, she saw Rianne and glared at her.

The wide oak doors of the dining room opened. Rianne didn't see the waiter who came through bearing a placard with a last name, nor the couple who rose to follow him inside, nor the *maître d'hôtel* who waited to show the couple to their table.

She saw part of a very large room behind him, filled with tables and diners who would stare at her if she went inside. Oh, God, would they also snicker behind their hands? Would they make sly, malicious remarks?

She couldn't catch her breath and her vision blurred. She became dizzy and teetered slightly.

Strong hands grasped her arms from behind and pulled her against the solid warmth of another body. "Are you able to walk?" Alex asked into her ear.

Rianne nodded, unable to speak.

"Good. I'm going to find us a quiet corner. We'll just sit for a while. That all right with you, darlin'?"

She nodded again, reassured by Alex's calm tone and the gentle strength of his hands.

Alex scanned the lobby until he found an empty corner with a settee and chairs.

Slipping his hand under Rianne's arm, he led her toward the corner. She walked like one mesmerized, her face pale, causing him even more worry.

What had brought this on? Damned if she wasn't the most complex woman he'd ever known. She swung from mood to mood, alternately demure, stubborn, fiery, and now . . . frightened. Definitely frightened. Of what? He urged her onto the settee. "For someone who insists she never faints, you've been doing a good job of it in the last twenty-four hours," he teased, deliberately seeking a lively response from her.

Her head jerked up. "I didn't faint!"

Alex smiled. Her color was returning and her eyes were brightening. "Right. You didn't, but you came close to it."

Her cheeks immediately bloomed with color. She bit her lip, but she didn't look away from him. There was still a lingering trace of—what was it in those sherry-brown eyes? Fear? Pain?

Haunted. That's how she looked. Haunted.

A feeling of protectiveness took root in Alex.

He fought it. He didn't need this. Rianne was Leslie's friend. He had no reason to become involved, even in a small way. He didn't *want* to!

He had his family and a circle of loyal friends—they were enough. He didn't need entanglement with a complex, sometimes fragile woman with a haunted past.

The smart course would be to hustle Rianne back upstairs and turn her over to his sister. Yes, that was what he would do.

He reached for her hand, but instead of assisting her to rise, he found himself asking gently, "Want to tell me about it?" *Bloody hell! What was he doing?*

"It was the crowd. I don't like crowds. I get nervous," she said in a rush. "I'm s—" Her voice fell as he gave her a warning look. She drew a deep breath. "All right, I won't say it. It's just that I didn't expect so many people. Some were staring at me, like those two ladies in the elevator. I felt as if—"

"As if?" he prompted.

"As if I were on display!" she burst out.

"I see." Alex idly played with her long, slim fingers. Her hands were small and soft, a pleasure to hold. "Did you stop to think that perhaps those people were all simply struck by the sight of a very pretty young woman in a lovely gown? That the men were wondering how to make her acquaintance and the women were jealously plotting how to prevent that from occurring?" He raised his eyebrows when she choked. "You don't believe me?"

"Certainly not!"

"Shall I prove it to you? Hmm, let me see . . ." He pursed his lips as he scanned the room. "Those young pups in the opposite corner—Do you see them?"

Rianne glanced in that direction. Alex was speaking of the group of men she had first noticed upon exiting the elevator. They were conversing, but their heads kept turning to and fro, their faces lighting up each time their gazes discovered a pretty girl. Even as Rianne watched, one jabbed another's ribs to direct his attention toward a striking brunette who had just swept out of the dining room with an older couple. "Yes, I do," Rianne told Alex as she turned back to him, puzzled.

Alex's gaze remained pinned on the young men. "Stay here. I'll be back in a moment," he told her.

"What are you going to do?" Rianne asked cautiously.

"I noticed their interest when they spotted you. I'll wager they'd like an introduction."

Rianne's jaw dropped. He couldn't mean it. Surely he wouldn't . . .

Alex rose. "Wait!" She reached for his sleeve and missed. He took two steps before she latched on to the hem of his coat. "Wait!" she cried again, and tugged fiercely.

He turned around. "No?"

She shook her head vigorously.

"That's a relief," Alex said as he straightened his cuff and sat down once again. "I don't think my ribs could take another assault." His eyes were gleaming when he met her gaze.

"You never intended to do it!" Rianne smacked his chest with her fan. "Oh, you are the devil incarnate, Alex Benedict!"

"I try my best," he said smugly, pleased that he'd managed to banish the ghosts. "Now, let's see about that dinner," he added as he caught the *maître d'hôtel*'s eye and beckoned.

Chapter 15

Rianne expected that they would eat in the public dining room after all, and she braced herself, determined to overcome this aversion she had to crowds.

Instead, she and Alex followed the *maître d'hôtel* through a quiet corridor and up a small flight of stairs. To her pleased surprise, she soon found herself seated at a small table in a private alcove several feet above the main dining room, out of sight of the other diners, thanks to tall potted plants between their table and the rail.

They ordered dinner and, while they waited, sipped the Champagne Alex had insisted upon. That is, Alex imbibed. Though Rianne held her crystal glass, she'd yet to drink from it.

"You don't care for Champagne?" he asked her.

She glanced up. "I'm not sure. I've never had it before." She raised the glass to her lips, then abruptly set it down.

Alex followed suit and sighed. "What is it now?" he asked. She took a deep breath and met his inquiring glance. "I'm very grateful for your consideration." She waved a hand to indicate the alcove. "You've ordered a wonderful dinner. Still, I feel as if I'm the condemned and it's my last meal. Can't we get this over with now?"

"Get what over with?"

"You haven't said a word about my appearance."

He quirked an eyebrow. "I distinctly recall telling Les that you looked delicious enough to eat."

"Ha! More than likely you'd chew me up and spit me out," she said dryly.

He laughed. Rianne wasn't amused. She reached for her glass and this time gulped half of the sparkling wine. Bubbles fizzed up her nose. "Oh!" she said in surprised approval. Tipping the glass, she drank the rest.

When she set the glass down, Alex was watching her, his lips twitching. "Like it, do you?" He snapped his fingers. A waiter magically appeared and refilled her goblet.

She stared at it longingly. "I really shouldn't," she said wistfully. "It makes me want to smile, and this is not a smiling matter."

"It isn't?"

Her eyelids rose. "You set up this little *tête-à-tête* to talk about my deception. I thought you were angry with me, yet I see that you're trying very hard not to laugh again. Why aren't you angry?" Alex was wondering that himself. Certainly that had been his inclination, but now . . . It was hard to stay angry at a woman who almost fainted at the sight of a few strangers who meant her no harm.

A woman, moreover, who could look at him, wide-eyed and breathless, as she was now, and distract him. "Why don't you tell me about Anne DuBois, and then I'll decide if I'm angry or not," he suggested.

He smiled as she took another sip of Champagne for courage. He listened to her brief story of leaving New Orleans to put a painful past behind her—she skimmed over that part without detail—and of how she had simply taken the most readily available transport and landed in Boston. She'd needed a way to support herself, and that was how she'd ended up at Chatham's.

"I knew I could teach French, but to convince the conventional Mrs. Busley, I had to become a middle-aged widow. Once I left the school, I never intended to continue the charade. But then you appeared and insisted that I visit Mrs. Hall. You must believe that I didn't set out to deceive any of you. It was just that . . ." Rianne shrugged. "I didn't have much money, and I needed time to find another way to make a living. I was afraid if I revealed myself to all of you, I'd have to leave. Then Leslie and Mrs. Hall asked me to be Leslie's traveling companion. I knew then that I had to tell them, and I did."

"And none of you thought that *I* deserved to know the truth?" Alex inquired dryly.

Rianne's cheeks took on a rosy hue. "They . . . we all thought that if you knew I was only twenty-three, you wouldn't accept me."

"You were right," Alex agreed, frowning. Twenty-three! "My Lord, you're young enough to *be* a student, not *teach* them!"

"There! You see? That's exactly why we didn't tell you!" Rianne exclaimed triumphantly.

To her dismay, Alex continued to frown. Was he going to tell her to leave now? The anxiety was making her mouth dry, so she drank more Champagne. Her hand jerked when he spoke.

"What were you thinking, traveling on your own at eighteen? Do you have any idea what could have befallen you?"

Rianne stared at him in astonishment. "I don't understand," she said slowly. "You don't seem to be angry because I deceived you, yet you're furious because I left New Orleans on my own?"

"Damned right, I am. It was careless and stupid. No, don't flare up at me." He was clearly displeased. "You're lucky you even got to Boston. Do you realize that?"

"Yes. I do now," she admitted reluctantly.

He relaxed at her admission. "About New Orleans—I'm assuming this 'painful past' involved a man. The one who was your guardian and . . . your guardian." For some reason, Alex couldn't quite say the word *husband,* so he omitted it. When Rianne nodded hesitantly, he continued. "Despite my curious nature and my assertion that I would learn everything there is to know about you, I realize I have no right to ask you for the particulars. We all have things in our past we'd rather forget—or try to. I only want your assurance that nothing in your past can harm Leslie in any way."

"There's nothing I would allow to harm her," Rianne told him. And since she didn't intend to reach New Orleans, what danger could there be?

"Good. Is there anything else I should know?"

Rianne met his gaze. "No," she replied honestly.

"Then we needn't discuss it again," he returned.

Rianne blinked. To say that she was surprised was an understatement. "Is—" She broke off as the waiter brought their first course. "That's it?" she asked after the man had left. "Does this mean that you aren't going to fire me?"

Alex shook out his napkin. "Only if you promise not to involve me in any more of your Grand Adventures. Last night was more than enough, thank you."

Relieved and happy, Rianne laughed. "It *was* quite an adventure, wasn't it? I'm eagerly looking forward to my next one."

Alex didn't respond. He was staring at her mouth. She couldn't imagine why. She knew she didn't have any spinach caught in her teeth. "Alex?" she said hesitantly.

His head jerked, as if he'd just realized that she was sitting across from him. "I don't even want to think about it," he said soberly as he reached for his fork.

Rianne had the strange feeling that he wasn't speaking of her Grand Adventure.

To Rianne's chagrin and Alex's amusement, they reached the elevator only to find that the same two couples they'd ridden down with were waiting, also. Rianne replied to the others' greetings with a shy smile, hoping she and Alex didn't end up in the same position.

Fortunately, Alex ushered her to one side, and they both ended up with their backs against the wall. Well, at least she wouldn't have to feel as if holes were being stared into her. Now she only had to face these people directly!

Alex watched Rianne carefully. She'd been lively during dinner; she'd appeared to enjoy her meal and had laughed at his comments, responding with her quick wit. She'd been fine when they finished dining and left the private alcove, but upon entering the elevator she became edgy again. She was standing with her head bent, twisting her fingers, aware that the two elderly ladies were surreptitiously eying her and her ring hand and speculating about her relationship with him.

Blasted women. He was irritated that Rianne's spirit was being dimmed by their curious stares. Rianne needed a distraction to bring her out of her troubled mood.

The elevator rose, and Alex bent over to whisper in Rianne's ear. "Since you already think I'm the devil, and I know there's an imp hiding within you, what say you to a little revenge?"

"What . . . ?"

Alex placed a finger over his lips and indicated the other four with a little questioning tilt of his head. She didn't have the slightest idea what he was up to, but his eyes were gleaming with mischief. Why not? she asked herself. It would be a pleasant change to be a participant in one of his games instead of the victim. She nodded.

"Sweetness," Alex said loudly in a deep drawl, "Ah'm afraid ah've neglected to tell you how enchanting you are this evenin'. Forgive me, *ma chérie,* but at times your beauty so overwhelms me that ah'm left speechless."

For one confused moment, Rianne wondered which of the other two women he could possibly be addressing. When her startled gaze met his, however, she was left in no doubt that he was speaking to *her!* His green eyes were filled with adoration, and so intently focused on her that she was mesmerized.

"Dearest," he continued in a tone so smooth it gave her goose bumps, "Ah find your shyness immensely appealing. It only adds to your charm. *Je t'aime, ma chérie.*" Rianne wasn't even aware that he'd taken her gloved hand and was pressing it to his lips, lingering over it. "Tell me you feel the same way about me," he murmured.

"Yes," Rianne breathed, not knowing what she'd agreed to; so captivated was she by the sound of his voice and his fervent words that she was oblivious to everything and everyone else—including the gasps and subdued whispers coming from the other two ladies.

Alex heard them, however, and sighed dramatically. "You have made me so happy," he murmured, and he swept Rianne into his arms.

She had time for one short breath as his face filled her vision, the hair falling across his forehead, the curve of his eyebrows, each and every one of his eyelashes . . .

And then there were only sparks of light as her own eyelids drooped, a whiff of masculine scent, the feel of Alex's body pressed close, and his mouth pressed even closer against hers, hot and slick, slanting over her lips, easing to skim over them, to stroke the edges of her mouth before coming back to cover it again.

He gathered her closer still. "Put your arms around me, Rianne," he whispered.

She obeyed mindlessly. Sensations attacked her from all sides. Her heart thumped madly, and her skin felt as if it were burning. It was all so overwhelming.

When his mouth suddenly left hers, she opened her eyes, dazed. Alex was bent over her. Two spots of bright color highlighted his cheeks. He was staring down at her with fierce intensity once again.

She stared back, unaware that her eyes were alight with confused wonder and pleasure.

Suddenly, he uttered a soft curse, and only when he jerked her upward did she realize she'd been arched backward over his arm.

The elevator door slid open, and the others exited. Rianne felt herself being urged forward, and stepped out of the car. She saw the grin the attendant swiftly wiped off his face as Alex turned to give him a gratuity. In a daze, she continued walking.

"My, but these Southerners are creatures of passion! Isn't that the most romantic thing you've ever heard?" one of the elderly ladies sighed. "Do you think they're married, Hildy?"

"Of course they are, May. She looked like a respectable woman. They're probably newlyweds," Hildy replied. "Harold never said things like that to me, did you, Harold?"

"Eh? What's that, m'dear?"

"I said—oh, never mind."

"Was he speaking to her in French?" May asked eagerly. "Oh, what do you think he said?" Her voice was a loud whisper.

"It could have been French. I'll wager he said something naughty to her."

May giggled, and their voices faded as they turned a corner.

Rianne almost turned, too, until Alex grasped her shoulders and pointed her in the right direction.

By the time he unlocked the door to the suite she was sharing with Leslie and pressed the key into her hand, she'd recovered enough to feel embarrassment."Thank you," she mumbled, staring blindly past Alex. "And thank you for . . . for dinner. It was . . . delicious."

"Rianne, look at me."

She didn't want to. But she didn't have any choice, as he grasped her chin and lifted her face to his.

Her embarrassment fled, for Alex's face was grim, his eyes burning with an odd mixture of anger and chagrin.

"I don't want you to misinterpret that kiss. I did it because those two nosy women were creating sordid scenarios in their empty little heads, and I couldn't resist getting back at them."

She stared up at him, unable to say a word.

"It was just a kiss. You realize that, don't you?" he urged.

Rianne nodded. He seemed about to say something more, then changed his mind. "Good night, then," he said and turned on his heel.

Rianne watched as he opened the door to his room. When he hesitated, waiting, she entered her room. After locking it, she stood with her back pressed against the door, the tips of her fingers stroking her swollen mouth.

He hadn't meant anything by his actions—she knew that—yet she couldn't prevent the rush of emotion that filled her.

Emotions that had been tightly contained for too long. Nor could she prevent the loosening of the constriction that had bound her heart.

He'd called her *sweetheart* in that deep drawl she liked so much, and *his darling* in French.

He'd looked at her as if he'd thought she was the most beautiful, wonderful creature on earth.

He'd *kissed* her! And, oh, what a glorious kiss it had been! Why, even now, she could taste him on her lips.

Oh, Lord! Whatever was the matter with her? It was one kiss. *Just one kiss* for heaven's sake, and Alex had warned her . . .

He'd warned her that it had meant nothing.

Of course it hadn't—to *him.*

But she was very much afraid that it did indeed mean something to her, because for a moment—just one moment—she'd seen in his eyes what glory they could have known, and already she mourned the loss.

Chapter 16

Bellesfield was a working plantation, as Rianne was soon to learn, but unlike any with which she had once been familiar.

They had left Atlanta in midmorning, after a late breakfast. Bellesfield's farm manager, Mr. Wilcox, had brought a buggy for the three of them, which Alex was driving, while Wilcox and another worker were in charge of the wagon loaded with their baggage.

As they reached the turnoff to the driveway leading to the house, Leslie pulled on Alex's sleeve. "Stop, please." At Alex's quizzical look she explained. "I remember walking up this road to the house, and I want to do it now."

Alex didn't even question it. "I'll walk with you," he offered.

"Will you come, too, Rianne?" Leslie asked.

"Of course. I'd like that."

Alex helped them both down and called to Wilcox to take the buggy. The three of them waited until it and the wagon had turned up the drive and disappeared from view. Leslie reached for Alex and Rianne's hands. Linked together, they began walking, slowly.

The entrance to the drive was almost tunnel-like, with thick stands of pines on both sides. The road gradually widened as it crawled up an incline, and at the top, two rows of stately, moss-covered oaks replaced the pines. As the three walkers reached the peak of the slope, Rianne saw that the oaks led directly to the house.

Upon catching sight of it, Leslie released their hands and moved closer to Alex to lay her cheek against his shoulder. He curled his arm around her waist, and Rianne stepped back, not wanting to intrude upon what was an emotional homecoming for Leslie. For Alex, too, perhaps. She felt that this was a private family moment.

"You didn't duplicate our house," Leslie said with relief.

Alex looked down at her. "No. No one will ever build another like it." His voice held a hint of regret.

Rianne had no idea what the original house had looked like, but she thought this one lovely, and it was much larger than she'd expected. A two-story blend of Georgian and Greek Revival styles, it dominated the rise, pristine yet imposing with its colonnaded verandah.

"This house serves two purposes," Alex said. "The west side contains the school's administration offices, while the east side comprises living quarters for the superintendent and his family, as well as guest quarters."

"What are those?" Leslie asked, pointing to the smaller white buildings set around the base of the sloping lawn that surrounded the house. Four on each side, they looked like charming little cottages, each with its own verandah. Though the dwellings were identical in form, flower pots and plants individualized landscaping around each.

"Those house the staff," Alex replied.

"But where are the students housed? Where are the classrooms, the—?"

Alex squeezed Leslie's waist. "Impatient as ever, aren't you? Everything else is behind the main house, on the other side of the knoll," he explained, laughing. "You'll have plenty of time to explore in the next couple of weeks. Right now I think I should introduce you to the superintendent and his wife."

He turned to look over his shoulder. "Coming?" he asked Rianne. The warmth he'd shown Leslie was gone. His tone was cool, his eyes remote.

Rianne sighed. He was still angry with her. Silly, really, since she hadn't been the one to instigate the kiss. It wasn't as if she'd *asked* to be kissed. She should be the one to be annoyed. For some male reason he blamed her, and he'd hardly spoken to her since. The morning after, he'd sent a message to Leslie, informing her that he had business matters to attend, and that he trusted she would be able to find suitable amusement for the one full day they'd be in Atlanta. He hadn't mentioned Rianne.

She'd told herself it didn't matter, but that was a lie.

His kiss had been a revelation in many ways. Though it hadn't been forced, it had certainly been unexpected. Since her experience with Lance, she'd assumed that she'd be revolted by another man's touch, but she hadn't been. She'd responded to Alex's kiss. Amazing!

Yet that wasn't half as—no, not even a fraction—as amazing as the knowledge that she'd come to care for Alex. Not as a friend, not as the brother of a friend, but in the way a woman cared for a man. She'd thought it would never happen, had carefully guarded her emotions so that it couldn't, yet the walls had crumbled with just one kiss.

One kiss, and for that he was treating her as if she'd committed a heinous crime.

At first she'd been hurt, but now she was becoming a bit fed up with his behavior. How long was he going to lay the blame at her feet for that kiss?

The superintendent, Donald Beld, and his wife, Sara,

were waiting for them on the front portico. Mrs. Beld greeted Alex with genuine affection and a kiss, introductions were made, and shortly thereafter Alex and Mr. Beld excused themselves.

Rianne and Leslie were left with Mrs. Beld. At first glance she seemed plain-looking, but she had lovely sky-blue eyes, and when she smiled and spoke in her gentle voice, her tranquil features took on a soft comeliness. Her movements were slow and graceful. One immediately felt comfortable in her presence.

"Leslie, I'm so happy to be able to welcome you back to Bellesfield. You'll find much changed, I'm sure, but the land remains the same. Rianne, I do hope you'll enjoy your stay here. We don't get visitors very often, especially ladies," she told them after she'd welcomed them into the house and offered iced tea and coffee, which they had gratefully accepted. "It will be lovely to have you both," she said as she led them toward a room she called her "hideaway."

"I need it, for I have two active children," Sara told them, laughing. "Josie, who's two, is napping right now. Jon—we call him Jonny—is almost ten. He's involved in everything that happens at Bellesfield. His curiosity is insatiable." She opened a door and stood back. "Please, make yourselves comfortable." Rianne and Leslie both gasped as they entered the room. Painted in soft, muted pastels, it had splashes of brilliant color in its sofa pillows and pots of green and flowering plants. But what really caught their eyes was the far wall, composed entirely of mullioned windows and several French doors that led onto the verandah, then out to a lovely garden boasting every hue of flower imaginable. White chairs and a table, surrounded by pots and pots of azaleas and camellias accentuated a feeling of privacy on this part of the verandah. It was so cleverly arranged that the room seemed to be an extension of the outdoors.

"What a wonderful room!" Rianne exclaimed.

"Was this Alex's idea, too?" Leslie asked.

"Yes. He's wonderfully talented, don't you think?"

At Rianne's questioning look, Leslie explained. "Didn't I tell you that Alex planned everything, from the house to the wells? Of course, he worked with an architectural firm, but the basic concept was his."

"I had no idea," Rianne murmured. The care and consideration given to each detail gave her new insight into Alex's character. Beneath that cynical exterior lay the heart of a man who appreciated beauty and artistry. And peace. For this sun-filled room was meant to soothe the soul and refresh the spirit.

Sara pushed a button near the door and, when a maid arrived, ordered the refreshments. Shortly, the first maid and one other returned with trays, which they soon arranged to Sara's satisfaction. "Very good. Stay a minute, girls." She turned to Rianne and Leslie. "Ladies, this is Mary Margaret—" she fondly patted the arm of the freckle-faced girl who wore a perpetual smile "—and this is Susan." The second girl, tall and thin with beautiful skin the color of beechwood, smiled shyly as Sara patted her arm, too. Both girls politely bowed and murmured, "Pleased to meet you, ma'am," to Rianne and Leslie in turn, before leaving the room.

Sara laughed at the bemused looks on Rianne and Leslie's faces. "They aren't strictly maids. They're students," she explained as she poured iced tea from a pitcher and added a mint leaf to each glass. "Like the others, they pay no tuition, but they're required to contribute to the running of Bellesfield for at least three hours daily. Donald and I both believe that the best way to learn is by example, and we try to match students with their interests. Since both girls intend to become housekeepers, they're learning how to manage a household by spending a period in each aspect of it, including cooking. Your visit will provide their first opportunity to practice with guests in residence."

"An interesting teaching method," Leslie remarked as she took the glass Sara offered. "Don't you think, Rianne?"

"Absolutely. I think it's a marvelous method of teaching."

"Rianne is a teacher herself," Leslie informed Sara. "She was my French instructor."

"Really?" Sara's eyes brightened with interest. "What a coincidence. We'll soon be holding a staff meeting to plan our next year's curriculum, and Donald and I had been thinking of adding French to it. Just the basics, you understand. This is a vocational school. Our students stay only one or two years before leaving us to find employment. Oh, some have gone on to university, but most enter into labor or domestic service. We thought it might be helpful for the domestic students to learn some French, since it's spoken in many households." She smiled at Rianne. "Perhaps we'll find time to speak of it again. I'd like to ask your opinion on how best to proceed."

"I'd be happy to help," Rianne offered.

After refreshments, Sara escorted them to their rooms. "Your windows face the back of the house," she explained as she pulled the drapes aside. "Despite the constant activity, it's a lovely view."

Rianne and Leslie both eagerly pressed to the window. Beyond the house was a crescent of brick buildings. The center one was three stories high and contained the classrooms, Sara explained, while the two double-storied buildings on either side connected to it by enclosed walkways were the dormitories, one for each sex.

Farther back, almost hidden by trees, was another complex of smaller buildings that served a variety of purposes and housed the equipment and machinery needed to run the large operation. Again, a taller building stood in the center. "That," Sara explained, "is the barn, with stables to the side. We raise and train Thoroughbreds here, did you know?"

Leslie's eyes lit. "Alex didn't tell me! Oh, it will be wonderful to ride about the property again." She turned to Rianne. "We'll ride to my secret places. There's a hill with a wonderful view, and—" She laughed at herself. "Listen to me. I can hardly wait."

Rianne smiled, hesitant to put a damper on Leslie's enthusiasm. Later she would tell her that she'd only once been on the back of a horse, and that had been a disastrous experience!

"As you can see, the area behind the big house is largely planted. There are actually two gardens, one for roses and one I call my 'hodgepodge' garden."

Rianne looked down, closer to the house. Below were magnolia trees, hedges, small private areas with benches, and so many flowers and flowering shrubs that it looked as if someone had stirred a rainbow in a giant pot and poured it right there. She spotted a couple of fountains, too, and where flowers and shrubs didn't cover the earth, a thick green lawn did. Paths inlaid with large flat stones led from one building to another.

As she watched, several people strolled the paths purposefully, yet no one seemed in a rush. It was a sprawling complex yet with no "institutional" flavor. It looked more like a small, well-cared-for village, the grounds beautifully landscaped but not overly formal. Everything fit together like the pieces of a carefully constructed puzzle.

Rianne was impressed—and surprised. An enormous amount of care and planning had gone into building not only the house but this entire school. Alex was very talented, indeed.

"Rianne?" Leslie called.

"Hmm?" She turned to find that Leslie and Sara were standing expectantly at the door. "I'm sorry. It's just so fascinating," she said as she went to join them.

Sara smiled. "Yes, Bellesfield is a lovely setting with a wonderful school. We've been able to accomplish a lot of good here, and we're very proud of it. Donald and I still bless the day Alex asked us to join the venture."

"That was in the summer of '66," Leslie offered. "I remember, because he came to Boston in August, then we didn't see him again for almost a year. He was too involved with the building of the school."

"He did wonders," Sara said. "Everyone, including Donald, thought it would take at least three years. Alex finished it in fourteen months by hiring Confederate veterans. He had a standing rule that not one was to be turned down, not even the handicapped. He found employment for all, and he paid good wages. In return, the men worked tirelessly for him. Many of them still do, in one capacity or another.

"Well, now I'll send Mary Margaret and Susan to help you unpack, and then you both might like to rest. Dinner is *en famille,* at seven. You'll meet my children and some of the staff then."

Dinner was indeed an informal, noisy affair, much like that of a huge, happy household. Seated at table were various staff members, Leslie, Rianne, Alex, the Belds, and their son, Jonny. Rather surprising, really, for most households rarely allowed the children at table. Sara explained that they did occasionally host more formal dinners, but she and Donald both felt that families should dine together whenever possible.

Their daughter, Josie, however, was too young. She'd been brought down earlier for introductions, and she was a darling, smiling child, the image of her mother. With a mass of blond curls and startling blue eyes, she charmed everyone. Jonny, on the other hand, was dark like his father, very polite, and more reserved than his bubbly sister.

The young mathematics instructor, Trevor Williams, sat on Rianne's right. On her other side was the school's pastor, Noah Moser, a gray-haired man of perhaps fifty, and next to him, his wife, Inez.

During dinner Rianne learned that Trevor was engaged to a girl in Atlanta, who was frequently the topic of his conversation. When he offered to show Rianne around the plantation the next afternoon, she accepted.

Everyone was friendly and interesting, yet Rianne found herself watching Alex, who sat at the other end of the long table. He seemed unusually subdued, almost to be brooding, which was puzzling.

He also spent a lot of time observing young Jonny. After dinner, when the others retired to what Sara referred to as the music-and-games room, both of them had been absent.

Hours later, the house was quiet, for everyone else was in bed. Still fully dressed, Rianne stood at a window in her room, staring out into the night, seeing nothing, really, but her ghostly reflection in the glass.

Perhaps because of her nap which she was unaccustomed to, she was still awake. She should be exhausted, for yesterday Leslie had pooh-poohed "doctor's orders" for rest and had dragged Rianne on an all-day shopping expedition. The two of them had eaten a late dinner in their suite, and Rianne had fallen asleep as soon as her head touched the pillow.

Now, she stirred restlessly. Though the window was open,

she felt too enclosed. A full moon shone tonight, and Rianne had a sudden desire to sit in a garden and breathe in the scents and listen to the sounds of the night. Impulsively, she turned and left the room.

Chapter 17

Rianne avoided the rose garden. She preferred the variety of blooms behind the sun room, anyway. Too, the gazebo there had beckoned to her earlier.

Approaching it, she was only a few feet from the entrance when the sudden glow of a cigar from within stopped her. Apparently someone else had claimed the gazebo for his own period of solitude.

She lifted her skirts and cautiously backtracked. She'd taken only a few steps when her hem caught on an oleander bush. Drat! She'd miscalculated and stepped off the path. She tried to pull herself loose without making any noise.

"You may as well join me, Rianne," Alex's voice called from the dark.

Rianne sighed. She should have known it was he. Now she couldn't leave without seeming either petty or cowardly.

Jerking her skirt free, she moved nearer, but only to lean against the gazebo frame. The moon broke through the clouds, casting enough light to reveal his face. "How did you know who it was?" she asked.

"Yours is the only light still on upstairs," Alex said dryly. "Stands to reason you're the only one awake."

"And you," she said as she glanced over her shoulder. Sure enough, the only two windows with light streaming through them were those in her room. She turned back to him.

"Yes, and me," he agreed.

"I'm sorry. I didn't mean to intrude. I'll leave."

Sparks momentarily hovered in the air when he tossed his cigar to the floor and squashed it with his boot. "You might as well come in and sit down. In fact, you might like to join me in a little liquid panacea." He held a half empty bottle up before his face, jiggling it so that she could hear the contents sloshing. "Kentucky bourbon. Finest in the world." He brought the bottle to his mouth and took a long draught. "Supposed to warm your blood and cure bodily ills." He chuckled mirthlessly. "Unfortunately, it doesn't do a thing for your soul." He extended the bottle in offering. Moonlight briefly glinted off it, then clouds drifted over and all was once again plunged into darkness. "Come, sit."

"I don't care for any bourbon, thank you, and I'd rather stay out here," Rianne said primly.

"Ah, the virtuous Madame DuBois has returned. No doubt she's frightened once again by the nearness of a male, especially one on the verge of inebriation." He sounded disgusted. "I won't ravish you, if that's your worry." His voice, coming out of the dark, sounded bitter.

His mood was so unlike him that Rianne changed her mind and entered the gazebo after all. "I'm not afraid of you, and I don't believe you'd ravish any woman," she replied calmly as she slipped onto the bench near the opening.

"You have no idea what infractions I'm capable of," he said.

"Which makes a man more guilty, do you suppose—harming someone with malice and deliberation, or failing to prevent an atrocity committed by another?"

She had no idea what the real topic was, but she knew he wasn't making idle chatter. "How can one decide amid so many uncertain areas?" she asked. "For instance, one might say the guilt of a party who deliberately renders harm is unquestionable, but is it always so? Take the matter of self-defense. If one knows that she—*he*—is about to be badly, horribly hurt, doesn't he have the right to protect himself in any manner available? Does that make him more or less guilty? As to the second—why, I would say that, unless the person knew beforehand that a harmful act would occur and didn't act, then he has no reason to feel guilt. His only crime, then, would be that of doing injustice to himself, should he carry such a burden."

Silence fell for several moments. "I'm not sure if that made sense," she said lamely.

Alex sighed. "No. I understood it perfectly. It's you who doesn't understand."

Rianne frowned. He was talking in riddles—had been since his first words—and she sensed he didn't intend to explain. "You're right. I don't."

"How could you?" he asked in a resigned tone. "You know very little of life. You're a lot more naive and innocent than I first surmised. You're probably as full of sweetness and light as I am empty of both."

A sliver of moonlight fell onto him again. He closed his eyes and eased his head against the wall, as if he were unbearably weary.

When he spoke again, his tone was one of resignation. "A man's allowed sweetness and light and happiness only once in his lifetime." He opened his eyes and found her unerringly, though she was still in shadow. "I have no desire to attempt to seek it again. You'd do well to remember that."

She still had no idea of what he was speaking, but the last part sounded like a warning. "Why are you telling me this?"

"Because you've been hurt in the past, and you're still vulnerable. You could be too easily hurt again. You're a young, attractive woman, Rianne, and there's passion lurking within you. I'm sure the man you knew in New Orleans never discovered it."

Ignoring Rianne's gasp, Alex continued to speak. "You kept it from him, didn't you? You tucked it away in that cocoon you wove around yourself." He took another swallow from the bottle, then swiped the back of his hand over his mouth. "Yes, it's still there waiting . . . waiting for the right man, and I—" He saluted her with the bottle "—am definitely not he."

"That's enough! You're making it sound as if . . . as if . . ."

"Yes?" he mocked.

"You're insinuating that I've . . . that I have designs on you. How dare you? And how dare you pass out sympathy and platitudes as if I'm a witless, pitiful female? I'm *not* infatuated with you!" she lied. "On the contrary, I'm quite sure I hate you!"

"Liar. I saw the look in your eyes after I kissed you. I recognized that look. I've been damned careful to avoid it in the past. But since you're now part of my present, I want you to stay the hell away from me!" he said harshly.

Rianne ignored the sudden stab of pain caused by his words. "Gladly! It will be easy, since I'm not a member of your 'majority'! "

"My what?"

"Those poor women who are blind and stupid and . . . and *desperate* enough to invite you into their boudoirs!"

This time his laugh was sincere. Rianne fumed, torn between kicking or slapping him before stomping away.

"Desperate?" he chuckled. "Hell, aren't we all? Sex is a balm, a way to forget the torments lurking in one's mind. I leave those 'poor women,' as you call them, happier and satisfied."

Rianne's anger vanished. Sudden insight told her that

Alex was speaking of his own anguish, she couldn't leave him here to wallow in it alone.

"Oh, yes," she said quietly. "But are you?"

"Happy and satisfied?" He chuckled again. "You really don't know much about men, do you? For a male all it takes is a warm, willing body." He took another swallow from the bottle. "Plenty of those about. A man doesn't have to look very far."

"I see. Then that's why you're sitting here, alone in the dark, with nothing but a bottle of bourbon to keep you company," she scoffed. "I don't believe you, Alex. I think you've chosen your women carefully and deliberately because you're afraid of forming an attachment. That's it, isn't it? Alex Benedict, the great lover, is a coward."

"Don't push, Rianne." His tone held a sharp warning.

Rianne ignored it. "Why not? Afraid I'll uncover your deep, dark secret?" Whatever it was that tormented Alex so, she doubted he'd shared it with anyone. Certainly not Leslie. "Afraid to show the real Alex? The one who's not as fearless and confident as he'd like everyone to believe?"

"I *said,* don't push!"

"Or maybe you're afraid I'll discover that you're nothing more than a man with real emotions that you keep hidden away from the world—and yourself."

"Dammit, Rianne—"

"Maybe you're afraid to let anyone know what you really feel, because if you open yourself up to others, then you open yourself up to more hurt.

"You see, Alex, I know you better than you think, because I see myself in you. For too long, just like you, I've kept my emotions in check. I'm not ashamed to admit that, just like you, I was afraid to let myself feel. The difference is, I'm finally learning that living in the past actually means dying a little more each day. And I've learned that I don't like being a coward. What about you, Alex?"

She jumped at the sudden sound of glass breaking. Alex had thrown the bottle of bourbon across the gazebo, striking the opposite wall. And then he was standing before her, so close she could smell the whiskey and tobacco on his breath.

"If you were a man, I'd kill you for that!"

"If you were a man, you'd admit that everything I've said is the truth."

"Truth! Bloody hell, you want to know the truth? All right, I'll tell you what the truth is. No, I'll show you, dammit!"

Grabbing her hand, Alex pulled her with him as he turned away from the house. Made clumsy by his long, angry strides, Rianne half-stumbled, half-ran behind him, but she didn't protest.

She had no idea where he was taking her; she knew only that she was about to discover the cause of his pain. She needed to know because she desperately wanted to help him, to take some of that pain away, if only he'd let her.

The moon lit the way as Alex led her past the school grounds and up a narrow path leading toward a small copse of trees. She was panting by the time they reached the top of the incline. Rianne gasped when she saw the enclosure, fenced in by beautifully wrought iron. The gate squeaked slightly as Alex pulled her within.

A white crypt stood in the center, guarding the many stones and statuettes surrounding it. Scattered among them were small patches of flowers and shrubs, all neatly laid out, the grass clipped, the stone paths so clean they looked as if they'd just been swept.

Alex's steps widened, and he dragged her behind him, toward an area to the right of the mausoleum. He halted, but kept pulling her forward, until he'd flung her in front of him.

She lost her balance and fell onto her knees—a foot from a gravestone topped by a beautifully carved statue. Rianne looked up and saw that the sculpture was of a mother and child, Madonna-like, and the face of the woman was so gentle, so serene that it brought tears to her eyes.

"You wanted to know," Alex said harshly from above her. "So look, dammit. Look!"

Her gaze fell to the inscription. Rianne's hand flew to her mouth, her gasp loud in the still air.

Mary Ellen Carter Benedict, it read, and the dates *1844—1865.* Beneath it was another name, *James Robert Benedict, Nine Months,* and below that, *Beloved wife and son. Only Angels Rest in Heaven.*

Rianne reached out trembling fingers to trace the grooves of the child's name. "My God!" she whispered. "Oh, my God."

"Now do you understand?" Alex's voice from behind her was harsh and bleak. "She was my wife, Jamie my son. I only saw him—got to hold him—twice. The first time he was five days old. The second time, he was five hours dead. Mary was clutching him in her arms, refusing to release him, even though she was dying, too. Jamie's skull had been fractured, while Mary . . .

"The war was over. General Lee had surrendered a week before. It took me that long to return to Bellesfield. It was late at night when I arrived, but I could see the flames from miles away. I knew it was my home. I damned near killed my horse to get here, but it was too late. Too late for me to do anything. I thought . . . at first I thought everyone had been killed, and I fell to the ground and howled my pain. Is that emotion enough for you, Rianne?"

"Alex . . ."

"God, yes, I cried. And when someone touched my

shoulder, I turned to see Sally, our black housekeeper, and hope returned. Mary Ellen was still alive, she told me. But when Sally led me to her cabin, what I found there was even worse than I could have imagined. My father was laid out on the floor, dead. He'd been shot in his study, trying to save my wife and child from bummers—marauders—the scourge of every army. They didn't give a damn that the war was over. They'd come to Bellesfield with no purpose but to raid and plunder—" Alex's voice fell "—and to rape. Five of them had their turns with Mary. This was after one of them had smashed my son's head against a wall because she'd refused to relinquish him. And then, when they were done, they set fire to Bellesfield and left.

"The bastards left, after destroying everything that meant the world to me." Alex closed his eyes. "I held Mary and Jamie in my arms until she died, an hour after I reached here. One damned hour. If I'd gotten home six hours earlier, they'd still all be alive. My father, my wife . . ." Alex's voice shook. "My son." He fell to his knees, also, and gently brushed his hand across Jamie's name. "My beautiful baby boy," he whispered, his voice cracking.

Rianne's heart broke for him. She wasn't sure he remembered she was there as he knelt, head bowed, lost in his grief.

She couldn't tell if he was praying or crying or simply remembering. She wanted to reach out and touch him, hold him tightly in her arms and comfort him, but she had no right to intrude, so she remained quiet, waiting, silent tears running down her face and dripping onto the earth that covered his loved ones.

After a long time, she heard his ragged sigh.

"Does Leslie know?" she asked in a subdued tone.

"No. She was only a child at the end of the war. She thinks that Father died of a heart attack and that Mary . . . that Mary

Ellen and Jamie died of a disease. That was traumatic enough. Les has never spoken about any of them since. I don't want her to know, do you understand?"

Rianne disagreed. "No, I don't. Leslie's a woman now. She should know the truth." Rianne gentled her tone. "You haven't told her because you couldn't bear to speak of it to anyone before now except, I assume, your Aunt Lorna."

"Yes," he said tersely.

"Oh, God, Alex," Rianne whispered, raising her head to look at him. "I'm sorry. I'm so terribly sorry."

A muscle twitched in his cheek. "Don't cry for me!" he growled.

Rianne swiped at her cheeks. "I'm not crying just for you. I'm crying for me, too. For everything we've both lost." Despite her efforts to control them, her tears kept falling. "And don't . . . don't tell me I can't. My tears are mine to give. You have no right to tell me who I can or can't cry for."

"I don't want or need your damned tears, don't you understand? They mean nothing to me. Nothing! Just as no woman can ever mean anything to me again."

Now Rianne did reach out to touch his sleeve. "Alex, it doesn't have to be that way."

He turned to face her, and Rianne drew back at his fierce expression. "Do I have to prove it to you? Do I?" He didn't wait for a reply but reached out and jerked her forward.

His mouth fell upon hers. His kiss was bruising and harsh as he slanted his lips over hers, uncaring whether she wanted it or not. His tongue forced her mouth open and delved selfishly within. Rianne wrapped her arms around him, letting him know that she would willingly accept this as an expression of his pain.

But as she held him close, he suddenly raised his head, and his eyes glittered down at her. "I could make love to you right here, next to my wife's grave, and it would still mean nothing. Do you understand?" he said harshly, his hands biting into her arms.

That, Rianne decided, was too much. "Stop it, Alex," she demanded, pushing at him.

"Stop? Stop? Why? I'm just getting started." And suddenly she was flat on her back. "Maybe I'm the man to unleash your passion after all. Maybe it's time to see just how many of *your* emotions I can arouse. What do you think, darlin'?"

"No! You can't—" Her protest became a gasp when, to her shock, he shoved his fingers into the neckline of her dress. The sound of ripping fabric was loud in the night. For an instant she froze. But then she slapped at his head. "Let me up! Do you hear me, Alex? Let me go!"

He did, releasing her abruptly and rolling over onto his back. "Now who's the coward?" he asked bitterly. "Were all those brave words mere rhetoric?"

Rianne scrambled to her feet. She glanced down, aghast at her torn bodice. She made an attempt to tuck it into her chemise as she backed away from him.

"Too bad," he said. "I was almost looking forward to sharing some of that happiness and satisfaction."

Rianne turned away and ran toward the gate.

"That's right, darlin', run!" Alex taunted cruelly. "If you know what's good for you, run like the wind!"

She did.

She wanted to slam her bedroom door shut, as if that would keep what had happened tonight at bay, lock out the memory of Alex's words and actions. But it was all burned into her memory, engraved on her heart.

No doubt he thought he'd frightened her away, but she'd fled because she'd been afraid that she would let him make love to her, because she'd desperately wanted to console him, to hold him and absorb his painful memories.

But it wouldn't have been real. She didn't want to become yet another object to him, one of his "majority." She couldn't let herself be that. She wanted him to make love to her because he cared!

Closing her door quietly, Rianne went to the windows. Instead of immediately pulling the curtains together, she stood very still, looking down. Was he still out there, watching her windows, watching *her?* The thought made her skin prickle, not in fear, but in anticipation. She took her time closing the curtains, then went to a rocking chair. Draped over it was a crocheted lap robe, which she wrapped around her arms and upper body before she sank into the seat and began rocking.

So now she knew.

She'd thought Alex a complex man—he could be both gentle and harsh, witty and serious, loving and cynical—but this was the first time he'd revealed his inner self to her. The awful guilt he carried.

How horrible it must have been for him! Was it any wonder that bitter memories haunted him?

His father, his wife. Most terrible of all, his son.

She pictured a little boy—black-haired, green-eyed, laughing as he played on the lawn, hiding in the garden to tease his mother, following his father. Events Alex had never had a chance to experience.

How utterly, utterly tragic.

And how tragic that Alex couldn't find his way to keeping the good memories in his heart and living a full life.

But who was she to judge? True, she had good memories of her parents and her early childhood, but she'd not had as much luck keeping her last memories of New Orleans from intruding upon her present. Still, she was at last making an effort. She was learning to laugh and cry and enjoy life again, while Alex . . .

She'd lived with fears long enough to recognize his. He *was* afraid. But not of memories or ghosts, not even of any living man. Except . . .

Rianne abruptly ceased rocking.

It was *she.* It was *she* he'd been avoiding the last few days, *her* he'd warned away.

My God, she thought, *he's afraid of me!* How ironic! How astonishing!

How *revealing* . . .

A smile spread slowly across her face. Alex was afraid of his feelings for her. Which must mean that he had some regard for her.

If only he knew he was in no danger from her. True, she had discovered she was in love with him, but she realized it could come to nothing. He was still in love with his dead wife, and Rianne had no idea how to compete with any woman, much less a dead one.

But over and above all that, she would be leaving him, and Leslie, soon. He didn't know that yet, of course, but when he did he'd be relieved.

But she was *not* going to deny her love, as she'd done earlier when he'd accused her of being infatuated with him. She wasn't going to flaunt it, but neither would she pretend it didn't exist. She was done with pretending.

She wanted this short time with him. She had only a few weeks to be near him, to hear his drawl, see his mouth curve, watch him walk in his purposeful manner. She even welcomed his anger, for it meant that he wasn't indifferent to her. If he wanted to tease her, he could. If he wanted to swear at her, she'd let him.

She would take everything he did and said, tie it together with an imaginary ribbon, and tuck the memories away for safekeeping, in her heart.

And be grateful she had that much.

Chapter 18

Alex was in a foul mood.

He'd made arrangements to meet Wilcox this morning and tour the fields, but he'd overslept—a rare occurrence. When he finally arrived downstairs, it was only to learn that the farm manager had awaited an hour, then departed.

Alex's stomach rebelled against breakfast, and two cups of black coffee didn't do much to rid him of a throbbing headache.

It had been a long time since he and Kentucky bourbon had been so friendly. A long, long time, he thought ruefully as he walked the path to the barn and stables.

He wasn't sure why last night had been different. He came to Bellesfield every year, sometimes twice a year, but he'd never suffered as deep a spell of melancholy as yesterday's. Memories abounded here. But he'd thought he'd put the past behind him, and he was damned proud of how he'd transformed Bellesfield.

Last night had been disastrous. He didn't know what inclination had urged him to sit in the gazebo, alone except for his bourbon, staring up at Rianne's window, refusing to admit he was in Sara Beld's garden because he knew Rianne preferred it to the rose garden.

He hadn't been willing her to come to him.

But she had, and he'd bared his soul to her, the only person to whom he'd ever related those horrific details. Not even Aunt Lorna knew everything.

But you told Rianne. Why Rianne?

Alex rubbed his aching temples. He really had to get rid of that blasted voice in his head!

"No! Wait! Don't do it! Please don't! Let me down!"

The feminine plea was Rianne's, and she sounded terrified. Alex sped across the lawn, leaping over shrubs and bushes, almost mowing down two students who barely managed to get out of his way.

He barged through the open barn doors panting, eyes blazing with fury, ready to commit murder. "What's going on?" he bellowed. "Where—"

"Oh, *no!*"

Alex slid to a stop in time to see Rianne sail over the back of a horse that was standing perfectly still. She landed on her bottom, looked dazed for a moment, and began laughing. But when she looked up at the horse and realized that it was practically on top of her, she almost fell on her face in her rush to escape, crawling madly on her hands and knees. Her split riding skirt got in her way, and she impatiently hiked it over her knees without even slowing down.

"Oh, my stars! Are you all right, Rianne?" The voice was Leslie's.

Alex hadn't seen his sister because she was standing on the other side of the horse, eyes wide, hand over her mouth. Another saddled horse stood patiently behind her. "What the devil is going on here?" he roared.

Leslie gasped, the horses shifted nervously, and Rianne immediately stopped crawling and glanced back over her shoulder. When she saw him there, she scrambled to her feet and pulled her skirt down. She faced him, her hat askew, looking like a guilty child. "Well, you see . . ."

"It's my fault, Alex." Leslie came around the horse to

stand in front of him. "I was about to give Rianne her first riding lesson. We decided not to use sidesaddles, and when she asked how we were supposed to mount them, I showed her the fastest way." Leslie laced her fingers together and formed a stirrup with her palms. "You know, the way you used to help me. Only I didn't realize that I was putting too much lift into it, and Rianne . . . well, you saw the result."

"What I saw was a woman frightened almost to death of a horse!" Alex yelled. "What were you thinking of, Les?"

"Oh, don't blame Leslie!" Rianne admonished, brushing straw and dirt off her brown riding habit. "I wanted to learn, and overcome a childhood fear. Actually, it was more my mother's fear than mine. Maman absolutely forbade Papa to teach me to ride. He *did* sneak me into the stable a time or two, but by then I'd caught her fear of horses." Rianne laughed. "Poor Papa! He was so disappointed that his only child would never be an equestrienne."

Leslie frowned. "Still, I should have been more careful. I prefer riding astride, but it might have been wiser to chose a sidesaddle for you. Are you sure you're not hurt?"

"Only my pride," Rianne said ruefully. "Stop blaming yourself, Leslie." She glanced at Alex. "And you," she added, "can stop blaming her, too. Falling was my fault. I didn't realize it would be so quick, and I forgot to swing my leg over, like Leslie told me to."

"I felt you going over, but I couldn't prevent it," Leslie said. "When I saw you disappear, I was so astonished, I couldn't move."

"I couldn't either, except to laugh, for I'd expected to end up on her back, not my . . . well, you know."

Leslie snickered. "You moved plenty fast after you looked up and saw Freyja above you."

"I was worried about her hooves. They were only inches

from my face, and Maman said that a horse's kick could kill a person, so I couldn't get away fast enough." Rianne giggled. "I probably looked like a giant crab."

Alex gritted his teeth. Rianne was enjoying a laugh at herself, while he felt like a complete ass. When he'd heard her screaming, he'd assumed that someone was molesting her. His heart was just resuming its normal beat after he'd run to her rescue.

But was she grateful for his concern? Not likely! "You two are completely mad!" he growled.

Rianne and Leslie turned to him, surprise on their faces.

"Alex," Leslie scolded. "Stop overreacting."

"I'm really all right," Rianne added quietly.

Alex snatched his hat off his head and slapped it against his thigh before shoving it back on. "Yes," he said grimly. "I can see that." He about-faced, then just as abruptly turned back. Grasping Rianne about the waist, he swung her up onto Freyja's back, shoved her left foot into the stirrup, then went to the other side of the horse and did the same with her right foot. Gathering the reins, he pushed them into her hands and curled her fingers around them.

"See that she doesn't kill herself," he ordered Leslie. "I may just want that little pleasure for myself one of these days."

Alex marched angrily out of the barn, muttering to himself.

Women! Leslie and Rianne were daft. Leslie was capable of creating trouble on her own, but now she had an accomplice in Rianne.

He was beginning to think he'd made a big mistake by not giving Rianne an extra month's pay and leaving her in Atlanta. He should have done it the morning after he'd kissed her.

Damn! He prided himself on his self-control, yet he'd foolishly given in to temptation.

It had started with that dinner in Atlanta. He'd watched Rianne eating and drinking with her delightful mouth, watched her pink tongue lick her lips, and all he'd been able to think about was whether those lips tasted as delicious, were as invitingly soft, as they looked.

He'd told himself that Rianne wouldn't taste or feel any different than a hundred other women he'd kissed. Then, fool that he was, he'd kissed her anyway.

He wanted to believe that he hadn't planned to do it; he'd been furious that the curious stares of strangers had put her in an anxious mood, and he'd simply wanted to jolt her out of it. He surely hadn't expected her uninhibited response. A slap wouldn't have surprised him. He'd even been prepared for it. What he hadn't anticipated was seeing that look of awed delight on her face. No shock, no anger, no confusion, but adoring sherry eyes, cheeks flushed with excitement, lips moist and rosy from the pressure of his mouth.

A woman could bring a man to his knees with a look like that. She'd work her way under his skin and cause an itch that wouldn't go away.

Well, it wasn't going to happen to him. He'd built up a thick skin over the years to prevent precisely that kind of entanglement. When a woman began gazing at him with more than physical passion in her eyes, he broke off their relationship immediately.

Oh, yes. He'd seen the signs before. Which was why—last night, when Rianne had appeared in the garden—he'd brutally quashed any thoughts she might have had along those lines.

One kiss. Just one little kiss, and the blasted woman believed herself in love with him.

What had happened to the Rianne who had an aversion to him in the beginning? The woman who could barely look at him when she spoke to him?

Why couldn't she have stayed plain Anne? Why'd she have to turn into an alluring female with flashing eyes, a smile that lit up a room, and a sense of humor she didn't mind aiming at herself? God help him!

Leslie and Rianne watched silently until Alex disappeared into the stables.

"Sure was doing a lot of muttering, wasn't he?" Leslie murmured. "Sounded like he was praying, too."

"You mean after he stopped growling?" Rianne replied.

Their gazes locked. They tried to keep straight faces, but soon they were snickering.

"I don't know why I'm finding this amusing," Rianne said, sobering. "Alex doesn't seem to like me very much right now."

"Nor me. I wonder what's made him so grouchy," Leslie mused.

Rianne didn't bother replying because she was pretty sure it was a combination of bourbon and herself.

She bit her lip, hesitating. Should she tell Leslie about what had really happened to Alex's family? No. Even though she strongly believed that Leslie had a right to know, it wasn't her place to tell her. It was Alex's. Here, at Bellesfield, would be the time for him to do so, but whether he would or not remained to be seen. She wasn't going to interfere.

And she wasn't going to let his temper and his moodiness dampen her Grand Adventure, either.

If he was worried that she'd push herself on him romantically, he was worrying in vain. She had no intention of doing so. But she wasn't going to run from him, either. And he was simply going to have to learn to live with that.

Leslie placed her hand on Rianne's knee, effectively breaking into her thoughts. "Do you want to continue with the lesson?" she asked. "I'll understand if you'd rather call it quits."

Rianne grinned down at her. "Of course I'd rather call it quits, but I won't."

"I knew you'd say that. This is going to be fun, my being your teacher. Lesson number one, coming up," Leslie said as she twisted her stirrup around, slipped her foot into it, sprang upwards, and threw her other leg over the saddle. She did it with such ease that Rianne was envious and sure she'd never become so accomplished.

"Twist the stirrup as I did," Leslie explained. "Once your foot is in it and you've grasped the saddle horn, it will rebound and give you the momentum to swing into the saddle." Rianne did so, and was surprised at how easy it was to mount in that manner.

Leslie was a patient teacher, and though Rianne never reached the point of relaxing completely, she began to feel more comfortable on Freyja's back. Freyja was a lovely horse, docile and responsive to the slightest touch on the reins.

But by the time they'd worked their way up to a trot, Rianne was ready to call it a day. "I'm n-n-never going t-to get the h-h-hang of this," she told Leslie as she bounced up and down. "I f-feel like a rub-rubber ball."

"You need to remember to use your stirrups and thighs to stabilize your body," Leslie assured her as she dismounted and held Freyja's reins so Rianne could do the same. "You're really doing quite well. In fact, I think you're ready to venture out of the training arena and the paddock tomorrow."

Rianne slid out of the saddle as she'd seen Leslie do. At least, she thought she did, but when her boots touched the ground, she found that her legs were wobbly. "Oh, dear." She laughed as she clung to the saddle. "I may have to take the crab position again to get back to the house."

"Having trouble, ladies?"

Rianne glanced over her shoulder to find Trevor Williams walking toward them. "Nothing drastic," she assured the Bellesfield teacher after the three of them exchanged greetings. "My legs are simply rebelling from riding."

His hazel eyes twinkled. "Need a hand?" he asked. "I'm on my way to the administrative building right now."

Rianne glanced questioningly at Leslie, who nodded. "Go on. I'll take the horses back to the stables and see you later."

Rianne let go of the saddle and gratefully accepted Trevor's arm. She tottered, regained her balance and leaned against him. "Thank you. Leslie warned me I'd probably be a bit stiff, even though we didn't do much more than walk the horses. I dread to think what I'll feel like after galloping." She laughed.

"You don't ride often?" he asked.

"This was my first time," she admitted as they slowly walked up the stone path. "I hope I recover by tomorrow."

"Walking off the soreness is the best remedy," he assured her. "Which reminds me—are you up to touring the grounds this afternoon?"

"Of course. I—" They heard a jingle of metal, and a huge shadow loomed over them, the heaving sides of a very large horse blocking their way. Rianne stepped back nervously and pressed closer to Trevor as the horse pranced before them.

Rianne's gaze took in the rider's polished black boots and the muscular thighs encased in snug pants. His coat was open and his shirt collar unbuttoned, revealing an expanse of tanned skin and a dark, curly thatch of chest hair.

"Finished with your riding lesson?" Alex asked dryly as he looked down upon them.

Rianne reluctantly tore her gaze from the intriguing view to shade her eyes before glancing up at him. Alex looked angrier than he had earlier. The bruised skin around his eye was turning yellow and orange, while his nose and cheeks were slightly windburned. His hair was disheveled. He looked wildly intimidating.

She didn't let that bother her. "Yes, and now I'm learning to walk again, with Trevor's help," she replied cheekily.

"Mornin', Mr. Benedict," Williams greeted him cheerfully.

The look Alex gave him should have quelled any man, but Trevor was made of stalwart material. He didn't wince or glance away, which won him new respect from Rianne.

"Oh? I was under the impression that you were a mathematics, not a walking, instructor, Mr. Williams," Alex said caustically.

"Yes," Trevor replied, unruffled, "but I'm fortunate to have other talents as well."

Alex's eyes narrowed. Rianne knew that he was deliberating over whether Trevor's words had a hidden meaning, and she felt undercurrents of challenge. She prudently remained silent.

"Most of us do," Alex finally replied. "However, I'm of the belief that it's often . . . *safer* for certain talents to remain untested. Wouldn't you agree?"

Trevor shrugged. "Sometimes. But wouldn't you agree that one should at least make an effort? One might fail yet not lose. On the other hand, one might venture and very well find unexpected gratification. Perhaps even splendor."

"Ah, but therein lies danger as well," Alex shot back, "for the blaze of splendor is short-lived, yet often consumes and destroys. I would be very cautious, Mr. Williams," he added sharply. "Very cautious indeed." With that warning, Alex gave a brief salute, tossed a narrowed glance at Rianne, and spurred his horse.

They watched him ride away, then resumed their walk. "Is there an understanding of some sort between you and Mr. Benedict?" Trevor asked Rianne.

"I'm sorry. What did you say?" she replied absently, having only Alex on her mind. She'd probably *never* understand him. Clearly he'd just warned Trevor off, which was confusing. Last night Alex had made it clear that he wanted nothing to do with her, so why should it matter to him if another man appeared interested in her? And didn't he know that Trevor was engaged to another woman?

Trevor repeated his question and Rianne shook her head in response. "Hardly," she told him. "In fact, we seem to clash more often than not."

"Then his behavior is most odd. It's obvious he retains a certain possessive attitude in regard to you."

"Isn't that interesting?" she replied.

It became even more interesting over the next several days.

For a man who'd told her to keep away from him, Alex kept appearing in Rianne's vicinity.

She strolled in the gardens with Trevor most evenings and found the young man intelligent, charming, and fun. She'd never had a male friend before, and it was a delightful new experience for her.

But each evening Alex stood on the verandah, smoking as he watched her and Trevor leave for their walk. Sometimes she'd catch his green gaze focused on her at dinnertime, too. Once, when the ladies were having coffee in Sara's sunroom, Rianne had glanced up to find Alex hovering in the doorway, watching her and little Josie, who sat in her lap, as they played pat-a-cake.

Though Rianne tried to pretend this odd behavior didn't bother her, she was slightly unnerved. Alex never specifically sought her out, never spoke to her in private. If he didn't want her attention, what *did* he want from her, for heaven's sake?

It was with some relief that she heard him announce at dinner one evening that he was riding to Atlanta on business the next morning for a day or two. Rianne felt as if she'd finally be able to breathe normally again.

The next day, after he'd left, visitors arrived at Bellesfield. It was a large party from a neighboring plantation, and Leslie was delighted to learn that among them was a young woman who'd been an old friend of hers.

"You could have knocked me over with a feather when Uncle told me that Alex had come to visit and brought you with him," Winifred Lewis told Leslie. "So, naturally I wanted to bring my fiancé and our friends to meet you."

"Wonderful! But first let me introduce *my* very dear friend to you," she said, pulling Rianne to her side.

Introductions were soon complete, and Sara ordered refreshments for all, then left the younger group to enjoy themselves.

It turned out that Winnie and her betrothed, David Griffin, had already had one engagement party in Atlanta, where she lived with her widowed mother. But her uncle had insisted on giving her a second party at his plantation so that he could invite his neighbors and friends. Since Winnie was his only heir and genuinely fond of him, she'd readily agreed.

"Uncle George had no idea what he'd gotten himself into, of course. We all descended on him like a swarm of locusts," she explained, laughing. "That's one of the reasons I dragged everyone over here with me. The poor dear will be able to sit in his battered old chair and take his nap in peace today. But tell me about yourself, Leslie. I know you've been living in Boston, but what have you been doing with yourself?"

Rianne left Leslie and Winnie to their chat, happy for Leslie. How difficult it must have been for her to leave her home and friends to live among strangers.

Then she smiled to herself. Wasn't that exactly what she'd done? How lucky for her that she and Leslie had become friends. If they hadn't, she would still be alone.

Rianne moved about the room, checking trays and pitchers and coffee servers and occasionally stopping to chat with someone. It was easy, since this was a friendly, laughing group.

"Excusez-moi. Je comprends que vous parlez français, mademoiselle."

Rianne turned to find a young man smiling at her hopefully. He was about her age, with dark, slicked-back hair, a small, dapper mustache, and earnest hazel eyes. *"Oui,"* she replied, smiling. "*Je parle français.* I speak French. How did you know?"

"Winnie's friend, Les-lie, tells me so when she and I are met. Winnie's fiancé, David, is *mon ami*—my friend. *C'est bon!* I would be most grateful if you allow me to—how do you say?—exercise my English with you."

"You wish to practice your English?"

"*Oui.* Prac-teez. I prac-teez on Paul"—he nodded toward another young man who was speaking to Leslie—"as we are zee traveling companions. But eet eez always good to prac-teez on *une femme charmante, oui?*"

Rianne laughed. "May I assume that your object is to *charm* women, rather than practice speaking to one?"

"Ah!" Jules tossed his hands in the air. "You understand!"

"Perfectly, Monsieur—?"

"Jules Lazar. Jules, please."

"Jules. Yes, we will speak in English so that you may practice. But you must call me Rianne."

"*Étonnant!* And you are from Boston, also?"

"Yes. That is, I've been living there for some years, though I was born in New Orleans."

His eyes lit up. "Ah! Paul and I are there next month." He asked eager questions about New Orleans. Knowing no other way to explain her woeful lack of knowledge, she told him that she'd left the city as a young girl. He accepted that, and they went on to have pleasant conversation until his friend, Paul, came to tell him that they were preparing to leave.

Jules rose, and Rianne offered her hand. "It was very nice to meet you, Jules. I hope you have a wonderful time in New Orleans."

"Ah, but this is not *adieu,* Rianne! I shall see you tomorrow evening."

"Tomorrow? I don't understand."

"Did you not know that one of zee reasons Winnie came was to invite Leslie and Monsieur and Madame Beld to her engagement party?"

"No, I didn't."

"But of course you have been invited, also. So you see, we shall see one another again, and we shall dance, *oui?*"

Jules was a friendly, charming young man, and she didn't want to dampen his eagerness, but she doubted that she'd be dancing. So she simply smiled and replied noncommittally, "Perhaps."

Chapter 19

"Oh, my! I think I'm going to be sick."

"Is it something you ate at dinner?" Leslie asked, alarmed.

"No. It's something I've put on—this new *me!*" Rianne spun about on the dressing table stool and looked at Leslie with a woeful expression. "I don't think I can do this, Leslie. My hands are shaking. My stomach is churning. I really *am* going to be sick."

"No, you're not. Why, you look beautiful! Heavens, Rianne, surely you've seen yourself dressed like this before."

"No. Never."

Leslie's jaw fell. "I don't understand. You're five years older than I am. Didn't you have a debut? I thought all French girls in New Orleans had debuts and went to parties and the opera and—"

"I didn't. I've never done any of those things."

"Oh, you poor girl," Leslie said sympathetically. "You haven't had a very happy life, have you?"

"Oh, please, don't pity me. I had the most loving parents any girl could hope for. Unfortunately, they both died too soon, and I lived a very secluded life after that, so I suppose I'm somewhat backward in social experience—which is why I'm so terrified now," Rianne admitted with a wan smile.

"But you've fit right in at Bellesfield, and yesterday afternoon you seemed comfortable with Winnie and her friends."

"Yes, but this is the first formal event I'll be attending as *myself.*" For years she'd worn Madame DuBois like a protective cloak, and now that she'd shed it, she had nothing beneath which to hide. She was such a coward! She wished she could be more like Leslie, full of confidence and socially adept.

What if everyone found her gauche? What if everyone stared at her pityingly? Rianne felt as if she were suffocating.

"I'll get you some water," Leslie said, concerned about Rianne's paleness. But when she went to the pitcher, she found it empty.

"I used it to water the flowers in the pot by my window," Rianne explained.

"I'll run into my room. I have some. In the meantime, take deep breaths," Leslie advised as she left.

"Deep breaths. Yes," Rianne muttered to herself. Really, she was being ridiculous. She'd stood up to big, bad men. She'd overcome her fear of horses. Well, almost. Surely she could face a crowded ballroom without panicking. She wouldn't even know most of the guests, so she had no reason to feel this apprehensive.

Then she recalled Leslie's birthday party—and what a fiasco that had been.

Leslie slipped back into the room and handed Rianne a full glass of water. She quickly gulped half of it down, then wished she hadn't when her stomach cramped.

"Feel better?" Leslie asked.

"No. I think I feel worse."

Leslie was amazed. She was having a difficult time reconciling this terrified woman to the calm, composed teacher she'd known for years. Still, Rianne's life had been nothing like her own very social one.

Something Rianne would never have if she didn't overcome her fear. Making up her mind, Leslie took her hand and pulled her to her feet. "I want to show you something." Leslie led Rianne to a full-length mirror and pushed her forward to stand before it. "You only took a quick glance before. What do you see now?"

"I see two—"

Leslie stepped aside. "No, look at only *yourself.* What do you see?"

Rianne stared at the reflection of the young woman in the mirror. She was wearing a fashionable evening gown of bronze Chambéry gauze and silk, its hem and back pleat trimmed with appliqué embroidery of roses—which she didn't mind, since they had no scent. The square neckline set off her shoulders and bosom nicely, and the color gave a glow to her skin. Well, there was certainly nothing wrong with the gown. It was the most beautiful one she'd ever owned.

Rianne scrutinized her hair. It was dressed in a sophisticated style, with curls pinned up at her crown and falling to her nape. She lowered her gaze to study her face. "Oh! Oh, no!" she said in a voice of dread.

"What is it?" Leslie asked, alarmed.

Rianne pointed to herself in the mirror. "I can't—I can't wear this dress," she choked, and then, to Leslie's astonishment, she began giggling.

Leslie stood frozen in consternation, wondering if Rianne was having hysterics. "Why not?" she asked cautiously. "It's absolutely gorgeous and it looks wonderful on you."

Rianne spun about to face her, still laughing. "I know. But it doesn't—it doesn't—" she sputtered. "It doesn't match my green face!" she chortled.

When Leslie finally caught on, she began laughing, too. Soon they were clasping hands and hopping up and down as they whirled about the room, laughing uproariously the entire time.

"You did look dreadful for a while," Leslie finally managed. "Your face was something like a lime. Oh, Rianne! I'm so glad you're here. You're so much fun to be with!"

"I am?"

Leslie leaned over to give Rianne a hug. "Yes, you are. This is wonderful! It's like having the sister I've always wanted."

Startled at this unexpected display of affection, Rianne almost pulled back. But Leslie was squeezing her too tightly and, well, it felt nice! She returned Leslie's affection with a tentative squeeze, unable to reply, choked up with emotion. The last person who had hugged her was Mimsie, and that was ages ago.

Alex had embraced her, yes, but it hadn't been genuine, so it didn't count.

Releasing Leslie, Rianne said, grinning, "At least this time Alex won't be around to see me make a fool of myself."

"You won't," Leslie told her firmly. "Just be yourself, relax and have fun. You'll do fine."

Rianne did better than fine.

From the moment she, in her russet gown, and Leslie in her ice-blue one, followed the Belds through the doorway into the ballroom, all eyes turned toward them. Rianne had one panicky moment when she considered fleeing, but before she could put the thought into action, she and Leslie were surrounded by several young men, all speaking together as they rushed to introduce themselves.

Taken aback, Rianne merely smiled, murmured her name in response, and nodded at dance requests as she and Leslie were hustled forward into the room. Shortly both women had glasses of Champagne in their hands as the men teased and flattered, vying for attention as they good-naturedly elbowed one another aside. Overwhelmed and wary at first, Rianne soon realized that these men weren't giving her sly looks or smirking behind their hands. They were simply young, enthusiastic and charming. She found herself relaxing, joining in the conversation and laughter.

"*Bonsoir,* Rianne!"

She turned to find Jules Lazar behind her. "Good evening, Jules. How nice to see you again."

Taking her hand, he bent to kiss her gloved knuckles, then grasped her other hand and stood back to appraise her. *"Je suis étonné!"* he exclaimed.

"What is it?" Rianne asked worriedly, wondering why he should be stunned. "Is something wrong with my gown?"

"Non, non!" He hastened to assure her. "Eet eez magnificent, as are you. The gown matches your wonderful eyes. I only meant that I am overwhelmed by your beauty, Rianne."

She blushed. "Leslie's beautiful. I'm ordinary," she said earnestly.

Jules was taken aback that she had no appreciation of her own appearance.

"Did I not explain that I am a connoisseur of woman? To be a connoisseur, one has to be most observant. Trust me. Mademoiselle Leslie is *une beauté classique*—a classical beauty—and a perfect white rose. You are *la belle papillonne*—illusive, tantalizing, and *vivant*—alive—with color."

Rianne fanned her cheeks, now warm with pleasure. "Goodness, Jules! I do believe you were only jesting when you claimed to be practicing your English, for your understanding of the language is exceptional. That's the nicest thing anyone has ever said to me." *Ha, so much for you, Alex Benedict!* she thought. "I don't know what to say in reply," she told him.

He studied her for a moment, then smiled. "You were born in New Orleans, *oui?*"

"Yes."

"Then you must do what all Southern belles do. You flutter your eyelashes and simper."

She laughed. "I'm afraid I don't know how to do either."

"Then you have only to smile. Eet will be enough to bring any man to his knees."

"Why, Jules, ah do believe ya'll are trying to charm me through flattery," she drawled.

Goodness! Where had that come from? She'd slipped into the slow, Southern articulation as naturally as if she'd never spoken with a Bostonian accent.

"But of course," he replied with a broad smile. "Now give to me your dance card, *s'il vous plaît.*"

The evening became a kaleidoscope of colorful, whirling gowns, an euphony of music and voices and laughter. Rianne and Leslie barely had time to catch their breath between dances. When they weren't dancing, they were surrounded by a bevy of eligible young men.

Rianne was having a wonderful time. She danced every dance, practiced flirting, and drank Champagne. If anyone had told her only hours ago, when she was racked with anxiety, that she—and Leslie, of course—would be the belles of the ball, she wouldn't have believed it.

Jules and Paul claimed her and Leslie for the late buffet, and afterward the four of them strolled through the gardens along with a number of other couples. Jules let it slip that he was a marquis, while Paul was the son of an English duke. They swore the women to secrecy, for after Winnie and David's wedding they planned to travel incognito for several months before returning to their separate homes to devote themselves to familial duty. They were intent on experiencing America without being pressured by social obligations.

"Ah, *oui.* Without *mamans* fleeing after us to catch us for their *jeune filles,*" Jules explained.

" 'Fleeing?' " Leslie asked.

"He means *chasing,*" Paul explained.

The four of them shared a laugh, and an enjoyable half hour together until the musical sounds of the orchestra again floated out the open verandah doors.

"Ah," Paul said, "the dancing is about to resume."

"So it is," Leslie agreed. "Well, come along then, Paul."

Linking her arm with his, she pulled him in the direction of the house. "I believe that little Mr. Jones is waiting for me, and you are to dance with his sister."

"Is she the tiny brunette whose head barely reaches my elbow?" Paul asked. "Gads, Leslie, it will be like dancing with my baby sister." Their voices faded as they disappeared along the path, as other couples were doing.

Rianne and Jules followed, but just before they reached the house, he slapped a palm to his forehead. "Oh, la la!" he exclaimed. "I suddenly remember that I am promised to that petite blonde with the bright blue eyes for this dance. Do you also have a partner, Rianne? Shall I escort you inside?"

"I believe I left the two dances after supper open, Jules, so I'll stay out here for a while. Even though it's cloudy, it's a beautiful night."

"You will be safe?"

"Of course," she laughed. "Ah do thank you for your concern, suh," she drawled as she curtsied gracefully, "but ah shall be perfectly safe out here by my li'l ol' self."

Jules clasped his hand over his chest. "Ah, zat accent! You do not know what it does to my heart," he teased. "I shall see you later, *oui?*"

"Oui." Rianne watched Jules enter the ballroom before she turned back to lean over the rail. Everyone else had disappeared inside, too, and she had the verandah to herself.

What a darling Jules was—attentive, flirtatious, and casual about it all. She had no romantic interest in him, nor, she was sure, he in her. He treated Leslie in the same manner. Still, it was nice to be admired by someone of the opposite sex.

As much as she liked Jules, however, it was pleasant to have a few moments alone. The better to savor her success. Heavens, what a surprising night this had turned out to be! She'd never expected to be quite so popular. It was all a bit overwhelming.

Deliciously so.

Humming to herself, Rianne whirled about the verandah in time to the music drifting from the ballroom. Then she skipped down the steps to the gardens.

Alex slipped into the crowded ballroom unnoticed. Standing next to the doorway, he searched the room for his sister. Since she stood taller than most women and had striking black hair, spotting her didn't take long. He smiled when he saw that her dance partner was four inches shorter than she. Still, Les was laughing, having a good time.

He scanned the room again, searching for Rianne, but he couldn't see her. She had to be in here somewhere. Perhaps near the far wall with that group of matronly ladies who were plainly keeping an eye on their charges.

Good. That was exactly where she should be, watching over Les. She had nothing else to do, since that insolent pup, Trevor Williams, wasn't hovering over her tonight.

Alex hadn't known about this engagement party until he'd returned to Bellesfield two hours ago and discovered that the Belds, Les, and Rianne had all been invited to Piney Woods. Some of the staff, including Williams, had gone to Atlanta for the weekend.

The only reason he was making an appearance here himself tonight was because George Lewis and his own father had been friends from boyhood. He intended to pay his respects, congratulate the bride-to-be, and leave. He didn't plan on dancing or socializing.

That was, not if he could prevent it. Already feminine glances were being aimed his way. George wasn't anywhere in sight. He and some of his cronies were probably tucked away in his study playing poker, no doubt.

Accepting a glass of Champagne from a passing waiter—he would have preferred a brandy, but that would have to wait—he edged around the periphery of the room rather than cross through the crowd. He'd go out the French doors to the verandah and enter the study from outside. No simpering little misses or predatory mamas would detain him.

From across the room, Sara Beld spotted him and waved. He acknowledged her with a nod and took a quick look to see if Rianne was with her. She wasn't, but Alex was confident she was somewhere in the ballroom. Despite her sometimes impertinent behavior, Rianne took her responsibilities seriously, and she would see to it that Leslie didn't get into any situation that might damage her reputation.

Too bad Rianne wasn't as smart about men. If she were, he wouldn't have to feel as responsible for her, nor keep a wary eye on Trevor Williams. The Bellesfield teacher had better not be playing with Rianne's feelings since he was already spoken for. Alex didn't want Rianne hurt and he was afraid she was already becoming too attached to the instructor.

Which was odd, Alex thought as he slipped out the French doors onto the verandah, since he'd been certain that she'd formed an attachment to *him.*

Could he possibly have been mistaken? She certainly didn't act like a woman infatuated. Though she hadn't made any effort to avoid him, she hadn't approached him again, either, since that night in the garden. In truth, she was doing a fine job of ignoring him.

He knew she was aware of him. Often, when he glanced in her direction, he'd catch her gaze on him, but that gaze was usually calm and considering rather than soulful, as might be expected from a woman in love. It was impossible to read what she was thinking.

Devil take it! What man ever understood a woman fully? What man wanted to? Women were creatures to be admired, appreciated, and made love to. He had no desire to delve into their minds or touch their hearts, and he refused to let his own be stirred.

He'd given his heart once.

He and Mary Ellen had practically grown up together, for she had been the only daughter of a neighboring planter. Then the Conflict had come, and Georgia seceded from the Union. Alex had been bound by honor and duty to join a cavalry unit, and so the wedding was expedited.

Mary Ellen had been only sixteen, he had just turned twenty.

They'd shared one brief week as husband and wife, had been able to snatch only a day or two together in the terrible years that followed.

The last time he'd made love to his wife had been almost a year before Appomattox, when he'd managed a leave and returned to Bellesfield for a brief visit.

The last time he'd held her in his arms had been as she lay dying, her slight body horribly bruised and ravaged.

Alex made a sound of disgust, angry at himself for feeling once again the helplessness and the pain.

It came upon him at times like this, when he least expected it. He didn't want to remember. He wanted forgetfulness. He wanted peace and laughter and the occasional warmth of a woman's body to keep the shadows at bay.

Alex turned and it was then that he heard humming and realized he wasn't alone.

Stepping to the verandah rail, he peered below and saw someone at the entrance to the garden path. The hurricane lamp emitted enough light to see that her gown was of a golden hue. It glimmered and gleamed as she whirled and turned. She was slim, and her graceful movements told him that she was young.

But not too young, he decided with satisfaction when he heard her soft, throaty laugh. She was no ingenue, certainly, or she'd never be alone in the garden. Was she waiting for her lover to make an appearance? Or could she be waiting for *any* man to come along? If that were the case, it was an auspicious opportunity for him.

Well, there was only one way to find out.

Setting his glass atop the rail, Alex walked to the steps leading down to the garden.

Chapter 20

"A beautiful woman should never have to dance alone."

Rianne spun about, tottering on her heels and almost losing her balance. A man stood above her, on the verandah, his tall form silhouetted by the light pouring out of the ballroom behind him.

So Jules had returned. She laughed softly. "Then by all means, suh, come and dance with li'l ol' me," she teased him.

He walked down the steps towards her. "No man could resist a request so sweetly voiced. It will be my pleasure."

It was Alex, not Jules! Rianne gasped and stepped back. Unfortunately, she backed right into the hurricane lamp, knocking it off its stand. It sputtered once, then went out, leaving her standing in darkness. "Oh, no!" she exclaimed.

"You have no need to be frightened," he said soothingly as he reached her side. "I promise I'm perfectly safe—unless, of course, you don't want me to be."

Rianne forgot the lamp as she wondered how she was supposed to respond to his light, flirting tone. Did it mean he was no longer angry with her? Or was he merely baiting her before shooting hurtful arrows at her once again?

Apparently he interpreted her silence as wariness, for he held out his hand as if to a frightened animal. "I promise I'm neither a figment of your imagination nor a ghost. Here, touch me. You'll see that I'm warm and living flesh."

Without volition, Rianne brushed his palm with the tips of her fingers.

"You see?" he said. Then his fingers curled around hers. "I fear that you, on the other hand, may be an angel, sent here to wreak havoc on mortal man."

"An angel—" Rianne broke off, confused. Did he know who she was? "Do I know you?" she asked tentatively, almost holding her breath.

"Not yet," he replied enigmatically, and she thought she saw his mouth curl in the dark.

"Not yet," she repeated lamely, breathlessly.

"Exactly," he replied with assurance. "We've not met, for I most certainly would have remembered."

So he really didn't know! Rianne choked back a giggle, but she couldn't prevent her lips from curving. She was almost tempted to tell him, just to see if she could deflate that cool confidence.

"I do, however," he continued, "intend that we should become better acquainted . . . much better." He executed a low bow. "Alex Benedict, at your service. And you, beautiful lady, are . . ."

Rianne flipped open her fan and held it over the lower half of her face. "Most definitely not an angel," she replied evasively. Goodness! Was this the way he introduced himself to all women?

"Then you must be a princess. Which is it to be, angel or princess?"

Oh, *really!* If he knew who she was, he'd call her a witch, no doubt. Or worse. "Whichever you choose, suh." This time Rianne purposely used her soft drawl, interested to see how far he'd carry this flirtation. "Though why you believe me to be either eludes me, since ah doubt you're able to tell what ah look like."

"Just before the lamp went out I saw a pure profile, and a mouth that curves enticingly."

Rianne knew he couldn't have seen much more than her silhouette! Jules and the others had practiced their male flattery on her and Leslie, and every other young woman in sight, but they had been mere amateurs compared to Alex. Did he flatter all women in this suave manner? He certainly hadn't done so with "Anne," and he'd probably swallow his tongue if he knew that he was speaking to *Ri*anne. She suppressed a chuckle at the thought. "Suh . . ."

"Alex."

"Suh," she repeated, trying to sound affronted, "you are much too forward."

"Why doesn't your tone sound convincing?"

She couldn't prevent the small laugh that escaped. "Ah'll try to do better next time," she retorted.

"Next time? That sounds promising."

"Ah beg your pardon?"

"Where do you come from?"

"Oh! Uh . . . Atlanta," she improvised.

"Is that your home?"

"Yes. *No!* That is, not permanently. I'm visiting, uh, friends for a time before traveling with them after Winnie's wedding."

"What's the family name of your friends? Perhaps I'm acquainted with them, too."

"Oh, I . . . I'm sure you're not," Rianne hedged.

"Ah," he said simply.

But a wealth of satisfaction tinged his voice, and Rianne wanted to smack him for it—and for always shooting challenges at her while giving her no time to think. "You ask far too many questions, suh. What's your purpose?"

"My purpose is to determine how much time we have."

"Time for what?"

"To become better acquainted."

"What makes you think I wish to become better acquainted with you?"

"You will," he responded confidently.

Rianne didn't know whether to laugh or kick him. Once more, he was the cocky, arrogant male.

"Since time is short, we shouldn't waste it, should we?" he suggested, and before Rianne realized what he was up to, he reached out and grasped her waist to draw her toward him.

"What are you doing?" she cried, jerking back.

His hands tightened. "As I said earlier, a beautiful woman should never dance alone, so I'm about to dance with you."

"The usual practice is for the gentleman to *ask,*" she protested.

He grinned down at her, unabashed. "I should confess that I'm not always a perfect gentleman. I prefer to take, and not ask, when I see something—or someone—I want."

With such limited experience, Rianne had no idea how to reply to his brash assurance. Then she recalled Jules's advice: "Just flutter your eyelashes and simper." The simpering seemed too childish, and she'd never fluttered her lashes at anyone before, but there was always a first time.

Rianne lifted her face and blinked several times in quick succession. "You are too bold, Mr. Benedict," she said coyly.

Alex stared, mesmerized, wondering what was wrong with the woman's eyes. Did she have some kind of strange affliction? For all he knew she was cross-eyed, too. All he'd really seen was her profile.

No matter. Women almost all felt alike in the dark. He liked this one's throaty, seductive voice. And she hadn't slapped him or stormed away, offended. She was, in fact, flirting back. A woman of experience. But if she wanted to pretend otherwise, he was willing to play along. With women, everything was a game, wasn't it?

He stepped back and bowed deeply. "Well, then, ma'am, may I have the honor of this dance?"

Rianne debated. It *was* only a dance, after all, and chances were, she'd never have this opportunity again to make up for their aborted waltz at Leslie's party. "Yes, you may, Mr. Benedict." She closed the fan, letting it dangle from her wrist.

His voice was a whisper in her ear as he drew her into his arms. "Listen to the music, angel, and relax," he told her when he felt her stiffen slightly.

Heavens, he was holding her much closer than was proper. Almost as close as when he'd kissed her . . .

He swung her into a wide step. "I promise you'll enjoy it."

She followed his lead, finding it hard to resist his smooth, seductive tone.

Seductive? Rianne missed a step. Oh, the rascal! That was exactly what he was trying to do: seduce her. Of course, he was a master at it. How many women had succumbed to his allure? How large was his "majority"?

Well, she couldn't let herself become one of them, but why not play his game for a while? She'd learned the art of flirting tonight. It would be interesting to see how Alex responded to her new-found abilities.

It would also give her another memory to tuck away in her heart.

She was taking a chance, of course. He'd be furious if he discovered who she was, but what could he really do? In a short time she'd be leaving anyway.

If he discovered her, she could claim that she'd wanted a bit of harmless revenge, and he'd have to grit his teeth and endure it, as she'd had to do with all his past sarcasm and condescension.

"Did I hear a small sigh?" Alex asked into her ear. "Are you not enjoying yourself?"

"Yes," she replied, raising her head. "Ah'm simply enjoying, as you requested."

"The dance? Or your partner?"

"Ah've never danced in a garden before. Even without a moon, it's exhilarating."

"And your partner?" he prompted.

"My partner is also . . . exhilarating," she said with deliberate breathlessness.

"Ah," he sighed. "Very good. We're making progress."

"Oh? Toward what end?"

"Toward an interesting interlude," he replied.

Rianne fell silent as she mentally debated the meaning of his words. Was he speaking of a flirtation?

Well, of course he was! Surely no man, not even Alex, would be so bold as to mean anything more, especially with a woman he'd just met.

Or thought he had.

"You've become very quiet," Alex said, breaking into her reverie.

"Ah'm considering your last statement," she replied honestly.

The waltz came to an end and Alex's hand, holding hers, slipped to her waist. He laughed and swung her about, forcing her to clutch his biceps. A beam of light from the salon fell onto his face. His eyes gleamed, and his teeth flashed as he looked down at her.

"Just say you'll spend the next few hours with me."

Oh, yes! Forever! Rianne thought dreamily. "It's not possible," she whispered reluctantly.

"Ah, but your tone belies your words. Perhaps a little more coaxing is in order." His head lowered until his mouth was mere inches from hers.

As before, Rianne was mesmerized by his voice and stared at his mouth as it lowered closer, closer . . .

This time, however, she wasn't taken unawares. This time, she knew what to expect.

Or so she thought.

The heated passion of his mouth thrilled her to her toes. It was such a wonderfully expressive mouth, promising untold wonders and secrets she could only guess at.

A hand slipped to her nape, another pressed her closer, so close that she could feel his heart beating against her own. Hers was thumping madly, but his beat slow and steadily.

She frowned in realization. The kiss had meant nothing to him.

What would it take to make him *feel* something? Angry, frustrated, Rianne lifted her arms to circle his neck and clutch him tightly. Without being asked, she opened her mouth to him and was both shocked and gratified when her tongue tangled with his. She pressed closer, desperate to make him feel what she felt.

Suddenly his mouth pulled away from hers. "What the hell . . . ?" she heard him exclaim, but she still clung tightly.

"What the bloody hell?" he repeated, and he reached up to pull her arms away from him and drag her into the light coming from the ballroom doors. "Rianne?" he asked incredulously. "What the devil do you think you're doing?"

She blinked and came back down to earth. "Kissing you?" she ventured.

"What kind of game are you playing?"

"Yours," she replied calmly. "As I recall, you started this."

"I didn't know who you were until we were already kissing, and I—" He broke off, as if he had been about to reveal something. "But you knew damned well who I was. Didn't it occur to you that, had I known, we never would have kissed?"

That stung, but she wasn't going to let him know that. "Truthfully? No."

"No?" He was taken aback by her answer and considered it for a moment. "Why not?" he asked.

"Why should I think that?" she retorted. "After all, by your own admission, you kiss many women. Unless, of course, the majority of 'the majority' don't enjoy your kisses." She shrugged casually. "Which wouldn't surprise me. You lack a certain . . . *finesse*." She forced a small, careless laugh through her lips.

"No woman's complained before," he bit out, vexed.

"Apparently they lacked the courage to be honest with you. Too bad. Had they not, you'd likely be much better at kissing."

"Better? No finesse?" he muttered. "Just what is it about my kisses that you find lacking?" he snapped.

"Well, you attack instead of wooing. A bit of gentleness can work wonders. You should practice it."

"I see. You're experienced at this sort of game, then?"

Rianne smoothed her skirt nonchalantly. "I've had my share of kisses," she said, not exactly lying. After all, Alex had kissed her twice.

"That's good. That's very good," Alex replied smoothly, causing her to glance up at him in surprise.

"It is?"

"Certainly. Since you're an expert, and you claim I'm not, I'd be a fool to let this opportunity slip away."

"Opportunity? Opportunity for what?"

His teeth flashed in a grin. "What do you think?" He took a step toward her. "You did insinuate that I needed tutoring, didn't you?" He took another step.

"I didn't mean . . . I didn't say . . . Stop!" Rianne edged backward. He followed. "I said *stop,* Alex!" He continued stalking her. "Now, really . . . Ohhh!"

He'd scooped her up in his arms and carried her down the path to a bench illuminated by another lamppost.

She wriggled and flailed, but to no avail. "Put me down, Alex!"

He didn't reply but went directly to the bench and slid onto it. Rianne immediately tried to squirm off his lap, but his arms were wrapped tightly around her waist. When she tried batting at his chest, he merely captured her wrists in one of his big hands.

"May as well give in," he said, chuckling.

She stilled, knowing resistance was fruitless. "What are you going to do?" she asked apprehensively.

"Why, practice, darlin'. Practice."

Rianne knew she could probably kick his shin. Or maybe clip his chin with the top of her head. She could even scream.

But she didn't do any of those things. Instead, she stared up at him expectantly.

"Someone ought to tell you that you should never look at a man that way unless you want to be kissed," Alex said as he stared into her eyes.

Her only response was a slow, challenging smile.

Alex's eyes narrowed. Releasing her hands—which she let lie in her lap—he brushed the tips of his fingers across her lips. "You have the softest mouth," he murmured. "Hard to resist."

He held her with a penetrating gaze as his fingers caressed her cheek, then moved down to follow the line of her jaw, circle her ear, then brush across her other cheek and trailed back to her mouth.

"Yes, indeed," he whispered. "Very kissable skin, too."

Something in his tone aroused Rianne's suspicions. Was he ridiculing her again? She opened her mouth to ask, but he leaned over her, his face but inches away.

Her "kissable" skin was prickling with awareness, her heart racing once again with anticipation. She parted her lips willingly.

Alex kissed the corner of her mouth, but when she turned toward him, his lips moved to her cheek, then proceeded to follow the same path his fingers had just taken.

He barely touched her, only skimming over her heated skin, his warm breath tickling, causing goose bumps to rise on her arms, and then his face was pressed against her neck and he was using his lips and his teeth to nibble on the sensitive area beneath her ear.

"How am I doing?" his amused voice whispered.

"You . . . I . . . Well, it's a decent start," she gasped.

"Hmm. Think it's time to move on to the next lesson?"

"I once knew a man," she volunteered in distraction, "who kissed my nose." It was her father, of course, but Alex didn't have to know that.

"Your nose, eh? It's a charming nose, but I think I can do better." And to her mingled shock and pleasure, he traced the edge of her low neckline with his tongue.

So many thrilling sensations were assaulting her that she could barely take them all in. "Alex!" she pleaded.

"Yes? Something wrong?"

Oh, the devil! He knew exactly what he was doing to her. "I thought," she said weakly, "that this was supposed to be a lesson in kissing. You haven't come close to taking your final test." As she'd hoped, her impudence spurred him on. His tongue trailed up her neck and over her chin.

"I'm getting there," Alex murmured just before he arrived

at her mouth. Still, he didn't kiss her immediately. His tongue tantalized and teased, until Rianne was ready to scream.

"You should . . . know something . . . about teachers," she panted.

"Oh? What's that?"

"Not all of them are patient," she told him. Then she reached up to grab his lapels and pull him closer. She sighed in relief and pleasure as his lips slid into place over hers. *Finally!*

Within seconds the kiss turned into a frenzied contest of pure sensual greed. He crooked his head one way; she crooked hers the other way. His mouth slanted over hers in one direction; she slanted hers in another, both of them wanting all the other had to offer, neither of them wanting it to stop.

It didn't, but Alex gentled his kiss. Perhaps because he needed to breathe, as did she.

It was no less exhilarating, however. To Rianne, this tender, soothing caress was even more arousing.

She dropped her hands to press them against his solid chest. Beneath her palms, his heart was now beating as rapidly as hers.

Well, this was more like it! she thought dreamily. She had no doubt that he was as moved as she was, and it was she who had accomplished it.

She murmured a soft protest when Alex finally broke away, but her protest turned into a sigh of startled pleasure when he nestled his face into the cleft between her breasts. His hands slid from her back up to her shoulders, then over, pushing the straps of her gown down and lowering its front.

Rianne gasped and stiffened as her gown slipped to her waist. For a moment, she felt a flash of fear—a memory of other hands, grasping, squeezing, digging cruelly into her flesh . . .

"It's all right, darlin'," Alex murmured against her skin.

And then his warm, big hands gently brushed over her sensitive breasts. Fear was replaced with aching pleasure, and her nipples responded by puckering in invitation. Her hands were in his hair, and she was pulling him closer and sighing, "Yes! Oh, *yes*."

Her head fell back as she offered herself to Alex. She moaned in pleasure as he nibbled and suckled one breast through her thin chemise while his free hand cupped and molded the other.

There were no words, only sensation and a richness of emotion unlike anything Rianne had ever experienced before.

Hands. Mouth. Tongue.

Longing. Desire. Tenderness.

Love.

Overwhelmed with feeling, Rianne lifted her hand to gently caress Alex's cheek. "Alex, my dearest . . ."

He froze. Then, with a muffled curse, he raised his head and shook her hand away from him.

Rianne was jerked out of her dreamy state. "Alex?"

He didn't reply but only tugged her gown back into place. Then he slid his arms under her knees and around her back and leapt to his feet.

"Alex? What—"

"Hush! Don't say a thing. Don't say another bloody word!"

He stormed toward the house, and when the light fell on his face, Rianne saw that he was tight-lipped and grim. "Oh, damn!" he kept repeating. When they reached the verandah, he practically tossed her onto it before stalking away.

Rianne stared at his rigid back, stunned. He was leaving!

He'd kissed her breathless, he'd caressed her intimately—and enjoyed both just as much as she had—and now he was leaving! Without a word!

She stalked along the verandah, keeping pace with him. "Come back here, Alex Benedict! You can't leave now." He ignored her.

She stamped her foot in frustration. "How dare you? Oh, you impossible man! You . . . you . . . You failed the test!" she shouted down at him. "Do you hear me, you failed, you . . ." He still didn't stop.

Furious, Rianne looked around for something to throw. The lounge chairs were too big, the pots of flowers too heavy, so she sat down and jerked her slippers off her feet. Leaping up, she threw one at him. It fell short, but the second hit him smack on the back of his head.

That stopped him, and she held her breath, waiting to see what he'd do. To her disappointment, he didn't turn around. He resumed walking and soon disappeared around the side of the house.

"Idiot!" she shouted after him.

Rianne stamped her foot again, then winced. Oh, darn! The least he could have done was tossed her slippers back to her. She lifted her skirts and looked down at her stockinged feet. There was no help for it; she'd have to retrieve them herself.

She turned to do so and was brought up short by the sight of a couple standing in the doorway of the ballroom, staring at her as if she were a madwoman. Their startled gazes fell to her unshod feet.

Rianne dropped her skirts and straightened her shoulders. "Bats," she said. "Place is full of bats. Threw my slippers at them to frighten them away."

Then, ignoring the other woman's shriek, Rianne sniffed

and walked past them with dignity.

By the time he reached the driveway, Alex was laughing.

What a woman!

What was he going to do with her?

Oh, he knew what he wanted to do, all right. He'd almost done it, too, right there in the garden.

He signaled briskly to one of the lads who'd been hired to watch the guests' horses. The others fell silent and kept their distance as they watched him cautiously, which only added to his amusement.

When his horse was brought to him, Alex tossed the boy a coin and mounted, then spurred Stonewall into a gallop. The horse sped down the driveway, leaving the startled lads staring after him.

No doubt they thought he was a lunatic.

They wouldn't be far wrong.

He was completely, utterly mad.

He should have walked away the moment he'd kissed Rianne and realized her identity.

Odd, that. He hadn't immediately recognized her muffled voice—with that mellow New Orleans dialect—behind the fan, but he'd recognized the taste and feel of her, the flowery scent she wore.

None of those things had remained long in his memory before—with other women.

But then, he couldn't recall ever wanting another woman as much as he now did Rianne. And he well knew that she wanted him.

So why fight it?

They were both mature, willing, sexually experienced adults. He sensed that she wasn't as experienced as he, but he also knew she hid a wealth of passion within her. Every kiss, every caress they'd shared hinted at it.

And damn, he wanted to be the man to free her from her restraints and let her soar.

She'd make an excellent mistress. She was lovely, passionate, and eager. Unjaded and still moldable. Overly intelligent, true; she'd learned to voice her opinions quite effectively. But her sense of humor matched his own irreverent one.

They'd fit well together as both friends and lovers. It didn't have to be anything more. It couldn't be. He'd already made that clear enough—more than once. Besides, *she'd* made it clear that she held no high opinion of marriage.

Perfect! That made it simple.

Chapter 21

What if?

What if, instead of collecting memories to take away with her, she actually *experienced* them as an ordinary woman?

For years she'd lived in nonexistence, inconspicuous, staid, obedient.

Not once in all that time had anyone asked her what she wanted or what would make her happy.

If anyone should ask her now, there could be only one answer: *Alex.*

Memories be damned. She wanted the real thing. She wanted it all, and her heart told her it was possible. There *was* hope, demonstrated by Alex's actions last night. Once again he hadn't been angry with her but with himself.

He was still fighting himself, fighting falling in love with her. He didn't want to, but Rianne was convinced it was possible, regardless.

Rianne smiled as she sat up and stretched languorously. She'd never fought for anything she wanted before, but she was going to do it now. And Alex wouldn't stand a chance.

Rianne's smile faded and turned into a frown. One obstacle remained. She couldn't very well refuse to continue on to New Orleans without telling him why.

She would have to find a way and a time to tell him the truth about her life there.

But, she didn't know all of it herself.

Rianne knocked on Leslie's door. When she received no response, she pushed it open and poked her head in. "Good morning, Leslie!" she chirped.

The lump on the bed stirred. Covers slipped down just enough to expose a tangled mop of black curls and Leslie's green eyes. "Can't be morning," she mumbled. "I feel as if I just got to sleep."

Rianne closed the door and walked to the bed. "It's not morning. It's actually closer to noon."

Leslie groaned and pulled the covers back over her head. "How can you be so cheerful when we didn't get home until two? You should still be in bed, too."

"It's a beautiful day. I don't want to waste any of it. If you come out from under those covers, you'll find that I brought you a cup of coffee."

The covers rustled as Leslie sat up. "Bless you!" She took the cup and saucer Rianne offered, sipped, then shut her eyes in bliss. "Mmm. I *must* be Southern—born to like this chicory-laden poison." She drank again. "Did we have plans for today?" she asked.

"Not really. Everyone else is being a bit lazy, too, since it's Sunday. I just thought you might be hungry, and there's a mouth-watering brunch laid out in the dining room. It's my understanding that we all help ourselves whenever we feel like it, and the offerings keep getting replenished."

"Have you eaten?"

"Can't you hear my stomach growling?"

"I thought that was mine. Give me half an hour and I'll be ready to go down with you."

"I'll be in the sun room. Sara's there with Josie, and I'm dying to play with the little sweet pea."

Rianne had seldom been around small children before Bellesfield, but she spent time with Josie each day, enchanted with the little girl. Josie apparently felt the same way about her, for whenever Rianne appeared, she would lift her arms and, much to everyone's amusement, scream, "Weenie! Weenie!" which was as close as she could get to pronouncing Rianne.

Today was no exception. Sara and two female staff members were lounging in the sun room, reading or conversing, and Rianne soon found herself sitting on the floor with Josie, rolling a ball back and forth. After a time, Josie became bored and crawled up into Rianne's lap to wrap her arms around her neck. " 'Side," she demanded, pointing to the French doors.

"You want to go for a stroll, is that it?"

Josie slid off her lap and began tugging on Rianne's arm. " 'Side, Weenie."

"Is that all right with you, Sara?" Rianne asked.

Sara glanced up from her book. "Only if you can bear it. Just don't let her bamboozle you into carrying her piggyback or avoiding her nap. She's already got Alex wrapped around her little finger, you know."

Rianne hadn't known. She couldn't recall having seen Alex with Josie. Rising, she took the little girl's hand. "All right. Outside it is. Come along, poppet."

Naturally, they'd walked only a short distance before Josie demanded to be carried. "Up, Weenie."

Rianne glanced guiltily over her shoulder to make sure they were out of sight of the house before complying. Josie immediately shoved her little fingers into Rianne's hair. "Ouch! Not that way, poppet. Here . . ." Rianne pried the fingers free and placed them about her neck. "And don't choke me, either."

They continued their walk down the path until Rianne heard laughter and boisterous shouts. Drawn by the sound, she traversed the path until she neared the end of the garden.

There was a baseball game going on. Or had been, she realized, as the participants gathered to shake hands and heckle one another. Alex was among them, she saw, and from his disheveled appearance, he'd obviously been a player. His black hair was falling over his sweat-glistened forehead in spiky disarray. His arm was draped over Jonny's shoulder as they stood side by side, the boy looking up at him in hero worship and speaking animatedly. Alex nodded, then glanced up, directly at Rianne with Josie on her back.

Their gazes locked. A quiver of awareness ran up Rianne's spine. Despite the others, it was as if they were the only two present.

"Weenie!" Josie was wriggling frantically, tugging on Rianne's hair again.

"What, darling?" Rianne said absently.

"Hosie wanna pway."

Rianne broke eye contact with Alex as Josie tried to slide off her back. She caught the imp and brought her forward. "Your Mommy said I had to bring you back in time for your nap."

"No! No! No nappy. Wanna pway wif Aweks."

Rianne shifted Josie into her arms. "How about this? We'll fly. Would you like to fly, sweetheart?" She swung the child back and forth in a wide arc, hoping to distract her. It worked. Josie giggled and shrieked and begged for more all the way back to the house. By the time the two of them stepped onto the verandah, Rianne was breathless, and her arms ached. Sara was waiting for them.

"Mama!" Josie shrieked.

"I see she's almost worn you out," Sara laughed as she took her daughter from Rianne's arms. Josie immediately stuck her thumb into her mouth and laid her cheek against her mother's shoulder, perfectly angelic now.

Rianne grinned. "I didn't realize a two-year-old could get so heavy. My arms feel as if I've been hefting coal," she admitted as she stretched them.

Sara's eyes twinkled as she appraised Rianne. "I'll bet your hair feels as if it's falling out, too."

"My hair?" Rianne reached up, found the loose strands, and flushed guiltily.

"I know," Sara laughed. "It's almost impossible to say no to this little baggage." She shifted Josie higher. "She's almost asleep. I'd better take her upstairs."

After Sara left, Rianne went to the mirror to repair the damage to her hair. She'd just finished when Leslie came into the room. "Good morning, everyone. Or should I say good afternoon?"

She received some good-natured ribbing from the other two women before she and Rianne left for the dining room. There, they exchanged greetings with the half dozen people lingering over coffee, but by the time they'd filled their own plates, the others had left. "I'd like to eat outside, if you don't mind," Leslie requested.

A servant brought a pot of fresh coffee for them and she and Rianne had barely sat down before Alex sauntered out, too, carrying his own full plate.

"Afternoon, ladies," he said as he pushed his hair back from his forehead and pulled out his chair. "I trust you slept well after your enjoyable exertions last night." He poured himself a cup of coffee. "They were enjoyable, weren't they?" Though he'd addressed both of them, he was looking at Rianne.

I will not blush. I will not blush. I will not blush. Rianne repeated the dictum like a prayer, also vowing, *Oh, you will pay for that, Alex Benedict!*

"Ah, it's my brother, the magician," Leslie said as she bit into a slice of bacon.

Alex raised his eyebrows in inquiry.

"Your disappearing act," his sister explained. "You showed up at the dance long enough to wave at me, but then I never saw you again. What happened to you?"

"I only came to pay my respects to George, but I wandered out into the garden, and, well . . ." He smiled devilishly. "Let's just say I found other distractions."

"Of a female nature, no doubt. Which reminds me . . ." Leslie turned to Rianne. "I also meant to ask where you disappeared last night. I don't recall seeing you for the longest time after supper."

"I was just going to remark on the coincidence. As did your brother, I wandered out into the garden."

Alex choked on a hushpuppy.

Rianne ignored him. "Only my experience wasn't as pleasant as Alex's, I'm sure. In fact, it was quite frightening."

"Really? What happened?"

"Would you believe I had a run-in with a wild animal? At least, that's what I think it was."

"Either of you care for more coffee?" Alex interjected loudly.

"No, thank you, Alex." Rianne gave him a honeyed smile.

Leslie shook her head. "What kind of animal?" she asked, wide-eyed.

"I'm not sure. It was rather dark out, you know. I was just minding my own business, when suddenly I heard this growling sound. Well, let me tell you, I was frightened out of my wits. I tried to move away, but it kept growling, and so I thought it best to keep still and hope *it* would go away instead."

"And did it?"

"Not for quite some time."

"Oh, my! Alex, are you listening to this?"

"I'm listening," he muttered, trying to catch Rianne's eye. She stubbornly refused to glance his way.

"Did you get a close look at it?" Leslie asked Rianne.

"Only its eyes. They were green." Rianne shuddered in remembered dread. "Horrible!"

Leslie gasped. "Could it have been a fox?"

Rianne pursed her lips in thought. "I don't think so. Foxes are too intelligent to get that close to humans, aren't they, Alex?" Now she did look his way, her expression one of innocence. When she received only a glare in return, she turned back to Leslie. "Besides, after some time, it stopped growling and began whining. Then it suddenly ran away."

"A dog, then. One of George's hounds. He's been raising them for years and has dozens, I swear."

"Of course! Why didn't I think of that? It was just an old hounddog, frightened by the music and the lights. The poor animal was probably looking for some reassurance and affection," Rianne said blithely.

"Still, it must have been a shock to suddenly be accosted by a strange animal in the dark."

"Yes, it certainly was. But there was no harm done. In fact, I think it's safe to say that the sorry old fellow was more frightened of me than I of him." She turned to Alex. "Isn't that the way with most animals?"

He narrowed his eyes at her. "Not all, I'm afraid. Many, especially those of a predatory nature, may pounce unexpectedly. One should always be alert when traipsing through unknown territory."

Her frown told Alex that she was contemplating his reply, wondering what he was really saying. He hid his smile behind his napkin. She'd figure it out soon enough. She was a clever little minx, she was, and she amused him. A worthy opponent. She'd also be a worthy lover.

It amazed him how she had evolved from a homely chrysalis into lovely, fascinating radiance. Of course, that radiance had actually been present all along; he simply hadn't seen it. Still, from the beginning, she had called to him. Maybe he'd recognized the sorrow she'd so carefully disguised.

Now, it seemed she'd dealt with her pain and was available—and he intended to avail himself of the feast.

"Sorry old hound, eh? Horrible green eyes?"

"Are you still harping on that? Goodness, but you hold grudges. That was days ago," Rianne reminded Alex as they slipped out of the music room and strolled toward Sara's hodgepodge garden.

"I'm still trying to get over the shock of your unexpected propensity for retaliation."

Rianne snickered. "You should have seen the look on your face when you thought I was going to tell Les that it was I you ran into in the garden."

"Speaking of which . . ." Alex glanced over his shoulder. "Come on," he said, grabbing her hand. "We're out of sight of the others now." They ran swiftly down the path together, laughing, until they arrived at the gazebo, breathless and exhilarated.

"Alone at last!" Alex said dramatically as he pulled her inside.

"Alex, stop!" Rianne quickly scooted along the bench until she was four feet from him. "I hear Reverend and Mrs. Moser coming down the path," she hissed.

Alex groaned. "Why is it that whenever I get you alone, someone shows up?"

"I don't know," Rianne whispered. "Do I look decent?" She was trying to smooth back her hair and straighten the collar of her dress at the same time.

Alex grinned at her anxiety. "About as decent as any woman who's just been thoroughly kissed—" A movement in the doorway caught his eye. "Good evening, Reverend. Mrs. Moser."

"Good evening to both of you. You don't mind if we join you, do you?" she asked.

"Of course not," Alex replied, watching Rianne shove the last pin into her hair before dropping her hands demurely into her lap.

"Please do," she said breathlessly, sending Alex a narrowed glance.

The Mosers began a casual conversation, to which Rianne responded and Alex tried to attend. In actuality, he was wondering how soon it would be before they'd leave and he'd have Rianne to himself again.

They'd had hardly a moment alone since the night of the Piney Woods ball. There were too many people at Bellesfield. Someone always appeared at the most inopportune moment, as now. All he'd managed thus far were a few stolen kisses.

He'd tried to take Rianne riding, just the two of them, but invariably someone, most often Leslie, invited herself along. He'd asked Rianne to walk in the garden in the evening. Someone would join them.

Because he wanted to be circumspect and avoid undue speculation, he was resigned to waiting a few more days, until they left for New Orleans.

Of course, then he'd have Leslie to deal with. Though he loved his sister fiercely, he almost wished she wasn't along. Perhaps once they reached New Orleans, he could persuade Les to spend most of her time with Uncle Burt's cousin, Louisa. He hadn't yet figured out what excuse Rianne could have for not always accompanying Les, but he'd come up with one.

Rianne responded politely to the reverend and his wife, but she, too, was wishing they would leave.

Wonder of wonders, Alex was courting her! It was what she'd hoped for, dreamed of. He seemed to have forgotten that he'd ever warned her away from him, seemed ready to admit his love for her. He hadn't said the words to her yet, but he would any day now.

She didn't mind waiting. Besides, she wasn't ready for anyone else to know about their relationship yet, either. She wanted to hug it to herself for a time, to bask in the glory of it. She especially wasn't ready to tell Leslie, for she wasn't sure how Leslie would take the news that her friend and her brother were in love with each other.

If only she and Alex could find more time alone, to talk. She wouldn't feel completely at ease until she'd told him about New Orleans, but thus far, she'd had no opportunity. They couldn't even make an assignation to meet late in the evening, for the long, balmy nights beckoned to everyone. Often it was past midnight when the house finally fell silent.

The sound of her name jerked Rianne out of her reverie. She sat up and realized she was still in the gazebo and that Reverend Moser had just spoken to her.

"I'm sorry. I'm afraid I was woolgathering. What did you say?"

"I asked if you've enjoyed your stay at Bellesfield."

"Oh, yes, very much. It's so lovely and so peaceful."

"I understand you're from New Orleans. Is Bellesfield anything like the plantations around there?"

"Hmm?" Rianne was staring at Alex, yearning to run her fingers through his thick, wavy hair.

"Noah, I think it's time for us to leave," Mrs Moser said.

"But, my dear, I'm very interested in—oomph!' He grabbed his side and turned to look at his wife in astonishment. "What did you do that for, Inez?"

"Noah, it is *time* for us to *go!*" she enunciated emphatically, tilting her head toward the other side of the gazebo, where Rianne and Alex were exchanging long glances.

"But it's only . . . Oh, Yes! I see. Yes, I believe it *is* time for us to return to our cottage."

Wishes for a good night were quickly exchanged, and Reverend and Mrs. Moser were soon hurrying back along the path.

Alex and Rianne glanced at each other again. "Oh, dear," she said. "You don't suppose they guessed, do you?"

Alex shrugged. "Probably, but they'd be the last people I'd worry about. Both of them frown on gossiping." Alex slid over until he was pressed close to her once again. "Now, where were we?" he murmured as he took her in his arms.

Rianne laughed at his eagerness, though she was equally so. "I believe you were here—" she touched her throat "—while I was about here," she said, nibbling on his earlobe.

"Oh, yes. How could I have forgotten?" The last part of his comment was muffled, since Alex's lips had already found her bodice once more.

"Mr. Benedict? Sir? Yoo hoo!"

Alex jerked away and muttered a soft curse.

"Where are you, sir?"

"It's Jonny," Alex said unnecessarily as he slid back to the spot he'd just left. "I'm in the gazebo," he called.

A panting Jonny soon made his appearance. "Evenin', Miss Rianne."

"Good evening, Jonny."

The boy turned to Alex. "Papa was going to take me

fishin' tomorrow, but now he has to go to Atlanta. Will you come with me instead?"

Alex reached out and ruffled the boy's hair. "Why not? The river still has catfish?"

"Oh, yes, sir!" Jonny's eyes shone with eagerness. "Last one I caught was this big!" He stretched his arms wide.

"Hmm. That's a big one, all right."

"May I come, too?" Rianne asked. "I think Leslie would like to, also. She mentioned going fishing a while back."

Jonny's face fell. "Do we have to take them?" he asked Alex in a loud whisper. "Girls don't know anything about fishin'."

"I'll have you know that my sister caught the biggest catfish in the county when she was your age," Alex said. "In fact, it probably still holds the record." As the boy had done, he spread his arms wide to indicate the creature's size.

"Really?" Jonny's eyes were agog.

Alex nodded. " 'Course, I had to help her pull it in. Girls aren't very strong," he added in a conspiratorial whisper, ignoring Rianne's snort of disgust. "They're weaker than men and need our help, you know."

"Yeah. They can't lift things or throw balls or anything."

"Right. So we have to be gentlemen and help them with most things."

Jonny nodded in male agreement. "Okay. I guess they can come along," he conceded.

"Thank you, Jonny," Rianne said solemnly. "I feel so much better, knowing you two strong men will be there."

"You're welcome, ma'am," the boy replied. "I gotta go, now, and get my fishin' stuff ready. 'Night, Mr. Benedict. You too, Miss Rianne." Jonny took off running and disappeared down the path.

Immediately Alex again slid across the bench. This time

Rianne stopped his embrace by planting her palm on his chest.

"*Weaker* than men? We need your help for *most* things?" she asked.

"Now, darlin', I couldn't very well lie to the boy, could I?"

"Oh, you are a devil! Just to prove that you're wrong, I'll make a wager with you. Bet I'll catch a bigger fish than you do."

"Have you ever been fishing before?"

"No. But I'm a fast learner."

"Hmm." Alex leaned over to nuzzle her neck. "Forget about fishing. I'd like to get back to the business at hand."

She splayed her palm over his face and playfully pushed it away. "I'm thinking about it."

He batted her arm away and went back to nuzzling. "Don't think. Time's a-wasting."

As if to reinforce his statement, Leslie's tinkling laughter pealed. Once again Rianne and Alex slid apart. Just in time—for Leslie and Trevor Williams suddenly appeared in the doorway of the gazebo.

"So this is where you two have gotten to," Leslie chirped.

"Damn," Alex muttered, loud enough only for Rianne's ears. "This place is a circus, and we're the main attraction. I give up."

Chapter 22

"Oh, yuck! No one said anything to me about worms!" Rianne squealed. She stared down at the squirming, gray mass in the bucket. "Nor that they'd be alive." She wrinkled her nose in revulsion.

Alex winked at Jonny. "You see, son? Didn't I tell you that women can't manage without men?"

Jonny grinned at him. "I see what you meant, sir."

Alex's eyes gleamed when he turned back to Rianne. "If you're nice to me, I'll bait your hook for you."

"What does 'nice' mean?" Rianne asked suspiciously.

He tilted his head and considered. "Well, for starters, you could gut and clean the fish we catch." He laughed at her look of horror. "Hmm. I see that's asking too much. What do you think, Jonny? Should we let her pass on that one?"

"Probably safer," Jonny replied, clearly enjoying this game.

"Right. Well, then, how about you cook the fish for me, Rianne? I warn you, I'm particular about how my catfish is cooked. It has to be dipped in egg, then in cornmeal seasoned with ground black pepper and a pinch each of thyme and basil—"

"Can't do it," Rianne replied, laughing. "For one thing, I don't have the slightest idea what most of those ingredients are. For another, I've never cooked anything."

"Not even an egg?"

Rianne shook her head.

"Can you boil water?"

She hesitated.

Alex slapped a hand to his forehead. "See? What did I tell you, Jon? Women are helpless. Helpless, and sometimes hopeless."

"I'd bite my tongue if I were you." Leslie hadn't said a thing until now, for she was busily readying her fishing pole. "Them's fightin' words."

Everyone laughed, and then they settled to do some serious fishing.

Despite the worms, Rianne found it a perfect morning. It was warm but not hot, and the sky was the purest blue she'd ever seen, dotted with huge, fluffy clouds. Crickets chirped, bees droned, and birds sang a medley of choruses.

The foursome spent two hours in peaceful contentment on the riverbank, lounging under a massive oak for shade. Alex had brought blankets and Leslie a picnic basket. Though they'd all eaten breakfast, it wasn't long before they devoured all the sandwiches, cheese, and apples the basket contained.

Other than eating, the only times they exerted themselves was when someone caught a fish. Jonny was the first, then Leslie, and then, to her own surprise, Rianne's pole dipped.

"I've got one!" she squealed, leaping to her feet. "What do I do? What do I do?" She grabbed her pole, and, to everyone else's amusement, jumped up and down in excitement. "Help me!"

Alex saw that she really did need help, so he sobered enough to get to his feet. "Don't drop the pole!" he ordered. "And don't jerk on it. Here, I'll show you."

Rianne was so thrilled about catching her first fish that she didn't even notice when Alex pressed close against her back to wrap his arms around her and cover her hands with his.

And after they'd pulled the fish in, she squirmed away to hop about in triumph.

"He's big, isn't he? Bigger than Jonny's and Leslie's, even."

"He sure is." Alex grinned at her exuberance. She was like a child who'd just received the most wondrous gift. Her delight made him feel good. Real good.

Maybe the right word was *happy*. Yes, that was it, he thought with surprise. He was happy because she was.

He was still smiling when he contentedly dozed off some time later—despite the fact that he'd taken considerable ribbing for being the only one who hadn't yet caught a fish.

Leslie looked down at her brother. "Trust Alex to find the most comfortable spot. You don't mind?"

"Not at all," Rianne replied. She *was* a bit surprised, though. After she'd gotten over her excitement, they'd retired under the tree again, she with her back against the trunk. Alex, without any ado, had simply lain down beside her and placed his head in her lap as if it were the most natural act. Rianne smiled down at him, unaware that Leslie's forehead was creased in thought as she studied them.

"Yes, well . . ."

Rianne glanced up at Leslie, wondering about her hesitant manner, but Leslie immediately glanced over her shoulder at Jonny, who was tossing twigs into the river a few feet away. "We'll leave you in peace, then. We're going to take a little walk." She chuckled. "Jon has a crush on me. I've impressed him with my hook-baiting abilities and my agreement to join him in an exploration for frogs and snakes."

Rianne nodded. "Actually, I'm impressed, too."

"I'm just full of surprises," Leslie told her. Then she shaded her eyes and looked up at the sky. "We may all be in for a surprise. Those clouds are getting dark and heavy." She wagged her fingers at Rianne and went to meet Jonny. The two of them strolled away, following the riverbank.

Rianne glanced up at the sky. The clouds Leslie had spoken of were still a ways off. Alex had plenty of time to take his nap.

She looked down at him and smiled. Though this was a rare opportunity for them to be alone, she was content simply to watch him sleep. He looked boyish, his face relaxed and vulnerable. Spiky lashes concealed his eyes, and strands of hair lay across his forehead. She gave in to temptation and tenderly brushed back his hair, but it sprang forward again, so she left it. How beloved his face had become to her.

Her gaze traveled down the long line of his body. His throat, the tanned skin revealed by his open collar. His chest, hard as a rock yet capable of refuge. His hands, strong yet gentle. His slim hips, powerful thighs . . .

She loved him! She hadn't known she could have feelings like this for anyone. She longed to bend and kiss his face and throat, all that she could see. She wanted to cradle him tenderly in her arms and have him hold her in return. Yet she also longed for him to make wild, passionate love to her.

For that's what it would be with Alex. He was intelligent and sophisticated, but he was also earthy. He would expect her to respond in kind. And she would, for there would be no room for fear with Alex.

Children, Rianne thought drowsily. A boy or a girl with Alex's dark hair and green eyes . . .

A soft touch on her cheek woke her. She opened her eyes slowly, slightly confused, until something brushed her cheek again. Then she glanced down and found Alex, awake. He grinned up at her. "Hello, sleepyhead."

"Look who's talking." Rianne knew he'd been watching

her sleep, just as she had, him. What had *his* thoughts been? she wondered.

As if reading her mind, Alex said, "Do you know how temptingly kissable you look when you sleep?" His fingers lightly stroked over her lips.

"Hey, you two!"

Alex raised his head to glance in the direction of the voice, then groaned and let it fall back onto Rianne's lap. "Not again! I'm beginning to think Bellesfield is too crowded."

Rianne laughed and waved at Leslie and Jonny. "Hello!" she called. "If you brought any frogs or snakes back with you, tell me now, so I can scramble up the tree."

"Nah. Couldn't catch any. They were too fast for us," Jonny replied as he and Leslie sat down.

"Did you go across the river?" Rianne asked.

"No, why do you ask?" Leslie wanted to know.

Rianne pointed to an outcropping on the other side of the river. It was quite high and topped by a lone pine, so that it resembled a steeple. "I saw that earlier and wondered about it."

"That's Church Rock. It's composed of granite," Leslie said. "A lovely spot. In the center of it is a small pool, with wild azaleas that bloom for months. There's even a cave of sorts. Alex and I used to play there as children." She laughed. "We thought it was our secret hideaway, but everyone knew about it, of course. Is it still the same, Jonny?"

"Yes. Sometimes I go over, too, when I want to be alone."

"It sounds lovely. How do you get there from here?" Rianne asked.

Alex sat up and pointed to a spot upstream. "The river's quite low there and has a bridge of rocks. We have no idea who built it. Probably the Indians, hundreds of years ago. Would you like to go across?"

Rianne eyed the rocks dubiously, unaware of the light in

his eyes. “I don’t know. Wouldn’t it be too easy to slip into the water?”

“Not if you’re careful.”

“You aren’t seriously thinking of it, are you?” Leslie asked Alex.

“Why not?”

She pointed to the sky. “Those clouds are moving closer. You’re taking a chance on getting caught in a storm.”

Alex scanned the sky. “I think we’re safe for another hour or so,” he said.

“Well, I’m ready to return now. Jonny and I thought we’d trade some of the catfish for a few of Cook’s peach tarts, right, Jon?”

“You bet!”

“You take the fish, Jon, and I’ll bring the rest,” Leslie directed as she rose to shake out the blanket she’d been sitting on.

Rianne was still studying the river. It seemed placid, except where it hit the rocks. There it surged, even spraying upward to form miniature sparkling rainbows. “How deep *is* the water?” she asked, biting her lip.

“Not very.” Alex studied her worried expression and decided to forgo telling her that beneath the surface the current ran swiftly. It was no problem for a strong swimmer, but . . . “Do you swim, Rianne?”

She shook her head, and he wasn’t surprised. Leaning forward, he scooped her up into his arms and turned toward the river, ignoring her startled squeal of surprise. “Then I guess it’s up to me to carry you across.”

“You’re mad, Alex!” Leslie laughed. “It will rain soon, and you’ll both get soaked and catch your death of cold.”

He about-faced. “Then give that blanket to Rianne,” he ordered. Leslie shook her head in amused resignation but complied. Alex shifted Rianne into a more secure position before turning about again and heading directly for the bridge of rocks.

"Stop!" Rianne shrieked. "I don't think I want to do this! You'll drop me in the river!"

Alex grinned down at her. "What? I've spent all morning convincing Jonny that men are braver and stronger than women and you expect me to *drop* you?" he teased. "Where's your faith in me?" As he'd hoped, she stopped squirming and wrapped her arms about his neck.

"I'll kill you if you drop me," she murmured against his chest. "That is, if I don't drown first."

"Darlin', I don't intend to let anything bad happen to you. I've got other activities in mind."

Alex wasn't worried about making it across the river; he'd done it hundreds of times in the past. Of course, he'd never had a woman in his arms. A woman who damned near had a choke-hold on him. The chance of falling in and drowning wasn't half as great as that of being strangled! He told her so. Rianne protested, but did loosen her hold. Still, each time he lifted a foot to step onto the next rock, she let out a muffled gasp. And she screamed when he took the final leap onto the bank.

"You can open your eyes now, sweetheart. We're across."

She slowly lifted her head and looked at him. Her eyes were so dark, they were almost black, and Alex realized that she really had been terrified. "You okay?" he asked gently.

She took a deep breath and nodded. "Sorry. I don't like water much. I fell into a stream when I was a toddler and almost drowned."

Ah! So that was it. Alex set her on her feet and gently smoothed her hair away from her face. "You don't have to be afraid when you're with me. I promise I'll always keep you safe." He was rewarded by a smile so sweet, he wanted to swallow it.

Snatching the blanket, he grabbed her hand and urged her forward.

The sun was still shining twenty minutes later when Alex helped Rianne over the last boulder and slipped his arm about her waist to pull her next to him. "Look down," he ordered. Rianne looked down—and stopped breathing.

A bowl-shaped indentation in the granite held a blue pool of water so clear she could see the bottom. Lush, verdant ferns bordered the pool, and beyond them, on the far side, was a patch of wild azaleas so brilliantly colored that they looked as if they'd been painted. The sound of dripping water caught Rianne's ear. She glanced up to find a small spring that seeped out of the moss-covered rock and trickled down into the pool. Lastly, she saw an opening in the rock—the grotto.

"Oh, my!" Rianne breathed. Leslie's description hadn't done this place justice.

"Does that mean you like it?" Alex asked unnecessarily.

"Oh, my!" Rianne repeated. Then she eagerly turned to him. "May we go down?"

"Your wish is my command, m'lady. Paradise awaits."

Still holding her hand, he led her down natural steps worn into the rock by feet of ages past. The path led first to the pool, then through the greenery to the cave.

The grotto wasn't very large, perhaps six by ten feet, with a ceiling only a few inches above Alex's head. Cool and surprisingly dry, its only signs of habitation were the remains of a fire that had been built in a small indentation in the floor, and a lantern and box of matches in a depression halfway up one wall. Dozens of smaller hollows pocked the walls, and Rianne saw that many held objects.

She peered into one and found that it contained several highly polished stones of varying sizes and hues. Another held faded feathers, yet another what appeared to be dried seeds. "Who put these things here?" she asked, curious, turning to Alex.

"Some are mine, some Leslie's. I wouldn't be surprised if others came from my father, and perhaps even *his* father and so on. The rest . . ." He shrugged. "Who knows? All I can tell you is that something about this place calls for—I don't know—a gift to say thank you, perhaps?"

"Oh, yes! I feel that, too. May I leave something, too, before we leave?"

"Absolutely."

"Let's look outside again, please."

Tossing the blanket upon the floor, Alex gave her a sweeping bow. "As you wish, m'lady," he said, but he also groaned. He'd finally brought her to a place where they could be alone and free of interruptions, and she was so enchanted by the scene that she could think of nothing else.

All *he'd* thought of all the way up here was how she'd look spread out naked upon the blanket for him.

Still, he didn't want to deny her present pleasure, even though he fully intended to give her more—of a different nature. The thought alone was enough to stir his body with anticipation.

He soon found himself sitting on his haunches at the entrance to the cave, observing Rianne as she found her way through the azaleas. In a moment she was sitting in their midst, only her head and shoulders visible, looking like one of the blossoms herself. The sun burnished her hair with red and gold; her cheeks were flushed, her eyes bright. Butterflies fluttered about her head, and when she lifted a hand, one large, colorful specimen alighted upon it and stretched its wings. Rianne laughed in delight.

Alex tried to brush away the contentment creeping over him. He tried to tell himself it was too dangerous, as were the warm, tender feelings that watching Rianne gave him.

Oh, he wanted some feelings, all right. He wanted to feel his blood urgently boiling, his heart pumping with carnal pleasure. His skin against Rianne's and his hands and fingers on her, touching, caressing, probing. His mouth and tongue, too, savoring the taste, the scent of her . . .

"Rianne."

When she turned to him, a question in her eyes at his low, serious tone, he slowly rose to his feet and extended a hand.

"Come to me."

She stared into his eyes for a moment, until hers filled with awareness. And then she stood, too, and made her way through the azaleas to him. Her gaze still locked with his, she placed her hand in his.

No questions, no coyness, no teasing.

She was his. She would do anything for him.

Alex backed slowly into the cave, leading her with him.

Chapter 23

Alex led Rianne to the center of the cave, his gaze still locked with hers.

Then he stopped and lifted her hand to his mouth, turning it over to press her palm against his lips before releasing it and reaching out to untie the ribbon she'd used to secure back her hair at her nape.

The freed ribbon floated to the ground, forgotten, as he brought her hair forward to mantle her shoulders, then rubbed a lock between his thumb and forefinger, savoring the texture.

"Pure silk," he murmured. "I can't wait to see if the rest of you feels the same."

Rianne's heart began tripping madly, yet her mind was oddly serene, without doubts, questions, or fears.

This was Alex, the man she loved and trusted.

This was what she wanted, and the wanting felt good and right. Yet she closed her eyes as Alex began unbuttoning her shirtwaist.

It was exquisite torture; he undid each button slowly, as if he were treasuring each moment, and his knuckles kept brushing against her breasts, until they were aching for more of his touch.

Alex reached the last button and pushed her shirtwaist over her shoulders to peel it off her, letting it fall to the floor while his hands slid to the back of her skirt and undid those buttons, too. Then he knelt before her to pull off her petticoats.

Cool air against her heated skin told Rianne that she stood in only her chemise and drawers.

Her composure fled as she felt Alex's warm breath against her thighs. Her legs began to tremble.

"Put your hands on my shoulders, Rianne," Alex ordered, his voice husky.

She did so, and felt the heat of his skin, his muscles bunching beneath the thin cloth of his shirt.

And then she felt . . . she felt . . .

Her eyes flew open, and she looked down at Alex's dark head pressed intimately against her, and even as she stared at him, befuddled, he clamped his fingers around her thighs, urging her to part them.

"Alex, no!" she gasped.

He might have ignored her objection, except that she was digging her fingernails into his skin. He looked up to see that she was staring over his head at the wall, mortification written all over her face.

He didn't even have her naked yet, and she was already shocked down to the tips of her toes! Which could only mean she was even less experienced than he'd surmised.

Alex almost laughed in elation. Oh, it was going to be a joy to initiate her, to pleasure her and teach her how to pleasure him.

But it seemed he might have to slow down right now.

That was all right. Anticipation would only make the loving sweeter!

"Rianne, look at me," he said quietly.

She shook her head.

"All right. Come down to me, then."

Now she did meet his eyes, and hers were filled with wariness and embarrassment. She quickly looked away again and bit her lip, hesitating.

"Come," he urged, taking her hands and tugging until she fell to her knees, too.

Alex slid his hands into her hair and held her head so that she had to face him. "It's all right, darlin'. We can save that for another time. But understand something: There's nothing wrong with anything we do together if it gives us both pleasure. Will you remember that?"

"I . . . yes. I'm sorry. I didn't . . . I just didn't expect . . ."

"You've never loved that way before?"

"No!" she exclaimed, stunned that he would even ask her such an intimate question.

To her surprise, Alex grinned. "That's fine," he said. "Better than fine."

"It is?" Now she was puzzled. "You don't mind?"

His thumbs idly traced circles on her temples. "No." He tilted his head and studied her thoughtfully. "All right. Let's try something else."

"What?" she asked, wary again.

"Well . . ." Effortlessly, he lifted her and straightened his legs before setting her down on his thighs, so that she was straddling him, her knees bent. He raised his own knees to bring her closer and support her back. "Take my shirt off, darlin'."

Rianne sighed with relief and smiled slowly. She couldn't wait to feel that hard bare chest and twine her fingers in those little whorls of hair and kiss his nipples as he'd kissed hers.

She made a faster job of it than he had, though. Alex laughed when she ripped his sleeve in her eager haste to pull the shirt off him.

A few moments later, however, he was no longer laughing.

He was gasping as she leaned toward him and began to nibble on his chest.

What a contradiction she was! Easily shocked one minute, so ardent the next. Eager little hands . . . hot, wet mouth . . .

What that delectable mouth was doing to him should be outlawed—and she'd gotten only as far as his chest!

"Whoa!" he said, laughing.

She glanced up at him hesitantly. "I'm not allowed to do that?" she asked, disappointed.

Alex's shoulders shook. "Didn't I say you were allowed to do anything you want? But if we don't slow down, this is going to be over before it starts." He pushed his hips upward slightly to demonstrate.

"Oh!" she breathed, her eyes widening when she felt the huge ridge of hard flesh under her buttocks. She wriggled experimentally and felt him jerk beneath her spasmodically. She grinned, delighted, feeling powerful. She liked the feeling so much that she shifted again and was rewarded by Alex's groan.

He said nothing more about slowing down. Instead, he was suddenly crushing her to him, flattening her breasts against his chest as he kissed her fervently. His tongue played with hers, exploring her mouth, and she gloried in his hot eagerness. His hands tangled in her hair as he cupped her head, his wonderful mouth now tracing paths across her nose, her cheeks, her ears.

Shivers of delight shook her body, and she moaned incoherently, pressing against him, wanting more.

He tugged her chemise down to her waist and bared her breasts to his burning gaze. Then his hands were eagerly cupping her, his thumbs stroking her nipples, causing such wonderful sensations that she thought she'd die from them.

But she didn't. She was too excited, too keen to learn what

else he could make her feel, and she arched her back, offering herself to him.

He took. He took her into his mouth and suckled, his teeth nipping at the tender flesh, then soothing it with his tongue, until Rianne emitted a low moan.

Alex glanced up to see that her eyes were closed, her head thrown back, her face flushed as her pink tongue flicked her top lip.

He was enthralled, but he wanted more. He could hardly wait to see her in the full throes of passion, as she came for him.

Still watching her, he slid his hands up her inner thighs until his fingers were parting the opening in her drawers. Rianne's eyes flew open the instant he slid one finger inside her drawers—and Alex smiled. "Lean back against my knees, love." His thumb unerringly found the tender nub of flesh.

Her eyes opened even wider. Oh! The things he was doing to her with his fingers! So deliciously wicked! So . . . So . . .

It came upon her with no warning. She felt herself helplessly rushing at unbelievable speed, soaring toward a place she'd never been before. She heard Alex's voice saying, "That's it. That's it, darlin'," and she fell helplessly back against his raised knees and relinquished herself to it, to him, feeling as if she were exploding, and she emitted a high-pitched cry.

When she next opened her eyes, she was curled up against Alex's chest. His arms were about her, and he was kissing her hair and whispering words of praise in her ear.

Still kissing her, he reached for the blanket and snapped it open behind her. Then he wrapped his arms around her again and pushed her backward until she was lying on it and he on top of her. "Lift your arms, love," he murmured against her neck.

She obeyed instantly. He pulled her camisole up over her head, then slipped his hands into the tops of her drawers and slid them down her legs.

She suffered only one instant of wary discomfiture at being naked before him. But then she decided it was much too late for embarrassment.

She didn't turn away when Alex stood to remove his pants. Nor when he looked down at her, in all his naked male splendor.

In fact, Rianne sat up to study him. He was, as she'd thought, well built and well toned. His chest she was already familiar with, but she was delighted with his narrow waist and hips, his muscled thighs and strong, long legs. Even his toes looked manly.

She'd saved the part in between for last, and now she raised her eyes and looked her fill.

My heavens! she thought. *No wonder I could feel him beneath me!* His manhood looked enormous as it jutted out proudly.

She didn't know she'd gasped until she heard Alex chuckle. He knelt beside her, took her hand, and placed it over his erect flesh. "Feel what you do to me, love," he told her as he curled her fingers around himself.

Rianne's mouth opened when he jerked again at her touch. She marveled at the feel of him, velvety soft yet so hard. She squeezed gently, curious, and he stiffened even more.

"Rianne!" he said hoarsely, and then he was pushing her back, lying down on top of her, kissing her, his hands caressing her breasts, her thighs, and once again Rianne felt that dizzying sensation sweep over her. She returned each kiss, each caress.

They were both deaf to the crashing thunder, blind to the flashes of lightning outside the cave. They were aware only of each other's sighs and murmurs, of skin touching skin. There was no world outside the cave. There was nothing but the two of them.

Alex drew her thighs apart and slipped between them. She felt the bones of his hips pressing against her, and then *that* part of him, probing, pushing gently.

He teased and tortured her, barely coming into her, then withdrawing. Rianne squirmed, wanting him fully inside her. He wanted that, too, she could tell, because he was panting and, astonishingly, she could feel him getting larger.

"Alex, please!"

Sweat beaded on his forehead, and she knew he was holding back, trying to control his passion for her sake.

"Alex, it's all right. Please. I want you *now.*"

He looked down at her, his eyes glazed with passion. "Yes," he muttered. "Now." And he pushed himself inside her.

Suddenly he froze.

"What the hell?" he growled.

He was still inside her, almost filling her, and Rianne almost cried out in frustration. She had been nearly there, to that place he'd taken her to before, and she wanted to reach it again. *Had to.*

Rianne instinctively clenched her muscles around him, locked her ankles behind his knees, and heaved her hips upward. She felt something tear inside her, but she ignored the sharp pain and held on to Alex with all her strength, until he swore softly and began to rock furiously himself. Until she'd reached the heights again and felt him explode within her, then groan loudly and collapse upon her.

They lay thus, entwined. Rianne felt limbless, as if she were floating, while Alex breathed heavily into her neck.

Then he raised his head, and his eyes were hot.

"You were a virgin! Bloody hell, you were a *virgin!*"

Basking in newly discovered sensuality, Rianne closed her eyes and sighed luxuriously.

"I know. Isn't it wonderful?"

Chapter 24

The only sound after her smug pronouncement was that of the rain pouring down outside and a steady dripping coming from somewhere farther back in the cave.

Still wearing a smile, Rianne opened her eyes—only to find that Alex's were shooting sparks of fierce, green fire down upon her. "*Wonderful?* What do you mean, *wonderful?*" he spat. "It's a damned catastrophe, that's what it is. How in bloody hell did it happen?" He rolled off her and sat up.

"How did what happen?" Rianne asked, confused at Alex's agitation. He was tugging on his hair as if he wanted to pull it out. What was wrong with him? They'd just shared the most unbelievable intimacy, and it had been magnificent. Glorious.

For her.

Apparently it hadn't meant as much to him.

But how could that be? He had been so tender, so loving, so . . . Rianne frowned. Had it meant *anything* to him?

A feeling of dread began to creep over her. "Alex?" Abruptly he was on his feet, pacing, unconcerned with his nakedness. "How in the devil could you be a virgin?" he shouted at her. "You've been married! You're a widow!"

Rianne sat up and reached for his shirt to clutch it to her bosom. "I never told you that," she said slowly. "The only person I ever said that to was Mrs. Busley, and that was only so she'd hire me."

He stopped pacing and stared down at her. "What are you saying? That you've never *been* married?"

"No. That is, yes, I've never been married." Ah, so that was it. Rianne sighed in relief. Since he'd thought her a widow, it would stand to reason he'd be somewhat surprised at her innocence.

Especially since it had come as a surprise to her, too.

This was, Rianne decided, the perfect opportunity to explain, to tell him all about New Orleans and Lance. "Alex, I—" she began.

"Do you know what you've done?" he rasped.

Rianne realized that Alex was furious. Utterly furious. She didn't understand. Shouldn't he be happy that he was her first lover? "Yes," she said slowly. "I've made love with the man I love, the man I thought—" Rianne bit her lip. She had a feeling that she'd made a horrible blunder, and she wasn't about to compound it by saying that she thought he loved her in return, or that she hoped he was the man she'd marry.

Alex snatched up his pants and stepped into them. "I gave you fair warning, didn't I?" he asked grimly as he closed the buttons. "I told you I'd never marry again. I thought you understood that. I thought you understood that the only commitment you'd get from me was my assurance that I'd always take care of you."

She felt ill. At last she understood his intentions. He'd thought her a woman of experience, one who would have known what to expect—and it certainly hadn't been marriage. Men didn't marry their—

"You intended for me to become your mistress," she stated flatly.

"Yes, dammit!" Alex went to stand at the grotto's entrance, his palms braced against the overhang as he looked out, unconcerned about the rain lashing against him.

The word echoed in Rianne's head. Mindlessly, she reached for her clothes and began to dress.

Mistress. As her mother had been to Lance's father.

Whore, Lance had called Claudine.

Mistress or whore. Was there really any difference? Both words left a bitter taste in Rianne's mouth.

It was then that she realized there was no hope. No dreams coming true, no future with Alex.

Thunder crashed outside again. A flash of lightning lit the interior of the cave.

Rianne wished it had struck her.

She wrapped her arms around her knees and rested her head on them, curling up inside herself, feeling as if she were shrinking, until she was only a tiny speck with a tinny voice. "Mistress," she said aloud. "He said that, too."

Alex turned to look at her. "Who?"

"Lance Paxton. My guardian. I made a mistake then, too. God, I must be stupid. But I suppose I should be thankful that it didn't take me five years to comprehend this time."

Realizing that matters were even more wrong than he'd thought, Alex came to kneel before her. "Five years for what, Rianne?" he asked quietly, containing his anger.

She didn't raise her head. "That's how long I spent trying to please Lance. From the time I was thirteen to the eve of my eighteenth birthday, he groomed me—in languages, deportment, dancing—to be the perfect hostess. I did everything he wanted, over and over again, until he finally approved, because I thought he was preparing me for our marriage. What did I know? I was but a child with childish dreams.

"Well, they were crushed the night he told me that he had no intention of marrying me. He told me I wasn't good enough. My mother . . ." Rianne raised her head and looked at Alex bleakly. "My mother had become his father's mistress to support us after my own father died." She shook her head sadly. "Poor Maman. Perhaps she could have managed on her own, but she had a child—me—you see. She had no choice."

"Rianne. I'm sorry, darlin'." Alex touched her cheek, but she jerked away and glared at him.

"Don't call me that anymore. You have no right. You're no better than Lance. He was laughing when he told me that he only wanted me for his mistress. Why aren't you laughing, Alex?"

"I'd never laugh at you to be cruel, Rianne."

"No, you use words, don't you?"

"Dammit, I'm not trying to deliberately hurt you!"

"Of course not. You don't have to *try.*" She began to laugh herself, bitterly, harshly, tears simultaneously streaming down her face.

Alex became alarmed. "Rianne, stop it!"

"But it *is* funny," she sputtered. "Don't you see how funny it is that I've repeated the same foolish mistake? The only difference . . ." she took a deep breath, striving for control. "The only difference is that I let you seduce me, while Lance tried to rape me."

"Oh, God!" Alex squeezed his eyelids shut in horror.

"Shall I tell you about it? Yes, why not? You tell me your ugly story, I tell you mine. I'd intended to tell you anyway, but not like this. You see, I can't go to New Orleans with you and Leslie. I can't ever go back. If I do, and Lance finds me, he'll kill me."

Alex's eyes flew open. "No other man is going to lay a hand on you in any way!"

"Such fierce words!" she mocked. "Are you always so protective of your mistresses?"

"Dammit, Rianne—"

She continued, as if she hadn't heard his interruption. "It was the eve of my eighteenth birthday. I was very excited. Lance had a gown made for me—white satin. Much like Leslie's birthday gown. Do you remember?"

"Yes. Go on," Alex urged.

"It was the most beautiful dress I'd ever seen . . ."

It had hung in her closet for over a month. It was virginal white, of course. She'd never worn anything else.

But this dress was special . . .

It was satin, cut in simple lines, but the sleeves and bodice and hem were trimmed with lace that had been stitched by nuns. They were the only ones who produced that particular lace made exclusively for Creole brides. Rianne knew that, because the dressmaker had mentioned it several times during the fittings.

"You can't wear it until the eve of your eighteenth birthday, pet," Lance had warned. "I'm taking you to your first opera, then dinner. Afterward, some time past midnight, we'll return here." He gave her one of those smiles that always made her stomach flutter. "It's going to be a special night—a very special occasion—for both of us."

He could only mean that the minister would be waiting when they came back to the house. Her heart thudded with excitement, but, as usual, she lowered her lashes and simply murmured, "Yes, Lance."

She was a bit surprised when Lance arrived at the cottage on the appointed night, for he wasn't alone. He had half a dozen young men with him—friends of his, he said. Rianne felt awkward and extremely self-conscious, for she'd never been in the company of other men.

She became even more so as the evening progressed. She loved the excitement and color and drama of the theater, but her enjoyment was dampened by the strange behavior of Lance's friends. They'd sent many sly looks in her direction and whispered behind their hands. She felt like an object on display. She couldn't enjoy her supper, either, for Lance and his friends imbibed freely of Champagne—she was allowed only fruit juice—and they became raucous. She felt an odd sort of anticipation in the air, but she assumed it was due to the wedding ceremony that was to follow, after she and Lance returned home.

But when they finally did go home, just after midnight, she couldn't understand why, if they were to be wed tonight, the minister was not there. And Lance's friends lingered, drinking and laughing and making crude comments as Lance took her upstairs.

She was even more confused when Lance escorted her straight to her bedroom and ushered her inside. He'd never before entered her room.

Mimsie was nowhere to be seen, but the room was filled with roses. Vases and vases of white roses heavily scented the air. "Oh!" Suddenly it struck Rianne that Lance had brought her here to freshen up while Mimsie and the minister and the others gathered below. She turned to him. "You wanted to surprise me, didn't you?" she teased.

Lance smiled, but a wave of uneasiness flitted over Rianne. It was the smile she didn't like, the one that said he was about to criticize her or chastise her.

But all he said was, "Oh, yes." And then he turned and locked the door to her room.

Rianne frowned. "Why are you locking the door, Lance? I'm not going anywhere until you say it's time."

"But it is time, pet," he told her as he approached her.

"But I . . . I don't understand. Aren't we returning below for the celebration?"

Lance stopped a few feet from her. "The only celebration," he chuckled, "is going to be up here. Do you like the roses?" he asked suddenly.

She nodded. "They're lovely, Lance. But there are so many of them!"

"There's Champagne, too," he said, nodding toward a small table. Sure enough, a bottle lay nestled in a bucket of ice, two crystal goblets nearby. "I know you were disappointed when I didn't allow you to have any wine at supper, but I wanted you clear-headed and fully aware for your initiation." "Initiation?" Her eyes followed Lance as he walked to her bureau and placed the contents of his pockets—some money and the key to her room—on top of it.

"That's what I said. So, we shall have Champagne after—"

"After . . . what?"

He turned to her, still wearing his sly smile. "You really don't know, do you? Come here, Rianne."

She obeyed, as she always had, though she was now confused and frightened.

"I suppose I can't blame you, since I warned Mimsie to keep her mouth shut and do as she was told. But just what did you expect was going to happen tonight?"

"I . . . I thought . . . I thought we were to be married," she stammered.

"My God, I knew you were naive, but I didn't realize you were stupid. Is that what you thought these last five years were about?"

She nodded. Lance threw back his head and laughed. And laughed and laughed. "Jesus, Rianne, even if I wanted to make you my wife, I couldn't. I was married over a year ago. To the plain, respectable, boring daughter of a prominent banker."

Rianne's eyes widened in shock. Her mouth gaped. Stunned, she could barely form a coherent thought.

"Angelique St. Onge is descended from a long line of Creoles, which makes her socially acceptable, while you're not. The daughter of a whore become my wife? Oh, that's rich. That's really rich!"

As stunned as she was, as trained as she was never to question him, Rianne was unable to prevent her cry of protest. "Don't call my mother that!"

"Why not? It was her role, after all. Just as it's going to be yours."

Rianne's heart plummeted, for she suddenly realized what he'd been planning for her all these years. She stared at him, horrified. "You have no right. I won't do it!"

"You have nothing to say about it. It cost me a bundle to get those false guardianship papers legalized. I've supported you, invested years in you. You'll do as you're told!"

She saw that no arguing, no pleading with him would help. She felt hollow, empty, shattered. She needed to get away from him. Yes, she'd find Mimsie, and they'd leave.

She turned to run, but he grasped her arm and roughly yanked her back. She tried to jerk free, and when she couldn't, she slapped him across the face.

That was a mistake. "You little bitch!" he growled, and he slapped her back, not once but several times. She fell against the bureau, knocking several objects onto the floor.

Her ears were ringing, yet she continued to fight him.

When her strength began to ebb, he laughed cruelly and taunted her. "This is the way you want it, eh? Well, I'll be happy to oblige!" He grabbed the neck of her white gown and tore the dress almost in half. Terrified, she found new strength. She scratched and bit and kicked until he finally slammed his fist into her jaw.

Rianne landed hard on the floor, so dizzy she could barely see Lance as he stood above her, pulling off his own clothes.

"You could have had it nice and soft, but, no, you have to be stubborn and foolish," he panted. "So be it." Naked, he leaned over to rip off her underclothes.

Blindly, in one last effort, Rianne kicked out at him. Her blow landed just above his groin and was strong enough to knock him onto his back. She scrambled to her knees, panting and sobbing in panic, and tried to crawl away from him, but he grabbed her ankle and jerked her back.

"You damned bitch! You're going to pay for that," he shouted, and suddenly his hands were around her neck, squeezing. She choked and gasped as darkness began to fill her vision.

Her arms flailed desperately, but her strength was almost gone, and her vision was dimming. Her fingernails scraped the carpet, seeking something, anything . . .

They closed over metal. By feel, she recognized her sewing scissors, small but sharp and pointed. She found the handle—and brought the scissors up to jab feebly at the air above her.

She heard a horrible scream. Her darkening vision was suddenly filled with red. Bright crimson, everywhere.

And then, mercifully, everything went black . . .

Rianne shuddered in remembrance and swiped at the tears running down her face. "I woke up to find Mimsie kneeling beside me, crying and begging me to get up. I had no idea how long I'd been unconscious or what Lance had done to me. All I knew was that I was covered in blood, horribly bruised and scratched, but alive. Lance wasn't in the room, but I could hear him below, shouting for a doctor, screaming that he was going to kill me. I'd cut his face, Mimsie told me. Badly.

"She helped me up and dressed me. There was no time to wash, to gather anything, but she—bless her heart—had packed a valise for me two days before. 'Just in case,' she said. She took Lance's money from the table and got me to the back stairs, where her brother, Carter, was waiting." Rianne rubbed her forehead. "How she came to be prepared, I don't know. I had no time to ask. I could hear Lance screaming at his friends, telling them to find me and drag me downstairs.

Carter and I fled. He took me to his house, tended my injuries, and then rushed me to the docks to find a ship. And that," Rianne concluded, "was how I ended up in Boston."

"The bastard deserves to be shot!" Alex snarled. "My God, Rianne. I'm sorry that happened to you." He lifted his hand toward her.

She reared back and slapped it away. "Don't touch me! I never want you to touch me again! And don't you dare give me that pitying look!"

"It's not a pitying look, dammit, it's admiration!"

"Oh, stop it!" she scoffed. "You don't have to flatter me anymore. You've already seduced me, remember?"

"How the hell can I forget?" he snapped.

Rianne scrambled to her feet. She couldn't take any more, she really couldn't. Alex despised her. Worse, he felt sorry for her. Oh, God, she needed to get away, to get back to the house, to her room where she could lock the door and shut out the rest of the world. Shut *him* out. "I want to leave," she said dully.

Alex frowned. "We need to talk, Rianne."

"Now," she said frantically. "I want to leave *now.*"

"All right. We'll talk later." Alex got to his feet and slipped into his shirt but left it undone when he saw that her own shirtwaist was hanging loosely from her shoulders. "Turn around so I can button you up," he told her gruffly. "You can't go back to the house looking this way."

She allowed him to move her about like a rag doll. When he was finished with her buttons, he scanned the floor until he spotted her hair ribbon. Bringing it back to her, he stepped behind her to gather her hair and tie the ribbon around it. It was only then that Rianne reacted.

"No!" She turned slowly and held out her hand. "Give it to me." She didn't look at Alex, only waited until he'd complied. Rianne took the bright ribbon to the wall and carefully placed it within one of the small hollows.

"It's my offering," she said quietly, her head bowed. "My thanks for the happiest moments of my life. Though they were brief, they were the greatest gift *I've* ever received."

Suddenly the tears poured out again, running down her cheeks and into her mouth, dripping onto the cave floor like raindrops.

Helpless to stop them, humiliated and mortified, she whirled about and ran to the exit.

Taken by surprise, Alex reached out to stop her, but she was too quick. She slipped past him and fled into the rain and up the path they'd taken.

"Rianne! Come back here!"

Slipping, sliding, banging her shins against the boulders, she scrambled, heedless of the danger. She needed to get away.

She finally crested the top of the outcropping and stood there, unable to think where to go. Though the rain had now diminished to a sprinkle, lightning still flashed around her. She ignored it, ignored the fact that she was standing on top of a granite peak, a perfect target.

The house. She wanted the sanctuary of the house.

She began to make her way down the slippery rocks, ignoring the rain, the lightning, and especially Alex.

Behind her, he shouted her name, then cursed loudly enough to be heard over the storm. That spurred her on, down the slope and toward the river, until she reached the bridge of rocks.

Only then did she glance back. Alex was running along the bank toward her, his open shirt flapping about him.

She didn't stop to think. Didn't want to think.

She stepped off the bank and onto the first boulder.

Chapter 25

She *almost* made it across.

Her foot slipped on the last boulder. She teetered for a moment—and then she toppled into the water.

Alex was forgotten as she struggled to keep her head above water. She thought she heard him shouting her name, but she was fighting the current. It was a losing battle. The rushing undertow swept her downstream while she bobbed up and down like a cork until her skirts pulled her under. Her flailing arms brought her back just high enough to gulp air.

She was swallowing more water than air. Her arms were already aching, her strength ebbing. It would be simpler to stop struggling and let herself be carried away.

She went under again, and this time she didn't try to gain the surface. She felt strangely calm, almost serene.

Then pain shot through her scalp, bringing her back to awareness. She began to struggle again, instinctively fighting the monster that had gotten hold of her.

She broke the surface, gasping and choking. The monster was Alex. He'd pulled her up by her hair, and now he wrapped one arm about her waist and began to swim toward shore.

It took forever, but at last he reached the bank. Still hanging on to her, he dragged her to solid ground, then collapsed beside her. They both lay there, coughing and spitting up water.

"What the hell," he eventually choked out, "did you think you were doing?"

Rianne opened her eyes to find his glittering down at her. She lowered her eyelids again. "Getting away from you?"

Alex cursed foully. Her eyes flew open when he suddenly jerked her upright and shook her.

"Dammit! You could have drowned!"

"Who would have cared? Certainly not you! What would you have done, Alex? Buried me beside your Mary Ellen? Oh, no. That's sacred ground, isn't it? In the garden, then? Or perhaps you would have found a distant spot in the woods—"

"Stop it! Stop it, damn you!" He shook her again, nearly hard enough to make her teeth snap together.

"*I care,* damn you!" he shouted. "That's the bloody problem. I love you, and it makes me so damned furious I could choke you for it!"

Rianne's jaw fell. Surely she was imagining his words. Nearly drowning had made her delirious.

"Did you hear me?" Alex growled. "I said I loved you, and—"

"And it makes you so furious you want to choke me. You really said that?"

"Yes, dammit!"

"Oh, Alex." She beamed up at him, a smile of joy. "Please don't choke me," she said. "It's been tried before and I don't like it much."

He sat up and pulled her against him to hug her so fiercely that she could barely breathe again. "Oh, God, I'm sorry! What a stupid thing to say! I'm sorry, sweetheart."

"You could simply have let me drown," she gasped into his ear.

He clasped the back of her head and pressed his cheek against hers. "Darlin'! Don't scare me like that again. I thought I was going to lose you. That's when I finally realized—slow as I am—how empty my life would be without you." He held her away a few inches to gaze into her eyes. "The truth is, I think I fell in love with you that night on the train, when you were so foolishly determined to protect me. I just didn't want to admit it. I was too . . ."

Rianne's eyes shone as she gently caressed his cheek. "Afraid. You can say it, Alex. I won't think any less of you. It will only make me love you more." She wrapped her arms around his neck and pressed the tip of her nose to his. "I've discovered something, too, you see, since I've known you. Fear is only overwhelming when you're alone, when you don't let others share it." She sighed. "But now we have each other, and together we can face anything. Oh, Alex, look over there!"

Alex turned his head.

"A rainbow!" she cried. "And it disappears right at Church Rock. Isn't that wonderful?"

He laughed at her delight and turned back to nuzzle her cheek. "Hmm. Wonderful," he agreed.

"Alex!" Rianne pushed him away and slapped him playfully on his chest. "You aren't paying attention!" she laughed. "What am I to do with you?"

He cocked his head and pursed his lips, considering. "Well, I can think of one thing . . ."

She slapped his chest again. "Not now! We're both sopping wet."

"You're right," he sighed as he took her hand and rose, pulling her with him. Still holding her hand, he led her in the direction of the house. "Beside, we've got plans to make."

Rianne glanced at him suspiciously. "What plans?"

"Wedding plans."

She stopped abruptly, forcing him to turn back to her.

"Are you asking me to marry you?"

He slapped his forehead in mock chagrin. "That's right. I should ask first, shouldn't I? Rianne—"

She jerked her hand from his. "If you're asking merely to make an honest woman of me . . ."

He grinned. "I was thinking more along the line of *you* making an honest man of *me.*"

"Alex! I'm serious. If that's the only reason you want to marry me, then I can't. Marry you, that is."

He saw that she was, indeed, serious. Her expression was almost woeful, in fact. "Can't, or won't?" he asked soberly.

She turned away. "All right, I won't. I don't want to marry you because you feel responsible for . . . for what happened back in the cave. Because you think it's the noble thing to do or . . ."

"Rianne?"

"Or because you're concerned what others might think, or . . ."

"Rianne?"

"Or . . ."

"Rianne!" he thundered.

She jumped but continued to face away from him. "What?" she asked in a subdued tone.

"Will you please look at me?" He sighed when she shook her head. "Dammit, Rianne, I admit I don't follow all the rigid rules of society, but it seems to me a man is supposed to propose to the woman he loves face to face, not to her back."

"I believe you love me, Alex, but I also understand how much you loved Mary Ellen. You've made it clear you never want to marry again, and I'm not critical of your feelings—truly I'm not. And I would absolutely *hate* for you to feel forced—Alex! What are you doing?" she shrieked.

"Shut up," he said mildly as he scooped her into his arms.

"For a woman who could hardly say a word when we first met, you talk too much."

"Well! You don't have to be insulting. I—"

"If you say one more word before we reach the house, I'm going to toss you to the ground and make furious love to you."

Rianne glanced ahead to see that the house was already in view. As would they be, if anyone was peering out the windows. She peeped up at Alex. He didn't seem angry, only determined. Having no doubt that he'd do as he threatened, she bit down on her bottom lip to keep from speaking.

Remaining silent wasn't difficult, for she felt more like crying than speaking again. She'd meant what she'd said. If Alex married her solely out of a sense of responsibility, she'd hate it. She couldn't do it.

But she couldn't let him go, either. Though the notion was against everything she believed, she'd willingly become his mistress, if that was what it would take to stay with him. It wouldn't be easy, but she would live with it if that was all Alex could offer. In time, he might change his mind about marriage.

She hoped so, with all her heart.

Leslie was the first to see them. She shrieked, drawing everyone else's attention to the French doors Alex had just pushed open.

He stood in the garden entrance of the sun room, Rianne in his arms. Bedraggled and dripping water, they looked like two shipwreck victims.

"Good heavens! What's happened to you two?" Leslie squealed, frozen in her chair.

Sara left hers and rushed to them, concerned. "Alex. Rianne. Are you all right?"

Rianne wiggled, but instead of releasing her, Alex winked

at her. "We're fine, Sara, though I think we could both use a hot bath and some dry clothing."

"Of course. I'll send Mary Margaret and Susan up to your rooms immediately."

"Wait, Sara." Alex glanced around, at her husband and Reverend and Inez Moser, who were still sitting in their chairs, slack-jawed. "Good," he said. "Everyone is here."

"You might have taken note of that sooner, Alex," Rianne said. "Put me down, please," she requested primly.

"Certainly, darlin'."

When he gently set her on her feet, Rianne lowered her head and immediately began to tug at her clinging skirt, which was tangled wetly about her legs. She was afraid to look at the others in the silent room. Surely they were all staring at her. Who wouldn't? She was a mess! Oh, Lord, she could only imagine what they were all thinking! Though Alex seemed to be making an attempt at explaining.

"This is something best done in private, something that should take place only between a gentleman and his lady, but since Rianne is somewhat reluctant . . ."

What *was* he saying? Rianne blinked when Alex appeared within her downcast gaze. She froze in disbelief.

Alex was *on his knees* before her! "What are you doing?" she demanded in a loud whisper. "Get up! Everyone's staring at us."

As if she hadn't spoken, he clasped her right hand in his. "Rianne, before these witnesses," he said very earnestly, "I'm asking you to be my wife."

Rianne's mouth dropped.

"I'm asking you to share your life with me. I can't promise you perfection, because I'm not, God knows, a perfect man. But I can offer you this: my unending love, given freely, without reservation, without doubts, without any shadows darkening my heart." Alex pressed her hand against his chest. "I can say this because my heart now belongs to you, my love."

Rianne pressed her free hand to her burning cheek.

"I know I've made some silly statements in the past about how determined I was to never marry again," Alex continued, "but the plain fact is, my love, that I've discovered that I'm incomplete without you. I want to wake up in the morning with you beside me . . ."

Rianne's blush deepened.

". . . I want to give you my children . . ."

She closed her eyes in embarrassment.

". . . I want to make you laugh with happiness and cry only with joy. Say you'll marry me. Please."

"Oh, my!" Sara gasped.

"Why, Alex, I didn't know you could be so romantic," Leslie said, awed.

Mrs. Moser clapped her hands. "Well done, Mr. Benedict!" she gushed.

"My dear," her husband reminded her dryly, "we have yet to hear the lady's reply."

Rianne was oblivious to these comments and too stunned to reply. She was still trying to comprehend that Alex, who could be so proud and unbending at times, had actually, on bended knee, proposed to her—in front of *everyone!* Had actually bared his emotions in front of everyone! Was still on his knees . . .

. . . And was now kissing her fingers one by one! "Won't you—" *kiss* "—please say—" *kiss* "—you'll marry me—" *kiss* "—before we both—" *kiss* "—catch our deaths of cold? Or, at the very least, before my bones permanently meld into this position?" Alex nipped her thumb.

That brought her back to her senses. Alex was gazing up at

her with a soulful expression, yet a smile teased the corners of his mouth.

Oh, the fool! The wonderful, wonderful fool! "Oh, Alex, do you really mean everything you said?" She sniffled, overcome with emotion.

"Dare I construe that as a yes? Does that mean I can get off my knees now?"

Rianne swiped at a lone tear. "Yes and yes, you lovely idiot! How can I say no, after that performance?"

"Thank God!" Alex said as he slowly rose. "I didn't know what I was going to do for an encore had you refused!"

Rianne gave Leslie a censored explanation as they climbed the stairs. Still chattering, she let Leslie help her undress, then into the tub. Soaping her sponge, she glanced at the usually talkative Leslie, who hadn't yet said a word. "Oh, dear! Have Alex and I shocked you terribly?" she asked.

"Heavens, no! You know I don't shock easily. It's . . ." Leslie waved a hand. "I'm just a bit surprised. I suppose I never expected Alex to fall in love again, even though I wondered if something was happening between you two when I saw him asleep with his head in your lap today."

"I doubt *he* expected to fall in love again, either," Rianne admitted wryly.

Leslie grinned. "Naturally, I'm not surprised *you* fell in love with my brother. How could you not?"

Rianne laughed in appreciation.

"I admit, I was a mite concerned when I watched you and Alex this afternoon, for Aunt Lorna and I both thought you might still be married, not a widow as you'd told Mrs. Busley," Leslie continued.

"Thankfully I'm not either." Rianne stroked the sponge over her shoulders and down her arms. "When I think of

Lance now, all I feel is revulsion."

"And no wonder! What a horrible thing to have to live through!" Leslie exclaimed. "But just think—if you hadn't, you never would have fled to Boston or Chatham's. And you'd never have met me or Alex, and he and you never would have fallen in love." She sighed. "Really, that part of your story is so romantic when you think of it."

Rianne laughed. "It didn't feel romantic all those times I wanted to slap your brother!"

Leslie grinned. "I know that feeling, too. He—" She glanced up as the door opened. "Speak of the devil!" She rose and took a stance between Alex and Rianne. "What do you think you're doing, Alex? You can't come in here!"

Behind her, Rianne abruptly slid down into the bath water. "I knocked, but no one answered," Alex defended. "Besides, if you've interrogated Rianne as well as I think you have," he said, "then you know that she hardly needs to be protected from me."

Leslie blushed. "Still," she persisted stubbornly, "you shouldn't be alone with her. *Especially* not while she's in her bath! It's most improper."

"Les . . ." Alex began impatiently.

His sister stood her ground. "You're the one who has always insisted on the proprieties. I've lived with your overprotectiveness for years, and I've never complained, have I?" At his raised eyebrows, she backed down a tad. "Well, almost never. Now Alex, you can just wait in Rianne's room until she's out of her bath and in a robe."

"All right!" Alex said, rolling his eyes. Then he tried to peer around her, but Les shifted her body to block his gaze. "Hurry up, darlin', will you? We need to talk," he called to Rianne.

Leslie glanced over her shoulder. "She can't hear you.

She's dunked her head beneath the bubbles and the bath water."

Alex waggled his brows. "Bubbles, huh?"

"Get out of here!" Leslie tried to sound stern but began giggling. "Hurry up, or she'll drown for real."

"I'm going!" Alex said as he whipped about. "Hurry it up, though, will you? We've got a wedding to plan for tomorrow."

Leslie grabbed his coattail and brought him to a halt. "Did you say *tomorrow?* Alex, that's impossible! There's far too much to do. Why, Rianne and I haven't even spoken about what she'll wear, and—"

A gurgling sound from behind her cut her off. "Oh, Lord! Go, before she drowns!" Alex quickly obeyed, and Leslie turned around to find water sloshing over the tub as Rianne waved frantically."Oh, my stars! She *is* drowning, and Alex will *kill* me!" Leslie muttered as she went to rescue her friend.

"I need at least three days."

Alex groaned.

Rianne was sitting on his lap, her body wrapped in a warm robe, her hair in a thick towel. "Alex," Rianne pointed out, "it isn't just me. Sara asked if she could plan a celebration, and she wants to bake a cake, and I haven't decided what to wear, and—"

Alex slapped his forehead. "I'm a dunce! Of course you'll want to go into Atlanta and do some shopping, buy a wedding gown—"

"Actually, no."

He leaned back to look at her in surprise. "No?"

Rianne shook her head. "I've already chosen a peach gown. It was a gift from your aunt Lorna." She shuddered delicately. "I swore I'd never wear white again, and I won't. You don't mind, do you?"

"Whatever you want is fine with me, darlin'." He knew her

reasons. "I'm sending a wire to Aunt in the morning to inform her of our wedding. Anything you want to say to her?"

"Yes. Tell her I send my love. And my apologies."

Alex quirked an eyebrow. "Apologies? For what?"

Rianne smiled secretively. "Oh, she'll understand. Besides, I intend to write her a long letter tomorrow."

"As you wish. Speaking of apologies, am *I* forgiven?"

"I'm still considering," she said with mock severity. "You did manage to make a public spectacle of both of us when you proposed."

"It was the only way I knew to make you realize how sincere I am, to prove that I love you madly. Fiercely. Unequivocally."

Rianne laughed. "All right. I'll forgive you. This time."

He snuggled her closer. "I'll do better the next time. I promise."

"The next time?"

"When we renew our vows on our twenty-fifth anniversary, with all our children and grandchildren gathered around."

She leaned back to look at him. "Grandchildren? Aren't you rushing things?" she teased.

"I'm going to rush them a lot more if you keep smiling at me that way."

"What way?"

"As if you've just discovered I'm a chocolate eclair and you can't wait to sink your teeth into me."

"I have, you are, and I can't." Rianne shoved her fingers into his hair and tried to pull his face to hers. Alex resisted. She gave him a questioning look. "No?"

He shook his head solemnly. "Sara and Les will both have my hide if I touch you again before we're married."

"Not even one little kiss?"

"Uh-uh. If I start kissing you, I won't be able to stop."

"They're both spoilsports," Rianne pouted. Then she brightened. "But how will they ever know?"

"They'll know because I won't be able to stop grinning." Rianne shrugged in defeat. She wasn't aware that the action made her robe fall open until she saw Alex's gaze drop. She glanced down. Her right breast was almost entirely exposed.

Beneath her, Alex's body stirred, and he groaned. "I'd better leave." His voice was raspy.

She shrugged her other shoulder. "Are you sure?" she asked, her own voice husky with invitation.

He groaned again. "Blast it, Rianne! I've already lost control once today. No other woman has ever done that to me before." His gaze was still pinned hungrily on her breasts, so he didn't see her eyes narrow dangerously. She shrugged again, and the robe fell to her waist. "God help me!" Alex prayed aloud. Then he leaned forward eagerly.

Rianne was off his lap so quickly that it made him blink. She was standing before him, pulling the lapels of her robe closed tightly to hide her bosom. "What—" Alex began.

"If you ever say another word about your *other women,*" she told him, her eyes shooting sparks of fury, "I'll cut your heart out."

Alex stared at her for a moment. Then, he stood, and a slow smile spread over his face. "Well," he said cheerfully, "at least it'll be quicker than a slow death."

He leaned to plant a quick kiss on her nose. He was grinning when he straightened and turned toward the door, leaving Rianne to gape after him.

"My little Amazon," he chuckled. He shook his head, opened the door, and began to laugh. "What a woman!"

Chapter 26

"Do you, Rianne DuBois—"

"Forrester."

"I beg your pardon?"

Beside her, Alex stirred. She could feel his eyes boring into her. "Forrester," she repeated. "My full and legal name is Rianne Charlotte Forrester."

"I see." Reverend Moser straightened his spectacles. "Do you, Rianne Charlotte Forrester, take Alexander James Benedict to be your lawfully wedded husband? Do you promise to love, honor and obey—"

"No."

A collective gasp went up from the witnesses behind the couple. Poor Reverend Moser looked even more befuddled. "No?" he asked disbelievingly.

"No. Remove the word *obey,*" Rianne said firmly, refusing to look at Alex, who was now pressed against her side. She could feel his shoulders shaking.

"Well, I, er . . ." Reverend Moser glanced helplessly at the groom, then sighed, relieved at the nod of permission he received. He turned back to Rianne.

"Do you promise to love, honor, and, er, be true . . ."

Rianne listened intently to the rest of the words, making sure the pastor wouldn't slip in anything else she was opposed to. When he was through, she smiled approvingly. "I do," she said clearly.

Mopping his brow, Reverend Moser then turned to Alex and repeated the vows, stuttering as he cast glances at Rianne. When it seemed she wouldn't correct him again, he rushed on. "And do you, Alexander," the minister continued, "promise to forsake all others and—"

"I promise," Alex cut in, "to forsake all others and to *never speak even one word of them* for as long as we both shall live."

Beside him, Rianne smiled in satisfaction.

They had the first argument of their married life that very night—their wedding night.

With the help of half a dozen other women on Bellesfield's staff, Sara and Leslie had spent hours preparing an empty cottage for them, so that they would have privacy.

It was lit with many candles and filled with fresh flowers from the hodgepodge garden. Alex had given orders that there be no roses. Not one. But perfume from the countless other blooms filled the air.

The wedding had taken place at one o'clock, despite Alex's impatience. He would have preferred ten in the morning, but the women had insisted that they needed more time, and he'd finally given in when it was pointed out to him that he was only *wasting* time by arguing.

Cake and punch had been served, and Alex had fretted then, too. But finally the couple was sent off to the cottage alone, to find covered dishes of food spread out on a table and Champagne on ice.

They'd ignored all but the bowl of fresh strawberries and the Champagne, which they'd taken with them into the bedroom.

Now, sated and properly exhausted after an hour of delectable delights—none of which involved food or drink—Alex and Rianne were sitting in their bed. Covered up to his waist by a sheet, Alex was propped up by pillows, while Rianne, who was wearing only his shirt, was straddling him, idly feeding him strawberries.

"I didn't have time to buy you a wedding gift," Alex suddenly said.

Rianne popped another strawberry into his mouth, then one into hers, washing it down with a sip of warm Champagne. "Nor I, you." Then she stared at him, her expression serious. "I've just thought of one you could give me, though."

He waggled his eyebrows at her.

"Not that!" she laughed. Then she corrected herself. "Well, yes, that, too. But what I'd really like is for you to tell Leslie the whole truth about your father's death and . . . and, well, you know."

Alex saw that she was in earnest. "You're right, sweetheart. It's time to let go of the ghosts. I *will* do it tomorrow. But I'll buy you a real gift when we reach New Orleans."

Rianne frowned and set her glass and the bowl on the bedside table.

"What?" Alex asked, watching her. "You don't want a proper bridal gift?"

"It's not that," she said slowly as she idly curled some of his chest hair around her fingers. "It's . . . Can't I stay here until you and Leslie return?"

Alex sat up straighter, causing her to bounce. "I thought you said you wanted to find Mimsie."

"Oh, I do!" Rianne had written countless letters to Mimsie through Carter, but she'd never received a reply. "But you could find her for me and bring her here, couldn't you?"

"You are *not* staying here, Rianne. You're my wife now. I didn't marry you to leave you behind. I want you with me at all times."

"But—"

"No *buts*."

"But, Alex," she persisted, ignoring his warning. "Leslie doesn't really need me, since you've decided she'll stay at Louisa's home." Leslie had told her as she helped Rianne dress for her wedding that that was what she and Alex had decided. "And since you have business to attend to, well . . ."

"No."

"Oh, you're so stubborn!" Her fingers traced a path down the center of his chest, toward the sheet. "Can't we at least talk about this?" she pouted.

He glowered at her. "You can talk to me, cajole me, try to bribe me with sex. I'm still going to say no."

Rianne jerked her fingers away and blushed furiously, ducking to hide her guilt.

He reached out to lift her chin, but she lowered her eyelids. "Rianne. Look at me, darlin'." He waited until she'd complied, and when he saw real apprehension in her eyes, he wrapped his arms about her and pulled her against him. "You're still afraid. What happened to our fighting fear together?"

"It's just that you don't know him, Alex. Lance can be very cruel."

"He isn't going to hurt you," Alex crooned as he smoothed back her hair. "He isn't even going to touch you. I swear it!"

She sighed.

He shifted her so that he could look into her face. "Don't you trust me?"

He sounded hurt. Rianne glanced up at him. He *looked* hurt.

She felt terrible. Throwing herself over him, she kissed his nose, his cheeks, his chin. "Of *course* I trust you, my love."

But later, as Alex breathed softly beside her, Rianne was still awake.

She did trust Alex. He was her husband, her lover, her friend. She trusted him implicitly.

But he didn't understand. Strangely enough, she wasn't as afraid of Lance's exacting revenge on her as she was of his ugliness coming between herself and Alex, of its tainting their marriage. And it would if she had to keep looking over her shoulder all the time they were in New Orleans.

If only she had some way to prevent it, to toss the ugly past away like unwanted garbage and start anew.

If only . . .

Two days later, just before breakfast, Leslie's door flew open. "Where the hell is she?" Alex demanded.

Leslie, who was sitting at her dressing table pinning up her hair, turned to face him. "Good morning to you, too, brother," she replied casually.

He stomped over to her and stood glaring down, his eyes fierce pools of green fire. "Don't be smart with me, Les. I woke up this morning to find my wife's side of the bed empty. Her closet seems emptier, too, but I didn't think too much about it until after I spent two hours traipsing about the plantation looking for her. *Where the hell is my wife?*"

Leslie sighed. "Don't glower at me that way. I'll tell you what you want to know if you give me some space."

He took one half step back, then crossed his arms over his chest and gritted his teeth as he waited.

Les rose and slid past him. "She's left for New Orleans," she told him resignedly. "I helped her pack yesterday, and she slipped out of your room shortly after midnight. Trevor Williams took her into Atlanta." Seeing the fury in Alex's eyes, she raised a hand. "Don't you dare yell at me or go after Trevor! Rianne threatened to do it all by herself if we didn't help. Would you rather we'd left her to make her way alone?"

Alex considered murdering Les and Williams both, but the fact was that he was learning more every day about his wife's stubbornness and determination. And, no, he wouldn't have wanted her on the road alone. But, damn, it hurt that she hadn't confided in him!

"Why?" he bit out. "What does she hope to do in New Orleans that couldn't wait until we were all there?" But he was afraid he already knew the answer.

Leslie confirmed it. "Alex, she wanted to rid herself of a painful past *before* you came. She wanted to confront Lance Paxton on her own and settle the animosity between them. She said it was the only way she'd feel free."

Alex's curses should have turned the air blue. "I'm leaving within the hour. You'll have to stay here until I can make other arrangements for you." He spun on his heel to leave.

Leslie hurried after him and grabbed hold of his sleeve. "Oh no, you don't! You're not leaving me behind, Alex!"

He whirled about. "Damn it, Les, I can't wait for you to pack and—"

"You don't have to." She waved at the trunks stacked against the wall next to the door and smiled at him. "I'm already packed. Have been for hours. And so are you. I did it while you were searching for Rianne."

Chapter 27

Nothing had changed. Bougainvillea still climbed the wrought iron posts and onto the second-floor railing. The same oleander bush still flowered in front. The same blue shutters, the same . . . Rianne shuddered. Did the cottage still belong to Lance, she wondered as she gazed at it through the carriage window.

She hadn't wanted to go near this cottage on rue Dauphine. She didn't really believe that Mimsie would have stayed with Lance, but she didn't know where else to look.

She'd already been to the street where Mimsie's brother, Carter, had taken her after that last night with Lance. But their tiny house was no longer there. Indeed, the street was entirely different, for a fire some years previously had destroyed most of the homes there.

She'd walked up and down the street, knocking on doors, to no avail. One woman told her that many of the former residents had moved away after the fire. No one seemed to know anything about a woman named Mimosa—Mimsie—or Carter Reed.

No, Rianne didn't want to be here, but the fear that Lance had taken his revenge on her beloved Mimsie kept playing in her mind, so here she was.

The carriage door opened. "I asked as you requested, ma'am," the driver told her. "The housekeeper swears she never heard of Mimosa Reed *or* Lance Paxton. She says the cottage belongs to her employer, a woman by the name of Janet Heston. I was informed that Mrs. Heston isn't at home right now," he added.

"I see." Rianne was torn between relief and worry. She glanced back at the cottage. A shadow in a second-floor window caught her eye, but when she peered closer only a curtain stirred—as if someone had been surreptitiously peeking out, then had stepped back quickly.

"Thank you," she told the driver. "You may take me back to my hotel now, please."

She had decided to stay in the same hotel Alex had told her he'd booked rooms in. She knew he'd be close behind her, and it had never been her intention to hide from him. She'd only hoped to be done with her business before he arrived.

But thus far she hadn't accomplished much of anything. This morning, her first day in New Orleans, she'd gone to the St. Louis Cemetery to visit her parents' gravesite. Their mausoleum was not large, but the marble was beautifully and simply engraved with entwined magnolia blossoms—Claudine Forrester's favorite.

Rianne's father had purchased the plot and ordered the crypt built before he'd gone off to war.

The remainder of the day had been spent looking for Mimsie.

Rianne was running out of time. She would have to go to the St. Onge Bank and confront Lance. She wasn't exactly sure what she'd say, but she was holding on to the hope that she'd exaggerated the fears she'd carried in her mind all these years. It was possible that Lance had already put the past behind him. And if not, well, she'd do whatever she must—apologize, beg his forgiveness, even grovel. Anything to find Mimsie.

By the time Rianne returned to her hotel, she was exhausted. She had a tray sent up, bathed, and climbed into bed and immediately fell asleep.

One minute she was dreaming of the garden at Bellesfield, the next she was wide awake, staring into the shadows of her room, her heart pounding with fear.

One of the shadows moved. Before she could take a breath to scream, a hand clamped over her mouth. She tried to jerk upright but was immediately pinned into place by a heavy body.

"Shh! If you scream, you'll wake the entire hotel."

Alex! His familiar scent filled her nostrils, and despite her resolve to handle her own problems her own way, she felt an enormous sense of relief that he was here. She reached up and pried his hand away from her mouth. "I'm not going to scream, but I just might give you a bloody nose for frightening me half to death, Alex Benedict!" she hissed.

"Then we're going to have a hell of a mess in here," he shot back as he rose and stepped away from her.

Rianne heard rustling sounds. "What are you doing?" she asked.

"I'm removing my clothes to keep from mussing them when I turn you over my knee for leaving me and coming here on your own!"

She supposed she couldn't blame him for wanting to, but . . . "Wait a minute!" she exclaimed in a loud whisper as he pulled the blankets aside to slide his naked body in beside her. She moved over to give him room. "You don't sound angry. Why don't you sound angry?" she asked suspiciously.

He gathered her into his arms and pulled her tightly against his chest, one hand cradling her head. "Angry? Try furious. Which is how I've felt since the moment I discovered you'd left Bellesfield. I still should be furious, but I'm just so damned relieved that you're here and that you're all right," he rasped into her ear.

"Mmph!" she muttered.

"Whatever made you do such a harebrained thing?"

"Mmmph!"

"What?" He leaned back slightly, just as she slapped her palm against his chest.

"I can't breathe!" she gasped. "Did you change your mind and decide to smother me, instead?"

"I thought of that, too." He sighed and pulled her close again, but not quite as tightly as the first time. "Damn, Rianne, you aged me ten years in one day! Don't ever scare me that way again!"

"I'm sorry, Alex," she said against his neck. "But I knew you wouldn't let me handle this myself, and—"

"Damn right! Didn't I tell you I'd take care of Paxton? Well, now that I'm here, you're to stay put. Here, in the hotel. You're not to so much as stick that pert nose out the door!" he said sternly.

"But—"

"No *buts!* You'll do as you're told this time!"

Rianne pushed away from him. "You have no right—"

"I have every right, dammit! You're my wife, and I—Ow! What'd you do that for?" She'd pinched his side and before he could react, slipped out of the bed.

She fisted her hands on her hips and loomed over him. "I will *not* stay inside this hotel. I didn't come back to New Orleans only to be kept a prisoner again, Alex! You can't do that to me. I won't let you."

Alex jerked upright. "You don't have a choice," he gritted, angry now. "I'll lock you in this room if I have to—to keep you safe, not hold you prisoner."

She stamped a foot in frustration. "Then I'll climb out the window!"

She sounded almost on the verge of hysteria, which was so unlike her, he simply stared up at her in shock. Then he realized that she was reliving her time with Lance Paxton, who'd taken freedom from her. And Alex knew he couldn't follow through on his threat.

"All right. We'll find another way." He held out his hand. "Come to bed, now, sweetheart."

"You promise?"

"I promise. Come now, love."

She slid back into bed and into his arms with a soft sigh. "It's just that I can't stand the thought of . . ."

Alex's hand slid from her waist down over her hip. He lowered his face to nuzzle her breast. "I know. It's all right, my love. Let's not talk about it any more tonight, Rianne."

"But—"

"Hush," he murmured lovingly as he tugged at the hem of her nightgown.

"But, Alex—" She broke off as his fingers slid from her knee up the tender inside of her thigh. Rianne sighed in pleasure as his touch left a trail of delicious fire.

"Don't talk," he ordered. "Just kiss me."

She grasped his hair and pulled his head back. "Now who's trying to bribe whom with sex?" she teased.

"Is it working?"

"Yes," she replied, pulling his face back to her breast.

"Oh, yes, indeed. It's working."

Alex smiled to himself. He didn't think it was the time to tell her that within an hour of leaving Bellesfield, he'd found a telegraph office and sent a wire to a detective agency in New Orleans—one often used by Brannon and Benedict. Rianne had been safely under surveillance the moment she'd stepped off the train.

The same firm was also under orders to investigate Lance Paxton. Alex had an early appointment with an agent tomorrow, in fact, to find out what information they already had for him.

He intended to learn everything he could about the bastard—his private life, his family and social standing, his finances.

Especially his finances.

There were more subtle and more effective means of destroying a certain type of man than killing him outright.

The next morning Rianne and Alex slept in—due in part to their exuberant reunion the night before. When Alex finally rose and kissed her on the cheek before going into the bathing room for his morning ablutions, Rianne smiled and snuggled back into her pillow. Some time later, he woke her with the delicious smell of café au lait and fresh, warm *beignets,* which they shared. Afterwards he left her to her own bath.

She'd just finished her toilette when she heard the murmur of voices from the sitting room of their suite. Leaving the bedroom, Rianne found Alex sharing more coffee with a stranger, whom he introduced as Riley Jackson, an investigator from the Pinkerton Detective Agency. Alex took Rianne's hand and pressed it to his lips. "We're going to find your Mimsie, darlin'."

Mr. Jackson was a small, nondescript-looking man, except for his shrewd hazel eyes and a dapper mustache, which he continued to stroke with his left hand while he took notes with his right. He was slow-talking and patient as he interrogated her. He sometimes nodded and murmured "Uh-huh" in a thoughtful way, and would then glance up to give her an encouraging smile and ask her another question. Rianne felt comfortable enough to tell him everything, even—at Alex's reassuring nod—the events of the night of her eighteenth birthday.

She felt much better after he'd left with a promise that the matter of finding Mimosa Reed was now his first priority.

Later that afternoon Rianne accompanied Alex to Louisa Newton's home, where Leslie was staying, to take her with them to Royal Street, where a branch office of Brannon and Benedict was situated. There, she and Leslie were introduced to the smiling staff, who seemed delighted that Alex was now married and that he'd brought his wife and sister to visit.

It was there, too, that Alex took them into a private office, sat them together on a sofa while he perched on the edge of the desk, and informed them that they were shortly to meet two men who were to become their constant shadows while in New Orleans. Leslie protested vehemently. Rianne said nothing but gave Alex a look that told him she knew perfectly well that he'd planned this in advance.

Alex aimed a stern look at his sister. "Have you forgotten, Les, that being here may not be the safest place for Rianne?"

"Oh!" Leslie turned to her sister-in-law. "I didn't forget, I just didn't think . . . What I thought was that Alex was being his usual over-protective self. I'm sorry, Rianne, for being so selfish."

She was so apologetic that Rianne smiled. "Your brother *is* a worry-wart," she said, patting Leslie's hand, "but in this case . . ." Her hand went to her throat as she turned to Alex. "*Do* you really think it's necessary?" she asked him.

Alex noted her nervous action. He didn't think she realized herself that each time her past was brought up or Paxton's name was mentioned, she instinctively, protectively stroked her throat.

A cold shudder ran up his spine. When he thought of a man's strong hands—that snake, Paxton's, hands—around that slim, fragile throat, he saw red.

"Lance Paxton still lives here, sweetheart. In fact, he's now a prominent man, thanks to his marriage into wealth and influence, but it's my understanding that his father-in-law, Pierre St. Onge, pulls all the strings. It's for that reason that I don't think there's any *real* danger," Alex said, hoping it wasn't a lie. "Paxton wouldn't want to jeopardize his standing in any way, whether it be social, financial or familial." Alex thought grimly of the dossier Jackson had handed over to him that morning. Paxton was very careful to maintain his public reputation, but he led a sordid secret life, too. Which made him vulnerable but also, perhaps, dangerous.

Still, Alex intended to be very cautious. Paxton wasn't stupid, his father-in-law even less so. They'd both eventually discover that someone was buying up their bank stock from other shareholders and insidiously burrowing into Lance's other business investments—including his less respectable ones.

"Alex?"

"Sorry. I was about to say that, much as I'd like to, I can't be with you every minute, sweetheart, and I don't want to dampen your enjoyment, nor Leslie's, during our stay here. So these men are to guard you when I can't. They're both long time employees of ours, and they know their jobs. Their large sizes hardly make them unobtrusive, and that's the whole point. No one will dare approach you while they're about."

Alex's eyes narrowed as he gave Rianne a penetrating look. "You know what the alternative is." She nodded in resignation. "Good, then keep in mind that neither of you is to go anywhere without them. Do you understand?"

"Alex," Rianne chided gently, "Leslie and I aren't children."

"True, but you *are* the stubbornnest two women I know," he teased in an effort to soften his words, "while I'm just a helpless, outnumbered, often outmaneuvered male."

As he'd intended, his words lightened the mood. He didn't really want to frighten them, after all.

They were interrupted by a knock on the door. Alex opened it to let two men in. Leslie and Rianne looked up. And up and up . . .

"Good Heavens!" Leslie gulped.

"Hercules and Goliath!" Rianne gasped.

The one with skin like glossy ebony turned and grinned at her with startlingly white teeth. "Exactly, ma'am," he said as he came to the sofa and extended his right hand. "Goliath Butler."

Rianne's hand disappeared into his huge palm. Likewise, Leslie's.

"And this," Alex said as he brought forth the other giant, "is Seamus O'Connor." This one was perhaps four inches shorter than Goliath, but his shoulders looked as wide as a house. His skin was ruddy, his hair almost orange, his eyes pale blue, and he wore a dark scowl that was suddenly and unexpectedly replaced by a twinkle, " 'Tis me grrreat pleasure, lydies," he rumbled.

"God help us," Leslie prayed.

"Amen!" Rianne tacked on.

Goliath and Conny, as he preferred to be called, lost their friendly demeanors and became dangerously grim the instant they accompanied Rianne and Leslie into public. As promised, they kept a short distance away but not so far that they wouldn't be able to reach either woman in only a few strides.

Alex hadn't understated their lack of inconspicuousness. It gave Rianne and Leslie and—they suspected—Goliath and Seamus, too—unlimited amusement as crowds parted in their wakes. Women gasped. Children scattered. Men quickly stepped aside.

During the day Rianne and Leslie were free to stroll or sight-see or shop whenever they wished. They found intriguing little shops, ate lunch or drank coffee at outdoor cafés, gorged on fresh, hot *beignets* and nibbled on luscious pralines.

In the evening Alex took them to the theater or the opera and to delightful restaurants. Tonight, in fact, they were dining at Tujague's with Louisa Newton and her daughter, Celeste, and Celeste's husband, Charles Rambeau.

Rianne was rediscovering the city of her birth and loving it. Her initial apprehension had vanished. There had been no sign of Lance. The only cloud was the fact that Riley Jackson was as yet unsuccessful in finding any trace of Mimsie. But Alex said that Jackson would have found a record of Mimsie's death, had that been the case, which lifted Rianne's spirits considerably. They'd find Mimsie sooner or later.

In the meantime, with at least one of the giants dogging her footsteps, it was impossible for Rianne *not* to relax and enjoy herself.

Which was probably why she was unprepared for what happened.

She and Leslie—and Goliath and Conny, of course—were at the French Market. Rianne was carrying a basket, intent on buying fresh fruit for everyone's breakfast. Conny was hovering a short distance behind her, while Leslie and Goliath were several stalls away.

Rianne reached for a plump peach. Just then someone jostled her arm and she dropped her basket. "Oh!" Rianne glanced up, but the only person near enough to have bumped her was a woman who was already bending to retrieve the basket. "Thank you so much," Rianne told her, holding out her hand. But when the woman straightened, she kept a tight grip on the basket and studied Rianne silently with chocolate eyes.

Rianne returned the scrutiny. The woman appeared to be in her mid-thirties, with an exquisite tawny complexion. Her clothes were modest but tasteful. She wore a traditional *tignon* wound about her hair, revealing only a dark widow's peak. She looked like a dozen other housekeepers shopping in the Market. She certainly didn't look like a thief.

Rianne frowned. The woman was acting like one, however. At the very least, she owed Rianne an apology, but, like the basket, it didn't seem to be forthcoming. "Excuse me, but you have my basket," Rianne pointed out pleasantly.

The woman took a peach from the basket and sniffed it before returning it and reaching for another. Though taken aback, Rianne stood her ground. "I'd like my basket back, if you please."

"Certainly." But instead of handing it over immediately, the woman reached into her sleeve and pulled out a folded piece of paper, which she tucked between the peaches. Only then did she hand over the basket. "I'd exchange these peaches if I were you, Mrs. Benedict. They're slightly overripe."

"How do you know my name?" Rianne gasped. "And what did you put in there?"

The woman's demeanor suddenly changed. She seemed nervous as she tossed a glance over her shoulder. "I'm sorry, but I can't stay to chatter."

"But—" Rianne was cut off as the basket was practically pushed into her hands.

"I'm to remind you that he doesn't like to be told *no*."

"Who?" But the woman was already hurrying away. Rianne stared after her until she disappeared into the crowd. What had that been about?

"You need some help, ma'am?"

Rianne glanced up to find Conny standing in front of her. "No, thank you. I'm ready to go, as soon as I've paid for these peaches." As she opened her wrist purse to pull out some bills, she shoved the folded paper inside.

After they'd rejoined the others, she made a vague excuse about being tired and wanting to return to the hotel.

Since Alex wasn't back yet, Conny planted himself in the sitting room while she rushed into her bedroom and unfolded the note.

Tonight, at Tujague's. Excuse yourself at eight sharp. Ask for the waiter, Henri.

The signature was merely a scrawled letter. *L.*

Chapter 28

"You're not hungry, sweetheart?" Alex asked.

Rianne glanced up to find that everyone was staring at her. "I'm . . . I'm not very fond of crabmeat," she improvised.

"But that's shrimp rémoulade on your plate, Rianne," Leslie pointed out. "Goodness, you *must* be tired."

"Who wouldn't be? Keeping up with you is exhausting! Even the giants were lagging today," Rianne retorted, forcing a light note into her voice. Everyone laughed, and directed their attention back to their meals.

Everyone except Alex, that was, who frowned as he studied his wife's features. She did look tired. Though she'd been napping when he returned to the hotel, she still had shadows under her eyes.

She'd been quiet all evening. Unusually quiet. Normally she had a chilled bottle of wine ready for his return to their rooms, and she'd sit on his lap while they sipped it and entertain him with tales of her day. Tonight, after he awakened her, she had apologized for "forgetting" the wine, and she'd taken an extended amount of time to dress for dinner, almost as if she'd been reluctant to venture out.

She suddenly turned to him. "What time is it?" she asked.

Alex glanced at his watch. "Almost eight. Are you feeling all right, darlin'?"

"Yes. Leslie and I have been out every day since we've

been here; all that activity is probably just catching up with me."

"Why don't you stay in tomorrow and rest?" Could she be pregnant already, Alex wondered.

Then he smiled. Of course she could be. God, they spent most of their private time together in bed.

"Perhaps I'll do that," Rianne replied. She felt the minutes ticking by. So slowly, yet too fast.

She was still reeling from the shock of receiving Lance's note. She couldn't understand how he'd found out she was here. She was Rianne Benedict now, not Forrester. She hadn't met anyone who had known her before. She hadn't known anyone other than servants. So how was it possible that he'd found her?

Her first inclination had been to ignore Lance's summons. But there was still Mimsie to consider. Surely he'd know where she was.

Her second thought had been to show Lance's note to Alex. But he would have insisted on meeting Lance himself—without her. That knowledge had brought her to the overriding reason she'd decided to meet Lance alone.

She didn't want to see him; she dreaded a face-to-face meeting, actually. But for too many years she'd lived in fear of him. She didn't want to live with it anymore. She was beginning a new life, a life far more wonderful than any she possibly could have dreamed. She wanted to be free to live it, and she knew the only way to do that was to face her fear—to confront Lance. If Alex went with her, she would be depending on him to protect her. She needed to do this alone.

She was, however, thankful that this meeting would be in public. If Lance tried anything, she could cause enough of a ruckus to make him look like a fool. No, Lance wouldn't dare touch her.

She abruptly set her napkin beside her plate. "Excuse me, I'm going to the powder room," she told the table at large.

"Would you like one of us to come with you?" Celeste asked.

"No!" Her abrupt response had everyone staring at her again. "That is, no—stay and eat your shrimp. I'll be back shortly."

Charles and Alex politely stood. "Perhaps . . ." Alex began.

"Really, Alex, this is a public restaurant with dozens of people about. I don't need you to hold my hand," she said, feigning embarrassment.

Alex, looking chagrined, sat down again. Rianne bent over to kiss his cheek. "I'll be back soon," she told him. "Promise."

The waiter, Henri, apparently knew who she was, for before she'd even asked for him, he approached her and bowed. "Madame Benedict. Come with me, please."

He led her swiftly through the kitchen and up the waiters' back stairway to the second floor. There, she followed him past tables of diners to a corner.

This table was set slightly apart from the others and almost backed up against the two walls. Only one candle lit it, and only one person sat there—a man whose face was hidden behind a menu.

Rianne tried to stare through it as Henri seated her.

A ringed hand rose. Fingers flicked, and a voice ordered curtly, "Pour some Champagne for the lady, Henri. This is a reunion."

"No!" Rianne turned to smile at the waiter. "No, thank you, Henri. I don't care for any Champagne."

He bowed again, threw a quick glance at the man, and left.

"Hello, my pet," Lance said as he lowered the menu.

Rianne stifled a moan.

His hair was just as blond, his eyes the same pale blue—except that they were now glittering fiercely at her. He was still quite handsome—except for the scar that began at the corner of his left eye and narrowed until it reached his earlobe. Oh, God, she hadn't known it would be so bad!

He lifted his hand to stroke the scar with long, white fingers. "A souvenir of our time together, eh?"

Rianne took a deep breath and struggled for composure. He *wanted* her to feel guilty. How silly she'd been to think she could face him herself and grovel if she had to. She'd never apologize to him again, no matter what.

"How did you know I was in New Orleans, Lance?" she asked with more calm than she felt. "Or that I'd be dining here tonight?"

"Ah, we are to skip the social niceties, then." He clicked his tongue ruefully. "I thought I'd taught you better."

"I'm not here to play your games, Lance."

"My, you've even acquired some backbone! Too bad. You were so easy to mold, so eager to please." Rianne began to push back her chair. "All right, pet. Calm down." He waited until she'd settled in her seat once again.

"How did I know? Actually," he chuckled, "it was all quite by accident. You see, I had someone following your husband, *Mrs. Benedict.* Imagine my surprise when my man came back with the information that Benedict had a wife, and her name just happened to be Rianne—a rather unusual name. So, being insatiably curious, I showed the man your photograph, and he affirmed that it was you. A bit older, but you, nonetheless. After that, it was simply a matter of paying for the right answers, such as the fact that your party had reservations here for tonight."

"You had Alex followed? Why?"

"Your husband made a substantial deposit in my little bank two weeks ago—so substantial that my father-in-law almost kissed his boots. Now why, I asked myself, would a man of Benedict's wealth—who owns a bank or two of his own, does he not?—put so much money in mine? It occurred to me that maybe your husband isn't as honest a gentleman as everyone thinks. Maybe he's taking bribes, or maybe he's siphoning money from Brannon and Benedict, hiding his actions from his partner. I like to know these little secrets, you see. Never can tell when I might put them to good use."

"Blackmail, you mean," Rianne said scornfully.

Lance shrugged. "Whatever. Anyway, it seemed a good idea to have him followed." He leaned back in his chair. "And now we come to you."

"Ah! I see. You think to blackmail *me*." She laughed softly. "It won't work, Lance. My husband knows all about you. Everything. There's nothing you can do to hurt me through him."

He lifted his glass and saluted her, but his smile was far too smug. "My, my! Such brave words! My little girl *has* changed."

"I was never *your* girl, little or otherwise. Get to the point, Lance. What is it you want?"

He set down his glass. "We have unfinished business between us, you and I." His lips curled in a parody of a smile as he stroked the scar on his cheek. "We never did complete your eighteenth birthday celebration, did we?"

This time Rianne did rise. Though she'd wanted to question him about Mimsie's whereabouts and wellbeing, she knew he would give her no answer. Punishing her, not laying the past to rest, was still his only desire. She would have to trust Alex's agent to track down Mimsie. "Good-bye, Lance.

I'd be lying if I said it's been a pleasure."

Lance snapped his fingers at someone behind her. When she looked over her shoulder, she saw two brawny, rough-looking men rising from the next table. She almost grinned. Compared to Goliath and Conny, they looked like mere children.

She turned back to Lance. "How typical," she said scathingly. "You never did like getting your hands dirty, as I recall. You're nothing more than a bully, but I'm no longer a naive, young girl dependent on you. Nor am I afraid of you."

"My men could have you out of here and into my carriage in mere minutes," he told her as he leaned back and casually sipped his Champagne.

A cloud of unease drifted over Rianne. She glanced back at the men. They hadn't moved, except that one was cracking his knuckles loudly enough to make her wince, while the other gave her a sneering smile that revealed a mouthful of ugly yellowed teeth.

"You wouldn't dare. There are too many people about. And Alex will come looking for me shortly. He'll ask questions. He'll know it was you," she retorted bravely, though her heart was beating madly.

Oh, God! Alex. She felt physically ill at the thought of what it would do to him if she disappeared.

"Ah, yes. Your husband," Lance sneered. "He moves about the city alone, you know. Not a good idea. So many ruffians about. Did you know that hardly a day passes when someone isn't murdered on the streets of New Orleans? A pity, but it happens." His eyes glittered in triumph when Rianne blanched. "Then there's your husband's sister, Leslie. I saw her when you arrived tonight. Tempting little morsel. So much so, in fact, that I might be tempted myself—before I share her with my friends."

Rianne leaned over the table. "Keep away from Leslie!" she hissed. "If you or any of your friends lay one finger on her, Alex will kill you, and I'll help him!"

Lance laughed, making it clear that her threat meant nothing to him. "Such fire! You know, perhaps I was wrong. There's something to be said for a fiery woman. So much more interesting. Tell me, is Leslie temperamental, too?"

"I'm warning you . . ."

She never saw his hand move until he'd grabbed her wrist and twisted it cruelly. "Sit down!" he ordered harshly. "Your attempts at bluffing are pitiable."

She had no choice. He slid his chair nearer to hers and brushed her cheek with his knuckles, making her flinch. "Why don't you ask me about Mimsie?"

Rianne's eyes widened. "Where is she?"

"She moved in with her brother after you left. Bad decision," he said, shaking his head. "I understand a fire broke out on their street soon thereafter. In fact, I do believe it may have even started in their shack. Heard there wasn't enough left to identify any remains."

"Oh, my God! *You* did it, didn't you? You killed her, you *bastard!*"

Conversation ceased as other diners turned in their direction. Lance immediately squeezed her wrist in warning. His insidious tone became a harsh whisper. "Keep your voice down!" Rianne tried to jerk free, but he only applied more pressure, digging his fingers into her cruelly. He held her so closely that she couldn't move. She felt suffocated and prayed she wouldn't faint.

"In two days," he hissed, "you'll come to the address I'll give you. You'll come alone. You'll tell no one, and you'll leave no messages." His eyes were filled with hate and lust as he looked down at her. "Do you understand?"

Rianne let her eyes indicate her acceptance. She had no intention of complying, but she needed time. She needed to find a way to protect Alex and Leslie from this monster.

His lips curled in a caricature of a smile. "It's good to see that you still know your proper role. Don't look so worried, pet. I promise I'll return you to your husband in good time. Of course, he may no longer want you after I'm finished with you."

Rianne closed her eyes. She knew what he meant. He might have wanted to kill her at one time, but now he wanted to make her pay for putting that scar on his face. He'd make her suffer, perhaps cut her, most certainly rape and defile her.

Lance could have no way of knowing what a cruel twist of irony that would be for Alex. Mary Ellen had been defiled, and now Lance intended the same for her.

"Good evening," said an affable voice.

Rianne's eyes flew open and locked on the face of the man who had just seated himself across from them. He didn't glance her way. His glacial gaze was locked with Lance's.

"You will," Alex said to him in the same, pleasant tone, "kindly take your filthy hand off my wife."

Chapter 29

"I asked you to let me handle Lance Paxton. You agreed. But did you do so? No. You waltzed off on your own—twice now, I might add—as if I didn't even exist. If Riley Jackson hadn't come to Tujague's when he did, compelling me to discover what was taking you so long, God knows what Paxton might have tried."

"Alex . . ."

"I can't trust you, Rianne," he grumbled as he turned her about to work on the buttons on her gown. "I should have refused to marry you until Reverend Moser put the word *obey* back into your wedding vows!"

"Ha! I wouldn't have married you if he had!" Rianne retorted. "I don't know why you can't stop scolding me," she pouted. "You acted as if nothing had occurred when we rejoined our guests, but the moment we were alone in the carriage, you start scolding." Cool air brushed her shoulders as Alex unfastened her last button.

Jerking his tie free, he slipped out of his jacket and began unbuttoning his own clothes. "I didn't want to ruin everyone else's evening."

Rianne let her dress fall to the floor. "Neither did I!" she said as she sat on the bed to slip off her shoes. She dragged her petticoats up over her knees to remove her garters. "But if I'd known you were going to nag me so, I'd have invited myself to spend the night at Louisa's."

"And I would have immediately uninvited you," Alex replied. His fingers stilled as he watched Rianne begin to roll a stocking down her slim calf. Reluctantly he dragged his eyes back to her face. "I can't understand why you didn't tell me about Paxton's note, or that you were meeting him."

"I've already told you why I felt it was something I needed to do alone." Rianne's hands stilled. "No, that's not all of it. I also didn't tell you because I was afraid . . . and embarrassed," she admitted.

Shirtless, Alex came to sit on his haunches before her. He studied her expression as he slid his hands under her petticoats to finish removing her stocking. "I can understand your fear, darlin'. Paxton's a bastard of the first order. But that was all the more reason for you to tell me."

"No, you *don't* understand! I no longer feared *Lance* as much as I feared what you'd see if you met him. I've been doing a lot of thinking while we've been in New Orleans. What I realized was that I was my own worst enemy."

His fingers stilled. "Explain."

"Keep in mind that I was only thirteen when it started, so I can forgive myself for the first few years. But later . . . I should have stood my ground and not allowed him to control me as he did. I should have had more character—"

Alex smiled as he curled his fingers about her ankle and lifted it to plant a kiss upon the arch of her foot.

"Stop that! It tickles. Where was I? I had spunk and a mind of my own when I was a girl. But somehow I let Lance squeeze it all out of me, until I had no backbone . . . no will. And I stayed that way—until I met you." She leaned down to cup his cheeks in her palms and bring her face almost to his. "You filled me up again, Alex. You filled me to overflowing." She smiled softly. "And you know what else?"

His throat felt scratchy. "No. What?"

"If," she said, letting her smile slowly turn into a frown, "you ever scold me this way again, I'll invite myself to be Louisa's or your aunt Lorna's *permanent* houseguest!" And with that, she pushed him hard enough to make him lose his balance.

He fell onto his back and lay there, too astonished to move. Eventually his chest began to rumble. A moment later, he was laughing.

Crossing her arms and knees, Rianne swung her foot while she waited for him to recover. He did, just enough to lift his torso and prop himself on his elbows to look up at her. "My little Amazon!" he said, shaking his head.

Rianne uncrossed her arms. "You'd do well to keep in mind that I've learned to stand up for myself. And there's one last thing . . ." she said, shaking a finger at him. "You never told me about *your* nefarious little plans for Lance, so you have no business chastising me."

"You're right. You're absolutely right," he agreed as he pushed himself up and kneewalked back to her. "I won't say another scolding word."

"Good." She extended her leg so that he could pull off her stocking. "Have you really ruined Lance?" she asked, curious.

"As well as I could manage in a couple of weeks—which is considerable. You, my dear, are now the majority stockholder in the bank Pierre St. Onge signed over to Paxton's management. You also own half a city block of prime commercial real estate, not to mention his riverfront plantation. As to the, er, less desirable investments he held—"

"You mean the gambling hall and the brothels?"

Alex nodded. "Those, too. Naturally, we'll close them down and sell or use the buildings for some other purpose."

"Naturally," Rianne agreed dryly. Then she laughed and

flopped onto her back. "We can build a new school with the proceeds, don't you think?"

"If that's what you want."

"That's what I want. Alex, you were absolutely magnificent, my love!" Rianne closed her eyes, remembering.

When she'd glanced up to see him sitting so calmly across from her and Lance, she'd almost fainted. And yet she'd also been relieved. *She'd* known that her husband was in a murderous rage, but she didn't think Lance had. Alex had been controlled and so . . . so *masterful!*

Lance had released her and leaned back in his chair, smiling nastily at Alex.

"Ah, your new keeper has arrived, pet," he'd jeered.

Though Alex's gaze never left Lance, Alex had calmly addressed Rianne. "I do hope you've concluded your little visit, my dear," he said. "Our guests are impatient for your return."

"I'm finished," she said firmly. When Alex didn't move, she glanced worriedly from him to Lance and back again. "You're coming, too, aren't you?"

The frigid green of Alex's eyes warmed as he shifted his gaze to her. "Paxton and I have some business to discuss. You're not to worry. Riley's here."

Business? What business? And why was Riley Jackson here? Rianne twisted about in her chair and was astonished to find that the Pinkerton agent was indeed not six feet behind her—at the same table with Lance's two henchmen. At first Rianne didn't understand why the other two looked as if they were frozen in place, their hands flat on the table in front of them as they stared at Riley. It wasn't until he smiled at her reassuringly and lifted the napkin covering his right hand that she saw he was concealing a pistol beneath the cloth.

Lance casually poured more Champagne into his glass

and slowly took a sip. "Reinforcements, Benedict? Afraid to meet me alone?"

"You're one to talk," Rianne snapped, "with those two gargoyles of yours!"

Alex's hand came over hers and squeezed gently. "Easy, love," he told her, ignoring Lance's insult.

Rianne turned back to Alex. "How is it that Riley's here?"

"He has some good news for you." Alex's gaze was once again pinned on Lance. "Want to tell her, Riley?"

"Be happy to. Found your friend and her brother, Mrs. Benedict. I won't tell you where they are just yet," he said with a quick glance at Lance, "but my colleague has spoken to them. I came straight here to tell you as soon as I received his telegram."

"Are you positive?" Rianne whispered.

"Absolutely. I've got the telegram in my pocket. It includes a message from Mimosa Carter to you. Want me to read it?"

"Please," she breathed, afraid to hope.

" 'Come as soon as you can, *ma petite papillonne d'or.*' "

Rianne's eyes brimmed. " *'My little golden butterfly.'* She always called me that." Rianne glared at Lance through her tears.

"You said they were dead! You told me they'd been killed in the fire! The fire *you* had set!"

Lance set down his glass and shrugged. "I did try, pet. Apparently the men I hired were inept idiots."

"You dirty liar!" she said contemptuously. "You'd do anything, say anything, to hurt me, wouldn't you?" Snatching up his goblet, she tossed the contents into his face. Alex could be unruffled; it didn't mean she was!

"Good move, darlin'," Alex drawled. "Might help lessen some of the stench around here. On the other hand, I have a feeling that it's going to get a lot worse in the next few minutes."

Rianne didn't doubt it would. Alex was very thorough.

As he was now, she thought whimsically as he slowly removed her other stocking. Rianne wriggled her toes as his hands slid up her leg.

Wait a minute! He'd already removed that stocking.

"Alex?"

"Yes, love?"

"When can we go to Shreveport to see Mimsie and Carter?"

"Hmm?"

"Mimsie." Rianne sat up. "I asked—" Her glance searched the room. "Alex?" Her petticoats fluttered. "What in the world are you—Ah!" She felt his seeking fingers, moving slowly on her. "Oh, *Alex!*"

Her petticoats were suddenly tossed up and shoved aside.

"You were asking?" he crooned as he planted a kiss on her lower belly.

Rianne flopped helplessly back onto the bed. "I was asking you," she gasped, "to please not stop!"

There was a spring in Rianne's step as she walked down the narrow street towards Louisa Newton's home. It was a beautiful morning.

Rianne turned a corner and met a woman walking in the opposite direction who smiled shyly and murmured a soft greeting. She was carrying a covered basket, and the delicious aromas drifting from it made Rianne's mouth water. She hoped Louisa's cook had made fresh *beignets*. She'd already had one this morning with Alex before he left for his office, but now she was ravenous again.

Rianne smiled at a startled cry behind her. Obviously the poor passerby had just met up with Conny!

Then she sighed. Despite his thorough humiliation of Lance, Alex still didn't trust the man. "Pierre St. Onge has promised that his daughter and her husband will be embarking on a long journey to Europe. Very long. But until I've received confirmation that Paxton is actually on a ship, miles into the Atlantic, Goliath and Conny are still to accompany you and Leslie everywhere."

Which was why Conny was still her guardian. Even so, Rianne felt as if she'd been released from prison.

Since her meeting with Lance, she'd been thrust into formalities and legalities and technicalities. She'd met with lawyers and accountants and property managers. She'd signed so many papers that she was convinced her hand was permanently crooked. Reams of papers. Bushels of papers. *Oceans* of papers.

Her head was still spinning with all the information that had been crammed into it. Alex, bless his heart, had wanted to be sure she understood *everything* before she signed her name.

She didn't care about all the *whereofs* and *therefores*. All she'd wanted was assurance that the wealth the papers represented was put to good use. She wanted none of it for herself, even though Alex had explained that a portion of it was actually her inheritance, for Lance's father had cheated her mother out of the real value of Belle Bayou. In that case, she'd told Alex, that particular portion could be divided equally among the city's orphanages.

At one time Rianne had been concerned about Lance's family and whether she was taking food out of their mouths.

Not so, Alex assured her. Lance had no children, and his wife was wealthy in her own right through a family trust—which, he hastened to add—Lance couldn't touch.

So the paperwork was completed, and Rianne was on her

way to Louisa's to have morning coffee with Leslie. Of course it was far too early to be calling, but this wasn't really a social call. Like most of New Orleans society, Louisa and Celeste slept late. Rianne and Leslie, however, were both early risers, so they'd gotten into the habit of having a quiet cup or two by themselves each morning.

Rianne was smiling as she rang the bell. Her smile turned into a frown when no one came to the door. She rang again. Still no response.

Glancing over her shoulder, she shrugged at Conny, who was leaning casually against the wrought iron gate of the house next door. Rianne turned back to knock again. She couldn't believe Louisa's servants were so lax this morning.

A lock clicked. Ah, at last! The door was pulled open, and Rianne found herself looking not at a servant, but at a disheveled Charles Rambeau. His collar was unbuttoned, his hair wasn't combed, and his face was creased with tension and worry.

"Rianne! Thank God!" He glanced over her shoulder and, upon seeing Conny, beckoned frantically for him to come forward. Then he grabbed her hand and practically pulled her off her feet.

Rianne stumbled against him. "Charles? What in the world is the matter?"

He waited until her companion had hurried to join them. "It's Leslie. She's disappeared!"

In the foyer, Celeste was consoling Goliath, who sat on a chair that was much too small for him. He was silent, holding his head in his hands, while loud feminine wails were heard from the direction of the kitchen.

"It's the new maid, Kitty," Charles explained. "Louisa is attempting to calm her, though the girl knows she's in trouble. From what we've unraveled thus far, it appears she was either bribed or threatened by Lance Paxton. She brought Goliath his coffee about two hours ago, as she usually does each morning, only this time she apparently slipped a sleeping potion into it."

"Oh, no!" Rianne breathed.

Goliath raised his head and nodded forlornly. He looked to still be half asleep. "I thought it was odd that the coffee was so sweet. Then, too, she hung about until I drank two cups. Usually she can't get away fast enough." He shrugged at Rianne's questioning look. "Scared of me, I guess. Anyways, last thing I remember is her staring down at me. I wasn't out long, but it was enough time for someone to snatch Miss Leslie. God, I'm sorry, ma'am. Your husband should shoot me for being such a fool."

Though Rianne was frightened for Leslie, she felt sorry for the big man. It wasn't his fault that one of Louisa's servants had apparently turned traitor. She patted his arm absently. "He won't. The important thing is that we find Leslie right away. Has anyone fetched the authorities and notified my husband?"

There hadn't been time; they'd just found Goliath. Conny was dispatched to do so, while Goliath and Charles went to search the house and the private courtyard behind it. Rianne followed a distraught Celeste up to Leslie's room.

It was in disarray. Her bedclothes were hanging off the side of the mattress and trailing onto the floor. A chair had been overturned. A pitcher lay broken and water seeped into the carpet.

A ladder leaned against her second floor balcony.

"Charles and I came to Leslie's room immediately after Goliath awakened us," a distraught Celeste explained. "This is exactly as we found it."

Rianne walked about the room, dread eating away at her.

"You found no note, no explanation?"

"Well, I . . . we didn't think to search the room. We only just discovered Leslie missing and—"

"I'll look around, Celeste. Why don't you go back down and comfort Louisa?" The elderly woman had been in tears when she came from the kitchen.

Celeste had barely left before Rianne began frantically searching through the items on top of Leslie's bureau. There was a message in this room. She knew it as surely as she knew who'd taken Leslie.

She found it tucked beneath Leslie's hairbrush.

Your birthday gift awaits. Come alone to your old home. Tell anyone, particularly your husband, and his sister dies.

This time no signature was necessary.

When Alex, breathless and grim, arrived an hour later with Conny, the house was in an uproar. Policemen were questioning everyone and tramping through Louisa's flower beds looking for clues—as if, he thought grimly—his sister was hiding under a rose bush!

Strangely enough, only Goliath was sitting quietly on the front stoop. His head was bent low, his hands hanging helplessly between his knees. When he saw Alex and Conny approaching, he slowly straightened and rose to his feet.

"Is my wife inside?" Alex asked without preamble.

Goliath mournfully shook his head. Then he extended his hand and opened his palm, offering a crumpled piece of paper. "Mr. Rambeau and I were searching the grounds when Mrs. Rambeau came running out with this. She said Mrs. Benedict told her to give it to you, and then she—Mrs. Benedict, that is—left."

Alex crumpled it even more after reading it and stuffing it into his pocket. He knew the name of the street Rianne had once lived on and, after inquiring, found that the carriage driver was familiar with it. Alex then began methodically giving orders and was still doing so as he, Conny, and Goliath rushed through the quiet streets.

Yet all the while his insides were churning with dread and fury. Rianne had left the note to let him know that she'd gone to her old cottage. The little fool! She'd taken it upon herself to try to protect Leslie.

His wife. His sister. Both in danger—perhaps even mortal danger. That Paxton was capable of murder, he had no doubt. The man was no different than those bastards who'd slaughtered his father, his baby boy, and Mary Ellen.

Alex felt as sick as he had felt upon returning to Bellesfield to find his family dead or dying. He'd failed them; he hadn't been able to protect them. He couldn't fail again!

But it *was* his fault, dammit! He was the one responsible for seeing to his wife and sister's safety. He thought he'd taken every precaution, yet he'd misjudged Paxton's desire for revenge. And he'd underrated Rianne's stubborn propensity to take matters into her own hands.

A clear image of her formed in his mind, pride and defiance written on her face after the dinner at Tujague's, as she'd said to him, "I've learned to stand up for myself."

She would, too. She'd find a way to stall whatever nefarious plans Paxton had in mind. She'd defy him until Alex arrived.

And here he was, feeling sorry for *himself!* Castigating himself with guilt. Just as he had all those years ago.

Everything was unexpectedly clear in his mind. What an idiot he was! What had happened at Bellesfield hadn't been his fault. It had been the war, that damned war and its aftermath. Fate. God's plan, if you will. And who was he, Alex Benedict, to arrogantly assume responsibility for God's actions? The awfulness at Bellesfield hadn't been in his power to prevent; it had *not* been the result of any action on his part or any lack thereof. Yet all these years he'd worn guilt like a shield—to cover his self-pity he now realized.

Well, he wasn't going to let it happen again.

"Get ready, men," he told Conny and Goliath grimly as the carriage began to slow. "The time has come."

Chapter 30

Where was it? *Where?* Rianne pulled Alex's shirts out of the armoire and tossed them onto the floor. She found nothing beneath them. She tore through another drawer, then another. Nothing.

Dammit! He'd brought it with him. She'd seen it, packed at the bottom of . . .

His small valise! The one containing his shaving gear.

She flew into the bathing room. Sure enough, Alex's leather case was tucked away in the gentleman's dresser.

She snatched it up and was relieved to find it satisfactorily heavy. A quick peek told her that she'd found what she was looking for.

The toothy gargoyle was waiting for her. He gave her a yellow smile. "He's waitin' inside. Said you'd know which room."

"Leslie? What about Leslie?"

His smile vanished. "That witch?" He rubbed his hand, drawing Rianne's attention to the filthy cloth wrapped around it. "She bit me. If'n I'd had her to myself for a time, I'd teach her a thing or two about bitin'." His grin was evil.

Rianne felt sick, but this was no time to show weakness. "If she's harmed in any way—"

He shrugged. "Ain't heard a peep outta her. Could be the boss is keepin' her too busy to talk. Hey, whatcha got in the bag?"

"Money. I brought all the cash I could get my hands on." She opened it to show him the loose bills but quickly snapped it shut again when his eyes shone with greed.

He looked away reluctantly. "Could just as well give it to me, girlie. Paxton don't want money. He wants you."

"That's for him to decide," she said coldly. "Are you going to let me by or not? He doesn't like to be kept waiting . . ." She let the insinuation speak for itself.

The ugly smile vanished. He stepped aside.

Gargoyle Number Two was at the top of the stairs. He said nothing, just cracked his knuckles as he watched her walk past.

Rianne stopped at the door to her old room and took a deep breath before she turned the knob and pushed open the door.

Framed by the open window behind her, Leslie was sitting in a chair beside the bed and facing the door, her wrists tied to it and her mouth gagged. Her eyes rolled wildly when she saw Rianne. There were bruises on her arms and a scratch on her cheek, but she seemed otherwise unhurt. Rianne prayed it was so. Leslie was still in her nightgown, but someone had tossed a man's coat over her shoulders.

Lance was sitting on the bed, propped up against the headboard, smoking a cigar. Despite his relaxed position, his eyes were bloodshot and held a fanatic look.

He took the cigar out of his mouth. "Good girl. I see you still hasten to obey me." He didn't smile. His voice was strained. "What's in the valise?"

Rianne closed the door and took two steps in his direction. "Money," she told him, and she held out the valise, offering it to him. "It's all I had on hand, but I can get more."

"You should, since you now have all of mine. But you see—" his mouth crooked in a tight smile "—that's not why I offered your sweet sister-in-law my hospitality."

Rianne withdrew the valise and kept hold of it. "Yes, I know. You're furious with Alex."

Lance's face turned a mottled red. "The bastard is going to pay for what he's done. As will you."

Rianne strived for calm. "I'll talk to Alex. He'll do whatever you want, I swear. Just let Leslie go. She has nothing to do with us."

Leslie shook her head frantically and made unintelligible noises as Lance tossed the cigar onto the floor and slid off the bed to crush it beneath his shoe. "I don't think so, pet. As I was considering finishing that birthday party, I decided it would be too boring with just the two of us. Which is why," he added as he slowly approached Leslie, "I've invited your sister-in-law."

Leslie's eyes shot murderous looks at him until he moved behind her, out of her line of vision. "You see," Lance continued, "I find I'm developing a taste for Benedict women."

"Just let her go, Lance. I'll do anything you want. Anything," Rianne pleaded.

"Nnh! Dnt!" Leslie's muffled voice was unintelligible, but her eyes spoke volumes as she beseeched Rianne.

"Ah! She wants to speak." Lance reached around Leslie to clench his fingers over her jaw and twist her head to face him. "You'll be nice if I take this gag off now, won't you?"

She nodded.

"Good." He released her jaw to jerk off the gag. Leslie licked her dry lips and tried to speak, but all that came out was a squeak. "Can't speak? Here . . ." Lance turned slightly and leaned to pick up a glass of water from the bedside table. Turning back to Leslie, he held it to her lips, forcing her to drink.

She coughed and cleared her throat. "Don't do it, Rianne! He doesn't intend to let either of us go!" she croaked.

Lance slapped her. Leslie's head rocked back, but she didn't make a sound as he stood over her. "That wasn't nice at all, Leslie. Now you've upset Rianne. Don't you want to be a guest at her party?" He straightened and turned back to face Rianne.

"You're wrong, Lance. I'm not at all upset," she replied calmly. "I'm not upset, because I have this." The click of the hammer as she cocked the Remington was surprisingly—and satisfyingly—loud. "You make one sound, one little peep to bring that gargoyle of yours in here, and I'll shoot you. Now, you're going to free Leslie, then go to the door and call him inside. Understand, Lance?"

Lance had frozen upon seeing the revolver, but now he began to laugh. "You're insane! Even if you were brave enough to pull the trigger—which I doubt—there's three of us and—"

She took a step nearer. "And I have six shots. How many of those do you suppose I could put into *you* before your henchmen get in here? One? Three? Or perhaps all of them? This close, I can't miss, Lance. It's only a matter of deciding where to shoot you," she said in a stone-cold tone. "A knee first? Both arms? Or maybe I'll just bring this to a quick end. What do you think, Les?"

"Shoot him where it matters most. He isn't a real man, anyway, so he won't need his—"

Lance's move was so lightning quick, Rianne saw only a silvery flash appear in his hand as he stepped to Leslie's side and grabbed her hair to jerk her head back.

And then the knife glinted at Leslie's throat.

Rianne froze in horror. Oh, God! Why hadn't she just shot him?

Lance slid the blade along Leslie's jaw, then higher, brushing it over her cheek before turning back to Rianne.

"How do you think she'll look, pet, with a scar like mine on her pretty face?" His own twisted into a grimace. "Put that weapon down, or I swear I'll do it!" he barked.

Leslie's sudden hoarse cry as she kicked out against the bed took both Rianne and Lance by surprise. Leslie's chair tangled with Lance's feet, and he lurched forward, throwing his knife hand up to catch his balance. Leslie jerked her hair free and thrust upward, slamming her shoulder into Lance's arm and sending the knife flying. Still tied to the chair, she fell to the floor, shrieking, "Shoot him, Rianne! Shoot him *now!*"

This time Rianne kept her eyes open as she pointed the Remington at Lance's chest and squeezed the trigger.

Rianne had braced herself for a loud report, but the boom that followed was more like a crash of thunder. She was so startled that she almost dropped the heavy weapon.

With a noise that loud, she expected Lance to be blown out the window, but to her baffled astonishment, he was still standing upright.

Dead men didn't stand. Nor did they swiftly move forward to grab the Remington from the shooter's hand and whirl her about to wrap an arm around her throat and hold that same revolver against her temple.

It happened so fast, Rianne didn't have time to wonder *why* Lance wasn't dead or where the bullet had gone. She lost almost all coherent thought as Leslie, still lying on the floor, gasped, "Alex!"

Lance's voice came from over Rianne's head. "Well, well. Look who else has joined the party. I didn't invite you, Benedict. Did you, pet?"

Rianne blinked. It *was* Alex standing in the doorway. And the deafening crash had resulted as he'd kicked open the door—now hanging crookedly on its hinges—not from the revolver.

From the quick movement of his eyes, he'd already taken in the scene. Lance, holding her tightly against him, the Remington at her temple; Leslie, hands still tied to the chair, lying on the floor, glancing worriedly from one person to another.

Rianne's eyes flew back to Alex. He flicked her a quick glance before once again aiming a savage stare at Lance. "It's a stalemate, Paxton. Your men are being detained by mine. This doesn't have to go any further if you let the women go."

"Stalemate? You may have ruined me, but now I'm in a position to take something away from you." Lance applied more pressure with the revolver, and Rianne winced. "Her! This is all *her* fault! Damn her, she's going to pay—and for scarring my face!" He was panting heavily in Rianne's ear, his voice beginning to quaver. "I should have killed her years ago!"

Rianne closed her eyes, convinced she was about to die.

"No!" Alex hadn't shouted, but his voice was still commanding. "No," he repeated with more restraint, though that restraint was belied by the burning fury in his eyes. "Let her go, Paxton. Let them both go, and you can walk out of here unmolested. I swear I won't come after you. And I'll return everything I took from you. Whatever you want."

"It's too late to make amends. St. Onge has already thrown me out of the bank, and my wife has locked me out of her house. All that's left for me is this little party." Rianne gagged as Lance's arm tightened over her throat. "*Did* you invite your husband?" he demanded.

"No," she gasped.

"Then tell him you don't want him here. Tell him to leave."

She shook her head. The gun left her temple and appeared in front of her, pointed directly at Alex. "Tell him!" Lance shouted. "Show him what an obedient little girl you can be."

"Please, Alex. Leave. Go away," she managed.

"Ah, you do remember your lessons after all," Lance crooned. "But you still look much too defiant, Rianne." He cocked the gun, still pointed at Alex. "Show me the proper behavior, or he dies."

Lance was losing control, Rianne thought frantically, and the only way to regain it was to subjugate and humiliate her. It didn't matter; she'd do anything to keep him from shooting Alex.

Rianne bent her head and clasped her hands before her.

"Please, Lance. Let them both go, and I'll do whatever you want. I swear! Please."

"Yes, that's the way! Shall we show him more, pet?"

"Rianne . . ." Alex's voice was filled with pain. "Don't."

She tried desperately to ignore his plea. "Yes, Lance. Whatever you say."

"Then tell him what you like to do most in the world, pet."

Rianne lowered her eyes. "To please you," she murmured.

"And what's your purpose in life?"

"To make you happy," she said through tight lips.

"Very good. You see, Benedict? She may be inept—as evidenced by her inability to shoot straight—but there's still time to train her fully." The barrel of the revolver brushed her cheek.

"Rianne!" Alex's sharp voice brought her head up. "Do you recall that night in the train?"

She stared at him, knowing he was sending her a message but unsure what it was. "Yes," she said hesitantly.

"How about the individual I introduced Gumm to?"

"I . . . I'm not sure."

"What the hell is this?" Lance growled. "Shut up!"

"Is that same individual here, now, in this room?" Alex

asked over Lance's objection. "If he is, his pockets are empty."

She stared at him for a moment, confused. Pockets? And then, she understood. The smile she beamed at her husband was radiant. "Yes!" she shouted.

"Well, hell, in that case . . ." Alex began to stalk forward.

"Stay back! Stay back, or I'll kill her!" Lance warned.

Alex smiled grimly and kept walking.

"I'll do it, damn you!" Lance screamed as he backed away, forcing Rianne with him. Once again, the Remington was at her temple, only this time Lance did squeeze the trigger.

He was astonished when nothing happened. He released her and stood, staring at the revolver in his hand.

Rianne was laughing as she stepped aside. Mr. Remington's pockets *were* empty!

Alex launched himself straight toward Lance, who glanced up and stumbled back—until he came up against the open window.

Alex couldn't stop in time. He slammed into Lance.

The empty Remington fell to the floor. Lance let out a short, piercing scream, and then toppled backwards—out the window.

The only sound that followed was a sickening thud from the brick courtyard below.

Epilogue

"*O-b-e-y*. Do you know what that spells?"

Rianne kissed Alex's left nipple. "Uh-uh. I was never very good at spelling."

"Then just say it. *Obey*. One easy word."

She kissed his right nipple. "I'm a little busy right now."

"Dammit, stop trying to distract me!"

She raised her head from his chest. "You don't like this?"

"Oh, I like it, darlin'." Alex grasped her waist tightly. She was lying on top of him, spread out over him like a soft, sweet-smelling, living blanket. "That doesn't mean I'm not still furious with you. I should put you over my knee and—"

"Hmm," Rianne interrupted, pursing her lips. "That sounds interesting." She effectively stopped his tirade by kissing him. And kissing him and kissing him. By the time she was through, he was too breathless to continue haranguing her.

"Alex," she said patiently, looking down at him, "it's over. I can't say I'm not glad Lance is out of our lives, and I'm sorry it ended that way. But it did, it's done, and now we need to look forward and plan our future together."

He sighed and pulled her head down to his chest. "You're right. It's just—dammit, Rianne, must I continue to beg you to never give me another scare like that? Have pity! I'm not as young as I used to be."

"Oh, pooh! You're as young as you need to be, and we're

going to have a wonderful life together. With children—lots of them. And grandchildren, too. Enough to always fill our lives with laughter and love."

"We'll have all of that," Alex promised as he squeezed her waist. "But I swear, when we repeat our wedding vows on our twenty-fifth anniversary, you're going to shout the word *obey* loud enough to make the rafters shake."

Of course, he didn't mean a word of it, but he wasn't about to tell her that. Not just yet, anyway. Secretly, he was so damned proud of her, he'd burst his buttons—if he were wearing a shirt. Despite what she'd been through since she was a small girl, she had more courage than most men. She was a woman any man would be proud to call his wife.

And she was *his*. His woman, his wife, his friend, his lover. Damn, but he was a lucky man. "Did you hear what I just said?" he asked gruffly, giving her a little nudge.

"Uh-huh. I'll think about it, my love," Rianne replied absently, and she smiled slyly against his chest as she snuggled closer.

By her calculations, she had twenty-four years, ten months, two weeks, and three days to consider.

Long enough for Alex to forget it.

"Alex?" Rianne raised her head from his chest and stretched upward, bringing her mouth tantalizingly near his. "Can we talk later?"

Their lips met in a kiss. Then just one kiss more. And then another and another and . . .